S

A KISS AND A PROMISE

It is 1917. Virginia Hewson is sixteen and so beautiful that Michael Gallagher, an Irishman fighting with the British Navy, falls in love with her on sight. The Hewson family is horrified but the young couple know their own minds and are set on marriage. Then Virginia has a baby—Stella Margaret —and when Michael returns from sea he takes one look at her and is convinced she is not his child. He agrees, reluctantly, to help to support her financially, but will do nothing else. With her world turned upside-down, will Virginia, a young mother, survive?

A KISS AND A PROMISE

Katie Flynn

First published 2003
by
William Heinemann
This Large Print edition published 2003
by
BBC Audiobooks Ltd
by arrangement with
Random House UK Limited

ISBN 0 7540 8714 X (Windsor Hardcover)
ISBN 0 7540 9372 7   (Paragon Softcover)

British Library Cataloguing in Publication Data available

Printed and bound in Great Britain by
Antony Rowe Ltd., Chippenham, Wiltshire

For Edna Cubitt, one of my oldest friends, with whom it is always great to reminisce and have a giggle.

PART I

CHAPTER ONE

APRIL 1917

Michael Gallagher came up on deck, still with the stuffiness of the seamen's mess in his nostrils, and took a deep breath of the cold night air. It was April, and in his imagination the breeze blowing across the Mersey was flower-scented and sweet. It reminded him of his home where, even now, primroses would be clustered around the brook which was the family water supply, whilst violets would be in bloom on the banks of the little lane that led to the village. Looking up, he reminded himself that the bright stars twinkling in the great arch of the dark sky above were the same as those his fellow countrymen would be seeing in far-off Kerry, and the thought made him long for his own place and his own people.

However, he had been fighting in the Royal Navy for eighteen months now and though he could not honestly say that he foresaw an early end to hostilities, he had made his bed and must lie in it. Furthermore, he knew that he would soon have some leave, and now that they were in dock he might actually have sufficient furlough to get to Kerry and back before his ship, HMS *Thunderbolt*, set out for America once more. He walked over to the rail and leaned on it, considering. The ship had come into Liverpool's Canning dock for repairs and that meant the crew would soon be sent ashore—as soon as the shipwrights came aboard, in fact—which meant, in its turn, that he might as well go straight to the Sailors' Home on Canning Place, and make sure of a bed.

But . . . it was a fine night, and though it was late, it was surely not so late that all the pubs would be shut? He had docked in Liverpool once before and remembered a jolly sort of place where his fellow countrymen tended to congregate . . . if he could just remember where it was. He did remember the creaking signboard and the size and joviality of the landlord, but as for its exact location . . . well, he would have to leave it to chance.

Usually, Michael would have been with his pals and they would all have left the ship at the same time, taken adjacent beds in the Sailors' Home and then gone out for a booze-up together, but tonight he had been in the seamen's mess, writing home, and had not wanted to leave his letter half finished. The ship had been on convoy duty, crossing and recrossing the Atlantic, so though he did get the chance to write to his parents when he was not on watch, posting such missives was a different matter, and therefore, he reminded himself now, his first duty was to find a post box.

Having made up his mind on this, he picked up his kitbag and began to make his way down the gangway. As he descended, a kitten, white as snow save for a pair of huge reflective eyes, came, tail-erect, across the short distance which separated them and gave a shrill, enquiring mew. It had probably been drawn to the quayside by the strong smell from fish boxes, Michael thought, but it would be disappointed, for the boxes were either empty or tightly closed. He felt in his pocket, but came up with nothing more exciting than a small square of chocolate. He guessed that the kitten

4

would not be interested in such an offering but squatted down anyway and held out a hand.

Immediately, the small creature came to him, rubbing against his fingers, then dashing off into the shadows, only to return seconds later, white whiskers bristling with excitement, snowy paws as silent as a breath on the cobbled surface. Clearly, it wanted companionship and a game rather than food.

'All right, little feller, you can sit on me shoulder until you get tired of doin' a balancin' act,' Michael said, bending to pick up the kitten. It immediately swarmed on to his shoulder as though it had understood every word and settled itself comfortably, tail neatly curled, paws together, whilst a rumbling purr vibrated against Michael's ear, making him laugh aloud. 'Ah well, I've always had a fondness for cats, so I have,' he informed it, beginning to stride towards the dock gates. 'You're a friendly wee feller so y'are, but don't I just wish you could talk! Then you could tell me the name o' the pub where us Irish fellers go . . . perhaps even take me there!'

With the kitten still perched on his shoulder, he had almost reached the dock gates when he saw a figure standing in the deep shadow directly outside the dock area. The kitten saw it too and its purr stopped as though a switch had been turned off. It leaped lightly off his shoulder and disappeared behind a stack of timber, one moment a little white ghost-cat, the next apparently gone without a trace.

The figure within the shadow moved and Michael stopped abruptly. Was he not a Kerry man, reared on superstition and with a strong belief in the supernatural? Now that he came to think of it, it was strange enough to find a white kitten on the quayside, let alone one which could disappear at will. And was not the female figure which came gliding out into the moonlight the very image of one of the faery creatures which haunted the bens and glens of his own country? She was very dark, her gleaming mass of black hair waist-length, her eyes frighteningly like pits in the pure oval of her face.

Involuntarily, Michael took a step backwards and the woman—or girl, rather, for he could see that she was very young—seemed to see him for the first time. She swung round, and now Michael saw, not only that she was young, but that she was very beautiful.

'Oh, how you startled me!' The girl's voice, soft and clear though it was, was reassuringly human, touched with the familiar Liverpudlian accent. 'I thought I was the only soul down here at this hour of the night, so I did.'

'Is it late?' Michael asked vaguely. He realised that he had no idea of the time but guessed from her tone that it must be after midnight. 'Come to that, it's terrible late for a young lady like yourself to be prowling the docks; dangerous, too. Why, you might get into all sorts of trouble; sailors can be wild when the drink's on them.'

'I was searchin' for Sunny,' the girl said. 'He's only young and he's terrible foolish. I were afraid he might see a movement in the water and jump before he'd thought, so to speak. You haven't seen him?'

Michael was about to reply that he had seen no one save herself when it occurred to him that he might have got hold of the wrong end of the stick.

6

'I've seen a little white cat, more of a kitten really, so I have,' he said cautiously. 'He were on me shoulder until you moved, but then he took fright and streaked off. He went behind that pile o' timber. Is your Sunny a little cat or are you searchin' for a young feller?'

The girl gave a trill of amusement and squatted down on the cobbles as Michael himself had done earlier. 'Sunny's a cat, o' course,' she said. She made a chirruping sound and held out her arms and Michael watched as the kitten emerged from its hiding place. It was still playing some private game of its own and rushed towards the girl, gathered itself as if to spring, and then abruptly tore away again, this time to scale a pile of abandoned fish boxes, its tail fluffed out with excitement.

The girl sighed and stood up. 'The moonlight's gorrin to his blood and he's mad as any March hare,' she said resignedly. 'He's been playin' the fool all the way down here, lettin' me get within a foot of him and then whiskin' away again. Oh dear, and I'm dreadfully tired.' She turned towards the cat again. 'Come to Stella, Sunny, and you shall have a whole saucer of conny-onny and a sardine as soon as I can lay me hands on one. Please, Sunny, don't give me no more hassle.'

Michael saw that the cat's whole attention was fixed on its young mistress and he moved swiftly, grabbing the animal round its waist before it had any idea that he was a threat. The girl gave a squeak of joy and tried to take the kitten from him but Michael, wrapping Sunny in the folds of his duffel coat, shook his head. 'He's drunk on moonlight and the dark and won't take to being

7

held easily,' he said. 'I was lookin' for a pub where I could get me a drink but I hadn't realised it was so late. Do you live far from here? Wherever you live, I might as well walk you home. I'd feel bad not keepin' an eye on you and your little cat so if it's all the same to you, miss, I'll tek the pair of ye to your door.'

The girl looked doubtful. 'I live in one of the courts off Rathbone Street. It's not far but, honest to God, there's no need for you to come. If you'll just hand me the cat . . .'

'I'm walkin' you home, so I am,' Michael said obstinately. 'You don't know me from Adam, but you'll be safe as houses, I can promise you that. Why, both me hands is engaged in suppressin' young Sunny here and holdin' me kitbag, so I'm not likely to give you trouble! Come to that, if it's as late as you say, they aren't goin' to welcome me at the Sailors' Home so I'll be findin' myself a nice park bench for the rest o' the night. Are there after bein' any park benches on Rathbone Street?'

The girl laughed and glanced shyly up at him, subjecting him to a brief, penetrating look before she smiled and fell into step beside him. 'Well, if you're sure you don't mind, I'd be glad of your company,' she admitted. 'As for benches, I can't think of a single one, but if you'd like to spread your bedroll on me mam's kitchen floor, I'm sure you'd be very welcome.'

It was Michael's turn to stare now and for one uneasy moment he wondered what sort of girl would let him into her home after such a short acquaintance. He knew there were dockside whores in Liverpool who would cheat a man of his last penny, and he had heard of a good many sailors who had been lured indoors only to find themselves accused of anything from rape to theft. Then men would magically appear in the girl's room, strip the sailor of anything of value, even his clothing, and either knock him unconscious and cart him down to the docks or simply eject him on to the street to find his own way home.

One look at his companion, however, convinced Michael that he could take her invitation at face value. She was very young and, he guessed, quite ignorant of men and their devious ways. It would not occur to her that there could be anything wrong in offering him the hospitality of her kitchen floor, and this meant that he could spend the rest of the night under a roof—thanks to Sunny the kitten— before making his way back to the docks as soon as it was light. There, he would enquire if it were possible for him to return to Kerry in the time it would take to repair the *Thunderbolt*. Of course he would have to wait until the girl's family were up so that he might explain how he came to be sleeping in their kitchen, but that would not hold him up for long. He turned to his companion. 'Thank you very much, I'd be happy to accept the loan of your floor,' he said gravely. 'Sure and I don't even know your name, but I'm Michael Gallagher, Ordinary Seaman aboard HMS *Thunderbolt*. She's in for repair at present, so I thought I'd mebbe go back to Ireland for a few days to see me mammy and daddy, if there's time enough, that is. I'd shake your hand but young Sunny's wrigglin' like an eel an' I dare not ease my grip on him or he'll be off like greased lightning.'

The girl laughed again. 'I'm Stella Bennett; I'm pleased to meet you, Mr Gallagher,' she said. 'I'm

9

the youngest of me family—I'm sixteen, goin' on seventeen—and all four of me brothers are in the Navy. George, Lewis and Fred are on the same ship, the *Wanderer*, and Bertie's on the *Eastern Princess*. What did you do before the war, Mr Gallagher?'

'I helped me daddy on our bit o' land and I worked at the fishin',' Michael said. 'It were a good life but I wanted some excitement, so as soon as I looked old enough I joined the Royal Navy and now I wonder why I bothered, because me life in Kerry was a good life and me daddy is hard pressed to run the place wit'out me. Still an' all, the war can't last for ever and one of these days I'll be goin' home to stay and not just to visit.'

'I've often wished we lived in the country,' Stella said. She sounded wistful. 'I'm real fond of animals —that's why me brother Lewis gave me Sunny— and I've often wished we could keep a dog or even a few hens, but Mam says the city's no place for animals and since me dad died there isn't much spare money. Me eldest sister, Lizzie, says Sunny's just one more mouth to feed but she shouldn't complain because I've gorra good little job in one of the big shops on Ranelagh Street, so I buys off the cat meat man out of me wages. Besides, when Sunny's bigger, I dare say he'll catch mice an' that—God knows, there's plenty of 'em in Victoria Court!'

'From the way he's fightin' me he could tackle a good-sized rat and beat it into submission,' Michael said, grinning. In actual fact, the little cat had settled down quite comfortably and his purr was reverberating through Michael's clothing. 'So you've four brothers . . . and here's me, an only

10

child. Still, as you're the youngest, I suppose most of 'em's left home. What about sisters? Oh yes, you mentioned Lizzie, didn't you?'

As they talked, they had been walking through the quiet, badly lit streets, Stella every now and then catching Michael's arm to guide him round a corner or through a narrow alley. As Michael asked his last question, they were passing beneath a gas lamp and in its subdued glow he saw her face upturned towards him, alight with gentle mischief, and he felt his heart give a queer little jump in his breast. She was so beautiful, so innocent, so altogether delightful!

'Sisters? Oh aye, I've got sisters all right. I'm the youngest of eight children. Lizzie's the oldest and the only one, besides meself, what lives at home now. The other two are married and livin' away. Lizzie helps me mam run the house, does the laundry, the messages and so on. I love her, of course I does, but she's always tellin' me off and complainin' about the way I behave, though I'm sure I try to be a good girl and do as I'm told.'

'I'm sure you do,' Michael said sincerely, meaning every word. He was astonished at her elder sister's blindness; surely one glance from those huge, dark eyes, fringed with black and curly lashes, would be sufficient to prove to anyone that Stella Bennett was an angel? He could not imagine her ever intentionally upsetting anyone, not even a bossy, fault-finding elder sister. He was about to tell her so when she dived under an archway, crossed a small cobbled yard, and stood on tiptoe to reach a big iron key down from a lintel above a front door. She opened it, took a few steps down a passage and turned right into a kitchen where a welcome warmth met them, together with the scent of baking, floor polish and the pleasant homely aroma of a banked-down fire. There was a lamp in the middle of the large table and Stella turned up the wick just as Michael gently stood the cat down on the floor. Sunny had obviously fallen quite deeply asleep in the warmth of Michael's duffel and now he stared round him for a moment, wide-eyed and curious, before jumping up on to the nearest chair and curling into a neat ball.

Michael glanced up at the large clock that hung above the mantel. Good God, it was past two in the morning, far too late for even the most accommodating boarding house. He hoped he would not be putting Stella in an invidious position by his presence on her kitchen floor, but it seemed he had little choice. There were few convenient park benches in this part of the city and besides, the thought of seeing her when he awoke in the morning made an overnight stay irresistible. Whether it was luck or the will of the gods, he had no means of knowing, but now he had met Stella Bennett he knew he would not willingly lose touch with her again.

'Would you like a cup o' tea, Mr Gallagher?' Stella said, her voice the lowest of low murmurs.

Michael glanced apprehensively towards the door which led to the rest of the house before answering in an equally muted tone: 'Sure and wouldn't I love one, Miss Bennett? But we don't want to be wakin' the rest of your family. It's no way to make meself loved, disturbin' folk.'

'Oh, Mr Gallagher, do you want the Bennetts to love you?' Stella said, flashing him a wickedly teasing glance as her lips tilted into the smile which

12

Michael had already decided was one of her chief charms. 'But they all sleep like the dead, even me brother George, and it won't take a minute to pull the kettle over the fire and freshen the pot.'

So there, in the warm and comfortable kitchen, the two young people shared a pot of tea and talked. They talked of everything under the sun, though mostly of themselves, and, on Michael's part at least, liking soon began to deepen into something very much warmer. Indeed, by the time he had laid out his bedroll on the hearthrug and whispered goodnight to his companion as she left the kitchen, he knew himself to be well on the way to falling in love for the first time in his life.

*   *   *

'Wharrever . . . ? By God, young feller, I near broke me bleedin' neck trippin' over your bedroll! You must be a pal of George's, I suppose, but why in the name of God didn't you share his room instead o' kippin' down on me kitchen floor? Oh mercy, I've stubbed me bleedin' toe and likely broke me ankle an' all! Gerrup an' tell me what you're a-doin' there.'

The woman's shrill voice acted like a bucket of cold water on poor Michael, still fathoms deep in sleep after his late night. He sat up, already mumbling an apology, and stared at the woman standing on her left foot and vigorously rubbing her right. For a moment, he could not remember exactly where he was, or why, but then the previous night's happenings came flooding back into his mind and he crawled out of his bedroll and began to pull on his jacket. It was tempting to accept her suggestion that he was George's friend, but he decided that honesty was the best policy. Taking a deep breath, he began to explain. 'No, Mrs Bennett, you've got me wrong. I—I was on me way to the Sailors' Home on Canning Place when I come across your youngest, a-searchin' for her cat. I—I reckoned it weren't safe for her to be on the streets alone so after we'd caught the cat, I brung her back here. By then it were too late for the Sailors' Home or any other lodging house, so when Miss Bennett said it would be all right for me to kip down on the floor . . .'

The older woman's eyebrows had shot up almost into her hair as he spoke but now she interrupted him, wagging her head sadly as she did so. 'You don't have to say no more, young feller; Stella is the kind o' girl who brings in half-drowned puppies, half-starved kids and scrawny kittens every day of the week, expectin' us to feed 'em and look after 'em. But it's the first time she's brung in a man what's fully growed, an' I ain't sure I like it. Did she tell you she were only sixteen?' She looked keenly into his face. 'And how old might you be, young feller? Not a deal older than her, I'd say. And I'm not Stella's mother, wharrever you may think; I'm her sister Lizzie.'

'I'm just eighteen, Miss Bennett, and I'm real sorry I took you for Miss Stella's mam,' Michael said humbly, realising that his mistake might yet cost him dear. 'The t'ing is, you were standin' with your back to the lamp so I couldn't see your face clear at all, at all.' He gave her what he hoped was an appealing smile. 'But I guess you'd rather have me space than me company right now; I'd better go to the Sailors' Home, where I belong.'

14

Lizzie Bennett smiled. Now that Michael could see her properly, for she had turned up the lamp, he realised that she was a good-looking woman with a quantity of dark hair which fell to her shoulders and twinkling brown eyes set in a round, rosy face. She appeared to be in her forties and could easily have been Stella's mother and he found himself wondering how old Mrs Bennett was and whether he would meet her, for Miss Lizzie did not look as though she meant to turn him out right now.

'It's all right, la', I'm not sending you on your way wi' no breakfast inside you,' Lizzie said. 'If I wanted young Stella to ring a peal round my ears, I might do it, but I'm of a peaceable disposition. The rest of the family will be down soon enough, so you go and have a wash at the sink and tidy yourself while I make the porridge.'

Michael obeyed gladly and presently found himself toasting bread before the kitchen fire and chatting away to Lizzie as though he had known her all his days. He told her about his life in Kerry, his home at Headland Farm and the fishing boat, the *Orla*, in which he and his father went to sea when conditions were right. She was intrigued, asking what the name *Orla* meant and expressing delight when Michael replied that it was Irish for Golden Princess, though he made her laugh by describing the elderly, tar-covered craft as being more like an old black dog than anything else.

By the time the rest of the family came clattering down the stairs, Michael and Lizzie were on the best of terms and though George, the only son at home right now, gave him a hard look from narrowed eyes, breakfast passed pleasantly. Mrs

15

Bennett was a white-haired woman with an untidy and bulging body beneath a much stained black dress and shawl. She had looked at him rather oddly when Stella introduced them but it was soon obvious that she doted on her youngest child and accepted Michael as her daughter's protégé.

She told Michael that she and Stella would soon be losing Lizzie, since her eldest daughter had taken a job in Birkenhead, where a new confectionery shop needed a competent manageress. She would be given the flat over the shop at a low rent and this, more than anything else, had persuaded her to take the position. 'We'll miss her, me and Stella, but we'll pull together to keep the place decent, and Lizzie won't be gone for another month so she's goin' to teach Stella how to cook before she goes. I'm not much of a cook now, though I were a dab hand at it when I were younger, but ever since Lizzie's been old enough she's took over the cookin' like. Fancy stuff at any rate,' she ended.

'Lizzie's a grand cook,' Stella said, between mouthfuls of porridge. She had come down to the kitchen in the grey and white striped poplin blouse and severe grey skirt which, she told Michael, were her working clothes but had enveloped herself in a large calico apron before beginning to eat. 'Lizzie works at Lunt's on the Scotland Road—I expect she told you—so it ain't often we have to make cakes and such, nor bread. Lizzie gets them at a special price, you see.'

'Aye, so she do. I reckon Stella ought to take on a job at Lunt's when our Lizzie goes so our supply of nice grub don't dry up,' George said gruffly. He grinned across at Michael; clearly his attitude to

16

the younger man had softened as the meal progressed. 'But of course, our Stella would rather swan around a posh shop, sellin' fancy leather gloves to fancy ladies at fancy prices. She don't like the idea of wearin' a uniform overall and sellin' sticky buns to sticky kids all day long, any more than she likes the idea of scrubbin' the floor.'

'They wouldn't want me,' Stella said smugly. 'They like older women. Anyway, when Lizzie goes, I'll be doin' me share of the housework which means scrubbing floors, I suppose.'

Presently, breakfast finished, the two sisters reached down hats and coats from the hooks beside the kitchen door and Michael jumped to his feet. 'I'd best be gettin' back to me ship,' he said, slinging his kitbag on to one shoulder and smiling at the assembled Bennetts. 'T'ank you for the loan of your kitchen floor; I've never slept better in me whole life. And t'anks for me breakfast . . . and for your kindness to a stranger in your city.'

George nodded and began to clear the table whilst Mrs Bennett took herself over to the sink. Michael left, walking between the two women, but presently Lizzie drew to a halt at the junction with Upper Duke Street. She kissed Stella warmly, giving her a slight hug as she did so and telling her to take care to be a good girl and not to forget to eat her carryout at dinnertime. Then she turned to Michael and held out a hand, shaking his warmly. 'No point in sayin' goodbye, since I've a feelin' we'll be seein' a good deal of you in Victoria Court,' she said gruffly. 'But you'll be off back to sea presently, no doubt?'

'Aye, in another ten days or so, I believe,' Michael said. 'I'll book meself into the Sailors'

17

Home but I'd be right grateful, Miss Lizzie, if—if I might trespass upon your hospitality again.' He had forgotten that he had intended to go home to Kerry. Now, his one desire was to be as near Stella as possible.

He was interrupted by the arrival of a tram clattering to a halt. It was a No. 3 and Lizzie immediately joined the short queue of people waiting to get aboard. 'Stella usually walks from here because it's not far to Ranelagh Street, but I go on by tram,' she said. 'Ta-ra then, Mr Gallagher.'

The two young people stood and watched the tram out of sight, then Stella tucked her small hand into the crook of Michael's elbow and they set off along the pavement, Michael quite dizzy at her closeness and Stella chattering away nineteen to the dozen. It seemed no time at all before they were in Ranelagh Street and Stella was preparing to go into Grundy's by the staff entrance, but as she was turning away, Michael caught hold of her sleeve. 'Miss Stella, what time do you finish tonight? Would—would it be all right if I was to come and meet you, escort you home?'

'But I thought you were wanting to go home to Ireland, weren't you?' Stella asked, her eyes widening. 'I was certain you'd only be in Liverpool for an hour or so today.'

Michael felt the hot blood rush into his cheeks; it was true, he had meant to go back to Ireland if time permitted, but that was before he had met Stella. He looked down at her and saw, from the teasing expression in her face, that he might as well be honest, since she had clearly already guessed his reason for changing his mind. 'Sure and aren't you

18

the cleverest colleen I ever did meet?' he said ruefully. 'Yes, I did mean to go back to me mammy and daddy if I'd time to spare, but now . . . well, any spare time I have I'd rather be spendin' with you.'

Stella gave a little gasp and Michael watched as rosy colour bloomed in her cheeks. For the first time, he allowed himself to hope that the feelings which had caught him unawares had touched her also. 'Is it the same for you, then?' she said wonderingly. 'There's always young fellers around our house and there's young men in Grundy's who've asked me if I'd like to go to the picture house or out dancing, but—but I've never felt like this before. I don't know whether it's right . . . Lizzie might think badly of me . . .'

'Lizzie made it pretty plain that she understood I'd be hangin' around for a bit,' Michael said frankly. 'What time shall I meet you?'

'Half past six,' Stella said, blushing rosily once more.

Michael grinned exultantly, happiness flooding him. 'See you at half past six, then.'

*   *   *

Lizzie, crammed into the tram, had liked Michael from the first but that did not mean she approved of his starting up some sort of relationship with her little sister. At sixteen, Stella was far too young to have a beau—except that she clearly had one, of course. Lizzie had only had to look at Michael to realise that he was smitten. Naturally there were others, a great many others. The local lads surrounded Stella like bees round a honey pot. The difference with this fellow was that Stella was

19

taking him seriously. Lizzie knew her sister as well as she knew herself and had unerringly read the signs: the brilliance of her eyes, the rosy flush in her cheeks and the way she kept stealing glances at Michael whenever she thought herself unobserved.

He was a grand-looking fellow too, over six feet tall, with curly black hair and eyes as dark as Stella's own. He had good white teeth, a strongly cleft chin, and his smile had an appealing quality to which Lizzie herself was not immune. If only he had not been Irish! Lizzie had nothing against the Irish—she came from Irish stock herself—but if she was right and the feeling between the two of them was as strong as she imagined, then one day Michael would take Stella away from her and Lizzie could not bear that. She had always known that Stella would marry and had hoped, for the girl's sake, that she would meet someone who could rescue her from the grinding poverty shared by most families living in the overcrowded and unhygienic courts. She had dreamed of Stella bringing home a solicitor's clerk or a local government officer, someone who would have a house in the suburbs, with a garden, and a view of something other than sooty bricks. With luck, there would be pleasant neighbours who would help the girl to settle into her new surroundings, and enough money to ensure the comfort of both Stella herself and any children that she might produce.

But an Irishman! If he had been from Dublin it would not have seemed so bad since such a personable young man would surely be able to get well-paid work somewhere in Liverpool. But a country boy from Kerry, whose father caught fish and grew potatoes for a living, was not at all the sort

20

of match that Lizzie had had in mind for Stella. The thought of her beloved little sister wearing a sacking apron and toiling in a great, wet field to dig up potatoes sent a pang of real pain through her heart. Her own grandmother had come from Irish farming stock and the tales of deprivation and near starvation suffered by such people had left an indelible mark on Lizzie's mind. I would do anything to prevent Stella suffering as Grandma suffered, she told herself fiercely. If only Michael were not so handsome!

Lizzie's thoughts were interrupted as the tram lurched to a halt and she suddenly realised that this was her stop. She fought her way off the vehicle and a soldier trod on her foot, reminding her sharply that there was a war on. Anything could happen in the next couple of years, she told herself, making her way along the crowded pavement. It was pointless meeting troubles halfway and making herself miserable over something which might never happen. Besides, was her own life not about to change? To be sure, Birkenhead was only a ferry ride away, but she would not be seeing as much of her darling once she was settled in her new job. And anyway, you never knew, Michael might take to city life like a duck to water, or Stella might meet someone else . . . or Michael's ship might be sunk and he might be drowned . . .

'Mornin', Miss Bennett! There's a lady on Sackville Street giving a party for around thirty people. She's asked us to give her a quote for six dozen milk rolls, three dozen fancies and a birthday cake. I told her you'd work something out and the lad would take a quote round to Sackville Street by eleven o'clock. Was that all

21

right?'

Miss Miller was a conscientious employee and would probably take Lizzie's place when she went off to Birkenhead, but she lacked self-confidence and Lizzie knew that this was something she should rectify so far as in her lay. Therefore, she smiled brightly at Miss Miller and told her that she had done exactly as she should. 'Though you are quite experienced enough now, Miss Miller, to have been able to do the quote yourself,' she added.

Miss Miller, a thin, intense young woman with mousy hair and light hazel eyes behind a pair of steel-rimmed spectacles, looked doubtful. 'Oh, but what about the discount, Miss Bennett?' she asked anxiously. 'We don't often have big orders except at Christmas time, and when we do, Mr Albert or yourself decides what discount should be given. I— I wouldn't want to overcharge someone . . . or undercharge them for that matter.'

'There! What a good job you said, Miss Miller, because once I leave you'll have to understand exactly how the discount system works.' She smiled at the other assistant, a fat and spotty teenager who would never have been employed by Lunt's in the usual way, since she was slow and could not add up without pencil and paper. However, all the bright youngsters were working in munitions or other war work and earning much more money than they could as shop assistants, so the firm had been glad to get anyone. 'You will take care of the shop, won't you, Miss Frost, whilst Miss Miller and I work on this quote together. If you need one of us, you only have to call.'

Lizzie accompanied Miss Miller into the tiny office and began to root out from her desk drawers

22

a number of bills and receipts and her large red order book. She would not now think of young Michael Gallagher, nor of her darling Stella; work had begun.

*   *   *

By the time the *Thunderbolt* sailed for New York once more, Michael and Stella were fathoms deep in love and knew it. Stella tried to tell herself that Lizzie's antagonism was merely due to the fact that she was secretly worrying over her own move to Birkenhead, for how could anyone not love Michael Gallagher? The ten days she had spent with him had been the happiest of her life and she had waved him off with such a feeling of desolation that she had scarcely known how to bear it.

But he would be back, of course he would, and she meant to write to him every single day, even though he might not get the letters with anything like such frequency. The *Thunderbolt* did not simply cross the Atlantic; it shepherded its flock of merchant shipping all over the world, wherever the Allies needed supplies, which meant that it might be many months before she saw him again. But he had told her that letters followed one around the globe and might be picked up at almost any port, hence her determination to write regularly.

'Customer, Miss Bennett!'

Stella, who had been tidying a pile of delicate lace handkerchiefs away in a drawer, turned immediately to face the counter, thanking Miss Murrell with a quick smile for drawing her attention. Miss Murrell was serving an irritable-looking lady with elbow-length kid gloves,

23

otherwise she would undoubtedly have attended to the customer herself, for he was a good-looking young man, despite having hair so red that Stella wondered it did not set fire to his boater. He tipped his hat, then leaned, confidentially, upon the wooden counter top.

'Good morning, sir. How can I help you?' Stella gave the customer her most engaging smile.

The young man smiled back and produced, from one pocket, a rather crumpled-looking suede glove in a shade between blue and grey. 'I'm trying to buy my mama a birthday present. I've borrowed one of her gloves for a colour match; is it possible that you might have a handbag in this shade?'

Stella looked doubtful but pulled open the big bottom drawer that contained all the handbags not already on display. 'I don't think I could find an exact match, sir,' she said regretfully. 'Oh . . . is the bag for evening wear? If so, we have several very pretty velvet ones . . .'

The young man, however, was shaking his head. 'No, not for evenings. My mama wants something practical for day wear,' he explained. 'Do you think something with a little more grey in it might be suitable?'

Stella did not think so; she thought a grey handbag with blue-grey gloves would look absolutely awful, but she was far too sensible to say so. Instead, she began producing navy handbags, which were the best she could offer, and thought they looked quite nice with the gloves though obviously not as nice as a matching bag would have done.

Finally, she was forced to advise her customer either to look elsewhere or to buy gloves as well as

24

a handbag, though she realised that this might not suit the lady, who sounded by no means easy to please for her son grew more flustered by the moment.

At the mention of trying elsewhere he looked rather relieved, and she suggested that he should try Lewis's, who had a larger handbag department than this one. 'Or you could go to Bunney's, on Church Street. They sell the most beautiful oriental gifts,' she assured him.

He cast a hasty glance round and then leaned towards her over the counter. He had an open, honest face with greenish-hazel eyes and these gazed imploringly into hers. 'I—I'm afraid I don't know Liverpool at all well, miss. Do you—do you have time off at midday? If so, and I were to buy you luncheon, would you do me the honour of—of accompanying me to Lewis's or Bunney's? I'm sure with your help I might find the very thing my mama wants, even if it isn't a handbag.'

Stella was about to advise him, rather sharply, to make up his own mind when she saw the desperate look in those green eyes. She said gently, 'Do you have no sister you could consult, sir, no aunts?'

The young man looked cast down. 'I have no female relatives, apart from my mama. The thing is, miss, my furlough is almost up. I go back to the trenches tomorrow and I wanted her to have a nice keepsake, something she really wanted, because . . . well, I expect you know what I mean.'

Stella's heart was touched. She knew all too well what her customer meant, for it was clear that he was an officer and it was widely known that the life expectancy of such a one was liable to be short. She felt sure that if Michael knew of the young man's

25

request, he would tell her at once to go with him to help choose the gift. What harm could there be in it, after all? Lizzie and her mother had both told her she should know more young men before she decided that Michael was the only person she would ever want to marry. They would be pleased to think she was taking their advice, and because of the strength of her own feelings, she knew that nothing would shake her love for Michael. So she looked up at the young man and gave him her sweetest smile. 'I see,' she said slowly. 'Yes, of course I'd be happy to help you choose a gift and equally happy to have luncheon with you, though I could not possibly let you pay for my meal. I shall be free in another twenty minutes, so if you would like to come round to the staff entrance on Cases Street at one o'clock . . .'

He agreed eagerly and when Stella emerged from the doors he was standing waiting, his hat tilted to the back of his head. She felt rather shy but her embarrassment soon dissipated when they entered a quiet dining rooms on Deane Street. Despite her objections, he insisted on buying her meal, which was as well, Stella reflected, since she had very little money on her. Over their food, she told the young man, who introduced himself as Peter Brett, all about her family and their lives. She would have liked to tell him about Michael but felt that this would be rather tactless since the last thing he would want to discuss would be the wretched, miserable war. He told her a little about himself; he had been to a very good school, had started at university but had volunteered for the army upon hearing of the death, in action, of one of his oldest friends.

26

'It seemed the right thing to do at the time, but now I think I must have been mad,' he said ruefully, between mouthfuls of pork chop and mashed potato. 'Still, what's done is done and everyone's getting war-weary. I don't imagine it will last much longer. Now tell me some more about your life outside Grundy's department store! Do you play tennis? Enjoy country walks? Knit for the troops? Or do you perhaps help at one of the local hospitals when you have time to spare?'

Stella laughed at the idea of spare time. 'I work six days of the week at Grundy's and on four of those days I am kept back to do stock checking, shelf stacking and the like, so I don't get away until eight or nine in the evening,' she told him. 'I've never played tennis in me life but I enjoy going to the picture house and seeing the film stars and I love the theatre. As for country walks, I think I would enjoy them. I used to like it when I were a kid and Lizzie took me on the tram to Fazakerley and we would walk out into the countryside. We took a carryout so's we could stay away all day and we used to pick great bunches of wild flowers, and paddle in the streams and catch tiddlers with a flour bag on a split cane. It were the loveliest thing we ever did—it's why I always wanted to live in the country, I suppose.'

'Well, there you are then,' Peter Brett said rather obscurely. He and Stella finished their meal almost simultaneously and both refused coffee, Stella glancing slightly anxiously at the big clock which hung above the door leading to the kitchen premises. They had not yet visited Lewis's or Bunney's and she dared not risk being late back after her break. To be sure, the war had made jobs

27

easier to find, but Stella did not like change and besides, she was happy at Grundy's. Miss Murrell was her best friend—outside shop hours she was Gwen to Stella—and she got on equally well with the supervisor and the floorwalker. She had no intention of losing her nice job, not even to help a young officer who would be travelling back to the trenches on the following day.

'Thank you very much for a delicious luncheon, Mr Brett,' she said formally as they left the dining rooms. She added, mischievously, as they turned towards Lewis's: 'I know I said I'd pay for meself, but I don't ever go out for a meal and I hadn't realised how expensive it would be. When you've only got ninepence in your purse, you can't offer to shell out one and six.'

They laughed together over Stella's cash shortage as they entered Lewis's and headed for the handbag counter.

CHAPTER TWO

1918

It was an icy cold January day and, once more, Stella was waiting for Michael's ship to dock. It was freezing down by the water and she knew that Michael's time ashore was liable to be short but, nevertheless, she was aglow with excitement, for this leave would be different from either of the others she had shared with him. This time, they would have somewhere to go, somewhere where they could be alone.

28

The fact that Lizzie and her mother constantly voiced their disapproval of her friendship with Michael had made both his previous leaves difficult, to say the least. Now that Lizzie was in Birkenhead, she was not always present when Stella brought Michael home, but Mrs Bennett did not attempt to make the young man welcome. In fact, she was so cold and unpleasant that the two young people felt they had to make themselves scarce as soon as they could and spent their time together walking the city streets, tucked up in a picture house when they had the money, or wandering round the markets, and making cups of tea in little cheap cafés last as long as possible.

Michael had always stayed at the Sailors' Home but he had a friend on board ship, called Toby, who lived in the city and on the last day of Michael's previous leave had suggested that, next time his pal was in Liverpool, he might like to have the use of the small back bedroom in his mother's house. 'You could bring your young lady there,' he had suggested and, seeing Michael's expression, had added hastily: 'No funny business, old feller. But it would be somewhere for the pair of youse to be together, like. I know her folk don't approve—she's awful young—but if you're set on marriage, and I know you are, what's the harm in being together in comfort?'

So now, Stella could look forward to Michael's leave without having to worry about her mother's attitude. Like a dutiful daughter, she would take him home to tea either today or tomorrow, depending on what time his ship docked, but if Mrs Bennett treated him as anything but an honoured guest, Stella had determined that she would warn

29

her mother that they would not return to Victoria Court again. When he was in Liverpool he usually called for her at the house since he did not like her hanging about outside the Sailors' Home, but now he would have an address of his own, a place it would be perfectly proper for her to visit and she intended to do so.

She had hoped that her mother might be more amenable after Lizzie had left for her new life in Birkenhead, but this had not proved to be the case. Mrs Bennett snubbed Michael whenever he was present and had been known to refer to him as 'that bog-trotter' when he was not. Gentle Stella had never told her mother what she thought of such rudeness but decided now that she would simply have to do so, for she and Michael meant to go and see the priest about a wedding. Not Father McKay, because he knew her far too well and might refuse to marry her—she was only seventeen after all—but a priest attached to a small church in the suburbs who, it was said, would marry you without too many questions asked. Stella sighed and rubbed her hands briskly up and down the sleeves of her shabby black coat. Why were parents so pig-headed? She and Michael loved one another deeply, she would not leave him for the richest and handsomest man in the land, so why could not her mother acknowledge this and wish them happy?

The docks were crowded as usual, but presently Stella was sure she could see the *Thunderbolt* nosing into a berth. Her heart began to bump unevenly. Soon, very soon, she would be in his arms again. She began to push her way towards where she hoped the gangway would be lowered.

'Phew!' As they left the small house in Victoria
Court, Michael let out his breath in a long whistle
of relief and put his arm round Stella's shoulders,
giving them a comforting hug. 'Your mam must
have got out of bed on the wrong side this
morning! I don't think it was anything I said,
because I scarcely opened me mouth. Why, she
even snapped at you when you said we might go to
see a film later.'

Stella took his hand and squeezed it. She felt
both miserable and guilty over her mother's
attitude, yet she could not quite suppress the
excitement which came over her whenever she
thought about the little room towards which they
were now heading. She had not seen it because
when Michael's ship had docked the previous day
there had not been time to catch the tram out to
Bootle. However, Michael had met her in her
dinner hour and had waxed positively lyrical over
the charms of the small room. ' 'Tis on the third
floor—it's an attic really, but Mrs Williams has got
it done up ever so nice,' he told her. 'It were Toby's
sister Margaret's room when she were at home, but
she got married and moved out last year. Mrs
Williams let it to a young couple for a bit but they
got a place of their own and she's not bothered to
fill it again yet. It's got flowered curtains at the
windows and a flowered counterpane on the bed.
There's a little paraffin stove what the young
couple used to keep the place warm and to cook
their meals on, though they had a share in the
kitchen, like. And there's two little easy chairs, a
wardrobe for your clothes, a washstand and a

cupboard for food. It'll be just like a home of our own I'm telling you.'

But right now, Stella must make Michael see that Mrs Bennett was not against Michael as a person. She simply did not want him marrying her daughter and taking her away from Liverpool.

She tried to explain this to Michael as the tram clattered its way through the city, heading for Bootle, but though Michael gave her a squeeze and said he quite understood, she thought that he, too, was looking forward to their sharing of the small room and was not as unhappy about her mother's attitude as he might otherwise have been.

They got off the tram at the junction of Stanley and Strand Roads and Michael looked consideringly at a fried fish shop which was doing good business. 'We could take some in for our supper,' he said. 'I know we had a good tea at your mam's, but you'll be hungry again before bedtime. We could heat them up over the oil stove, I dare say.'

Stella cast a quick glance at him then hastily looked away. Surely he did not expect her to stay until his bedtime? She knew he would take her home, which meant they would pass the fried fish shop and might buy themselves a paper of chips to eat on the tram. So she shook her head and assured him that she would not be hungry again before bedtime. Then, arms linked, they continued to hurry towards Marsh Lane and their goal.

*   *   *

It was a lovely room, even nicer than Michael's description had been, and Stella bustled about,

32

pretending to be a housewife in her own little home, examining everything from the mugs in the cupboard to the sheets and blankets on the beautiful double bed. She had met Mrs Williams and had thought her an admirable person, for the older woman had seemed to take it for granted that she and Michael were a couple. She said she hoped to see plenty of the younger woman when the *Thunderbolt* went back to sea, and when she left them, Stella felt she had made a friend.

It was midnight before she got back to Victoria Court. She half expected to find her mother waiting up for her but, clearly, Mrs Bennett had taken it for granted that her daughter would be home when the show at the picture house finished and had not bothered to wait up. As she undressed and climbed into her own little bed, a daring plan formed itself in Stella's mind. Michael would only be ashore for another three days and she decided there could be no harm in spending almost all of those three days with him. She could prepare and cook them meals in the Marsh Lane room, which would be considerably cheaper than eating out. In fact, she decided she would stay with him almost all night, and catch the first tram back to Victoria Court in the morning. Since Lizzie had left home, Mrs Bennett had got into the habit of remaining in bed until Stella had made the breakfast porridge, brewed the tea and cut her carryout. Then Stella would shout up the stairs: 'Breakfast's ready, Mam,' and her mother would come fumbling down in her voluminous nightdress, draping a couple of thick shawls around her shoulders and declaring that she would pay Stella back for making breakfast by preparing a high tea fit for a king. So, if Stella was careful, her mother would never know that she had not slept at home but would simply assume that her daughter had come in fairly late after the pictures or a dance and seeing Michael off back to the Sailors' Home.

All day at work, Stella smiled brightly at the customers and sang beneath her breath as she tucked away gloves, scarves, umbrellas and similar articles in their appropriate places. When her working day was finished, she met Michael outside the staff entrance and the two of them returned to Marsh Lane with the makings of a meal which Stella had bought in her lunch hour. So it was over steak pie and mash that she outlined her plans and was gratified to see Michael's delight, though she wondered a little when he began to tell her that he would take great care of her, that nothing would go wrong and that she was the dearest creature on earth, so she was.

In addition to their supper Stella had bought three brown eggs and half a loaf of bread. The first tram next morning would be clattering along Stanley Road at about six o'clock, heading for the city, and Stella meant to be aboard it, but she intended to cook her man a good breakfast before she left him, even if it did mean getting up at five o'clock. She knew that Michael owned an old alarm clock and decided she had best set it for five otherwise she might oversleep. She meant to insist that Michael slept in the bed whilst she would snuggle down on the two little easy chairs, pushed together. After all, he was bigger and heavier than she and was paying rent for the room, so it would be very unfair if she occupied the bed and left him trying to sleep in his bedroll, laid out upon the

34

floor. The weather was still bitterly cold, and snug though their room was when the oil stove was lit, she guessed that it would get pretty chilly once the fire was out. Up on the chairs, with Michael's bedroll round her, she would be warm enough, but anyone lying on the floor would feel draughts both from the long, sloping attic window and from the ill-fitting door. No, no, it simply would not do; she would insist that Michael slept in the bed.

It never occurred to her for one moment that they might share it.

*   *   *

Three days later, Michael and Stella said a sad farewell to their little room and caught the tram together, but this time Stella did not go straight home to rumple her unslept-in bed and make her mother's porridge. She would go to the docks first and see Michael aboard the *Thunderbolt*, and then she would make her way to Victoria Court. If her mother discovered she had been deceived, then there might be trouble, but nothing on earth, Stella decided, would stop her from saying a proper goodbye to her man.

For now she felt truly married to Michael, even though no banns had been called and no ceremony of marriage had been performed. Ever since that first night, when Michael had gathered her up in his arms and carried her to bed, she had known only exquisite happiness and an overwhelming feeling that she was doing the right thing. Oh, she knew that, morally, what she and Michael were doing was very wrong, would have horrified everyone had they known, but it no longer seemed to matter. They meant to marry, but because of her family's objections they could not do so yet. Well, if she was going to have a baby as a result of being with Michael, then she knew her family well enough to anticipate their reaction. Everyone, even Father McKay, would insist that she and Michael married immediately. 'For the child's sake,' they would say severely, and folk would count up on their fingers and maybe smile slyly at one another when the baby was born, but they would not call it a bastard nor, in their hearts, think any the worse of her and Michael.

The tram was full, for there were many early workers making for the city centre from Bootle, but Michael and Stella had managed to get a seat on one of the long wooden benches and now, as Stella looked up into Michael's face, a strange thing happened. A picture flashed into her mind, a picture of a long, low room with oddly shaped windows. It was rather dim in the room, and crowded too, with men hanging up what looked like bundles of canvas and rope. Stella suddenly realised that the men were slinging hammocks, that this must be a scene aboard his ship which Michael had described to her. She thought, with a slight shock, that this was not the first time she had seen pictures of something Michael had described . . . or had he? Certainly, he had talked about his life on board ship at some length but never, she now realised, in the detail of the pictures which formed in her mind. He had told her about the places and people she saw, but only vaguely, never with the exactitude of her visions, if you could call them that. She began to speak to him, and as soon as she did so the picture disappeared and all she saw were the bodies of the men strap-hanging and Michael's gentle, loving face as he looked down at her.

'They never tell us where we're bound until we're well clear of land, but you will write, won't you, sweetheart? As you know, letters catch up with us eventually, even if I do get five or ten at the same time. But if you number the outside of the envelopes, I can read them in the right order. This furlough has been grand, so it has. The best four days of me entire life, but in a way it'll make the missin' of you worse. Mrs Williams will have to let the room because I can't afford to pay her rent when we're not there, but she says if it's occupied next time I'm in port, we can have the other attic room, the really small one, for a shillin' or two. Ah, here's our stop.'

The tram drew into the Pier Head and there was a mass exodus, during which Stella's toes got trodden on and elbows landed painfully until Michael put a protective arm about her and drew her close to his side. It was still very early, the street lamps reflecting in the dark water. Once they got clear of the Pier Head itself, there were fewer people about. Sailors were making their way back to their ships, a few cats gathered round the strong-smelling piled up fish boxes and hopeful urchins, eager to earn a ha'penny, offered to 'Carry your kitbag, sir?' in piping tones.

They reached the end of the gangway and, heedless of onlookers, Michael swung Stella into his arms and kissed her soundly. Then he stood her down and cupped her face in his hands. 'With my body, I thee worship,' he said softly. 'Take care of yourself, alanna, and remember . . .' he lowered his voice to a husky whisper, '. . . if you should be finding yourself in the family way, be sure to let me know quick, and tell your mam I'm ready and willin' to make an honest woman of you next time I'm in port. Once we're wed, we'll take the room on permanent if that's what you'd like.'

'I hope I *am* going to have a baby,' Stella said. It sounded shocking, put so bluntly, but she told herself she was only speaking the truth. 'If it's the only way to get us married, then it's good enough for me. And I'd love the little room, only—only I'd be rather lonely when you're at sea, darling Michael.'

'That's true, but I don't think this war's goin' to last much longer. And once it's over, we shan't be wantin' the little room because we'll marry and go back to Ireland,' Michael said. 'Oh, me darlin' girl, I must get aboard and sling me hammock and reserve a space for Toby. He'll be comin' later. Oh, Stella, I love you so much, it hurts.'

Stella smiled tremulously. 'Me too,' she said. 'I—I love you so much that sometimes I seem to see what you're thinking. Oh, darling Michael, take good care of yourself and come back to me quick, quick!'

*   *   *

A month after Michael had left, Stella was setting out a selection of scarves for a customer when Miss Murrell nudged her in the ribs. 'Here comes a friend of yours,' she whispered. 'Shall I take over here for you? I'll be bound he's wanting to speak to you because it can't be his mam's birthday every day of the week!'

'No thank you, Miss Murrell,' Stella said politely,

giving her friend an indignant glance. Miss Murrell knew very well that one did not abandon a customer to another sales lady, not even if the Lord Mayor of Liverpool was waiting to be served. However, she did glance in the direction her friend had indicated, and knew the young man at once, despite a change in his appearance. It was Mr Brett, the young officer who had taken her out for luncheon, and he was on crutches, one foot and most of his leg heavily plastered.

He saw at once that she was busy and limped slowly past, giving her a rueful grin over her customer's head which she returned with a quick and sympathetic smile. Poor Mr Brett! But at least he was alive, although clearly injured—and badly enough to be brought home, too. Stella had heard that the hospitals in France were full to bursting and was glad that he had been judged sufficiently well to return to Blighty. She found herself hoping that he would ask her out again so that she might tell him a little about Michael. She would have liked to have confided in Gwen Murrell, but hesitated to do so in other than vague terms. Miss Murrell came from a similar background to her own. She lived in a crowded terraced house not far from Victoria Court, shopped in the same shops, frequented the same picture houses and knew many of the same people. She knew that Stella was seeing a seaman of whom her family did not approve, knew that her friend was set on marriage, but did not know Michael's name, or that they were lovers. Indeed, Stella did not mean to tell Mr Brett of the intimacy between her and her young man, but anything she told him would remain strictly between the two of them, mainly because their lives ran on parallel lines which would never touch. Furthermore, one of her mother's favourite arguments was that she, Stella, had simply never known any man well, apart from Michael. On the spur of the moment, she decided that it might be a good thing to talk about this young officer, perhaps to take him home. Then it would be all the more convincing when she stubbornly insisted on marrying Michael, for there was no doubt about it, Mr Brett was a far better match than ever poor Michael could be. He lived in a large house in a smart and expensive neighbourhood. His father was a banker and his elder brother was at Cambridge, studying law. Stella knew little about his mother, save for her taste in gloves and handbags, but from the way Mr Brett spoke of her, she was used to having her own way and had probably never dusted a shelf or baked a cake in her entire life.

How delighted Mam would be if I married into that little lot, Stella thought now, with an inward smile, still bending solicitously over her customer. She herself would hate it, of course, feel like a fish out water, but that would simply never occur to her mother. Mam would just see a golden future for the daughter she adored. She would tell herself that Stella, too, would never need to dust a shelf or bake a cake, would be a real lady with a big house and scores of servants. She would boast about her daughter's brand new motor car, about the charitable works she would undertake to keep boredom at bay. When the babies came along, there would be a smart nursemaid to push the big perambulator and the children would wear beautiful clothes and go to expensive schools. And

40

I'd never have to wash a nappy, Stella thought with an inward giggle. Wasn't it ridiculous how one's imagination could run on, given the slightest opportunity? What a good thing she was deeply in love with Michael and unlikely to be swayed by the worldly goods which her imagination had just laid before her!

'You'll take the pink *and* the grey? I think madam has made a wise choice,' Stella said glibly, picking up the two delicate chiffon scarves, fine as wreaths of mist, and beginning to pack them in tissue. 'That will be eight and tenpence, please, madam—do you have an account with us?'

The woman gave her account number and Stella, aware of the supervisor whose sharp ears appeared to hear every word her staff uttered, asked if madam would like to see some gloves in the same shades. To her great relief, the customer replied courteously, but firmly, that the scarves would be all and presently left.

Mr Brett, who had been hovering, came forward, swinging along on his crutches, and stopped in front of Stella. 'Same time, same place?' he asked rather breathlessly, and Stella realised that he had noticed the supervisor's beady-eyed attention.

Stella might have prevaricated a little, might even have decided that it would be better not to go out with him again, but the presence of Miss Ellison put a stop to any such hesitation. Stella only had time to say, in a hissing whisper: 'All right, then; one o'clock at the staff entrance,' before the supervisor bore down upon her. Mr Brett turned away leisurely, as though he had all the time in the world, and began to limp across the shop floor.

'Miss Bennett! I really cannot allow you to

41

entertain your—your gentlemen friends whilst you are supposed to be working,' the older woman began, but Stella broke in at once.

'I'm *so* sorry, Miss Ellison; the young gentleman was asking me if I could tell him the way to the gents' toilets.' She turned her wide, limpid gaze upon the older woman. 'Would it have been more correct to send him to you for such information? I told him the floorwalker would direct him.'

Miss Ellison went turkey-cock red and glared balefully before turning away without another word, but after a decent interval Miss Murrell came over to her, grinning from ear to ear. 'I ain't never seen no one cut the carpet from under Miss E. like what you can,' she hissed gleefully. 'That'll make her think twice before she tries to interfere if one of us gets a male customer again. I wonder if she believed you, though.'

'I don't care whether she did or not,' Stella replied tranquilly, but with a lurking twinkle in her eyes. 'I'm going to meet him for luncheon, like before. He's awful nice and ever so generous.'

'I thought your naval beau was the only feller you cared about,' Miss Murrell remarked, as the two of them began refolding the rejected scarves and replacing them in the long drawer beneath the counter. 'I thought you was as good as engaged and goin' to get married just as soon as you could.'

'So we are,' Stella said defensively. 'But I thought it wouldn't hurt to throw a bit of dust into me mam's eyes. She's always nagging me to see a bit more of other fellers, and though Mr Brett is only a friend I reckon it'll please her. But it's all right, I'm going to tell him all about Michael over our meal.'

42

It was a mild and sunny day, with a brisk March wind blowing in their faces, when Stella and Mr Brett caught the train up to Southport. Stella had been seeing a lot of Mr Brett, and he had suggested a trip to the seaside resort on her day off. Mr Brett—only by now she called him Peter—was still on crutches, and it seemed as though he was glad of any quiet diversion which would take his mind off the pain in his foot—and also off his return to the trenches which, he guessed, would not be long delayed once the plaster cast came off.

As Stella had intended, she had told him all about Michael without giving away that they were lovers, and had found him a sympathetic and interested listener. He told her that he himself had grown very fond of a young nurse when he had first been sent into hospital, and hoped to renew the acquaintance one day. It made Stella feel even more at ease in his pleasant and undemanding company and the staff at Grundy's grew accustomed to seeing him hovering at the staff entrance as the door closed.

Despite her earlier intention to take the young officer home, Stella had not done so. Now that Lizzie no longer lived with them, the small house in the court wore a neglected air and the kitchen was often downright dirty. Mrs Bennett resented what she regarded as unnecessary housework, and though she cooked a meal every night for herself and her daughter, the food was uninspiring.

However, as Stella and Peter Brett walked companionably along Lord Street, she was astonished to hear herself hailed. 'Stella Bennett! Are you so toffee-nosed that you're goin' to walk straight past your own sister? And what are you doing in Southport, may I ask?'

It was Lizzie, looking very smart in a navy coat with a hat trimmed with a wreath of pale blue roses around the brim. She was with another woman of about her own age, also smartly dressed in a tweed suit with a little cape around the shoulders.

'Lizzie!' Stella squeaked. She gave her sister a hug and a kiss, then stepped back. 'Come to that, what are *you* doing in Southport? Me and my friend, Mr Brett, have come up for a look round the shops and a stroll along the prom. It's my day off and he's—he's still not well enough to rejoin his regiment.' She turned to her escort, aware that her cheeks were hot. 'But I'm forgetting my manners. Mr Brett, this is my eldest sister, Miss Lizzie Bennett. Lizzie, Mr Brett.'

'And I'm forgetting mine,' Lizzie said heartily. 'How d'you do, Mr Brett? And this is my friend, Miss Parsons.'

The four of them chatted idly for a short while and then Lizzie said that she and Miss Parsons must be going. 'We aren't on our day off like you youngsters are,' she explained. 'We've come up to take a look at some property. The boss is thinking of starting up in Southport so Miss Parsons and myself is giving the once-over to three vacant shops and we've only seen one of them so far.' She held out a hand towards Stella's companion. 'Nice to meet you, Mr Brett.' She turned to her sister. 'Tell Mam I'll be over on Sunday and do try to get her to buy a decent joint of pork; the meat we had last time I were home were tough as old shoe leather.'

44

Stella laughed and promised to see to it, and she and Peter Brett went on their way. Stella was not sure whether to be glad or sorry that they had met up with her sister but decided that it was probably a good thing. Lizzie would report back to Mam and perhaps her mother would stop nagging her over her insistence that she meant to marry Michael. At any event, it might take some of the pressure off her. Mrs Bennett had several times suggested that she should bring Mr Brett home and Stella knew that her mother only half believed in her 'officer beau'. Now that Lizzie had actually met him, however, any doubts would surely be laid to rest.

*   *   *

Lizzie had been astonished by the encounter. Naturally, she had heard, both from her mother and from Stella, that her sister had become friendly with a young officer and she had never for one moment doubted his existence, since she knew that her darling Stella would never lie to her. The young officer existed all right, but she had not expected him to be quite so well spoken, self-confident and charming or, if the truth were known, quite so—so redheaded! But his unaccented voice thrilled her, and the way he looked at Stella . . . any other girl would have been in seventh heaven, Lizzie told herself severely. If only, oh if only Stella had not met that wretched Irish seaman first! But Michael Gallagher was far away, sailing heaven knew what distant seas, and Mr Brett was right here. Surely he would not be returning to the Front for a good while yet? He was still on crutches, still limping badly. Oh, if only he would sweep Stella off her

45

feet, propose marriage, show her the sort of life he could offer her!

'Miss Bennett, wharrever are you thinkin' about? That's three times I've asked you if you'd care for another cup o' tea, and not so much as one word in answer have I got!'

Miss Parsons's voice was plaintive and Lizzie hurriedly hauled her mind back to the present, to the neat little tearoom where she and her fellow employee were sharing a big brown pot of tea and a plate of fancy cakes. 'My dear, I'm that sorry,' she said contritely. 'Me mind were elsewhere . . . yes, another cup of tea would be very nice. And perhaps . . . yes, perhaps one of them pink iced buns.'

'Your mind were with your little sister and her beau,' Miss Parsons said shrewdly. 'You've thought o' nothin' else since we met 'em.'

'We-ell, yes, that's true,' Lizzie admitted. 'He seems a nice young feller, and you can tell he's right fond of Stella. But . . . I don't know . . .'

'Oh well, she's young yet, and not likely to be considerin' marriage, or her future,' Miss Parsons said comfortably, pouring tea. 'She'll be havin' a good time, and wi' looks like hers . . . well, who can blame her?'

Lizzie helped herself to the bun with the pink frosting and bit into it. 'Who indeed?' she echoed rather thickly. 'I dare say you're right and she's just—just gettin' to know several fellers to gerra bit more experience, like. She's a good girl, our Stella.'

*   *   *

Stella was in her room getting ready for work.

Outside the window, a light drizzle was falling and she sighed, selecting her dark raincoat instead of the lighter garment she had planned to wear. It was May, and high time that they had some nice weather.

Glancing down at herself, Stella was pleased to see that there was no obvious sign of her pregnancy for she knew that, by now, she was almost five months gone. She found herself dreading the moment when she would have to admit to her mother and Lizzie that she was in the family way. She and Michael had planned for this, seeing it as their only hope of an early wedding, but now that the moment had come Stella was secretly afraid that admitting she was expecting a baby would make her sound like a bad girl with no thought for her mother's feelings, but only a sort of greed. This was not true; she and Michael were deeply in love, but she knew there were people who would look at her differently once they heard about her condition.

However, it was something that would have to be faced, though no one had yet commented on the slight thickening of her supple waist, and her bouts of morning sickness had been of short duration; indeed, pregnancy seemed to suit her, giving her a glow, so that friends remarked how well she looked.

Gwen Murrell was walking out with a young man from the Sports Department and for the first time in her life spending her money on something other than pretty clothes, so the two girls haunted shops like Bunney's where household goods could occasionally be bought very cheaply. Miss Murrell's young man was not happy at home and had suggested that he and Miss Murrell should aim for an early wedding, even if it meant a lot of scrimping and saving right now. Accordingly, the bottom drawers of both girls were gradually growing, and it obviously did not occur to Miss Murrell that her friend was nest building.

It would not be so bad breaking the news to her mother if she had Michael's support, Stella told herself as she clattered down the stairs. His immediate offer to marry her without delay would calm a good deal of her mother's anger and the fact that Michael had promised they would move into a room of their own meant that the family would not have to face the condemnation of neighbours and friends. By the time the baby was born, Stella assured herself philosophically, as she entered the kitchen, she would be a married lady with a home and husband of her own. Oh, folk might count on their fingers and look knowing, but she found she no longer cared about that. Her mother was one of a large family—six boys and eight girls—and Stella knew very well that at least three of her aunts, and probably more, had had to get married.

'You ready for the off, Stella love?' Mrs Bennett was sitting at the kitchen table, spooning the porridge Stella had made earlier into her mouth, and spoke rather thickly through it. She glanced up at the clock on the mantel. 'Have you got time for a cuppa afore youse go? I reckon there's a good five minutes before the next No. 1 comes along.'

'No, I don't think I'd better, Mam,' Stella said with real regret; she could have done with another cup of tea. 'Miss Ellison likes us to be in early—it puts her in a good mood.' She swung open the kitchen door. 'See you tonight, Mam,' she called

48

over her shoulder, slamming the door behind her and setting off, though not for the tram stop. She had realised months before that any letter from Michael which was delivered at her home was either hidden or destroyed, and rather than create a full-blown row had made other arrangements for her post. Now, her letters came to the corner shop where Mrs Mullins stuck them under the counter and handed them over whenever Stella called in. She was a fat and friendly woman and thought it very romantic to be helping a pair of star-crossed lovers, so never said anything to Mrs Bennett about the arrangement.

Now, Stella ducked into the shop and looked hopefully across at Mrs Mullins, who immediately produced an envelope from under the counter. 'There you are, m' dear,' she said cheerfully, handing it over. 'I hope as how it's good news; it's about time the old *Thunderbolt* came into port again, ain't it?'

Stella agreed fervently and hurried out of the shop. There was a queue at the tram stop, which meant the No. 1 had not yet arrived. She joined the end of it and began to open the letter. It was not a long one but so far as she was concerned any communication from Michael was something to be savoured and enjoyed. The tram came along and the queue drew back, cursing as water sprayed up from its wheels, then everyone scrambled aboard and Stella, following, stuffed the letter into her pocket, unable to prevent a big smile from spreading across her face. Michael was delighted that they were going to become parents, and the ship was heading for Liverpool at last! The convoy over which she stood guard would be returning to

49

sea with its cargo of much-needed food supplies within three or four days. It was not long, and it would mean that she and Michael could face her mother together. All the way to work, Stella smiled and smiled and thought longingly of the little attic room in Marsh Lane. Was it possible to arrange to wed in three days? She supposed it must be. Then they would get married and nothing her mother could do after that would part them.

Satisfied, Stella dreamed happily of the days to come.

*   *   *

After a couple of days of euphoria, Stella made a brave decision. She realised that there was no time to be wasted if she and Michael were indeed to marry before he returned to sea. Therefore, she must tell her mother immediately so that they might go together to see Father McKay. Once he realised that she was expecting Michael's baby, he would be as eager to get a wedding arranged as she. All Stella's sensitive soul shrank from the task of having to tell her mother without Michael's support, but she told herself not to be a coward, and two weeks before Michael's ship was due to dock she decided to take the bull by the horns.

It was a Sunday and she and her mother had just got back from Mass and were preparing the Sunday dinner. Lizzie was going to join them and suddenly Stella decided that she would tell her mother before her sister arrived rather than after. It might mean that she had to go through two lots of reproaches, two lots of gnashing teeth and rending garments, but she thought it would be fairer both to her mam and to Lizzie if they heard her news one at a time. What was more, her mother proceeded to give her an ideal opportunity for such a revelation by remarking that Minnie Thelwell, at No. 24, was clearly expecting another baby, though God knew how she would manage since she already had four kids under five and a husband fighting somewhere in France.

'An' if young Joseph Thelwell has got a brain in his head, he'll do a bit of countin' up and realise he probably ain't the father,' Mrs Bennett was saying grimly as she pushed a large pan of potatoes over the heat. 'Mind, he's a good lad and she's a trifle weak-minded, so mebbe, by the time he's home next . . .'

'I'm having a baby, too, Mam,' Stella cut in, her voice a little high and strained but still determinedly cheerful. 'It ain't for a while yet, but Michael and meself want to marry when he next comes home. He'll be back in two weeks.' She glanced across at her mother who appeared to have been turned to stone in front of the stove, with one hand still on the pan handle. 'I—I thought you and meself might go along to the Presbytery this afternoon and have a word with the Father. I—I don't know much about such things as special licences, but Michael thought we might need one. D'you think the Father will be able to tell us what best to do?'

Mrs Bennett did not reply at once but she did turn a little in order to stare unbelievingly at her daughter. 'It's a joke, ain't it?' she said huskily. 'You're havin' me on because of what I said about Minnie Thelwell. It were wrong of me, because she

51

ain't a bad gal, but—but it were wrong of you, our Stella, to gimme such a fright.' To Stella's horror, large tears welled up in her mother's eyes and trickled down her cheeks. 'Stella? Tell your old mam it ain't true!'

'I'm sorry, Mam, really sorry, but if you're honest, you must know that for Michael and me it were the only way,' Stella said humbly. 'I didn't want to be a bad girl, but what else could we do? You made him so unwelcome that I dreaded bringing him home and we both knew you'd never let us get married, not without us runnin' off to Scotland or somewhere, and Michael's not home for long enough. So—so we decided that it were gettin' pregnant or waitin' four years, and we couldn't either of us bear that.'

Mrs Bennett sat down heavily in the nearest fireside chair. The cat, Sunny, immediately jumped into her lap but though Mrs Bennett automatically began to stroke his gleaming back, she did not take her tear-wet eyes from her daughter's face. 'So now it's my fault, is it?' she said bitterly. 'I might have known it would be my fault. Oh, Stella, how could you? I always tell everyone wharra good gal you are and now . . . to have people starin' an' callin' names . . .'

Stella had been preparing suet pastry for an apple dumpling. Now she ran across the room and put her arms about her mother, regardless of her floury hands. 'But Mam, if Michael and meself get married then no one's goin' to say things—why should they? An awful lot of women are in the family way when they walk up the aisle.'

'Yes, I know; I were expectin' Lizzie meself when your dad and I wed,' Mrs Bennett admitted in a

52

lugubrious tone. 'But—but that were different. We wanted somethin' better for you, Lizzie an' me. There were that young officer, Lizzie told me about him, she said he were a grand, handsome feller and well-to-do. Why oh why, queen, couldn't you have settled on a feller like that, instead of a bog-trottin' Irishman what'll carry you off to Conny-wotsit to toil out your days in the spud fields an' never see your old mam again, very likely.'

'Oh, Mam, I don't love Mr Brett an' never shall and I love Michael very much,' Stella said. 'And marrying Michael won't be like that anyway. I'm not going to leave you, not while the war's on. Once the war's over, you'll have the lads back, I know you will, so you won't be lonely. Very likely, when George marries, he an' his wife will move in with you; it 'ud be company for you, someone to do the cooking and look after you when you're old.'

'I'm old now,' Mrs Bennett wailed, rubbing at her eyes with her fat and rather dirty hands. 'I'm as old as the bleedin' hills but I've led a good life—apart from gettin' in the family way with Lizzie—an' now look how I'm repaid! Me youngest child what everyone knows is the most beautiful gal in Liverpool an' she throws herself away on a . . .'

'Don't say it again, Mam, or I'll get real upset,' Stella said warningly. 'I'm going to marry Michael and it won't do for you to keep calling him names. If you do, I really *will* move out because he'll be my husband and no one could bear hearing their mother call their husband bad names.'

Mrs Bennett sniffed and dabbed at her eyes again with the edge of her shawl, but Stella could see that the worst of the shock was over and her mother was growing, if not reconciled, at least used

53

to the idea that her youngest child was going to be married. 'Ho, so I aren't to call your precious Michael names, aren't I?' she said belligerently. 'And why not, pray? Are you goin' to tell me he didn't have no hand in gettin' this baby? He's behaved as bad as you—worse—so I'm entitled to call a few names, I think.'

'Then you'd best call me a few at the same time, Mam,' Stella said steadily, though she could feel the heat rising in her cheeks. 'I'm a slut and a bad girl and I'm going to have a little bastard; is that what you're thinking?'

This was too much for Mrs Bennett. She turned in her chair, disturbing Sunny who jumped down with an affronted air, and gave her daughter a hearty hug. 'No, of course you ain't a slut an' the baby won't be a bastard, not once you and that—that . . .' she caught her daughter's eye and grinned suddenly, '. . . not once you and that decent young Irishman is wed,' she ended.

'Right. An' shall you and me go to see Father McKay and get things sorted out when we finish our dinners?' Stella asked hopefully. She returned to her suet pastry, rolling it out and then lining the basin with it, before tipping in the prepared apple pieces. Once it was full, she added sugar, then placed the rest of the pastry on top and sealed it down. She was about to envelop it in a pudding cloth when the back door opened and her eldest sister's cheerful voice remarked that it was perishin' cold for May, so she had brought them a nice steak pudding which they could boil up for their tea.

Stella sighed; now she would have to tell her story all over again, doubtless to the same shock

54

and recriminations. But there was no point in putting things off. As her sister began to divest herself of her coat, Stella said in a small voice: 'Mam and meself were just agreein' that we'd go round to see Father McKay after dinner. We need his advice, because . . .'

CHAPTER THREE

Father McKay would have married them, had he been able to do so, but it was simply not possible because Michael's ship arrived in Liverpool well before it should have docked, and was due to leave in rather less than two days. This time, however, because of the forthcoming marriage, Michael was actually invited to stay in Victoria Court, and since the room at Marsh Lane was not available he was happy enough to accept.

He felt a trifle uneasy, though his mother-in-law to be kept her lip buttoned for the most part; but since he was home mid-week he did not have to run the gauntlet of Lizzie's disapproval, for there was no doubt that Lizzie did disapprove, would have urged her mother to forbid the match, had it not been for Stella's condition.

Stella had told him, as they walked back to Victoria Court from the docks, that he would be sleeping in the boys' room and not sharing her own small bed. 'It wouldn't be fair on my mam,' she said righteously, and then spoiled the high tone of her remark by adding: 'But I'll sneak in once Mam's asleep because we love one another and want to be together, don't we?'

Michael agreed, and was so nice to Mrs Bennett that she began to look on him with a little more favour. He did everything in his power to encourage this. Although he was in Liverpool for such a short time, he made sure that it was he who brought in coal from the shed and logs from the woodpile, and he who worked the pump which crouched over the low stone sink.

When Stella came to him that first night, he held her gently in his arms, longing for her but worried in case lovemaking might harm the baby. Stella had no idea, but she had suddenly become aware that life was short and opportunities must not be allowed to slip away. Minnie Thelwell's husband, Joseph, had been killed in France barely a week before. Now there would be no one to query the fatherhood of her child or to help her rear her family. Stella had gone round to see her and had done what she could to comfort the older girl, but with very little success. 'It's a judgement on me,' Minnie had wailed, with the telegram, already so tear-blotched that it was scarcely readable, in one hand. 'I went wi' another chap 'cos my Joe hadn't been home for so long. I didn't love the feller— hardly knew him, in fact—but I were desperate for money 'cos Joe's allotment hadn't come through and—and he offered me five bob . . . oh, Stella, I wish with all me heart I'd not done it!'

Once, Stella would have been appalled by Minnie's story, but now she felt she understood it very much better. To go to bed with a man for money was far worse than what she and Michael had done, she acknowledged that, yet she knew that she herself would commit a crime in order to save Michael from being hungry or cold. And

Michael's child was already dear to her. If that child was hungry, crying for food, and she had no other means of earning, perhaps it was possible that she, too, might sink her pride in order to buy bread.

She did not think, however, that she should share this philosophy with Michael and, indeed, was ashamed of herself for having let such a thought even enter her head. The trouble was, having heard Minnie's sad little story, she had begun to realise, for the first time, that Michael, too, was just a pawn in the great game of war. His ship might be sunk by enemy action, he might be swept overboard by an enormous wave, a torpedo could strike the ship or gunfire from an enemy vessel might kill him as he worked on deck. She had heard of seamen being killed in dockside brawls, dying in a dozen different ways, gone for ever because of some foolish accident which would never have happened in peacetime.

On the day following his return she had meant to go to work as usual but decided she could not bear to do so. He would be here so short a time, and was so precious to her! So she paid little Laurie Gittins to take a message to Miss Ellison saying that she was sick but would return to work as soon as she was fit enough. Then the pair of them set off for a full day out together, catching a tram which took them into the beautiful May countryside. Stella had packed a picnic which they ate sitting on a stile, content with each other's company and enjoying the sweet smell of the air whilst they talked and talked and talked, for it was as though each could never learn enough about the other. And then there was Michael's home to be described in loving

57

detail, the brownish photograph of his parents on their wedding day to be mulled over to see which one he most closely resembled, the tales which Mrs Bennett had told her daughter about the father she could not remember.

It was a wonderful, unforgettable day, yet when it was over and Stella lay in her own small bed, waiting for the moment when her mother's snores would echo through the thin partition between their bedrooms, announcing that it would be safe for her to go to Michael up in the large attic room her brothers had once shared, she was filled with a dreadful sadness, a feeling that fate had something dark and distressing in store for her.

She fought the feeling alone for a while, then made her way slowly and carefully up the creaking attic stairs and slid into Michael's bed. He was waiting for her, and took her at once into a warm embrace, but even his arms, his closeness, could not entirely dispel her feeling of unnamed dread.

'You're crying, alanna,' Michael said presently, his big, warm palm clearing the tears from her cheek. 'You mustn't cry! Oh, sure and I know we've not managed to get married this time, and I'll be gone tomorrow so I shall, but that's no reason to cry! Wit' a bit o' luck I'll be back in port again before the babe's born, and you're over the worst, haven't you said so a dozen times? Your mam knows, your sister Lizzie knows, even the priest knows . . . and we'll be married just as soon as may be, haven't I promised it over and over?'

'Ye-es,' Stella snuffled, pushing her head into the hollow of his shoulder and trying to sound more confident than she felt. 'Oh, but I don't want you to go back to the *Thunderbolt* tomorrow, my darlin'

58

Michael! I don't want to have the baby all by meself, with only my mam to help me! Suppose . . . oh, suppose something awful happens to me? Women do die in childbirth! Or—or suppose something happens to *you*, my dear love? I'd not want to live if you were killed.'

'Now this is silly so it is. You're workin' yourself into a state, girleen, and there's no need for it, indeed there is not! I've got through the war so far—the *Thunderbolt* is a lucky ship so she is—and I mean to go on to the bitter end wit'out a scratch so I do. As for dyin' in childbirth, I forbid it, d'you hear? You're goin' to be just fine, and I'll be sendin' money back to you so's you can have the kid in hospital if you want; or, if not, so you can have a good doctor in attendance and not one of them old gals what reckon to birth babies when they've a pint of gin inside 'em and no idea of modern methods.'

This made Stella laugh and presently, in a tangle of limbs and with her thumb in her mouth, she fell asleep. They woke in good time in the morning so that Stella was back in her own room a long while before Mrs Bennett so much as stirred, and was downstairs making the breakfast early, so that Michael might have egg and bacon before he left. But as she bustled about the kitchen she was still anxious, and when at last they set off for the dock she had to be very firm with herself not to show her feelings to Michael. She clung to his arm, gazing up into his face as though she might never see it again. Once more, Stella had meant to go in to work as soon as she had seen Michael to the dock, but she found herself most unwilling to do so, for though she had said nothing to Michael her dreams had

59

been frightening the previous night, with a ship afire, men jumping from her sides and being lost in the dark waters, and the terrifying noise of the rough sea, the roaring flames and men's despairing cries turning it into a nightmare. No, she would stay with Michael just as long as she could.

So the two of them sat on a pile of planks until Michael had to leave, then they kissed hungrily and Michael ran up the gangway and disappeared into the bowels of the vessel whilst Stella was left to make her way home, sick with fear for him.

That night her dreams were in truth nightmares; she came down to the kitchen to make her mother's breakfast, pale and shaking, for she had had a ghastly one in which a ghostly Michael had woken her from a sound sleep to announce that he was dead and would never see either her or their newborn babe again. Making porridge and brewing the tea, Stella tried to convince herself that such dreams were the result of her unhappiness at seeing him leave, knowing the danger into which he and the *Thunderbolt* went, that everything would be just fine. But she was still miserably unconvinced when her mother came slapping downstairs in her old slippers, with one fewer shawl than usual because it was a warm day.

'Don't be daft, queen,' Mrs Bennett said cheerfully, when Stella admitted that she had had bad dreams and feared for Michael's safety. 'He's a grand, strong young feller and the ship's a sturdy sort o' vessel. Stop worritin' over nothin' and write him a cheerful letter. As for the babe, aren't you just like meself, with a grand pair of hips for childbearing and good health beside? To my knowledge—and I should know if anyone does—

you've never ailed a day in your life!'

This was true; despite a frail, almost ethereal appearance, Stella had never suffered anything more serious than a head cold, and that had disappeared in less than three days. And Michael was strong and could, he had told her, swim like a fish. No use worrying, no use making herself ill over foolish fancies.

Yet for many weeks, as her body thickened and the child within her quickened, Stella was convinced that she had held and kissed Michael for the last time, that she would never see him again. But his letters continued to arrive sporadically, and there was no bad news about the *Thunderbolt*, and when, at the end of September, Stella's labours began, she was beginning to hope. She took to her bed and the midwife was summoned, and before the doctor could arrive Stella's baby was born, a fine strong little girl, perfect in every way. She was doted on by her mother and grandmother, and her Aunt Lizzie came hurrying over from Birkenhead to worship at this very new shrine. Stella had left Grundy's when her condition became obvious, but her friends called on her and most envied her the beautiful, healthy baby.

'I'm calling her Virginia Margaret,' Stella wrote to Michael. 'She's the dearest thing in the world, apart from you, darling Michael, and the prettiest. She has skin like milk, huge blue eyes—only they may change to brown, because Mam says all babies have blue eyes—and a rosebud mouth. Her hair is silky, soft and sweet smelling, and her little nose . . . well, it's a little button really, but you can tell it will be the nicest, neatest nose a girl could desire when she's a bit older. Oh, you're going to love her so

61

much, Michael . . . only you aren't to love her more than you love me—that's not allowed. I want to call her Virginia because it's such a pretty name, but I suppose they'll call her Ginny for short; folk from Liverpool always shorten names. Mam and Lizzie say Virginia is too fancy—what do you think? Mam wanted to call me Virginia, but everyone thought it was too fancy then, and Lizzie said it made her think of Gin and Tonic. But our little girl . . . well, she definitely has a look about her of yourself . . . I can't wait to see your face when you find what a pretty creature we've made between us!'

Because of her overwhelming happiness at the baby's birth and perhaps also because she was so busy, Stella's nightmares had become a thing of the past. With great placidity she fed and changed her baby, walking up and down with Virginia over her shoulder when the little mite had wind, washing an interminable supply of nappies and taking the child for airings in an ancient perambulator she had bought second-hand from Paddy's Market. She had never been a keen needlewoman, but now she bought cheap off-cuts and end-of-roll material and painstakingly stitched baby gowns. She knitted tiny jackets and little pink bootees and, as the weeks passed, she got herself a job, cleaning and serving behind the counter at a local pub to augment the money Michael sent. She took the baby with her at such times because, fond though her mother claimed to be of the baby, her standards of care were not high and Stella knew that her mother could—and would—sleep through the baby's most indignant howls.

Cleaning and serving in a pub was harder work and far less congenial than her job at Grundy's had been, but it was more convenient. Grundy's would never have permitted her to take the baby to work and Stella could not bear even the thought of being parted, for hours at a time, from her little one. So she fashioned a sling to carry the baby and scrubbed floors, made up fires and carted heavy coals and water with the greatest good humour and was very happy.

*　　*　　*

Michael received the letter, which had followed him from port to port, and told all his pals that his intended had had a baby. Some of them gave him odd looks but most congratulated him. Friends like Toby knew he had meant to marry on his last leave and felt sorry for the little girl he had left behind, still unwed, when the *Thunderbolt* sailed, but they did not say so to Michael and perhaps, knowing that her man was at sea, the critics would be less censorious than they might otherwise have been, or so they hoped.

It was common knowledge amongst the sailors now that the war must be drawing to a close. They had seen few enemy ships for many months, and though they knew that there were still submarine packs lurking beneath the surface of the waves, they had seen no sign of them on this convoy. The naval ships circled the heavily laden merchantmen, impatient now to get back to port with their much-needed cargoes.

Michael was looking forward eagerly to their return to Liverpool, counting the days, his eyes straining eagerly ahead for any sight of land. Storms might have held them up, but the weather was calm, the waves seeming almost to caress the sides of the *Thunderbolt*.

He was on watch, staring up at the arch of the night sky, at the brilliance of the stars, when the first intimation came that there was going to be a change in the weather. A little breeze had been blowing steadily against his left cheek and now, almost imperceptibly, he was aware that it was changing, coming from a different direction. He glanced up at the sky once more, but there wasn't a cloud in sight. Yet the wind was definitely freshening. Michael knew his watch was coming to an end and hoped that if there was to be a change in the weather, it would not turn out to be a storm, which would make sleeping difficult. He had no desire to find himself thrown out of his hammock within an hour or so of entering it. But though the wind continued to be gusty, it seemed as though a storm was not imminent, for the sky remained clear.

Nearby, someone cleared his throat. Michael glanced around him, but could see no one. Odd! He walked over to the rail and peered down into the blackness below, and to his surprise he saw a sleek shape in the water, bobbing alongside the *Thunderbolt*, seeming to look back at Michael out of a pair of huge, liquid eyes.

A seal! Michael forgot about the wind change, the fact that his watch was almost over. At home, fishing trips were often accompanied by a seal or two. Some fishermen hated them, declaring that they took the catch, but the Gallaghers thought that there were fish enough in the sea for all, and liked the company of the huge, gentle creatures.

Michael leaned further over the rail. 'Hello, me

64

young pal,' he said gently. 'And are you after warnin' me that there's to be a change in the weather? Because if so, I'd already seen a sign or two . . .'

He had no sooner said the words than there was a tremendous explosion. Fragments of metal were hurled into the air and the ship began to list heavily. Michael was thrown to the deck, hurled against the rail, and for one moment could not think what had happened. Then he remembered the wolf pack, remembered too that both sides had sown the seas with mines . . . one or other, either a torpedo or a mine, must have hit them, for he could hear the sea roaring into the hull of the ship, feel the vessel's list to starboard.

You have to hand it to the British seamen, Michael thought, as the men began to stream up from below. There was no sign of panic, no one was trying to shove others aside in their effort to reach their boat stations. Despite the enormous shock the scene was moderately calm, with officers adjuring the men to form orderly queues for the lifeboats.

Michael was joining the end of just such a queue when there was another enormous explosion. It nearly knocked him off his feet but he clung to a stanchion, guessing at once what had happened, for now the ship was sinking fast. Most likely another torpedo had been fired and had entered the magazine, starting a raging fire which was now blowing away so much of the hull that the ship was almost literally torn in half. No time now to form orderly queues let alone launch boats. The ship was going under too fast for such niceties. Within minutes of the explosion, Michael found himself in the water. He knew he must get away from the sinking vessel which could so easily drag him under, but the darkness was complete and he could not tell in which direction safety—or comparative safety—lay.

He glanced around him but the sea was now quite choppy and though silhouettes of other ships in the convoy occasionally came into view when he reached a crest, they were speedily lost as he plunged once more into a trough. A plank hit him, crashing heavily into the side of his head and making him feel sick and dizzy for a moment. Then he realised that it might save his life and turned wildly to stare after it as it bobbed away out of reach.

It seemed to him that he swam and floated for hours without seeing any sign of other men, but then he had a bit of luck. An oar floated past and this time he grabbed it and wedged it beneath his arms, unutterably relieved to be able to stop swimming if only for a moment.

The sea no longer seemed quite so rough and Michael felt a deep and terrible weariness overcoming him. He mustn't sleep . . . he mustn't sleep . . .

*   *   *

'It's over! Them Germans have signed a paper—an armistice they call it—and the guns stopped firing yesterday!' Mrs Bennett's normally pale and rather puddingy face was flushed with excitement, her eyes bright with it. 'When d'you reckon your young feller will be home to make an honest woman of you, eh?'

66

The two women were in the kitchen. Stella was at the table breastfeeding Virginia whilst Mrs Bennett gobbled porridge. They smiled at one another, though it was an effort for Stella to smile at all right now. She was desperately worried about Michael, and despite her deep and abiding love for the baby in her arms she was still sure that he was, at any rate, in some sort of danger. Once more her placid nights had retreated under a hail of nightmares, all concerned with fire and enormous waves. She had been down to the shipping offices constantly, trying to get news, but so far she had been unsuccessful. Despite the fact that Germany had sued for peace at the end of October, the newspapers were full of conflicting reports. It seemed wicked, as well as absurd, that though peace had been agreed, the guns still thundered out their message of death until eleven o'clock on the eleventh day of the eleventh month. A cruel, needless way for perhaps hundreds of men to die, not defending their country, not even attacking the enemy, but simply dying so that some politician, somewhere, could boast that the armistice had been signed and the war ended at the exact hour of his choosing.

Rather impatiently, Mrs Bennett repeated her last remark. 'I spoke to you, Madam Toffee Nose! I said when d'you think your young man'll come home?'

'Oh, Mam, I've told you, I don't know,' Stella said with what patience she could muster. 'But when Virginia's finished drinking, I'll go down to the shipping office, see whether there's any news. Last time I went, they told me the *Thunderbolt* had turned for home, but they've had no wireless

67

messages from her for ten days. It could be a technical fault, the feller said, and maybe, as she gets nearer home, she'll be able to contact another ship. But until she does, we're all in the dark.'

'All right, all right,' Mrs Bennett grumbled. 'I just hope you hears before Victory Day—that's the fifteenth—because there's bound to be parties and all sorts of carryings-on and the last thing folks will want is to see your long face.'

It was easily the nastiest thing her mother had ever said to her and Stella's eyes widened in shock. Then she saw her mother's anxious look and knew that she had only spoken so sharply because she was worried, perhaps not so much about Michael as about Stella herself. The baby had finished and Stella put her across her shoulder, stood up, and went and gave her mother a hug. 'I'm sorry, Mam,' she said gently. 'It's been a hard time for the whole family; you've lost one son, and a son-in-law, but you've managed to keep pretty cheerful on the whole. I *am* worried about Michael, who wouldn't be, but I'll still try to keep smiling for your sake. And now I'd best get down to the Admiralty office.'

And presently, with baby Virginia tucked warmly into the old perambulator, Stella made her way down Duke Street to Canning Place and the Admiralty office. She was a familiar figure in there by now and usually greeted by the elderly clerk with a smile. But this morning, he looked up quickly, nodded, and then began to arrange the papers on his desk with meticulous care, eyes downcast. Stella's heart sank into her boots but she spoke as cheerfully as she could.

'Good morning, Mr Fry! Any news of the *Thunderbolt*?'

'Aye. HMS *Bideford* signalled that the *Thunderbolt* had been torpedoed but other ships in the convoy picked up a good few survivors.' He looked up at her fleetingly then, his rather small eyes behind his steel-rimmed spectacles full of sympathy. 'We've had no names as yet, but you mustn't despair, miss. Just you pray your young feller's one of them lucky ones what got fished out of the 'oggin.'

Stella turned away. She felt quite cold. She remembered the strong feeling she had had when they had parted the previous July, that she would never see Michael again. Oh, God, and the nightmares! The flames, the scorching heat, the cries . . . and then the darkness of the water, the waves crashing down, the fear . . . but she remembered her promise to her mother and, at the door, turned resolutely back to give Mr Fry the benefit of her brightest—and most artificial—smile. 'I'm sure you're right, Mr Fry, and when the lists of names come through, his will be amongst them,' she said, with only the slightest tremor in her voice. 'But I'll pray very hard, just in case.'

*   *   *

Victory Day dawned, but there had been no word at the shipping office, no list of survivors. 'Since shipping will be making its way back to port, that may not mean much,' Mr Fry had said wisely the previous day, when she had gone down to the docks in the vain hope of some good news. 'You go off and enjoy the victory celebrations tomorrow, my dear; it's been a terrible time for you, a terrible time, but I'm sure we'll have some news soon.'

69

There were to be fireworks, street parties, no end of jollity. Some of the troops had already come home; Stella had seen them in the streets, pale and hollow-eyed, their skin grey and unhealthy-looking, their eyes dull. She remembered the last time she had seen Michael, how well he looked, how bronzed and strong. If he came home, she supposed he would look very different now, because the ordeal of being shipwrecked would surely put its mark upon him as plainly as soldiers were marked by their experiences in France. But then she had dragged her mind away from such thoughts and, pushing the big perambulator before her, returned to Victoria Court, where she had admitted to her mother that there was still no news.

'Mr Fry says to enjoy the celebrations, but I don't think I want to,' she said, picking the baby out of the pram and holding the child's still sleeping body in her arms. 'To tell you the truth, Mam, I'm not feelin' so good. I think I've mebbe gorra head cold comin' on, so it'll be best to stay indoors, in the warm.'

Mrs Bennett looked at her doubtfully. 'I'm sorry there weren't no good news for youse, queen, but I think you ought to wait until the mornin' before you decide to stay cooped up in the house. A victory don't happen every day o' the week, you know, and in the years to come that littl'un . . .' she pointed to the child in her daughter's arms, '. . . will ask you what you did on Victory Day, and . . .'

Despite herself, Stella giggled. 'Oh, Mam, you remind me of that awful recruiting poster—d'you remember it?' She raised her voice to a squeak. "What did you do in the war, Daddy?" But I really do feel as if . . . oh, all right, I'll see how I feel

70

tomorrow.'

Now Stella and her mother were sitting at the kitchen table, preparing vegetables for their evening meal, for Lizzie and a couple of her friends were going to end their celebrations with a visit to Victoria Court, when there was a knock on the door.

'Come in,' Mrs Bennett bawled cheerfully. She guessed it would be a neighbour or a relative, and looked astonished when a total stranger came hesitantly into the room.

Stella, however, recognised him at once. 'Mr Fry!' she exclaimed. 'Oh, Mr Fry, have you—have you had news?' Her hand flew to her throat and she could feel her heart beating there as though it had leaped from her chest. She dropped the potato she was peeling and jumped to her feet. 'I can't . . . I don't know what . . .'

'Aye, we've a list of survivors,' Mr Fry said hesitantly. 'Your—your young man *is* Able Seaman Michael Sean Gallagher?'

'That's right,' Mrs Bennett said, when Stella found herself suddenly incapable of speech. 'Aye, that's right, Mr—Mr Fry, is it?'

'That's right,' Mr Fry echoed. 'Able Seaman Gallagher is on the list of those picked up by HMS . . . look out!'

For even as the words she had longed to hear came from his lips, Stella pitched forward, hearing his voice growing smaller as she plunged into unconsciousness.

*   *   *

'You're all right, chuck. It were the shock, though

71

God knows you couldn't have had better news if you'd been the Queen herself,' a voice was saying. 'Why, Stella, the war's over, you've got a lovely, healthy baby, and now your feller's comin' back to you. I ask you, is that a reason to faint and scare us half to death?'

Stella opened her eyes; her sister Lizzie stood close, bending over the sofa on to which she must have been lifted. In the background her mother was ushering someone out of the kitchen door . . . now who could that be?

The man, for it was a man, turned in the doorway and everything came back to Stella in a rush. It was Mr Fry, and he had brought her good news, the best possible news! She struggled to a sitting position, though even that small action made her feel dizzy and sick again. 'Mr Fry . . . you are so good, so kind! Oh, you've come all the way from the shipping office and—and I didn't offer you so much as a cup o' tea . . . Mam, is there something . . . ?'

Mr Fry turned and smiled self-consciously across at her. 'The offices is closed for Victory Day. We got the lists last night, but it were too late to come and tell you then, so since I only live a few streets away I thought I'd pop over this morning,' he said. 'Thanks for the offer, queen, but I'm off home now, to start me own celebrations. No doubt you'll call in some time during the week, to get all the details. I think Mr Gallagher will probably be back in port in a few weeks—perhaps even less.'

'Thank God,' Stella said devoutly. She closed her eyes, quite literally thanking God inside her head, and heard the soft click of the front door closing behind their visitor. She opened her eyes again and

72

immediately the kitchen swung dizzily around her and Lizzie's anxious face swelled like a balloon before shrinking to a more normal size. 'Oh, what a fool I've been; I were so sure that me darlin' wouldn't be comin' home to me, that I'd never see him again! Oh, Lizzie, the *relief*! He's been saved, and I'm so very, very happy! I'll gerrup off this perishin' sofa just as soon as I've had a drink, because I'm rare thirsty and I reckon a cup o' tea would just settle my queasy stomach.'

'I'm pourin' it this instant,' Mrs Bennett said. 'Truth to tell, queen, I feel a bit oozy-dozy meself. I reckon it's the excitement . . . but now you know your feller's safe you'll be able to enjoy today, same's I shall.'

*   *   *

Michael stood on the deck of the frigate *Viola* and watched as the shoreline grew closer. His heart gave a lurch as details became clear. The Liver birds, wings upraised, looked down on the shipping, which was crammed into the Mersey so closely that it was difficult to see a passage of clear water, and Michael, in his borrowed clothing, felt the excitement growing in him. The war was over, his child had been born, and very soon now, he and the girl he loved would be married. All right, it was the wrong way round, he knew that of course, but there was no need for his parents to know that he and Stella had jumped the gun. The Gallaghers were set in their ways. Michael thought they would have condemned Stella as a fast girl, a bad girl, if they had known that the baby had come before the wedding. But there was no need for them to know.

73

He would carry Stella and the child back to Ireland, introduce them as his wife and child, and his parents would never question the order in which things had happened. So, he concluded, as the ship began to nose into the dock like a rabbit seeking its burrow, they would be able to start their married life in Kerry without having to fear spiteful gossip.

He supposed that they would have to spend some time in Liverpool before he could take them back to Ireland, but he had no intention of settling there, not even for a few months. No, he wanted his home now; his real home, and he wanted it for Stella and the child as well. The great city was no place, to his way of thinking, in which to bring up a family—and he was sure that he and Stella would have other children as well as . . . what had they named her . . . the small Virginia. He grinned to himself at the fancy name. Never mind, if it was what Stella wanted, then it was good enough for him.

The dock was getting nearer but Michael had no gear to pack so he stayed where he was, leaning on the rail, watching the people going about their business on the crowded quayside. He wondered what his mother-in-law to be would say when he told her that he was carrying her beloved youngest back to Ireland just as soon as possible. He guessed she would not welcome such plans, but then until his last leave she had never scrupled to show him how much she disliked and disapproved of him, so she would just have to accept that the 'bog-trotter' had every right to live in his own country, and to take his wife and child along with him. Yes, he had heard that muttered 'bog-trotter', more than once,

74

on Mrs Bennett's lips when she thought him too far away to catch her words, and had resented it. He would take his Stella home to Ireland without a pang of conscience after the way the old witch had treated him.

But he had best ask if he could go ashore, for already the gangway was being lowered and seamen, kitbags over their shoulders, were queuing up to leave the *Viola*. Michael took one last look at the crowded dockside—but it was too much to hope that Stella would know upon which vessel he had come home, let alone when she was due to dock—and went below. Not long now and you'll hold her in your arms, he told himself exultantly. Not long now.

*   *   *

Michael thundered down the gangway, crossed on to the Goree and Strand Street and came to Canning Place. From there it was a quick journey up the Duke Street hill until he turned right into Rathbone Street. He was on fire with anticipation, could not wait to see her face when he burst into the kitchen. He was quite breathless by the time he reached the court; nothing mattered now but seeing her, holding her . . .

It was the middle of the afternoon, and a chilly December day. He was surprised by how quiet the street was, and the court itself . . . well, without even thinking about it, he had expected crowds of small kids, people coming and going, all the usual bustle of an overcrowded, rundown area in a large city. There were four or five children, dirty and ragged, playing some game on the big, filthy paving

75

stones, and a woman with a shopping bag passed him and grinned, showing a number of grey, uneven teeth, but other than that the court was quiet.

Michael slowed down, puzzled. He was outside the Bennett's house now, and saw that they had somehow acquired new curtains. The windows were veiled in white . . . in *white*? Now that he came to look more closely he realised that they were not curtains. Someone had hung bed sheets across the windows . . . now what on earth could that signify? He went up to the front door and, suddenly, he remembered a scene from his last return when he had noticed white sheeting hung across someone else's window, and had asked Stella for an explanation.

She had looked at him for a moment as though he was completely mad, but then she had relaxed, shaking her head at him. 'Customs are different, I suppose, in all countries, even though we speak the same language. It's mourning, chuck. Poor Minnie's Joseph was killed last week.'

God, it meant a death in the family, of course! Pictures flashed through his mind. His baby? Surely not. Stella had told him how healthy and beautiful she was. But Mrs Bennett was old . . . it must be Stella's mam. He was very sorry, of course he was, but these things happened. He hurried across the paving stones and knocked on the door. He was shaking, which was ridiculous . . .

He could hear footsteps. Dragging footsteps. They sounded as though someone very old was coming to the door. Michael was suddenly aware that he felt sick and dizzy, that he hardly dared look up but was keeping his eyes focused on his shoes. When the door opened and Mrs Bennett stood framed in the doorway he simply stared at her, wetting dry lips with a tongue suddenly almost as dry. In her turn she stared at him without a word before standing aside and gesturing him into the house. Michael did not move but looked a desperate, unbelieving question.

'It were only two hours ago that she died,' Mrs Bennett said huskily. 'They're both gone, my girls. Lizzie went yesterday . . . she come over to help nurse Stella as soon as I gorra message to her, sayin' the poor child had got this terrible flu what the troops has brung back from France. She were pulled down by breastfeeding, I reckon, 'cos there were no way she would let me give the kid a bottle. Why, this mornin', she dragged herself out of bed to change the kid's nappy, though she was hot with the fever and so trembly that I had to fasten the pin for fear she'd pierce the kid's stomach. Oh, you poor feller, an' you never even knew she were ailin'! Wharra homecomin'!'

Michael went on staring. It was a dream—no, a nightmare. This could not be happening. He must have misunderstood the old woman . . . she meant that Lizzie, poor, kind maiden-aunt Lizzie, was dead of the flu. He knew that Mrs Bennett had never liked him; she was simply trying to test him out in some cruel, twisted way. She was not serious, could not possibly mean that his darling girl, the mother of his child, his dearest Stella, was . . .

'Dead? Stella?' It was his own voice, slow and cracked, incredulous.

The old woman standing in the doorway nodded. Her hair hung down in witch locks, her skin was grey; she looked—oh, a hundred years old, a thousand. And suddenly he knew that she was telling him the plain, unvarnished truth. He took a couple of steps away from the house and put his face in his hands. And felt the slow, hot tears in his palms . . .

He began to walk, stumbingly, back out of the court and along Rathbone Street. He had no plan in mind; he just wanted to get away from the house which had once held his love. But a hand caught his elbow, tugging him to a stop. A large, urgent hand. He turned to jerk himself free and saw that it was George Bennett, the only male member of the family he had ever met. George's face was tear-blubbered, swollen, and it made Michael realise that no matter how bad he felt, he must not just turn away from the grief-stricken family. Stella would not have wanted it. He could almost hear her gentle voice in his ear, telling him that he must stand by them, must give them what support he could for her sake, for the sake of the wonderful love they had shared. But George was speaking.

'I'm real sorry, old feller. It's been a terrible shock for all of us, but we've known it were—were on the cards after Lizzie died. I came ashore four days ago and I did me best, honest to God I did. I gorra doctor for the pair of 'em, but it weren't no use. Lizzie went in the early hours of the morning. I think Mam had snoozed off; you can't blame her because until I came ashore there were only her to nurse the pair of 'em. Neighbours have helped, of course, doin' the messages and the cookin', washing and dryin' the sheets and so on, but until I got back Mam did all the real nursin' herself. Come on in, old feller, you've had a terrible shock and you should sit down whiles you take it in. Then

78

you'll want to see Stella . . . and the kid, o' course.'

George was a big man, as tall as Michael and a good deal stouter, but had he been the puniest feller on the face of the earth Michael would have gone with him. Indeed, he was glad of the other man's company, especially when he was led up the stairs and into Stella's small bedroom. He stopped in the doorway, then went forward and stood by the bed, looking down at Stella's small, pale face, surrounded by a cloud of black hair and looking so gentle, so peaceful, that for one wild moment he thought she only slept. Then he touched her cheek and it was cold and another glance told him that this was no longer his Stella. There was a look of cool remoteness about the small face which it had never worn in life, and Michael bent and kissed the cold forehead, then turned away. Two hours! If he had come just two hours earlier, he might have been able to tell her how much he loved her, but regrets were useless. Two hours earlier, his ship had not even docked; he had come as fast as he could and now all he could do was to bear his grief as bravely as possible and do whatever he could to help old Mrs Bennett over the next few days.

At his side, George cleared his throat. 'Your little daughter's not here right now. The gal what worked with our Stella has took her out in the perambulator. She's gettin' the messages for me mam and seein' the babby gets fresh air at the same time. It seems they're quite willing to give her an hour or so off each morning since the flu is sweepin' the whole city and customers is short.'

'The baby's all right then?' Michael said, without much interest. The baby, which had meant so much when Stella had been alive, now simply seemed an additional burden. He found himself wishing devoutly that it had been the child who had died, but such thoughts were wicked as well as useless, so he turned to George. 'I'm awful sorry, George, because you've lost both your sisters an' I know you were real fond of 'em. Don't you think it would be better if I booked into the Sailors' Home? The way things are, I'm just a reminder for your mam and truth to tell, she never wanted Stella and meself to marry, so though I'm willing to help in any way I can, I'd be glad to make meself scarce if you give me the nod.'

They had descended the stairs by this time and were standing in the narrow hall, George with his hand on the kitchen door. When Michael finished speaking George said roundly that Michael was welcome at No. 17 and would be for as long as he chose to stay. 'The thing is, our mam had big ideas for Stella and Lizzie encouraged her. They wanted to see the poor gal married to a duke or an earl—some chance—so no ordinary feller could possibly have been good enough. But that's all over now and you're welcome to stay wi' us for as long as it takes.'

Accordingly, Michael followed the older man into the kitchen, sat down at the table and was given a large tin mug of tea and a slice of dry-looking currant cake. He drank the tea thirstily but when he tried to eat a piece of cake, he choked and found that he could not swallow, and presently he got to his feet. 'I'll have to go back to my ship and find out what's to become of me and when I'm needed,' he said gruffly. 'I think they'll send me back to Ireland as soon as they can because they'll not be wantin' me, not now the dear old

80

Thunderbolt's forty fathoms under the waves.' He sketched a salute at the two Bennetts solidly munching cake. 'Do you want me to nip into Waugh's undertakers on the Scottie to—to make arrangements, like?'

But mother and son assured him that this would not be necessary, that they would handle it, and Michael left them, immensely relieved to be out of the house and away from the dreadful presence of what lay quiet and still in the small room upstairs.

Outside, a light rain had begun to fall. Michael turned up the collar of his duffel coat, ducked his head and was almost out on to Rathbone Street once more when a skinny girl, pushing a large, old-fashioned perambulator, came round the corner at a trot. She was wearing a big mackintosh, with a waterproof hat pulled well down over her eyes, and did not see him, with the result that the pram hit him in the shins, causing him to give a protesting gasp. The girl stopped short, then began to apologise, pushing back her raincoat so that she might see him better.

'Oh Gawd, I'm ever so sorry, mister,' she gabbled. 'I didn't see you because I had me head down—did I hurt you very much? Oh Gawd, look at me messages!' The collision had been violent enough to send a number of bags and packages spilling out on to the puddled paving and both she and Michael bent to retrieve them, knocking their heads sharply together as they did so and causing the girl to stagger back with a squawk. 'There, an' all you was doin' was trying to help,' she said remorsefully. 'I'm not usually so clumsy, but I've had a terrible day. Me best friend's died of this here flu, leaving a little baby—the one I've got in the perambulator—so Grundy's have give me time off to help out. Me pal's mam is real old and . . .'

Michael interrupted. 'I've just come from the Bennetts'; you must be Stella's friend,' he said. He bent over the perambulator and peered in but could only see a small mound beneath the blankets. 'Is she—is she anything like Stella?'

'No, I don't think so,' the girl replied. She leaned into the pram and pulled the blankets off the baby, propping it up against the pillows. Michael stared in total disbelief. So far as its face went, the baby looked like all babies, but it had a great plume of bright ginger hair and eyebrows and eyelashes so white as to be almost invisible. There must have been some mistake, Michael thought wildly, still staring at the child. This could not possibly be his baby, the baby to which Stella had given birth, not with hair the colour of a bunch of new carrots. Why, he himself had hair the colour of coal, and so did Stella. They both had eyes so dark that they were almost black, but this child's eyes were round and blue. He turned and looked dumbly at the girl beside him, not knowing what to say, but she seemed to notice nothing strange.

'I think she's the image of her dad,' she announced flatly. 'By the looks of you, you're a Bennett yourself, so you'll know that none of them's got red hair, but the young soldier who used to take Stella out whenever he was home, he had fiery red hair.'

Michael took a deep, steadying breath. 'Who— who was he?' he asked hoarsely. 'I mean what were his name? Where can I find him?'

'I dunno as I remember his full name,' the girl said doubtfully. 'It were a short sort of name; he were a lieutenant. But you can't get in touch with him because he were killed only a couple of months before Armistice Day. And what's to become of the baby I can't imagine,' she ended.

Michael stared at the occupant of the perambulator, trying to see some resemblance to Stella, but could discern no such thing. Was it possible that the baby had somehow been changed so that some other woman had their baby, his and Stella's, and his poor love had been landed with this weird-looking, redheaded brat? For now that he looked hard at the baby, he thought it was very odd-looking indeed. Its wide eyebrows had an upward tilt and the corners of its eyes were tilted up too. Its skin was so pale that he could clearly see the blue veins at its temples and though the nose was just the usual little dab of putty, when it suddenly smiled at him he saw that its mouth, too, had an upward tilt, giving it an elfin look.

'It ain't . . .' Michael hastily shut his mouth on what would have been an unforgivable remark, but now that he had seen the child—Ginny, was it—he was sure that it was not of his getting. He could not imagine for one moment that Stella had played him false, gone with another man. He thought that perhaps their baby had died and Mrs Bennett—or even Lizzie—had begged, borrowed or stolen another baby from somewhere and managed to convince Stella that it was her own child. But he did not mean to say anything until he had had a good, long think, so he helped the girl to pick up her messages and went on his way. He would go down to the docks and sort out what was to become of him in the next few weeks and when that was settled, he would decide what was best to do.

CHAPTER FOUR

Michael had thought long and hard all that afternoon whilst hanging about in the shipping offices, signing a great many papers and listening to a great many people telling him that they had not yet sorted out what would happen next to the survivors of shipwrecked vessels. Since Michael had only joined for the duration he was, theoretically, free to go home, but if he did so he would lose several months' pay, and even in his eagerness to escape from Victoria Court he realised that this would not be fair to anyone, including himself.

Since George had been so pressing, Michael was still sleeping under the Bennetts' roof, though the funeral had taken place a week ago, and he was becoming increasingly eager to move on. He had never quite dared to voice his opinion that Ginny was no get of his for not only was it an insult to Stella, but he could see that George would take it sadly amiss. The older man was huge and at the mere breath of such a suggestion would doubtless beat Michael to a pulp. And I wouldn't blame him, Michael told himself. If anyone else tried to speak evil of my mammy, then I'd beat them to a pulp meself.

And what of Gwen Murrell's remarks about the redheaded soldier who had visited Stella when he was home on leave? He now knew the girl's name, though he had made very sure that he did not encounter her again. It was pretty obvious that she had never told the Bennetts of her suspicions and equally obvious that they had not told her that

84

Michael himself was the supposed father of the child. In fact the more he thought about the whole situation, the more he longed to get away, back to Kerry where he belonged. In the end, a fortnight after he had first returned to Liverpool, he talked the whole thing over with his friend Toby, who had been picked out of the sea by the frigate *Viola* only an hour or so before Michael's own rescue.

It was a couple of days after Christmas and the two young men were sitting in the pale December sunshine on a wooden bench in Sefton Park, watching a nanny and her two small charges throwing bread for the ducks. 'Sure and I wouldn't even dream of suggesting that this redheaded soldier meant anything to Stella,' Michael explained. 'The truth is, she was so innocent that—that she might have not realised . . . oh, hang it, I won't believe she slept with anyone else, not if she'd left me with half a dozen redheaded babies! But Toby, what am I to do? I can't stay here, I've got to go back to my people in Kerry. I'm willing to send money back to Mrs Bennett but I can't, and won't, take that kid back to me mammy and try to pretend it's mine when, in my heart, I have such doubts.'

'D'you think it's a changeling? One of them pixicated kids what the fairies change over in their cradles?' Toby asked, only half-jokingly. 'To be frank, old feller, you've got two choices, unless you fancy it were the Angel Gabriel what fathered little Ginny! Either she's yourn, or she ain't. If she is, then you surely can't deny her, and if she ain't, then you cut and run, with my blessing at any rate.'

'What if I pay? An allotment, like, same as we did in the Navy? I'd send it straight to the old girl, so she could buy extra food and that when the kid

85

gets bigger,' Michael said desperately. 'If she were mine—if she looked like me—then I suppose I'd have to take her back home and me mammy would be landed with the task of bringing her up. If she were a boy now, I reckon I could cope . . .'

'But she doesn't and she ain't,' Toby interrupted. 'Have you told Mrs Bennett that you don't think the kid's yours? Or George?'

'No, and I'm not going to,' Michael said, suddenly realising that he had made up his mind and was really only asking Toby for his opinion in the hope that his friend would think as he did. 'I shan't have to tell George anything because his ship sailed yesterday and all I need tell Mrs Bennett, surely, is that I'm going to send money for the kid. It ain't as if me and Stella managed to get married, because we didn't. Mammy and Daddy are too old to get landed wi' a baby and we live a long way from the nearest village. Bringing up a baby out there would be terrible hard. I'd do me best but it wouldn't work. No, little Virginia's best off here, living with her gran, and I dare say, when Stella's brothers marry, their wives will give a hand. So I'll get myself a berth aboard an Irish ferry just as soon as I can.'

'Are you going to tell Mrs Bennett that you're leaving?' Toby asked suspiciously. 'I think you should, old feller.'

'I will,' Michael promised. But next day, when he told Stella's mother that his contract with the Royal Navy was finished and he would be returning to Ireland, he managed to make it sound as though he would be back in Liverpool as soon as he'd settled things with his parents. Certainly the old lady had no idea that Michael was planning to abandon his

86

child to her tender mercies. As it was, she waved him off quite happily and it was not until several days later that she realised he had not given her an address.

'But these bleedin' Irish are all the same; they come up from the bog, scarce able to talk the King's English, and probably don't even know what an address is,' she said disgustedly to a neighbour, as the two of them queued outside a greengrocer's shop. 'Mind you, he ain't all bad. He left me three quid, for the kid I suppose, but milk only costs a few pence, and she don't want anythin' else yet. And I dare say he'll gerrin touch afore the money runs out,' she finished.

*   *   *

When Michael had left Liverpool, it had been cold and grey, and when the ferry deposited him in Dublin it was cold and grey still, yet to Michael there was a softness in the air which he had not noticed in the city of Liverpool. It cost him a pang to look around at the bustling streets of Dublin, however, because he had thought he would be bringing Stella here, proudly showing her his country's capital city. As it was, he looked around him with only moderate interest. If Stella had been alive, he would have considered trying to find a job in Dublin, but now there was simply no point. City living was not for him, never had been. Now, all his thoughts were centred on the farm in Kerry which he had not seen for so long.

He had been paid off by the Navy, and because his wages had been so overdue he had collected a tidy sum, so he could have caught a train, which would have taken him home in a matter of hours. Instead, he decided to tramp it. He knew he would get lifts from time to time because his fellow countrymen were always anxious to help one another, and once he was on the road he was glad he had taken the decision to walk. The first person to stop for him was a baker, driving out to replenish his stocks of a certain type of wheat flour. The baker was a talkative little man and when Michael was afoot once more, he knew most of what there was to know about Mr Flanagan, his seven children and his ingenious little wife who made all their clothes and kept the house spotless, yet worked in the bakery six days a week.

Despite the fact that it was still winter, it was mild enough for Michael to creep into a haystack on one occasion when darkness found him far from the nearest village or farm, but apart from that he found someone willing to give him a bed every night. He always offered to pay but when they discovered that he was a sailor and had been fighting the Huns, they assured him that payment was not necessary; they were glad to do their bit for such a one as he.

It took him two weeks to cross the country and all that time he was in a fever to get home. He could not forget Stella, did not want to forget her, but in the back of his mind he believed that once he was home again, the pain of loss would diminish and the recollection of her lovely face and sweet, gentle ways would gradually fade. So when he found himself walking up the narrow lane, with steep banks on either side, that led to his home, his heart gave a bound of joy. He would return to his old life and his old ways, look to his parents and old friends for companionship and start to forget the misery of the war and the worse misery of losing Stella.

He rounded the corner of the lane and there was the cottage. It had not changed at all. The white cob walls were kept clean by the salt-laden breeze coming off the sea, which was only a matter of twenty or thirty yards from the end of their orchard, and the thatched roof overhung the windows like the shaggy hair overhanging the eyes of an old English sheepdog. Because of the strong winds which drove inshore from the Atlantic, the thatch was criss-crossed with ropes which were attached to boulders and it was this alone, during winter gales, which kept the thatch in place. As it was January, a thread of blue smoke came from the chimney and there was no one working in the garden. It was a fine day, however, the pale blue sky arching overhead, so probably Michael's daddy would be out in his fishing boat and his mammy occupied within doors.

Michael raised his hand to the latch and was halfway through the small wicket gate when something whacked him in the back with such ferocity that he nearly fell over. Even as he turned to see who—or what—had hit him, he knew. It was old Dan, his father's sheepdog, and one of his own best friends, for boy and dog had spent many hours together as Michael roamed the woods, meadows and coastline, searching for gulls' eggs, collecting blackberries or nuts, or sitting patiently on the rocks and casting out a line in the hope that some fat and foolish fish would take his bait.

The dog was yelping with excitement, jumping up and trying to lick Michael's face, and when

Michael put both arms round him and lifted him off his feet he was in ecstasy, licking Michael's countenance so thoroughly that not an inch of it remained dry.

'Well, so that's what all the fuss was about! You've had your turn, Danny, now leave the boy alone so's he can give his old mammy a great big hug.'

Unnoticed, Maeve Gallagher had emerged from the cottage and now stood no more than a few feet away, beaming. She was a thin and wiry woman of medium height, grey-haired, and with the seamed and sunburned face of one who spent as much time outdoors as in. Michael, who had not seen her for more than two years, felt his heart contract with love. She was grand, was his mammy—he wondered how he could have stayed away from her for so long. He put the dog down carefully, then gave his mother a hard hug, wondering why on earth he had thought that she would be unsympathetic towards the child Stella had borne. She was smiling with pleasure now, urging him inside the cottage, saying that they had a deal of catching up to do and might as well begin at once. 'Your daddy's taken the *Orla* out to see if he can get a few fish,' she explained. 'Oh, Michael, sure and it's wonderful to see you home again, safe and sound, after the terrible time you've had. But I'm that sorry about your young lady. You didn't say much in your letter but I know you thought a great deal of her. Do you want to tell me about it, son, or is it still too new, too raw?'

'You would have loved her, Mammy,' Michael said huskily. 'She wasn't just beautiful, she was gentle and kind. I think she would have taken to

90

country livin' like a duck to water, but it wasn't to be.'

'Your letter said flu and we've heard, since you wrote, that the disease is sweeping the whole of Europe,' his mother said. She gestured him to sit down at the table and went over to where the kettle hung on a chain above the peat fire, a thin thread of steam coming from it. 'But you'll be wantin' a nice cup o' tay and a piece of buttered brack before you do anything else.' As she spoke, she was pouring water into the big brown pot into which she had already tipped a tiny spoonful of tea leaves. 'You've come home at the hungriest time o' year, Michael me love, which means there's not a great deal of work waitin' to be done and I think that's a good thing. After what you've been through, rest and quiet and your own folk round you is what you'll be needin' most.'

Michael, agreeing contentedly, bit into the brack, then took a drink of his tea. It *was* good to be home, he told himself, and everything here would be homemade from the brack itself to the big calico apron which his mother always wore in the house. They were too far from the nearest town—and too poor—to buy when they could make and Mammy's brack and her lovely stews and bread and apple pies were a great deal tastier than those which Mrs Bennett bought from her local shops.

Presently, his mother finished her tea and went over to the low stone sink. She must have been scrubbing potatoes for the midday meal when she heard Danny's welcome, for now she eyed the vegetables in the pan, then reached into a sack beneath the sink and added a couple of generous handfuls to those already in the bowl. 'This was for supper when your daddy's home,' she told him over her shoulder. 'But I reckon I'll make a meal just for the two of us now, so what do you fancy? The hens don't lay well at this time of year but I've three eggs, plenty of spuds and cabbage and a piece of salted cod.'

'A fried egg and a few fried potatoes would be grand, so they would,' Michael said yearningly. Fresh eggs were almost unobtainable in Liverpool, or had been up to the time he had left; in fact food shortages were endemic. Mrs Bennett had told him that, a few months earlier, King George himself had urged his subjects not to eat so much bread since wheat was having to be brought into the country from abroad. Apparently, the King had also said that his own family was strictly rationing the food they ate, though Michael had taken that with a pinch of salt. Many, many times, he had heard his father talking of rich landowners who preached propriety to their tenants whilst keeping two or three mistresses tucked away somewhere and he knew, from personal experience, that the rich in Liverpool would demand that the poor should make do on a loaf per family, per week, whilst themselves living off the fat of the land. Marie Antoinette's much quoted remark, 'Let them eat cake,' was as true today as it had been then, because the rich simply had no idea how the poor fared. Nor how totally impossible it was for them to deny themselves bread and eat cake in its place.

However, his mother was reaching up to the smoky rafters overhead and bringing down— Michael's mouth watered—a flitch of home-cured bacon. 'I'll cut us a couple of slices of this as well,' she said triumphantly, clearly reading the greedy look on his face and enjoying it. 'They say bacon's rationed in cities but Daddy killed a pig last autumn and there's still some fine meat salted or smoked to see us through the winter. Sure and we don't have shop bought clothes or shop bought food out in the country here, but we eat better'n town folks, I'm sure o' that.'

Michael was sure of it too and, for a moment, he thought uneasily of the odd little red-haired child who was going to be brought up in a dirty house in a dirty court by a dirty old woman who seldom did a hand's turn if she could avoid it. He looked around the shining kitchen. It had an earth floor and an open fire, but there were rag rugs underfoot and the delft on the press sparkled with cleanliness. Hanging from the rafters overhead were strings of onions, bunches of dried herbs and, of course, the flitch of bacon. Despite the fact that it was January, a row of geraniums bloomed on the window sill and though the wooden chairs had been carved by his father years before, out of cast-up driftwood, they were made comfortable as well as attractive by a number of bright cushions. These were stuffed with feathers from the ducks and hens, which his mother plucked and saved whenever she killed a bird for the table, and added a great deal to the ease of anyone sitting in those chairs for long.

Lazily watching as his mother began to slice potatoes, Michael thought of the other rooms in the cottage. If you went out of the kitchen door and turned to the left, you would reach the bedrooms; one quite large, one medium sized and one very small. The large room was used mainly for storage

93

and Michael remembered, with a pang of real pain, how he had planned to install himself, Stella and the child in that room, just as soon as he had enough money to buy a double bed and a bit of furniture. He rarely entered his parents' room but knew his own very well indeed, for until he had joined the Navy he had never slept a night away from it. Like the kitchen, it was earth-floored and extremely clean, the gingham curtains at the window faded and patched but still capable of keeping a good deal of cold out. His bed had been too small for him for some years but he thought, wistfully now, of the sheer comfort of it. His mammy had made the feather mattress into which he sank each night, just as she had made the patchwork quilt which covered him.

If you turned to the right when you left the kitchen, you would enter the parlour, the 'best' room. On Sundays, his mother served tea and sandwiches at four o'clock and this unlikely meal was always taken in the parlour, for before her marriage Maeve Gallagher had worked as a maidservant in a big house outside Limerick. There, every day of the week, she had served the rich family with tea, dainty cucumber sandwiches and tiny cakes in their 'white drawing room', and when she got a home of her own she had decided that she would carry the afternoon tea tradition from Limerick to Kerry. Clearly, it would be impossible to do so on any day but Sunday, and at first Sean Gallagher had laughed at his wife's fancies, as he called them. But soon enough, tea in the parlour had become a Sunday tradition for the Gallaghers and though he had never said so, Michael thought that his father secretly approved and enjoyed the weekly ritual.

Maeve Gallagher had been thirty-five before she had given birth to a live child and Sean only a year older. In common with many other Irish couples, the two had had a very long engagement because they wanted some money behind them before they got married. They were to share Sean's parents' home, could scarcely do anything else since the old man could not have run the farm without his son's help, and their savings had enabled them to build an extra room on the end of the farmhouse.

Maeve's parents lived outside Limerick, many miles from the tiny holding where Sean had been brought up, but she, too, came from a rural background and was no stranger to the many and varied tasks demanded of a smallholder's wife. When Michael had been small, his grandparents had been the owners of the property, his own parents merely working it for them. But both Sean and Maeve were hard and dedicated workers, determined to get on. They had gradually bought land, increasing the size of their property whenever they were able to do so. Sean bought stock but made sure he only bought the best, even if it meant temporary hardship for his family, and when his parents died he was astonished to realise that they had been putting money away for years in an old tin box, under their marital bed. He had used the money to buy fruit trees so that the stretch of ground in which he had previously grown cabbage and potatoes could become the orchard it was today.

'Right you are then, Michael! Get outside of this and when you've ate it, we'll have a walk around and I can show you the changes we've made since you've been gone.'

His mother's voice startled Michael out of his reverie and he looked with real appreciation at the laden plate she was placing before him. She had always been a first rate cook, the sort of woman who can make a delicious dish out of almost nothing, but today she had used the best ingredients, for everything on the table was home-grown. Maeve's plate was nowhere near as heaped as Michael's own but the two of them finished the meal almost simultaneously, washing it down with tin mugs of tea. When they had done, Maeve took their plates over to the sink, then went to the back door and hooked down the serviceable old coat which she wore for outside work. It had once been Sean's but she liked the roominess of it and refused to buy something more suited to her smaller stature. Michael pulled on his own duffel and followed her out of the cottage, smiling to himself at the odd picture she made with his father's old coat almost big enough to wrap round her twice, and so long that she was continually lifting the skirts in order that they should not drag in the mud.

The two of them then proceeded to examine every foot of the property, and examine it minutely, what was more. Maeve's flock of poultry had trebled in size since Michael had left and he thought there were probably more ducks on the pond his father had dug out from the stream which clattered under a tiny stone bridge. He supposed that the pond, or pool rather, was not actually on their property but on common ground, however, no one had ever disputed their right to the ducks. They could scarcely do so since the mallards had been wild but became tame after his mother had fed them throughout every winter. Sometimes the Gallaghers had duck eggs but this did not happen often since the ducks were not as obliging as the hens and tended to nest in a far more secretive manner.

Michael commented on the increase in the pig population—two enormous sows inhabited the stone-built sty at the end of the orchard, each with bonaveens nuzzling her fat sides—and remarked that he thought his father's flock of sheep had also increased.

Maeve smiled with a touch of slyness. 'Aye. When the inspectors came round, your daddy took some of the ewes and half the lambs off to the common beyond the village and didn't bring them back till the nosy fellers had gone,' she explained. 'And we hid the second sow and her bonaveens in a cave down on the shore.' She smiled reminiscently, her eyes slitting with amusement. 'Sure and that was a business, so it was! I drove the sow and her little 'uns in the cart until we reached the cave mouth, but penning them up inside . . .' she rolled her eyes expressively, '. . . it were the hardest thing I've ever done. The old sow took fright and kept chargin' at me and tryin' to herd her bonaveens out of the cave and back on to the shore, but I had your daddy's old ash plant and she didn't fancy a slap across the head with that, so I won, in the end. But she squealed loud enough to be heard ten miles off and wasn't I mortal afraid that she'd give the game away and bring the Ministry fellers down about my ears.'

Michael laughed with her, though he felt a trifle guilty at so doing. He saw no reason why farming

97

folk, who were never considered by their rulers to be of any importance whatsoever, should be forced to hand over beasts they had reared or crops they had grown, simply because there was a war on. But he did wish that he had been able to get home after he had met Stella. He had not really heeded how hard rationing had hit city people until after Stella's death, when he had been in Liverpool for weeks. If only he had thought, he could have come back to the farm after he had first met Stella, and then returned to England, laden with good things—bacon, honey, butter, even eggs—and perhaps if he had done so Stella might have been strong enough to withstand the flu, might have been alive today.

But such thoughts led only to misery and despair and Michael dismissed them summarily from his mind. Instead, he asked how Maeve had got the big sow and her offspring back into the cart when the time came to return them to their home because he knew, from experience, how hard it is to load one reluctant pig, let alone a dozen or so.

'It were a rare circus, to be sure,' his mother said ruefully, her eyes still shining with remembered amusement. 'Pigs is always contrary, and of course they're mortal fond of shellfish, and certain sorts of seaweed, so once they were able to leave the cave, they didn't fancy leaving the shore at all, at all. In fact Sheila—that's the name your daddy has give to the sow I took to the shore—was a real devil and I could not get her back in the cart. I tried liftin' the bonaveens in, hopin' she'd follow, but would she? Not she! In the end, your daddy came down, wondering what was up, what with the din Sheila and the little 'uns were kicking up. We didn't get

98

her in the cart even then, but we drove them up the cliff path and round into the front garden, then down the side path by the peat pile and back to their sty. Then your daddy and I just stood and laughed because I looked like an old scarecrow, splattered wi' mud and sand, my hair all down from its bun and my skirt wet to the waist wi' seawater, for that wicked old sow thought nothin' of chargin' me into the waves to keep me from catchin' her.'

'How about if we go down to the shore now?' Michael said presently as they returned to the cottage once more. 'Are there still mussels on the rocks? If so, we could take a pail and get some, give us an excuse for a walk along the shore.'

Maeve agreed, though reminded him she would have to be back in time to milk their three cows, and presently mother and son were busily picking mussels off the rocks and, on Michael's part at least, watching the sun sink into the Atlantic in a glow of rose and gold. He thought he had never seen anything more beautiful and realised that he had spent his whole life amid such breathtaking scenes and was appreciating them now, for the first time, because he was seeing them through the eyes of a stranger. As they clattered the mussels into the pail, Michael found himself beginning to tell his mother about Stella and the Bennetts, though he had not intended to do so quite so soon. He started at the very beginning, when he had come ashore and seen the young, white cat and been almost frightened by the slight, dark-clad figure of a young girl . . .

But though he told her more than he had ever told anyone else, he did not breathe a word about the baby, suddenly convinced that if he did so

99

Maeve would insist that the child should be brought back to Ireland where she belonged. He had known all along, really, that his mother would love her, but the truth was, he felt nothing but resentment towards the tiny, redheaded brat. If Stella had not been breastfeeding, he was sure she would have recovered from the flu. Her mother had constantly boasted that her daughter had never ailed, never lost a day's work through being sick. Why, then, should she catch the disease, let alone die from it? The baby would be a constant reminder that she had played her part in Stella's death and what was more, as soon as his mother realised that the child was not at all like himself, or Stella, she might stop being sorry that his love had died; in fact, she might think that he had had a lucky escape. He did not doubt that she would bring Virginia up to the best of her ability, but there would always be the feeling that her son had been entrapped by a bad woman who only wanted a father for her illegitimate child. Michael knew that he could not bear that. Better that his mother's picture of Stella should remain unsullied and that the child should stay in Liverpool.

'Well, we've got enough mussels for a good supper,' Maeve said breezily. She tried to lift the bucket then grimaced at him. 'You can carry these up to the cottage, Michael me love, and start cleaning 'em while I bring the cows down to the yard for milking. Danny will give me a hand with herding them—not that they'll need much herding—and you can drive them back again, when the milking's over.'

'And I'll help you milk 'em,' Michael said contentedly, as they began to climb the short cliff path. 'Oh, Mam, it's grand to be home, so it is!'

* * *

When the knock came at the door, Mrs Bennett almost missed it because the baby was grizzling again, beginning to cry in that desperate, infuriating way that a hungry baby will. Mrs Bennett had been ignoring the noise for ten minutes, but it was beginning to get on her nerves which was why, she told herself virtuously, she had been taking a nip out of the Guinness bottle when the knock had sounded. Now, she whipped the large black bottle off the table and inserted it carefully into the coal hod. That done, she hurried across the kitchen, seized the kettle from the fire and began to pour water into the teapot, calling out as she did so: 'Come in, love, it's on the latch.'

The door opened and a small girl looked tentatively into the room. She was a thin child with mousy hair and a small, nondescript face, saved from total plainness by a pair of very large, clear, hazel eyes. She was wearing a man's tweed jacket, which had been cut down to more or less fit her, over a droopy gingham dress, with cracked boots several sizes too large on her small feet. But she grinned cheerfully at Mrs Bennett and came right into the room, sidling towards the fire and raising her voice to be heard above the baby's wails. 'Whazza marrer wi' the baby, Miz Bennett? She ain't half a-bawlin'.'

Mrs Bennett looked approvingly at her visitor, though someone less experienced in the ways of the court might have queried why she was not clad more warmly, for the March day was chilly.

However, she continued to splash water into the teapot, saying as she did so: 'Oh, she's hungry, but I ain't got nothin' for her in the house.' She gave the child a questioning glance. 'Wharrizit, Addy? Your mam sent ya, did she? I axed her earlier if you'd get me messages today.'

'Aye,' the child said in a piping treble. 'She didn't say what you was wantin', but please, Mrs Bennett, if there's lots, can I take Ginny and the pram? I's only eight an' I can't carry a lorra stuff in me arms and me mam wants a big bag o' spuds and a cabbage, as well as a screw o' tea and two penn'orth of buttermilk.'

The child had to raise her voice because of the baby's wails and Mrs Bennett's eyes brightened. 'Wharra good thing you come when you did, chuck,' she said, having a little difficulty with her words, but managing to get them out in more or less the right order. 'It's time li'l—li'l Gi-Ginny . . .' She jerked her thumb at the now roaring baby, giving up the attempt to pronounce the child's name. 'She wants feedin' and I ain't gorrany milluck,' she bawled. 'You can ge' me some an'—an' feed the little bugger while you're about it.' She beamed triumphantly down at the small Addy. 'Awright?'

Addy nodded and held out a hand. For a moment, Mrs Bennett just stared down at it, then she clicked her tongue reprovingly at herself and reached into the pocket of her dress. She produced a handful of small change and counted it out on to the kitchen table, saying sonorously as she did so: 'Two pun o' spuds, conny-onny for the baby, an ounce o' tea and a cabbage. Will 'at do?'

She gestured towards the small heap of coins as

she spoke. Addy scooped up the cash and pushed it into her pocket. 'If it don't, I'll leave off the tea,' she said cheerfully. She crossed the room, seized the handle of the perambulator and pushed it towards the door. 'See you later, Miz Bennett.'

* * *

Addy thumped the perambulator down the three steps on to the flagstones and was heading for Rathbone Street when Miss Tillett, Mrs Bennett's neighbour, stopped her. She peered into the perambulator then withdrew her head hastily.

'That baby needs changin'; she reeks of stale piddle,' she said. 'How's the old gal today, eh?'

'The worse for drink,' Addy said baldly. 'She thinks I don't notice, but she were pourin' water into an empty teapot and she gorrall her words muddled like, when she were tellin' me what to buy.'

Miss Tillett tutted disapprovingly. She had been a nurse before she retired from the profession and kept her own small house immaculate, cleaning through every single day. She said this was for the sake of her lodgers—she had two of them— but Addy knew it was because Miss Tillett liked cleanliness and hated dirt and the problems connected with it. She also knew that Miss Tillett disapproved of the state of many of the homes in the court, including Addy's own. But since she was always on hand to help a neighbour in distress, her lectures on the evils of dirt and a poor diet were taken in good part and most of the women, including Addy's mother, did their best to take her advice. Poverty, however, prevented them

103

from following such advice as closely as Miss Tillett would have liked.

The baby had stopped screaming as soon as the perambulator was moved but now, because Addy was standing still, she began to mutter. Addy hastily jiggled the handle but it was no use. The baby wanted feeding—needed feeding—and would not shut up until she felt the rubber teat enter her mouth. Addy was about to move on when Miss Tillett stopped her.

'Bring the baby into my place,' she said authoritatively. 'I've got some conny-onny she can have and some cream to spread on her poor little bum. I don't suppose the old girl gave you a clean nappy?'

Addy sniffed scornfully. Nappies were a luxury beyond the reach of most inhabitants of the court. Babies wore any rag of suitable size and Ginny would be no exception. After all, Mrs Bennett was only her granny and you couldn't expect a granny to lash out on nappies when she'd been landed with an extra mouth to feed. Addy said as much to Miss Tillett as she bumped the perambulator up the steps and into the older woman's kitchen, but Miss Tillett shook her head. 'I know poor Stella died a few months back, but I also know the father has sent at least two postal orders so far, so there's no excuse for the old girl neglecting Ginny.'

As she spoke, Miss Tillett had taken the bottle from the perambulator and was making up a jug of conny-onny and hot water. When this was done, she picked up the child and held her under one arm whilst she hastily spread the kitchen table with newspapers. Then she laid the baby upon the papers and began to remove the sodden and stinking bundle of rags from the child's nether regions. Ginny paused in her screaming for a moment as she felt the cool air on her exposed skin and Miss Tillett exclaimed with disgust, pointing to the baby's thin buttocks and lower stomach which were covered with red running sores. 'Look at that! If this child lives another month with that old witch neglecting her, it will be a perishing miracle.' She turned to Addy. 'Fetch me a bowl of warm water, a bit of soap and a clean towel, would you, queen? You'll find everything in the cupboard beside the oven. Then if you go under the sink, you'll find a pile of old towels and sheets and that. I'll tear one up to make a nappy. Then you can sit her on your lap and give her the bottle while I fetch some soothing cream out of me bag.'

Addy settled herself in one of the comfy fireside chairs and took the baby, who had reached the hiccuping stage, but the distressing sounds stopped as soon as she sucked in the first mouthful of warm milk and peace descended on the kitchen. Whilst she fed Ginny, Addy looked at her long and hard. Poor little bugger, she thought tenderly, seeing the stick-like thinness of the little arms and legs and the dreadful sores which, now that she looked closely, she realised extended from the child's waist to her ankles. She was not a pretty baby but Addy knew that babies change as they grow older and anyway, what did prettiness matter? Poor little Ginny deserved a chance to live, and abruptly Addy decided that if she, herself, could help the baby then she would do so. The drunken old woman next door would probably be glad enough of any sort of free help and Addy knew that her own fat and comfortable mother would be as outraged as

Miss Tillett if she knew the state the baby was in. I can go in every day after school, Addy planned busily as the level of the milk sank in the bottle. I can beg bits of rag off the neighbours and take the dirty bits back for Mam to wash and if the old woman runs out of conny-onny again, I'll—I'll threaten to tell the scuffers that she's starvin' the kid. I'll tell her I know about the money as well so she needn't try to pretend she can't afford milk. Why, I'd take the baby away from her altogether if I could—I wonder if the old gal would mind?

She put the point to Miss Tillett, who smiled approvingly at her promise to 'see the baby right' but shook her head at Addy's suggestion that they might keep the baby themselves. 'She won't let that happen, chuck,' she said sadly. 'Young Michael's sending money every month for the baby's upkeep. I know it all goes the same way, mostly to the Jug and Bottle, but if the baby was living with someone else and Michael found out, the money might not arrive any more. If Lizzie were alive . . . but you can't expect young fellers like George and Lewis to know about babies and what they need.'

Addy's happy imaginings of having a real live doll in the house to take care of disappeared and she thought, regretfully, that it would not have been fair on her own mam. After all, in term time, both herself and her three brothers and two sisters were at school, and since Dad was a seaman and rarely home for longer than a few days, all the responsibility would have fallen upon her mother.

'Here we are then.' Miss Tillett had returned to the room, flourishing her nurse's bag which, as Addy knew, was kept well stocked with bandages, iodine and various unguents with which she

106

anointed any ills that came her way. 'I see she's finished the milk already. Give her to me, Addy, and I'll bring her wind up before I put some ointment on her wounds.'

'Wounds?' Addy echoed doubtfully. 'I thought it were only soldiers what got wounds.'

Miss Tillett laughed. 'You're probably right; I meant sores.' The child gave a couple of enormous burps and then her head thudded on to Miss Tillett's shoulder and Addy saw that Ginny slept. In fact, she slept all through the anointing of her person, the adjusting of the towelling around her nether regions and the placing of her back in the perambulator. Addy thanked Miss Tillett sincerely for everything she had done and promised to bring the child back whenever she could do so; Miss Tillett had said that she wanted to check that the sores were healing but knew if she went round to No. 17 the old woman would regard her interest as interference and would make sure she kept Ginny out of Miss Tillett's sight in future.

Feeling very grown up and responsible, Addy then wheeled the perambulator into the court and under the archway which led on to Rathbone Street. She felt as though she and Miss Tillett were conspirators, joined together in an alliance against horrid old Mrs Bennett to save the tiny princess, Ginny, from her gran's wicked wiles. The fact that tiny Ginny neither looked nor acted like a princess did not matter. Addy rather admired the baby's bright red hair but thought the child's bony, knobbly little face looked rather like a turnip. However, her teacher at school, whom Addy much admired, was fond of saying that beauty is only skin deep and that pretty looks are not always accompanied by pretty ways. Therefore, she would continue to think of Ginny as a beleaguered princess, shut up in a crumbling castle, under the guardianship of a wicked old witch—Addy read a lot of fairy tales—and would be proud to do her best for the child.

In the perambulator, Ginny slumbered, a dreamy smile on her small lips. 'If I could worm your dad's address out of the old woman, I'd write to him and tell him where his money goes,' Addy said, addressing the sleeper. 'Still, me and Miss Tillett are going to take good care of you, so don't worry your little self; we're your pals, we are!'

She continued to chatter away to the baby until she reached the grocer's on Washington Street. She had a wistful look in the window first, then put the brake on the perambulator and trotted into the shop, knowing that her dreaming must now stop as the serious business of getting the messages began.

PART II

CHAPTER FIVE

AUGUST 1928

It was a warm, bright day in late August. Ginny Bennett wandered slowly up Byrom Street. She had arrived at this point after a pleasant stroll through the city, peering in windows, examining the Adelphi Hotel and Lime Street Station as she passed them, detouring slightly so that she might walk through St John's Garden, and finally ending on Byrom Street, which was her chosen destination.

Ginny was wearing what she always wore in summer, a drab and extremely dirty cotton dress. She was barefoot and this was something which she intended to remedy as soon as possible, for children were no longer allowed to attend school without shoes or boots and Ginny was desperately anxious to return to school with her playmates at the end of the summer.

She had missed a great deal of school because Mrs Bennett could always think of a good reason to keep her at home. Ginny had not minded too much in the early days but she had begun to realise of late that there were things she was going to need to know which could only be learned in school. There was another reason for her desire to begin to attend school regularly; her class was to have a new teacher, a Miss Mabel Derbyshire, and though only a couple of the girls had met her when she came for her interview, they were tremendously impressed. 'She's young, and awful pretty, and she

111

ain't the sort what will go at you wi' a ruler or a cane,' one of the girls reported. 'She's gorra nice voice and a nice way wi' her an' all. I reckon we're real lucky to have Miss Derbyshire to teach us.'

And now there was the problem of shoes; children attending school must, the authorities said, have shoes. Several times, Ginny had obtained shoes from various sources, usually badly worn plimsolls with soles so thin she could feel every pebble through them, and gaping holes at toe and heel. Such footwear came from friends who had outgrown them or even from Paddy's Market, where they could be obtained, usually, for as little as a penny. But with a new young teacher about to start at the school, everyone, and that included Ginny, wanted to make a good impression.

Once, Ginny had had a good, stout pair of shoes. Miss Tillett had got them for her and she had been proud of them, had actually worn them for two whole days before her grandmother, running short of cash, had either sold or pawned them; at any rate, Ginny had never seen them again. She had been young then, only six, but now that she was nearly ten, Ginny had learned her lesson well. It was useless acquiring anything good; Granny Bennett would simply sell it when she was short of a bob or two. The old woman was cunning as a fox. She would wait until Ginny was asleep and then she would pinch anything that she thought was sellable. Shoes or boots were best because she must have known she would be unlikely to get anything from the sale of Ginny's disgusting cotton dress or ragged knickers. And anyway, she needed Ginny to get her messages and, lately, to cook her some sort of meal, because Mrs Bennett was beginning to go downhill, healthwise. She had had a very strange turn back in June and had ended up in hospital where the doctors had told her to leave the drink alone or pay the price, which would be an early death.

Fright had forced Granny Bennett to abandon her ways for a while, especially since her sons were now refusing to contribute towards the upkeep of 17 Victoria Court. They had families of their own and did not intend to allow their mother to drown in a sea of Guinness, George had told her severely. They would pay up again when she stopped drinking.

'It were that bleedin' cocky doctor at the hospital what give the game away,' Mrs Bennett had said savagely to Ginny, when she learned of her sons' decision. 'It's like what they say in the Bible . . . an ungrateful child is worse'n a serpent's tooth . . . ain't that what the Bible say? And what do they think we'll live on, the pair of us, if they don't give their poor old mam a few coppers now and then? Fresh air?'

Ginny, thinking ruefully that her grandmother seemed to expect *her* to live on fresh air whilst she herself wallowed in Guinness, tried to look sympathetic and then put her foot in it by reminding Granny Bennett of the little brown envelopes which came across the sea from Ireland, regular as clockwork, every month. 'They come from my dad, don't they?' she had said casually and had waited, far from casually, for the answer. Her granny had never mentioned the name of the man who sent the money, had always denied to Ginny's face that it was her father, but Ginny was no fool. She had known for at least four years that every

113

child has to have a father, had guessed from talk overheard that her father was still alive and living in Ireland. After that, it was a simple matter to question Addy, who had not scrupled to tell her that Michael Gallagher was a grand feller and sent money every month.

Unfortunately, Addy had never set eyes on Michael so could not describe him to his daughter, but she had known Ginny's mother pretty well and confirmed that Stella had been beautiful as any princess, with a mane of shining, black hair and big, dark eyes.

'So me red hair must have come from me dad,' Ginny had mused aloud. And Addy had said that she supposed it must. Now, whenever Ginny pictured the sender of the envelopes, he was tall and red-haired, with blazingly blue eyes and white skin which freckled in summer, very like her own.

Mrs Bennett, of course, was no help whatsoever. To be sure, she gave Ginny money for messages but always made certain that there was never enough change for a decent pair of shoes and Ginny was determined that she would return to school complete with proper footwear. A great number of children in her position went to school in clogs, which the scuffers provided free, and Ginny knew very well that she had only to ask and a pair of clogs, the right size, would be handed to her. No one would buy such clogs off Granny Bennett, so she would be safe enough in that regard, but Ginny was proud. The thought of actually advertising her impoverished state really hurt her, particularly when she remembered that her kind and generous father sent money every month so that she need not be a charge on Granny

114

Bennett. She had boasted about her father, that was the trouble, telling the kids in the court how wonderful he was, how he lived on a big farm in Ireland, owned boats and cars, and would send for her one day, when she was full grown. All children fantasise and accept each other's tall stories without question, even knowing their own to be fibs. Johnny Briggs told everyone about his rich Uncle Ken, who had gone to America when the war had ended and made a fortune. Janet Tanner told everyone that she spent her holidays on her elder brother's farm in the Welsh hills, although in fact, as Ginny knew, she spent them baby-minding for her sister, Kate, in a court off the Scotland Road. Danny Levitt said his family owned the jam factory and his mam sat in an office telling other people what to do all day. Ginny herself, of course, could only boast about her father, but that was good enough to make her dread the thought of the stigma of police clogs. She would tell the children that her father had bought the shoes and everyone would believe her as she believed Johnny Briggs, Janet Tanner and Danny Levitt, though she did take Danny's stories with a pinch of salt. He and she were best friends, spending most of their waking hours together during the school holidays. In fact it had been Danny who had suggested that she should find a hiding place outside the house for any money she earned and might like to share his own secret spot.

At the end of Victoria Court towered the back of an enormous warehouse. Smoke-blackened and smelly, it reared storeys above the houses in the court and though it was used for ball games, the part against which the privy was built held no interest for anyone. Except for Ginny and Danny, that was. Right at the bottom, in the corner created by the privy, there was a loose brick. Years ago, Danny had told her proudly, he had eased it away from its fellows in order to hide small objects in the gap behind it. Wise now to her grandmother's unpleasant ways, he had let Ginny into the secret, realising that she had even more need of it than he, and so far no one else had guessed that the brick was any different from the rest of the wall.

They had to visit their hidey-hole under the cover of darkness, but a trip to the privy was necessary before going to bed. Ginny waited until her grandmother was asleep before letting herself out of the door and crossing the yard like a shadow, wrapped in a dark shawl. Having made sure she was unobserved, she would then find the brick, her fingers recognising it even though her eyes could not make it out, and ease it from its place. Then she would add any pennies and ha'pennies she had earned to her small hoard and replace the brick.

Last night had been different though; last night she had been withdrawing her savings from the bank, so to speak, and today she meant to buy that all-important pair of shoes. Of course she would be unable to take them home, she knew that. But she had a friend of her own age—and in her own class at school—whose father kept the grocer's shop on the corner of Washington Street. Annie had told her mother about Ginny's predicament and Mrs Wait had agreed to keep the shoes provided they had been honestly acquired. Ginny, who in desperate moments had seriously considered prigging a pair, had earnestly assured her friend that the shoes would be bought with her very own money, sent her by her father, and Annie had reported back that not only would her mother keep the shoes, she would also take care of anything else which Ginny was afraid to take home. Granny Bennett was well known—and well disliked—by most of the small tradesmen in the surrounding streets, for she was not above asking for tick until the end of the month and then 'forgetting' to pay up.

Annie had offered to accompany Ginny on her shoe buying expedition, as indeed had Danny, but when it came to the point, neither was available on this bright August day. Annie had two little sisters and Mrs Wait was taking them to New Brighton for a day out; a treat which Annie could not possibly have missed. The kindly Waits had offered to take Ginny as well, urging her to put off her purchase for just one day, but Ginny had made up her mind that she would buy the shoes as soon as she had saved ten shillings and feared that, if she went to the seaside with the Waits, she would spend some of her hard-earned money on ices or a paper of chips. And the money *was* hard-earned too; she had chopped kindling, run messages, minded babies—in fact, done anything which would earn her a penny or two.

Danny, who was almost two years older than she, had had the enormous good fortune to get a holiday job, delivering bread for a local baker. It was not particularly well paid but Danny had assured her that the 'perks' were good. At the end of the week, he was given any stale bread or buns which had not been sold, and when you were the eldest of a large family of hungry girls and boys this was not to be sneezed at. And since today was

Saturday, and therefore the end of the week, it would have been downright wicked even to suggest that Danny might accompany her.

So here she was, in Byrom Street, hoping to be able to buy a decent pair of shoes with the money she had been saving up. She slowed as she approached Scott and Metcalfe's shoe shop. The window was big and shiny with a special section for children's boots and shoes. Ginny moved across to it, examining the wares on offer with a critical eye. She wanted stout lace-ups because they would last longer than the pretty, shiny strap shoes on display. On the other hand, strap shoes were cheaper and her feet were growing as fast as the rest of her. It would be all right to cut holes in the toes as her feet grew, she supposed . . . might it be better to choose a cheap, cardboardy pair for 7/6d which would allow her to put a whole half crown back behind the brick in anticipation of other needs.

Sighing over the difficulties of choice, Ginny made her way into the shop. It was bright and cheerful with the walls lined with shoeboxes and two long mirrors so that customers trying on shoes could take a good look at themselves. There were customers already sitting in the smart little gilded chairs whilst young ladies kneeled before them, helping them into the shoes of their choice. One little girl, in a pink coat and matching hat, was trying on ballet shoes of pink satin and another child, about Ginny's own age, was being fitted with elegant party shoes of patent leather with pom-poms on the toes and the fashionable Cuban heel. The other customers were all adults so Ginny moved to the section of the shop where the two girls sat, guessing that children would probably

118

have an area to themselves. She wondered whether she should sit down, and was just about to do so when a middle-aged woman, wearing pince-nez spectacles on her long pink nose, came hurrying towards her. She was making shooing motions but Ginny stood her ground, though she hastily pulled a handful of loose change out of her pocket.

'Out, out, out!' the woman said. 'This is a respectable shop and we don't want children hanging about, waiting to run off with the stock, no doubt.' She looked at the money in Ginny's hand and gave a scornful sniff. 'Where did you get that from, eh? I don't doubt you thieved it from someone!'

Ginny felt the hot colour rush into her cheeks but she still stood her ground. 'I don't steal, not from anyone,' she said loftily, trying to keep her voice steady. 'And I'm here to buy meself school shoes . . . what's wrong wi' that?'

'Where's your mam?' the woman demanded. It was obvious that she had expected Ginny to cut and run, and when Ginny had done no such thing it had surprised her. 'Kids don't come in here to buy their own shoes, their mams come with 'em, so where's yours?'

'Dead,' Ginny said baldly. 'I live with me gran, but she's been poorly so she sent me out to get me own shoes. I dunno what size I am, but I know what shoes cost—I looked in the window—and I've got enough money for the pair I want.'

The woman was less sure now; Ginny could see the uncertainty in the beady eyes behind the gold-rimmed spectacles. 'We-ell, I don't know . . . I suppose I could show you a pair, though if you don't know what size you want, I'd have to . . .' Her

119

eyes went down and settled, triumphantly, on Ginny's bare and dirty feet. 'Why, you nasty little ragamuffin, this is a decent shop for decent people! I ain't puttin' a pair of our good shoes on those feet! I doubt they've seen soap and water in the whole of your life . . . folk who buy shoes here wear shoes and stockings, so I'll thank you to take yourself off.'

Ginny became uneasily aware that everyone was staring at her, and when she looked round she realised that what the woman said was true. The girl buying the party shoes was wearing long, beige, silk stockings and the child with the ballet shoes wore white ones. All the adults had stockings as a matter of course and Ginny realised, belatedly, that she should not have chosen such a posh shop. If she had kept on going, reached Great Homer or the Scottie, she could have got something just as good and probably far cheaper. And on the Scottie, they would be used to kids coming in to buy cheap shoes. However, there was nothing she could do about it now except to leave with what grace she could muster.

She was halfway to the door when someone shouted from the back of the shop. Ginny glanced back; it was a tall, heavily built man with a face like a bulldog, all wrinkled jowls, frown and squashed-looking nose. 'Don't lerrer gerraway,' he bawled angrily. 'If she's been tryin' to thieve from the shop then it's the scuffers who should be telled . . . no use bein' soft on her just 'cos she's a gal! Stop thief, stop thief!'

He came towards her, meaty hands ready to grab, his short bow legs carrying the big and powerful body forward at a surprisingly fast rate.

120

Ginny heard the woman who had refused to serve her begin to say, rather uncertainly, that she rather thought Mr Bostock had got it wrong, that the kid was a real little ragamuffin all right, but . . . only the man charged on and Ginny suddenly decided that this was no place to linger. She doubted very much whether she would be allowed to give any sort of explanation once the big man got his hands on her . . . and she knew she could outdistance him; better to get well clear while she had the chance!

Accordingly, she shot out of the doorway and on to the pavement, turned right and scooted, whilst all around her the cry went up: 'Stop thief!' 'Whazzat?' 'Thievin' shoes from that there shop . . .' 'Stop her . . . it's the redheaded one, the one what just fairly flew past us . . .' 'Too much of that sort of thing . . .' 'Tradespeople have gorra stick together . . .'

The remarks came thick and fast but Ginny paid no heed to them, for now panic had her in its grip. She felt as guilty as though she had, in fact, tried to steal shoes and simply tore along the pavement as fast as she could, eager only to get away. The rights and wrongs of the situation no longer seemed to matter, for she was the hunted and they, the hunters, would not stop to ask questions if they caught her. She simply ran, head down, as fast as she possibly could.

She might have escaped them all had it not been for a tram, coming to a halt beside her. She swerved to avoid the queue of people at the stop, slipped on something wet and messy on the paving stones, and crashed heavily down amongst the feet and shopping baskets. She tried to scramble

121

up again, to continue her flight, but as she did so dizziness overcame her and she plunged into blackness.

It could only have lasted a matter of seconds, that momentary loss of consciousness, and then she began to scramble to her feet once more, suddenly aware that someone was holding her wrist in an iron grip. Helping her to her feet? One glance was sufficient to put that hope to flight. No rescuer this, but the bulldog, a vicious gleam in his small eyes and his mouth opening to explain, since one or two of the people in the tram queue were murmuring it were a shame, and what were that great hulking brute of a feller doing, grabbin' a-holt o' the little gal like that?

But the explanation was already on his lips. He was the manager of the biggest shoe shop on Byrom Street . . . they must know it . . . and one of his staff had caught the little bitch stealin' a pair of his decent shoes . . . he could not allow that sort of thing; if every guttersnipe in the city thought him a soft touch . . .

There was a muffled giggle at that. Ginny glanced at the faces surrounding her and saw that not one of them thought the bulldog likely to be a soft touch, no sir! Therc was sympathy in some of the eyes which met her own, but their oweners were beginning to disperse, some to climb aboard the tram, others to move up, nearer the head of the queue.

'Where's the shoes then, mister? The shoes you say she prigged?'

It was a boy, probably no older than herself, and he was glaring at the bulldog as though, for two pins, he would thump him one. And . . . oh, thank heaven, Ginny thought fervently; someone prepared to take her side, to speak up for her. But it would not do to let her pleasure and relief show, so she merely shot him a speaking glance in which gratitude and despair, she suspected, were nicely mingled, for though grateful for his intervention she did not think the bulldog would take much notice of a young boy.

He might not have done, either, but the rest of the queue were adding their voices to his. Yes, where were the shoes? He could scarcely drag her to the police station if he had no evidence, no stolen shoes to show! This, however, did not daunt the bulldog, nor encourage him to loosen his hold on her wrist.

'I'm tekkin' her back to me shop. No doubt she threw away the shoes as soon as she gorroutside me premises,' he said. 'If I find the shoes then it's straight to the station, an' I'll see she gets what she deserves. If I don't find 'em then I'll bleedin' well hand out me own sort o' punishment. She won't forget that in a hurry, I'm tellin' you; it'll mek her think twice afore robbin' again.'

But this, it seemed, was too much both for Ginny herself and for another member of the bus queue. A young woman stepped forward and laid a hand on the bulldog's arm. She was tall and slim, with shining fair hair cut in a fashionable bob and a sweet, gentle face. She was frowning now, though, and looking at the bulldog with real dislike.

'Take your hands off the child,' she said quietly. 'There are no stolen shoes here and so far the only voice we've heard has been yours—and very loud and unpleasant it was, too.' She turned to Ginny. 'Can you tell me what happened, dear? Speak out,

123

now.'

Ginny took a deep breath and marshalled her thoughts. 'I went into his shop to buy meself some shoes for school, when the new term starts,' she said loudly, so that everyone could hear. 'I'd been savin' up for weeks and weeks, all me message-money, pennies what I were give for mindin' babies, the money I got for choppin' kindlin' wood and sellin' it round the courts . . .'

'A likely story,' the bulldog growled. 'If you've got money—*if*, I say—then it's money what you stole off some poor shopkeeper, I don't doubt.'

'Hold your tongue, sir,' the young woman said. She spoke sharply and with authority, and Ginny gaped at her. How brave she was—and how very beautiful, with her straight ash blonde hair, pale complexion and cornflower blue eyes. But she had not finished with the bulldog yet, so Ginny continued to listen appreciatively. 'It is no business of yours where the money came from, though I've no doubt this young person came by it honestly. Why should it be otherwise? And if I were to go into your shop—which is now extremely unlikely—would you ask me where the money I was about to hand over for my new shoes came from? Would you suggest that it was not come by honestly? Then why should you do so just because the would-be purchaser is a child?'

The bulldog mumbled something under his breath; Ginny could not catch it but thought he had probably said something to the effect that children couldn't earn enough money for shoes, because the young woman promptly contradicted him.

'No doubt, when you were young, you had parents who bought you everything you either

124

wanted or needed,' she said crisply. 'But few kids today are in that fortunate position. I don't think there's one member of my class—I'm a teacher— who doesn't try to earn a few pence in the summer holidays. But that's beside the point.' She turned to Ginny. Eyes blue as forget-me-not flowers shone with compassion, yet Ginny could also see humour in their depths. 'Can you show us your shoe money, dear, or were you forced to abandon it when you were being chased by this—this *gentleman*?'

How nice it was to hear the bulldog being called a gentleman in such a tone that it was very clearly not meant as a compliment, Ginny thought gleefully, pulling the large collection of small change out of the pocket of her dress and displaying it to one and all. 'There's ten bob altogether,' she said triumphantly. 'And I *did* work hard for it, honest to God, miss. But the woman in the shoe shop wouldn't let me try anything on, 'cos I were barefoot, so I said I were sorry to have troubled her . . . nice as pie I was, thinkin' it would ha' been better to go along to John Lee's on the Scottie. I thought the shoes there would be every bit as good, an'—an' perhaps the shop ladies an' gents would be a bit more . . . well, mebbe they'd understand kids can't always afford stockings as well as shoes.'

There was a mutter of appreciation from the tram queue; clearly, they felt that Ginny had got a bit of her own back by this remark. Feeling more confident with every minute, she continued with her story. 'So anyway, I were turnin' away, meanin' to get along to the Scottie just as quickly as I could, when that—that *gentleman*—started shouting stop thief. He came towards me . . . the shop lady tried

125

to explain but he wouldn't listen, not he! So I ran . .
. though I'm no perishin' thief, I swear it on the
Bible, and if the shop lady hadn't been so toffee-
nosed and hoity-toity I'd ha' bought the shoes even
wi'out tryin' 'em on.'

'I don't believe a word of it,' the bulldog declared,
but Ginny could hear the uncertainty in his tone.
'Some o' these bloody guttersnipes could talk their
way out o' a murder charge at the Old Bailey; why,
they've lied all their lives, so lyin' comes natural to
'em.'

There was a shocked mutter at this remark; even
the tight-lipped old ladies who had looked
accusingly at Ginny, even the other shopkeepers
who had joined in the chase, looked disapproving
over the spiteful speech. And the schoolteacher
stepped forward until there could not have been
more than six inches between her pretty, straight
little nose and the bulldog's horrid protuberance.
'So you are pretending you still think that the child
stole the money? From some firm like your own,
no doubt, which trades in pennies and ha'pennies!
Why, you stupid, ignorant man, no one steals
pennies and ha'pennies, let alone farthings!'

This seemed to convince even the most sceptical.
A shopkeeper, still in his striped apron—he must
be a butcher, Ginny thought—said roundly that the
young lady was right and that the bulldog owed the
kid an apology. 'Then no more need be said,' he
added majestically. 'For I believe the law wouldn't
look too kindly, Mr Bostock, on a false accusation.
And as for you takin' the law into your own hands .
. . and wi'out a smidgen of proof—well, you could
be in serious trouble, you know.'

'It's awright, I won't prosecute him this time,'

126

Ginny said magnanimously, and was rewarded by the gale of laughter which greeted the remark. 'And now, if you don't mind, I'll be on me way. I've gorra pair o' shoes to buy before the day's out.'

The young teacher laughed with the rest, but when Ginny began to thank her, to say that she had feared prison at least as a result of the bulldog's malevolence, she shook her head, smiling down at the younger girl. 'The police would never have believed him, not once you showed them all your loose change, and even if they had, they wouldn't have shot you into prison, they'd just have told you off and visited your mam to warn her what you'd been doing. Only I do think you should have come shoe-shopping with either your mother or your father, because there are people, like Mr Bostock, who take advantage of a child alone.'

'Me mam's dead,' Ginny said briefly. 'And me dad's gorra farm over in Ireland. I'm goin' to live there one day, when I'm growed, but for now I live wi' me gran—that's Granny Bennett—in Victoria Court, off Rathbone Street.'

'Couldn't she have come shopping with you?' the young woman asked. Another tram drew up beside them and she took Ginny's hand. 'I'll treat you to a tram-ride then we can continue this conversation. Jump aboard!'

Very happily, Ginny obeyed, and soon they were upstairs on one of the front seats, Ginny chattering away and explaining everything, for she wanted her new friend to know exactly how things stood.

'Gran bends her elbow a trifle,' she said. 'And— well, she's norran early riser . . . and she'd want to know where I'd got the money for shoes from,' she added in a rush. 'To tell the truth, miss, I don't

127

mean to lerrer know I've got good shoes for school—when I do get 'em, I mean—because if she knows, likely she'll take 'em over.'

'Take them over? But what good would they be to her? Your feet can't possibly . . . oh, I see.'

'Yes, that's right. She'd either pawn 'em or sell 'em, next time she's short o' cash. So you see I had to come by meself. Oh, a pal had meant to come wi' me, but her mam's taken her and her sisters to New Brighton for the day. They asked me if I'd like to go along, but I wanted to get me shoes. If I'd known . . . but then Annie Wait's just a kid, like me, so it would still have happened, I dare say.'

'You're probably right,' the teacher said, after a moment's thought. 'But I think you'll find that if I go into the shop with you, we'll have no trouble. Would that be all right by you? There are several good shoe shops on the Scotland Road where you'll be well treated, I'm sure.'

'Oh, miss,' Ginny said tremulously. She had all but made up her mind that she would have to buy cheap gym shoes from a market stall and give up the idea of real, strong shoes. 'Oh, miss, would you really? I'd be that grateful! I were just thinkin' that I didn't fancy going into a shoe shop ever again after . . . well, after what happened earlier. But weren't you on your way somewhere? I don't want to hold you up.'

The teacher laughed. 'I was going to buy myself a new briefcase, but that won't take all day and I will almost certainly get what I want on Scotland Road. You see, I'm starting at a new school in the autumn term, teaching rather older girls than the ones I taught in Wigan, and I thought I'd need more books and so on, hence the new briefcase.'

128

'Oh, you were at Wigan, were you? I don't know it. Then where's you goin' next, miss?'

'The Rathbone Street Council School. I don't suppose you know it, but . . .'

'Know it?' Ginny laughed exultantly. 'It's *my* school, miss! And one o' the reasons I wanted decent shoes was because we're havin' a new teacher this September. Well, if that ain't the strangest thing! Are you goin' to teach Standard VI by any chance?'

'That's right. Well, whoever would have thought it? We are obviously fated to know one another, dear, so we'd best introduce ourselves. I'm . . .'

But Ginny was before her. 'You're Miss Derbyshire, Miss Mabel Derbyshire,' she said triumphantly. 'When you came to the school last June two of the girls from our class saw you . . . oh, miss!'

Miss Derbyshire laughed again. 'Well, what it is to be famous,' she said lightly. 'And you are . . . ?'

'I'm Ginny Bennett,' Ginny said promptly. 'I live in Victoria Court wi' my gran. The girls said you were going to lodge in the neighbourhood . . . have you found somewhere?'

'I'm looking for a place of my own, so if you hear of a nice little house going for a reasonable rent you can let me know,' Miss Derbyshire said. 'But until then I'm lodging in Canning Street, and getting to know the city. It's a grand place and the shops on the Scotland Road seem to sell everything. Ah, I think we should get off here, if we're to buy your shoes at the shop I've got in mind.'

*   *   *

129

It was late afternoon before Ginny returned to her own area and then she came walking on clouds. She had had a marvellous day, almost the best day she could ever remember. Miss Derbyshire had not only gone with her to buy the shoes but had insisted that the shop lent Ginny a pair of stockings and had seen to it that she tried on at least a dozen pairs before making her choice. In fact Ginny had been so dazzled by the splendid footwear that she had been quite unable to choose, and had been grateful when Miss Derbyshire and the assistant had advised her to take one particular pair.

'They're on special offer, miss,' the young gentleman assistant had said. 'It's the last pair in that pertickler style, you see, so the boss knocked one and six off the price.' He had gazed, adoringly, up at Miss Derbyshire as he spoke, then turned his attention back to Ginny. 'It's a fair savin', one and six—why, you could buy yourself a shoe cleaning kit for one and fourpence. Or some nice woollen stockings for when winter comes.'

As it happened, the sturdy black shoes were as handsome as any of the others and felt very comfortable, so Ginny had been glad to buy them. She had watched, closely, as the young man had wrapped them in tissue paper and put them in a beautiful green and white shoebox with a picture of two smart little children—both wearing new shoes —on the lid. Then he slipped the box into a long brown paper bag and began to solemnly count the pile of coins which Ginny had placed carefully upon the counter. Naturally, she had abstracted 1/6d, since she had known the exact sum in her pocket, but she watched, a trifle anxiously, as the

130

young man counted; after all, her money had led an adventurous life today, what with being chased through the street, knocked to the ground at the tram stop and then hauled upright by the bulldog. Ginny now knew his name was Mr Bostock, but to her he would always be the bulldog.

However, the young man had begun to put the money into the till, saying as he did so: 'That's it, correct to the last farthing. Now you must go off and spend the one and a tanner on something you really want,' and he had smiled in the friendliest fashion at them both, before crossing to the door of the shop and holding it open for them.

That should have been the end of it, but the day had continued on its blissful course. Miss Derbyshire had suggested that they should go into Miss Harriet Young's dining rooms and share a pot of tea. Ginny had looked down at her dirty dress and bare feet and said, bashfully, that she did not think . . . but Miss Derbyshire, it seemed, was equal to anything. 'Perhaps it might be better if we patronised one of the small neighbourhood establishments,' she said tactfully. 'After all, you did not know you were going to be invited out for a cup of tea and a bun when you left home this morning.'

Ginny agreed, rather doubtfully, that this was so and wondered, with a good deal of apprehension, what a 'neighbourhood establishment' could possibly mean. Her apprehension, however, was unfounded; she had realised it as soon as they turned into one of the large and bustling eating houses frequented by the store holders and market traders of the area. Miss Derbyshire had looked around her with a kindling eye. 'I only found out about these places, and the ones you call canny houses, last week, from another teacher who shares my lodgings,' she had said, confidentially. 'They give such excellent value! So now, whenever I'm in the area I pop in and have a snack. Mrs Evans, she's my landlady, provides breakfast and an evening meal, but nothing at midday.'

Once in the eating house, Miss Derbyshire had ordered the meal of the day for them both. It was beef stew and dumplings accompanied by a floury mound of mashed potato, with a slice of apple pie to follow and all washed down with several cups of tea from a large brown pot. Seeing that she was now mistress of 1/6d, Ginny had offered to pay her share, but Miss Derbyshire would not hear of it. 'But if you come shopping with me for my briefcase, you can buy us both a cup of tea at about four o'clock, when we shall be glad of it,' she had said. 'And after that, we shall have to turn our steps homeward. Mrs Evans is very particular about punctuality at mealtimes. She serves the evening meal at six, and woe betide anyone who is late!'

After their meal, they had wandered up and down the Scottie examining windows until they reached a shop which sold leather goods. Miss Derbyshire picked out two beautiful briefcases and then asked Ginny which one she preferred. Ginny, her bosom swelling with pride, said she thought the light one the prettiest, but the dark one more serviceable, and after examining both cases closely Miss Derbyshire opted for the darker one.

'And now for that cup of tea,' she had said gaily as they left the leather shop. 'And then we'll catch a tram back to Canning Street. What is going to happen to your shoes though, my dear? I'm sure you wrong your grandmother when you say she would take them from you, but if it would help, I suppose I might take charge of them for you and bring them to school each day.'

Ginny was delighted at the suggestion but realised, even if Miss Derbyshire did not, that it would not do at all. Her schoolfellows would soon begin to dub her 'teacher's pet' and to say nasty things about Miss Derbyshire's preference for redheaded nobodies who thought themselves above their company and so on. So she had thanked Miss Derbyshire earnestly, whilst assuring her that the shoes already had a good alternative home. 'D'you know Wait's, the grocer's shop on the corner of Washington Street?' she asked. 'Well, Annie Wait's in my class—our class, I should say. She's me best pal and her mam's ever so kind. They're going to keep the shoes for me—when they ain't on my feet, that is.'

Miss Derbyshire had agreed that this was an even better idea, and when the tram came to a halt at the junction of Great George and Upper Duke Street they climbed down and set off together towards their respective homes, parting when they reached the cathedral. Ginny would have gone further and accompanied Miss Derbyshire all the way back to her lodgings in Canning Street, but though Miss Derbyshire might be a stranger to the city of Liverpool, she still knew very well where Rathbone Street was and smilingly told Ginny to 'Hop along home now, dear. You mustn't be late for your tea any more than I must be late for mine.'

Ginny had realised that this was a polite dismissal; Miss Derbyshire had been very good to her, but she would not want one of her future pupils hanging around by her lodgings. So Ginny

133

had taken her dismissal in good part and was now wandering back towards the Waits' shop, where she meant to leave her lovely new shoes. It would be a wrench to part with them because it was another ten days before the start of term, but keeping them by her would simply result in losing them altogether, so Ginny headed for Washington Street. When she got there, she guessed at once that Mrs Wait and the children had not yet returned from New Brighton. Mr Wait was serving an enormous woman carrying a huge brown shopping basket and his assistant, skinny little Alice Fowler, was running back and forth, filling a box from a piece of paper which she held in her hand. Someone had obviously left an order and Alice was dealing with it. There were three other women waiting to be served, one of whom kept glancing impatiently at the clock above the counter.

Ginny, hovering between counter and door, was in a quandary. She did not like to interrupt Mr Wait and had no intention of letting Alice into the secret of the shoes. On the other hand, she dared not go home with her purchase, so what to do? But the problem was solved for her when Mr Wait caught her eye as the enormous woman turned away and began to surge towards the door. 'You back already, Ginny?' he asked jovially. 'Got them messages me good lady asked you to fetch for her? That's fine, just fine. Nip up to the flat would you, queen, and dump it on the sofy in the parlour. 'Twon't take you a moment; Mrs Wait will settle up wi' you later.' Mr Wait turned to his next customer, an elderly man wearing a heavy overcoat, despite the warmth of the weather. 'Yes, Mr Gibbs, and what can I do for you this fine day?'

Immensely relieved, Ginny scuttled up the stairs and dumped her beautiful new shoes on the sofa. She was about to leave the room again when the desire to see them once more made her delve inside the brown paper bag, but she only allowed herself to lift the lid of the box and glance quickly within. That wretched bulldog had made her aware, as nothing else could, of the dangers which a kid of her age could face if she did anything in the least suspicious. The Waits were good, kind people, but if something happened in the flat, if a plate was found to be broken or a teaspoon missing, it would be easy to tell themselves that young Ginny Bennett had been rather a long time upstairs, leaving her packages as Mr Wait had bidden her.

And anyway, I've still got 1/2d to spend, Ginny reminded herself buoyantly, as she ran down the stairs. 'Thanks, Mr Wait,' she shouted, and emerged on to the pavement once more. I could buy no end of things, she told herself. I wouldn't mind some new woolly stockings—they'd look prime with me shoes—but I suppose what I really ought to do with the money is make it work for me, like Danny always says. If he had a few pence over, Danny would buy something cheap and sell it a bit dearer. Sometimes he bought shrimps from the Charlotte Street Market and hawked them round the courts; once he had bought a huge jar of pickled onions—going cheap because the lid was insecure—and decanted them into four well-washed jam jars. He had made paper tops to fit over the tin lids of the jars and again had sold them to housewives in the courts, telling them— untruthfully but solemnly—that his Aunt Peggy, who lived in the country, had grown and pickled

135

these onions herself and weren't they cheap at the price now?

Chuckling over her pal's inventiveness, Ginny considered what she should buy but decided, finally, that it had better be as many second-hand stockings as she could afford, from Paddy's Market. She had seen her legs clad in the borrowed stockings that afternoon, and had realised how nice they looked. What was more, everyone knew that shoes rubbed one's heels if you wore them barefoot, but with a nice pair of old Ma Halligan's woollen stockings she would be as smart as, or smarter than, anyone else at the Rathbone Street School.

* * *

Granny Bennett sat in her dirty and neglected kitchen, staring morosely at her large and filthy feet. She had not let a drop of liquor pass her lips for three whole days, but the urge to cast caution to the winds and to stagger down to the Livingstone Arms and order a pint of Guinness was strong. The doctor's advice had scared her stiff at the time and she had vowed, with tears in her eyes, to take the pledge. But that had been six weeks ago—more— and now her fear had receded when compared with her desire for liquor. She had slipped off the wagon half a dozen times in the past couple of weeks but, oddly enough, she had not been tempted to continue drinking past the first two or three glasses. She had discovered that if she took her mind off it, she could hold out against the urge to drink for some while. Better, a neighbour had made her up a quantity of lemonade—horrible

136

stuff—but if she filled herself up with it, then one quite small glass of porter satisfied her for a while, at least.

This afternoon, however, the lemonade had all gone and Michael's money was in her purse, still unspent. Since the boys had stopped supporting her, she had begun to rely heavily on the brown envelope which came so regularly each month, and because she no longer drank had been managing quite well on it. George, who came round about once a fortnight, usually with a home-baked pie or cake from his wife, had seen the difference in her and had congratulated her on her good sense. Even Lewis, her youngest—and favourite—son had commented on how much better she looked, when he had popped in with a big stone bottle of ginger beer—ugh—and a bag of bulls-eyes, sent by his wife Amy.

The door, opening softly, brought Granny Bennett back to the present. As though thinking of him had conjured him up, George stood in the doorway, paused there for a moment, and then entered the room. He was carrying a large fruit cake and grinned encouragingly at his mother as he put it down on the kitchen table.

'How you doin', Mam?' he said cheerfully. 'I come in quiet like, in case you was havin' a snooze, but I see you're awake. Mary baked you a cake— it's still warm from the oven—so I thought we'd have a slice with a cuppa.' He then went and pulled the kettle over the fire since his mother merely stared owlishly at him, not attempting to move. ' 'Twon't take a minute to mash the tea, and slicin' the cake will be even quicker.' He glanced around the room. 'Where's our Ginny? Out off on the spree I s'pose wi' her pals.' He chuckled. 'That young Danny, he's a right caution, ain't he? Always up to something . . . but there's no harm in him and he takes good care o' Ginny.'

Mrs Bennett sniffed but accepted the cup of strong tea her son handed her and began to eat the cake, hoping that by so doing she would ease the longing for liquor, which was beginning to be insupportable. 'Ginny? I never know where the bleedin' kid is, nor I don't care,' she said sourly. 'She's just a burden and she's not my responsibility. What do her father do, eh? Never comes near nor by, never give me his address so I can't get in touch . . . an' you boys are no better. That snivellin' kid eats me out o' house an' home—I'm sure she takes money for herself when she goes for me messages. I does me best to clothe and feed her an' what thanks do I get for it? There's times when I remember me darlin' Stella and I downright hates the kid. I tell you, George, if it hadn't been for Miss Clever Ginny, our Stella 'ud be alive today.'

'Mam, how can you tell such lies?' George asked, his broad and honest face reflecting his shock at his mother's words. 'You make it sound as though our Stella died in childbirth, which weren't the case at all. It were the flu that killed her, not the kid, an' you don't want to go bearin' a grudge for what happened ten years ago, anyway.'

'Yes I do,' Mrs Bennett said mutinously. 'If Stella hadn't dragged herself out o' bed to feed that bawlin' brat, she'd of had the strength to fight the flu an' get well again. Why, she never ailed in her life! And anyway, if you're so interested in the kid, why don't you take her on? I've had enough of her. I want rid!'

138

George looked baffled. 'But Mam, who'd do your messages, light your fire, put hot food on the table? I know Ginny's only a kid, but I don't believe you can manage without her, even so. An' then there's the money her pa sends. If someone else took Ginny, then they'd take the money too.'

'They would not!' Granny Bennett said aggressively, swelling with anger at the mere suggestion. 'I've—I've earned that money, bringin' the kid up for him, an' I don't mean anyone else to get their hands on it.' She looked at George with sharpened attention. 'You an' Mary don't do so bad; that canny house she runs is always busy, so I've been told, and you've got your regular job with the Council. Why don't you take the kid if you're so interested in her? You wouldn't need the bog-trotter's money. You an' Mary are well-to-do.'

'Mary an' me's got four kids of our own,' George reminded his mother, 'and little Polly needs more attention than other children.' Polly had been born with a weak heart and a sight defect so severe that she could barely see a couple of feet in front of her.

Mrs Bennett, however, merely sniffed again. 'One more wouldn't make no difference; she could look after Polly for you. Still an' all, I suppose the kid does have her uses.' She looked piteously across at her son. 'I dussen't use the fry pan no more, 'cos me hands is too feeble to grasp it wi'out shakin' an' I don't want boilin' fat all down meself. I'm not too steady on me pins, either, so doin' me own messages ain't possible. 'Course, I dusts round an' so on, but I can't cope wi' washin' sheets an' such.'

'There you are, you see? You couldn't manage without Ginny and you're fond of her really, under-

139

neath,' George said triumphantly. 'If you can just keep off the drink, and let Ginny help you, you'll live to be a hundred yet, Mam. An' speakin' o' the drink, you've done real well to keep off the booze for so long and I'm proud of you.' George took another mouthful of cake and then, looking rather self-conscious, continued. 'Mary an' me's been a bit worried over our Ginny, to tell you the truth, Mam. I see her in the street a week ago and I were quite shocked; the kid looked downright peaky and her dress were filthy. The truth is, Mam, she's hasn't been gerrin' enough to eat, 'cos you were spendin' the money down at the old Jug and Bottle. But now I reckon she'll be plumpin' up, eh?'

'She's always been a scrawny kid. I could stuff her to the gills wi' good things an' she'd still be a scrawny kid,' Mrs Bennett said with finality. 'As for her dress, she could wash it at night and purrit on next day, couldn't she? But she's too fond of playin' out to waste time on washin' clothes.'

George looked horrified. 'D'you mean to say our Ginny's only got the one dress? Oh, Mam, what would our Stella think if she knew that? What would her pa think if he knew, come to that? The money he sends is for the kid, you know, and a second-hand dress off Paddy's Market don't cost a fortune. Why, school starts in a week or so, an' she can't go to school in that rag of a dress.'

Mrs Bennett heaved herself to her feet and waddled over to the kitchen door, flinging it open. The money in the pocket of her bedraggled black skirt was beginning to burn a hole; if she did not blow some of it on a large glass of Guinness with a chaser of rum, she would most probably die on the spot. 'George Bennett, you can gerrout of me

140

house and the sooner the better,' she shouted dramatically. 'If you've come to criticise your old mam, who's doin' her best against fearful odds, then you can bloody well make yourself scarce. You're a prig and a bully, tryin' to make me feel guilty for what's no fault o' mine. I feed the kid up like a Christmas turkey an' I give her decent clothes. An' what does she do? She grows an' grows, like a perishin' weed, that's what she does, an' you blame me for it! Now gerrout!'

George, his mother knew, was an easy-going sort of feller, but not above shouting back if he was sufficiently provoked, so she did not wait for him to leave the house, but left it herself. She thundered across the court, her feet slapping on the dirty paving stones, and out on to Rathbone Street, turning automatically in the direction of the Livingstone Arms. Behind her, she heard George shouting angrily, but she ignored him. Silly bugger, she was his mother, dammit, not one of his bleedin' kids. She would tell him he must learn to show respect if he ever dared to come into her house again. It would have been different, she told herself as she entered the pub, if he had still been paying her an allowance; then, he would have been justified in criticising her. It did occur to her, as she dragged her purse out of her pocket, that George's next action might have been to reinstate the allowance since he had seen for himself that she had not been drinking. Well, if that had been his intention, she was sorry to have thwarted it, but it was his fault, after all. He had defended Ginny and criticised his mam, and so far as Mrs Bennett was concerned, that was unforgivable. Well, unforgivable unless it was also accompanied by

141

cash.

'Evenin', Miz Bennett. You're early. Quite a stranger, too, but when the dibs is down, food comes first, eh? Now what can I get you?'

The landlord was a cheery, middle-aged man, bald as a coot and with a swivelling eye which disconcerted new customers. Mrs Bennett, however, knew him well and in any event did not care if he had one eye on her and the other on the ceiling, so long as he sold her a drink.

'A small rum and a large Guinness,' she said briskly. She showed him the note in her hand since she thought he hesitated, adding: 'An' make it quick, Mr Barraclough, 'cos I'm as dry as the Sahara desert.'

The landlord complied and Mrs Bennett paid, scooped up her change and downed the rum in one large swallow. She had meant to take the Guinness over to a table and savour it slowly, but somehow it had all disappeared before she had even turned away from the bar. She stared, owlishly, at the empty glasses, then pushed them across to Mr Barraclough. 'Same again,' she said rather thickly. 'Same again, landlord.'

*   *   *

When Mrs Bennett left the Livingstone Arms that night, she was very drunk indeed, and not one penny of Michael's money remained in her possession. In fact, had any money remained she would not have left the pub, for in the mood of rage and defiance which had possessed her after George's visit, she would have considered it a failing to have returned home sober. As it was, she

142

staggered from the pub with a bottle of Guinness tucked into her skirt pocket and made her way, unsteadily, across the court. By now, she had reached the maudlin stage and was weeping sadly to herself. 'I'm mish-mish-mishunderstood,' she mumbled, hiccuping. 'I've quarrelled wi' me eldest son and it's all the fault o' that nasty brat. Why, oh why, couldn't she ha' died instead o' me darlin' Stella? Oh, if only Stella were alive today, she'd see her poor old mam right. She wouldn't lerrem blame me for what ain't my fault . . . she'd know why I hates that bleedin' kid wi'out expectin' me to lower meself by tellin' her. Oh, Stella, Stella, why did you up and die?'

CHAPTER SIX

When Ginny returned to Victoria Court, the house was empty but she guessed that George had been visiting because there was three-quarters of a large fruit cake sitting in the middle of the table, though the teapot standing next to the cake had been cold, she judged, for a couple of hours at least. She also guessed, with an inward groan, where her grandmother was. For had not Ginny taken her father's brown envelope from the postman that very morning? She had offered to do Gran's messages before going off on her own concerns and had grudgingly been given enough money for a bag of potatoes, a couple of carrots, a turnip and a box of Oxo cubes. She had suggested that she might buy some scrag end if Gran would part with a little more money—she was sick to death of blind scouse—but Mrs Bennett, who had pocketed the envelope without blinking an eyelash, promptly said that there were no money available for such luxuries.

Ginny had brought the groceries home, peeled and chopped the vegetables and put them in a pan, sprinkling two Oxo cubes into the water. She had not, however, put the pan over the fire, knowing her grandmother might well go off and leave it cooking until the pan was dry and the vegetables burned. Instead, she had stood it under the low stone sink and asked if there was anything else Granny Bennett wanted.

'I want you out o' here,' her grandmother had growled nastily. 'Don't you go hangin' around the house hopin' to nick some o' me money for wharrever it is you're after, 'cos you won't get nothin'. Clear orff, d'you hear me?'

'Yes, I hear you,' Ginny had said in a tired voice. She could not remember the last time Granny Bennett had even been a bit nice to her but her additional nastiness was due, Ginny realised, to the fact that she was on the wagon. Ginny, who knew very well what it was to be hungry, imagined that wanting drink so badly must be even worse. There had been times when she had cried with the hunger pains in her stomach so, presumably, drink pains must be even more horrid.

Guessing that Granny Bennett was now in the pub, however, did not make Ginny's own lot any rosier. She knew Gran would drink herself into a good mood and would then proceed to drink yet more until she was in a bad mood. Only when all the money was gone would she come staggering home, and by then it behoved Ginny to be well out

144

of the way, preferably tucked up in bed, for her grandmother would not essay the stairs when she had a load of Guinness aboard.

So when Ginny roused to hear her grandmother blundering about downstairs, she made no attempt to get out of bed. Granny Bennett was shouting and swearing as she lurched into the kitchen and began to bang about in the cupboards. Ginny guessed she was searching for something to eat and ignored the racket as she ignored the drunken command to 'Come down out o' that, gal, an' find your gran some grub.' Experience had taught her that drunks may think they want food but are seldom able to eat it when it arrives and she had no intention, anyway, of getting within arm's length of Granny Bennett, who packed a wicked punch when in her cups.

Next morning, Ginny got up at her usual time and went downstairs to start the breakfast. Granny Bennett was sprawled on the filthy, faded little sofa, snoring so loudly that it was a wonder she did not wake herself up. Ginny cast her an incurious glance, then something made her look more intently. The old woman was a very odd colour indeed. Her whole face and the hands protruding from beneath her shawl were a bright, artificial-looking pink, and all of a sudden Ginny took fright. Her grandmother hated her and Ginny was not too fond of the old girl either, but she had no desire to share the house with a corpse. Whilst Granny Bennett was clearly not dead—the snores proved that—there was certainly something very wrong.

Filling the kettle and placing it upon the fire, Ginny wondered what she should do. If Miss Tillett had still been alive, she would have gone next door, but her old friend had died two years previously and the people now living there, the Borrages, were far too involved in their own affairs to be of much use.

The trouble with calling a doctor was that it would cost money and Ginny had bought her stockings and was now penniless. There were other people in the court, of course, but she hesitated to call on them, knowing how furious her grandmother would be if the neighbours gossiped to one another about her drunken state. She was still hesitating over what to do for the best when she heard the front door opening. She had sunk into a chair to think her problem over, but now she jumped to her feet. It had to be family—anyone else would have knocked—and she could only hope that it would be George. She had two uncles still living in the area, George and Lewis, and though she scarcely knew either of them well—Lewis seldom visited and George only twice a month—she felt more at ease with the older man. Uncle George was tall and dark with receding hair. He was also stout and Ginny never doubted his goodness of heart. Uncle Lewis was very different. He had wavy yellow hair of which he was inordinately proud, for Ginny had noticed that he was always flicking it off his face and smoothing it back with both hands whilst pressing the waves in with his fingers. He had very bright, blue eyes, a mouth which smiled easily and a strongly cleft chin, yet despite the fact that he was by far the handsomest of her uncles, Ginny thought him less trustable than plain and plodding Uncle George.

Now, she opened the kitchen door so abruptly that her Uncle George, for it was he, almost fell into the room. He stared at her for a moment, then spoke. 'Is me mam all right? I were tellin' my Mary that we'd had a row, Mam and me, and I told her that the old gal stalked off, swearin' an' shoutin', in the direction of the pub. My Mary were a nurse once, and she said it were downright dangerous for someone to cut out the booze for weeks and then go off on a bender. So I come round early, before going to work, to check out . . .' At this point, the deafening snores caught his attention for the first time and he gave a relieved grin. 'I hear she's alive an' in good voice! Well, mebbe she didn't drink all her money away, so I better be off.'

He half turned as if to leave the room but Ginny grabbed his arm urgently. 'I know she's snorin', but I think she's maybe really ill,' she said. 'She's ever such a funny colour, Uncle George, and she's not woke up though I've been clattering around the kitchen, wondering what to do for the best for ten minutes at least. Come and tek a look at her.'

To do her Uncle George credit, Ginny thought, he took one look at his mother and produced a florin from his pocket. 'Go and get Dr Barker; show him the money an' say as it's urgent,' he said. 'I never seen a human face that colour before so I reckon it's a job for the doctor. Hop along, queen.'

*   *   *

Granny Bennett opened her eyes and gazed groggily around her. Where the devil was she? She had a vague memory of very unpleasant things happening to her, being dragged and bullied and pushed about and told she must walk. Someone had given her a great deal of horrible salty water

147

. . . she had vomited, wept and wailed, hit out. But that had been a long time ago—hours, weeks?—and now she appeared to be tucked up in a bed, beneath a coverlet so white that it hurt her eyes.

'Mam? Oh, thank God, she's come round.'

Granny Bennett moved her head with considerable difficulty until she could see the speaker. It was her son, George, and as soon as she met his eyes he grinned, relief shining out of his face. 'Oh, Mam, we all thought you was a goner this time. Wharrever made you go on the booze when you've been good for so long? Dr Barker's warned you over and over that the drink would be the death of you an' this time it damn nearly was. If—if you're going to say it were because we had a row, then I'm real sorry, but tell me, what have you got against our Ginny? You made it pretty clear, yesterday, that you really hate the kid, even though she's useful to you. Why, if it weren't for the money her pa sends, I do believe you'd have turned her out on the street or sent her to an orphan asylum. So what is it, eh? You wouldn't tell me yesterday, but I reckon you're more amenable today.'

Mrs Bennett stared at him for a long moment. The trouble was, the story was quite a complicated one and she did not feel like justifying herself right now; she was too tired. On the other hand, though, if George understood the reason for her dislike of her granddaughter, then perhaps he might do something about it. Slowly, she began to speak.

'Oh, George, it's all such a long time ago, but it's as clear in my mind as if it were yesterday. Have you ever heard anyone mention your Aunt Violet?'

Obviously baffled, George shook his head. 'I didn't know I had an Aunt Violet,' he said. 'Were

148

she your sister, Mam? Come to that, I thought you were the only girl in a family of boys, so I suppose she must have been Dad's sister.'

Mrs Bennett sighed. 'Violet were my sister. She were two years younger than me but we were close as could be. We went everywhere together; to dances, the theatre, on day trips . . . everywhere. When we were old enough to go courtin' . . . oh well, I suppose it's no surprise if I tell you, we fell for the same young feller. He were called Neil McAllister and—and I thought he were the bee's knees. He were my young man at the start but after he met Violet, he changed. Then one day, I woke up to find a note on me pillow. She and Neil had lit off, gone to America. I told everyone I didn't give a damn, that she was welcome to him, but I vowed to forget her, cut her off completely.

'When they were settled in like, she wrote, begging me to forgive her, sayin' I must go to America as their guest. Oh, five or six letters she wrote, but I never replied to one of 'em. Even when I met and married your dad, I couldn't forgive her for what she'd done. So you see, when Ginny were born . . . well, it were more than I could bear.'

'But Mam, what's this got to do wi' our Ginny?' George asked. 'I'm sure she's never heard tell of this Violet, same as me.'

Mrs Bennett stared very hard at her son; was he mad or something? Couldn't he see how Ginny was a constant reminder of the hated Violet, who had taken her man? But she must be patient with him. 'Ginny is the very image of Violet. She's got Violet's ginger curls—I hate ginger hair—and all them horrible little freckles . . . why, even her eyes is the same, blue instead of a decent brown, with

149

them ugly white lashes. It weren't so bad when she were a baby, but first off she killed my Stella and then she got more 'n' more like our Violet. She even talks like her—Violet were always the clever one, always top o' the class, though she were younger than meself. But I didn't mind that, we liked being different in some ways, I just minded her takin' my feller.'

'But our dad was crazy about you, Mam,' George pointed out. 'You've told us over and over what a grand feller he was and how happy he made you. Once you'd got him, why did you grudge your sister that feller, Neil?'

'Dunno, doesn't matter,' his mother muttered. She had known this story was going to tire her, and tire her it certainly had. But at least George now knew why she hated Ginny and perhaps he would help her in some way. If he sent Ginny to live with Lewis and took his old mam in, she thought hopefully, then life would definitely improve. Of course she would not have wanted to live with George and Mary had she been her normal self, because they would not have approved of her drinking. But right now, the horrors of having the drink forced out of her system, and the illness which had followed, were clearing her mind. She knew she would never let another drink pass her lips. She was a reformed character. She would get rid of the nasty brat, move in with one of her sons—she would even hand over some of Michael's monthly money—and drink nothing but tea for the rest of her life. That way, she told herself drowsily, I really *will* live to be a hundred.

*   *   *

150

Michael stood at the rail of the ship looking down on the crowded quayside. He was waiting for his friend, Nobby Clarke, because the two of them had decided that today was the day they would go ashore. Someone had told them that there was a local market in which various native-made goods were sold and since they both wanted small things to take home to parents, girls, relatives and so on, it seemed an ideal opportunity.

'Everything's dirt cheap,' one of the older men had assured them. 'Of course, you have to bargain, but if you stick to your guns you'll get something pretty decent for a few coppers. I always visit the market when I'm ashore.'

So here was Michael, standing at the rail, with the hot African sun beating down on his head, wondering what gifts he could buy for his parents. Mammy liked pretty things, preferably something she could wear, whereas his daddy liked what you might call curios, strange objects which he could place upon the mantel or take into town in his pocket to show his pals on market day.

Market day! Michael had stayed on the farm for three long years after his return from Liverpool, but at the end of that time the sheer boredom, the hard work and the lack of any spare money had got him down to such an extent that he had become morose, his unhappiness showing clearly enough for his mother to remark on it.

'The trouble is, you've had a taste of the outside world,' she had observed. 'You left here a boy, content with the farm, a few pals and an occasional meeting with a pretty girl. You went away and saw the world, realised there was more to life than growing potatoes and turnips, feeding pigs and cows and wringing a hen's neck for a special dinner a couple of times a year. And then, of course, you found love, and perhaps that was the biggest change of all. You've done well, lad, to stick it for three years with never a complaint but I think the time has come when you should go away, if only for a few months. Other lads do, you know; in November, they take a berth on a coaster or even on one of the big liners, and don't come back till March or April. It's the quietest time of year for a farmer but this place isn't huge and, as you know all too well, farming is an uncertain business. We may do well one year but the next we'll be scraping the bottom of the barrel to feed ourselves, let alone have something over to sell from stock. If you go to sea again, no doubt you'll send us back some of the money you earn, and in a bad year that would be more use to us than your labour.'

Michael had not realised how irksome the narrow life on the land had become. Even his leisure time was boring, particularly in the winter. In summer, he would go for long rambles on the cliffs, collect seabirds' eggs, fish from the rocks, or go out in the *Orla* with his father, trawling the sea loughs, even adventuring out to the Atlantic fishing grounds when the weather was clement.

In winter, there really was not enough work to keep the three of them occupied. Feeding the stock, ploughing their oddly shaped little fields, fetching in peat for the fire and water from the well, were tasks that he and his father shared out meticulously, but it still left long periods when there was really very little to do. But he felt that to

152

leap at his mother's suggestion would seem ungrateful, so when he did speak, it was hesitantly. 'Oh, aye, winters are a bit trying, but what would Daddy say? Sure and isn't it himself who'd have most of the work on his hands? He might think I were running out on him—on you both, come to that.'

It had been a fine September evening, almost seven years earlier, and he and his mother had been sitting on the rocks, fishing for anything they could get. Maeve had looked up at him and smiled. There was so much sympathy and understanding in her face that Michael had to fight back tears. His mammy understood all right. She knew how he missed Stella, how he longed for her constantly, how he found other girls pale shadows when compared with the woman he had loved and lost. And she had clearly also realised that the repetitive, but often backbreaking, work on the farm enabled him to think too much.

Sean had never paid his son a wage, nor had Michael expected him to. Farmers always told their sons that they were working for their own benefit in later years and, since this was true in most cases, sons did not complain. Michael had had to ask for the allowance which he sent to Liverpool every month, but had explained that Stella's mother was very old and relied on the money as her only source of income. Both Maeve and Sean had accepted this without question, having no reason to doubt his word, and had never wondered, aloud, why he should do such a thing; it was common practice in Ireland, as in England, to support one's parents in their old age. He had missed the independence that his naval pay had given him, though, as well as

153

missing his shipmates and the excitement of seeing the world for the first time.

'Running out on us?' His mother gave a snort of laughter. 'We managed without you whilst you were fighting the war and, as I've already said, if you could allow us a little money . . .' Michael leaned over and squeezed her shoulders. She was a wonderful woman, so she was; she knew him better than he knew himself!

'Oh, Mammy, of course I'll send money home, you know that. And—and if you really mean it . . . well, it would do me the world of good to get away.'

So he had signed on with the *Mary Louise*, a cargo ship, which had come into Castlemaine harbour to take local produce on board, and had remained with her ever since. She was liable to be away from her home port for six months or more at a time, since she would deliver one cargo and pick up another, taking it to its destination, wherever that might lie, and relying upon loading another cargo for a different destination as soon as she had room in her holds. Michael had sailed with her to many strange and exotic ports, was well paid for his long absences and thoroughly enjoyed the life.

He had been home no more than half a dozen times during the seven years he had sailed on the *Mary Louise*, since that first momentous decision to return to sea.

One reason why he felt no guilt, now, over his prolonged absence was because a distant cousin, Declan, had come to the farm. At the time, Declan had been twelve and had been sent by his ailing mother when the doctors had told her she would not live to see the year out. 'I know you'll be good to me son, and won't grudge him his food, for that's all I'm asking,' she had written pathetically. 'His father left me when Declan was a toddler, and when I go he'll be alone in the world. You were always a good woman, Maeve, so I've no fear that you won't do right by my son. God bless you. Siobhan.'

As soon as Declan was strong enough, he became Sean's right-hand man and on his eighteenth birthday the family had begun to pay him a wage. 'He'll never replace you, Michael, but we felt it only fair to pay him what we'd have paid any worker who weren't a close relative,' Michael's mother had written. 'I know you won't want to come back until you decide to settle down, but when you do, there's room for us all. Your daddy has a decent flock of sheep, grazing on the common land, and he and Declan have been bringing in good catches of cod, enough to salt down what we don't use ourselves, to sell in the market.'

Her letter had gone on to talk about other farming matters but it had eased Michael's conscience. He knew he would go home one day, but that day had not yet come. Perhaps he might remain with the ship until age forced him to leave the sea, but when he did go back, it was good to know that there would be a strong, younger man to help him run the old place.

'Sorry to keep you waiting, Michael. I got collared by old Dixon; he wanted some stores brought up to the galley, which held me up a bit. Still, I'm here now. Shall we go?' It was Nobby, breathless but grinning, and toting a canvas kitbag which he patted significantly as the two of them clattered down the gangway. 'Several of the fellers have asked me to pick up fruit, if we see anything suitable, and Cook wants any sort of green vegetables—do they grow cabbage in West Africa?—so I brung this along.'

'You won't get many cabbages in that,' Michael observed as they reached the quay, but Nobby shook his head and punched Michael on the shoulder. 'You mad? I'm not carting cabbages, or not the number Cook wants anyhow. I'll tell 'em to deliver a couple of boxes—more if they've got 'em—and Cook'll pay when they arrive. Cor, ain't it hot, though?'

Michael agreed that it was, and presently they reached the market. It was held on a huge open space dotted with palm trees and was a hive of activity. Extraordinary things were being sold and for some time Michael and Nobby merely wandered, allowing their eyes to dwell incredulously on such items as dried and smoked snake, rats which had been skinned and jointed for the table, and other lumps of gory meat which they could not identify. This did not matter much, however, since most of the meat was crawling with flies, and looked thoroughly unappetising—if not inedible—to a European eye.

There were also stalls selling lengths of gaudy cotton and voile materials with colours so brilliant that they hurt the eye, as well as displays of local crafts. Some of the woodcarvings were extraordinarily clever and Michael bought a number of beautifully carved little barrels which fitted into one another, for the sheer pleasure of handling such an exquisite object. There were seven barrels in all and inside the last was a tiny wooden figurine. The biggest barrel was no more than three inches high and Michael, pocketing it and parting with the small sum of money required, told Nobby that it was just the sort of thing his father liked. He then bought a length of pale blue material, patterned with brilliant birds. It would make up into a nice full summer skirt, which his mother could wear with a dark blouse, and was exotic enough to mean her friends would guess that it came from her seafaring son.

He was considerably exercised in his mind over what he should buy for Declan, for the skinny boy was now a sturdy young man. Finally, he decided on a clasp knife with a carved ivory handle, into which the blade fitted snugly. It would be a useful tool about the farm, but it was also beautiful and unusual and would, he thought, give the young man pleasure.

They found vegetable and fruit stalls and bought a goodly supply of each, not forgetting to order the cabbages for the cook. Then Nobby suggested that they might buy some lemonade and some rum, mix them together to make a long, cooling drink, and sit under the trees for a while, for the heat was now intense and both young men were tired. Michael was doubtful about the wisdom of the lemonade—local water could not always be relied upon—but Nobby saw a soda fountain with a familiar brand name, so they bought that instead and mixed it with a very potent local rum. The drink brought sweat pricking out on their brows but also seemed to make the heat more bearable, and they sat down on a small knoll, only feet away from the stalls, to watch the comings and goings of the crowd and enjoy a little breeze which occasionally wafted over them.

Michael found himself watching a tall, elegant woman in a long pastel-coloured sari, a fold of which she had drawn over her head. She appeared to be of Indian blood for she had a narrow, aquiline nose, skin as pale as any European and a red caste mark in the middle of her forehead. Michael thought she was beautiful and sat up in order to see her better. She was accompanied by a young girl of maybe seven or eight who, like herself, was paler-skinned than the locals, though she had a quantity of dusty, frizzy, brownish-black hair. She was quite a pretty child, though clad in a stained cotton shift, ragged about the hem, and, naturally, was barefoot. She was carrying a huge basket, heavily laden with various types of root vegetables, and was obviously finding it as much as she could do to lift it, for she would stagger a few paces and then stand it down on the ground whilst sweat streamed down her face and neck.

It can't be mother and daughter surely, Michael asked himself, as the ill-assorted couple came level with him. No mother would expect her child to cope with such a weight alone; she would give her a hand. No, I suppose the poor little creature is some sort of maidservant, but even so, if that woman had an ounce of pity in her nature . . .

The woman paused by a stall selling carved wooden stools, cane-bottomed chairs and sturdy tables and the child, with an obvious sigh of relief, let the basket down with a thump. Unfortunately, she had chosen uneven ground and the basket tipped, allowing a small melon to roll across the dirt track between the stalls. The child gave a startled squeak and scurried after the fruit, picking it up and dusting it down tenderly, but when she

158

went to replace it in the basket the older woman pounced on her, snatched the melon from her grip and threw it down on the track, then began to hit the girl as hard as she could across the face and shoulders, ignoring the child's muffled cries and clearly feeling no pity for the thin, half-starved little creature.

There were several mumbled protests from the surrounding stallholders but the only people who moved were Michael and Nobby. They leaped to their feet and charged down upon the woman, shouting 'Stop that!' and 'Leave her alone, you wicked bully', the last being Michael's contribution.

The woman straightened up, her face still flushed with rage. Michael had thought her handsome, but now there was so much malignancy in the pale face that all his admiration fled. He picked the child up—she was light as a bird—and held her protectively against his chest, glaring at the woman as he did so. 'What has she done that was so terrible?' he demanded hotly. 'The melon rolled out of the basket because it was too full— and it were you who filled it, not the kid—and she picked it up, quick as quick, and tried to put it back in the basket.'

The woman's large black eyes blazed with fury. 'She is a bad girl,' she said in only slightly accented English. 'But I may beat her if I wish to do so; it is certainly none of your business.'

'Just because she's a child and clearly ill-nourished and unable to defend herself, that does not give anyone the right to lay hands on her,' Michael said stiffly. 'If her parents knew . . .'

The woman laughed harshly. 'Parents?' she said jeeringly. 'I am her parent, or the only parent she has ever known. She is the child of my dead sister and was left in my charge. She is lazy and spiteful—a good-for-nothing. Now put her down before I call the police.'

Michael stood the child on the ground, feeling such helpless rage boil within him that he was tempted to strike the woman but guessed that this would only make things worse for the child. Instead, he said haughtily: 'What is your name and the name of the child? I shall report this matter to the authorities.'

He had not expected any result from such a threat but, to his delight, the woman looked startled and afraid. 'I meant no harm . . . it was just that the melon is one of my favourite fruits . . . I do assure you, she's not a good girl, she does many bad things. She steals, she lies . . .'

'Your name?' Michael said remorselessly. He was beginning to enjoy himself. 'I meant what I said—I mean to report you to the authorities for . . .' But before the woman could answer, the child had seized her opportunity. She slipped off into the crowd, disappearing like a raindrop into a puddle, and the woman grabbed her basket and also set off, though in the opposite direction.

'Well, I reckon that's the last we shall see of them,' Nobby said with some satisfaction. 'I reckon you scared her so she'll think twice before she hits a young kid again. As for that story . . . the one that the child was her niece . . . I don't believe a word of it. The kid was one of them poor little urchins what hang about on the outskirts of places like this, offering to carry bags or baskets for a few pence. She'll think twice before gettin' involved wi' a woman like that again. Now, what next?'

Michael stood still for a moment, gnawing his lip and staring in the direction the little girl had taken. Then he shrugged his shoulders; they were not here for days, just hours, and there was nothing more he could do about the child. At least we saved her from one beating, he thought, as Nobby led the way into a new area of the market. It can't be true, though—that the woman is the girl's aunt. No one would treat a relative like that! Or would they? Strange and terrible things happened sometimes; it was impossible to say for sure that a woman would not beat a child to whom she was related.

For some time he simply followed Nobby amongst the stalls, a deep frown etched on his forehead. But at last his friend spoke. 'Whatever's the matter, Mike? You ain't still thinkin' about that kid, are you? We can't do nothin', except forget it . . . dammit, we did what we could, which was more than the locals were prepared to do!'

'I know,' Michael said morosely. He took a deep breath and stopped, swinging his friend round to face him. 'Nobby, you're a good friend, so you are. Can you keep a secret?'

'See this wet, see this dry, cut me throat if I dare to lie,' Nobby said promptly, drawing a wetted finger across his throat in the age-old childish gesture. 'What's up, old feller? That bloody woman upset you good an' proper, didn't she?'

It was a statement really, but Michael nodded. 'Yes, she did. You see, I've . . . well, I've got a daughter of me own so I have. Of course, she's only a baby . . .' He stopped short, realisation suddenly dawning; whenever he thought of Ginny he saw her as a tiny baby, but years had passed . . . she must be almost ten, if his calculations were right! 'No, she

161

were a baby when I saw her last,' he amended hastily. 'She's gettin' on for ten now. And the way that woman hit the kid . . . oh, Nobby, I left young Ginny wi' her gran, but suppose, just suppose, that the old shawly teks a dislike to her, or passes her on to someone else, an orphan asylum, even? Suppose my sprog's liable to be treated the way—the way that woman treated that young 'un just now? My—my girl died in the flu epidemic when the baby was only weeks old. She lived in the 'Pool; the gran has always seen to the baby . . . I send money regular, but I've never been back, never set eyes on the kid . . . and now—now I've got to *do* something, find out if she's all right, or I'll never forgive meself!'

Nobby stared at him. 'You've got a kid?' he said incredulously. 'But then so have dozens of fellers . . . only they don't keep 'em quiet, see no reason to do so, I suppose. But why are you tellin' me now? Don't say that little scene back there . . .' he gestured with his chin to the spot they had recently left, 'has given you the idea that your kid needs you? Because it seems she's done all right for nearly ten years!'

'I don't know how she's done,' Michael admitted wretchedly. 'I—I send the money, but they don't know what ship I'm on, or how to get in touch wi' me. And seein' that woman, the way she acted . . . well, it's made me think I've behaved badly.'

'No worse than most fellers who find a girl's in the family way and don't want to marry her,' Nobby replied with unconscious callousness. 'I guess I wouldn't want to marry just because . . .'

Michael let Nobby continue, even if he did have the wrong end of the stick. He did not feel like explaining further. It was easier to let Nobby

162

assume that he'd run rather than wed; and it was certainly true that he had run rather than find himself saddled with a child. He said nothing further on the subject, therefore, apart from telling Nobby that he rather thought, when the ship was in home waters once more, that he would just check, make sure his daughter was all right.

The two young men continued to wander amongst the stalls until they came to a section of the market where livestock was being sold and bartered. There were sheep, a great many goats, skinny, horned cattle, hens, ducks and geese, and even a section for more exotic creatures. They saw brilliantly coloured parrots sitting staring out of the bars with bright, curious eyes, and a mongoose, equally curious, examining the passers-by without a hint of fear. But it was the little birds which caught the young men's attention. Tiny, finch-like creatures with vivid crimson plumage; others white as snow with big, dark eyes and small sharp beaks, others still, yellow as daffodils, with white crests, and all of them crammed into cages too small so that there was no opportunity to so much as stretch their wings, let alone fly.

When they left the market much later that afternoon, they carried no livestock with them. They had bought one of the cages full of tiny birds but had left the market and released them in the surrounding countryside. 'I've been brought up to believe it's wrong to cage a bird, an' I can't change at my time of life,' Michael had told his friend. 'We'll keep no prisoners, Nobby. But one of these days, I'll buy my little daughter a kitten because— because her mammy were mortal fond of kittens, so she was.'

Nobby looked at Michael shrewdly as they boarded the craft and saw that he was still upset. 'I just thank the good Lord the kid got away before you made a proper fool of yourself. You're soft, Gallagher, that's the trouble.' He sighed deeply over his friend's attitude as they went below.

*   *   *

When he got into his bunk that night, Michael found himself unable to sleep. Pictures of a skinny child being beaten up kept intruding and when he did finally doze in the early hours of the morning, his dreams were no better than his waking thoughts. Guilt, deep and terrible, almost swamped him. He reproached himself continually because he had not made proper arrangements for his child. It was all very well to tell himself that no better guardian could be found for a child lacking a mother than a grandmother; the fact was, he knew Mrs Bennett, knew she disliked and despised him, should have wondered whether, as the child grew older, she would dislike and despise her, too. In his dreams, Mrs Bennett became a monster, swelling with rage whenever the child crossed her path, beating her no matter how hard she endeavoured to stop her, screaming abuse at her if the child skipped out of arm's reach.

By morning, Michael was pale and hollow-eyed. Nobby remarked on it as the two of them began their first job of the day, which was to release the mooring ropes as the *Mary Louise* took the tide and nosed out of the port. 'You ain't still worritin' over that kid o' yours, are you, mate?' he asked, as the bows of the ship met the waves and began to move

164

to their rhythm. 'That's called pointless worritin', 'cos there ain't a thing you can do about it until we make landfall again in good old Blighty.'

'Don't I know it?' Michael said gloomily. 'And since we're only out of the Port o' London a month, it'll probably be five months, maybe six, before we're back again.'

'And maybe, after five or six months, you'll have come to your bleedin' senses and see that there ain't nothin' you can do at this late stage,' Nobby said bluntly. 'If the gran's been good to the gal, she won't want you interferin'. Mind you, you said she were old, didn't you? Mebbe the gran's dead an' the kid's wi' some other relative. Did your young lady have brothers and sisters?'

'Yes, lots,' Michael said, his brow clearing. 'She had four brothers in the Navy and three sisters. The oldest sister died a couple o' days before Stella, in that flu epidemic. The oldest brother, George, were a grand chap, so he was. He wouldn't let harm come to no child o' Stella's.'

'Well, there you are then,' Nobby said buoyantly. 'George'll look after your little lass so quit worritin'. The six months will pass in a flash, you'll see, an' though I guess you'll want to check up on the kid, I bet you'll find her happy as Larry. So let's see you grin.'

'You've made me feel a lot easier in me mind,' Michael said, beginning to smile.

'Gerra move on, you fellers!' A loud voice interrupted. 'Swab this perishin' deck before the waves start comin' inboard and muckin' it up again. You can check the hatches while you're doin' it.' The bo'sun was a cheerful Liverpudlian with a round face, weathered by sun, wind and rain to a

165

uniform puce. Despite his colouring, he was an easy-going man, but when he did issue orders, he expected them to be carried out at once. Michael and Nobby jumped to obey.

*   *   *

'Only two more days of blissful freedom, Mabs, and then it's noses to the grindstone time again. Have you finished preparing for your new class? You'll have a lot more to do than me, because your kids are older.'

Miss Mabel Derbyshire and her friend and colleague, Sandra Holmes, were in the kitchen of the big old house on Canning Street. Their landlady, Mrs Evans, provided them each morning with a breakfast of porridge, tea and toast and she served a meal each evening, but at lunchtime, during the holidays at least, her lodgers were at liberty to buy their own food which they then might cook in her large and pleasant kitchen. When term time started, the teachers would have a meal on the school premises, but during the holidays the kitchen became a meeting place at noon. Mrs Evans would not take gentleman lodgers and made no secret of the fact that she preferred teachers or nurses to other professions. This was pleasant for the girls, who speedily became friends and formed into groups over mutual interests.

Normally, at this time, Mabs and Sandy—she was always called Sandy—would have shared their meal with Emily Butterworth and Nora Hayes, but today Emily and Nora had gone shopping for equipment which they would need when school started in two days' time.

166

'My kids are also total strangers so far as I'm concerned. Oh, except for one—the one I told you about, Sandy. But I got the impression that she'd not spent much time in school—she lives with her gran who needs a great deal of help—so I don't suppose she'll be of much use to me so far as introducing me to school ways is concerned. But I've done my best to prepare some fairly simple lessons which should determine how much the children have learned—and remembered—from last year. I did wonder about PE, but the school doesn't have much playground, does it? Still, I suppose we can do exercises and play games such as Tip, or Rescue—anything to get rid of some of their energy!'

Sandy, who was to take the admission class, laughed. She and Mabel had been at school and then at college together and were both determined to remain together if it were humanly possible. Once they had started to work in Wigan, they had realised that rural poverty was nothing compared to the poverty of an inner city, but the knowledge had not put them off teaching. Indeed, it had fuelled their desire rather than weakening it. The Wigan school had been in a very poor area, and in such an old building that they were in daily dread of its collapsing around their ears. Still, the kids were great and I was very happy there, Mabel thought now, which must be why, when we decided to move on, we applied for Rathbone Street School, though of course we were influenced by the fact that there were two jobs going rather than one. In any case, we would both have applied for jobs in the same area so that, at least, we could have lodged together.

She was still thinking how lucky they had been when Sandy gave a shriek. 'Are you or are you not watching the perishin' toast?' she shouted. 'I smell burning.'

Mabel gave an equally ear-splitting scream and dived across the kitchen, pulling the grill pan out from under the flame just as the edges of two of the four pieces of toast actually caught fire. She grabbed a fish slice and beat the toast until it merely smouldered, then turned the slices and began to sprinkle grated cheese on the uncooked sides. 'Sorry, sorry, I was dreaming,' she told her friend.

'I'm quite looking forward to the start of the new term,' Sandy said, just as the kettle boiled. She took it off the stove, which was a modern gas one, a great improvement on the one they had been using when they had shared a room in Wigan, and began to make a pot of tea. 'In schools like this the kids really respond to teaching, and though I'm no saint, I went into teaching in order to make things better.'

'Yes, well, whatever the reason, we'll soon know if we've done the right thing,' Mabel said. The cheese was bubbling nicely and she switched off the grill and arranged the slices of toast on two plates. 'Do you want some pickle with this, or a nice big blob of tomato ketchup?'

'I think I'll go for pickle this time,' Sandy said, beginning to pour two cups of tea. 'What do you think of our revered headmistress, eh? She's not much like Miss Bristow, is she?'

Mabel thought about the past few years. She and Sandy had lived in the same tiny Suffolk village and gone to the old-fashioned little village school.

There had only been two teachers, Miss Brown, who taught the children until they were nine or ten and Miss Bristow, the headmistress. Both teachers had the soft accents of rural Suffolk, and had ruled their pupils mainly by threats of 'tellin' your mum and dad what a bad child you've been' when someone proved obdurate. It was a mixed school, though the teachers preferred the girls to sit on one side of the aisle which divided each room into two, and the boys on the other. Infants, of course, mixed far more freely, and in the playground it was pretty well a free-for-all, though again girls tended to keep to themselves, despising the rougher games which the boys enjoyed.

Sandra and Mabel had both come from large families where money was scarce. They lived in adjacent cottages a short walk from the centre of the village and their fathers were farm labourers who made ends meet by growing a good deal of their own food in the long, narrow cottage gardens. There were seven young Holmeses and five young Derbyshires, and it had speedily become obvious to both girls that if they were ever to escape from the rural poverty which surrounded them, they would have to work hard at school.

Miss Bristow had thoroughly approved of their desire to better themselves, particularly since most of their fellow pupils were not in the least interested in education but spent their time in school gazing out of the window and longing for the end of the day. So she had arranged for them to have what she called 'extra tuition' after school for half an hour each day, and had actually invited them into her own home—the schoolhouse, attached to the school itself—during the holidays

169

to learn to play on her old upright piano, to go further into the mysteries of mathematics than the school could take the generality of its pupils, and to read her large library of assorted books. She had never charged their parents for any of this help, though Mr Holmes and Mr Derbyshire, well aware of the dearth of good jobs in the small village and the cost of transport to anywhere else, had seen that the teacher was supplied with eggs from their hens, vegetables from their gardens and fruit from their trees, even if it meant sometimes having to tighten their own belts.

When the time had come for the two girls to leave, Miss Bristow had suggested that they become pupil teachers, for the numbers at the school had grown from thirty to fifty, and she and Miss Brown were very stretched as a result. As pupil teachers the girls learned invaluable lessons in discipline, whilst they continued to work with Miss Bristow at holiday times and after classes were over. Then, when they were eighteen, she had told them of a one-year college course which would gain them a proper teaching certificate, if they had decided teaching was the career of their choice.

The year in college had been happy beyond their wildest dreams, and they had worked harder than ever, emerging at the age of nineteen with excellent references from all their college teachers, and with the teaching certificates which would ensure them jobs in the profession of their choice.

Naturally enough, they had begun to look for work immediately, and would have had little difficulty, had it not been for the fact that they were determined to stay together. They realised, of course, that they could scarcely hope to get jobs which would enable them to live at home, for the village was tiny, many miles from the nearest town, and had a thrice weekly bus service. So they had looked and looked, and when they found the school in Wigan which wanted teachers for Standards I and II respectively, they had applied at once, and got the jobs. They had moved into lodgings, but after two years Mabel had decided she would like to teach rather older children so they had begun to scan the education journals again. They had eventually found the advertisement for an infant teacher and a person to teach Standard VI at Rathbone Street School in Liverpool. They had applied, been granted interviews, and been offered the jobs; so here they were, settling into lodgings once more.

'Mabel! I asked you what you thought of Miss Mackie and you went off into a dream. She's very different from Miss Bristow, but I reckon she'll turn out to be all right, don't you?'

'Yes, I think so,' Mabel said absently. Their new headmistress was neither elderly nor soft-spoken, as Miss Bristow had been. Miss Mackie was probably forty or so, with a strong Liverpool accent which the girls had found difficult to understand at first. She had thin, greying hair, pulled off her large bony face and fastened at the nape of her neck in a hard little bun, and a pair of glasses, gold rimmed and very small, which seemed to spend most of their time on a narrow piece of black ribbon hanging round her neck. She wore sensible flat shoes, masculine-looking pin-stripe suits in grey or navy and was capable of out-shouting the noisiest pupils. She had warned both girls that punishment, frequently needed, was handed out by all teachers

171

in the form of a ruler on the palm of the hand, but in special cases, where a member of staff sent an erring child to the head teacher's study, she wielded a cane with great effect, either on the palm of the hand or across the backs of the legs.

'I don't believe in overdoing the cane,' she had told them when they came to look round the school, 'but this is a tough area, young ladies, and you'll find some of the children do not take kindly to any form of authority. If you give an order and they flout it and go unpunished, then you'll find they never obey you again. Naturally, this cannot be allowed, so corporal punishment is a sad necessity. Unless you can achieve instant obedience for any command you may give, a few smart blows with the ruler is much more effective than a thousand words.'

Neither girl had much relished this advice, for the children in their previous school had not needed such methods to keep them in line, but looking at the area surrounding the Rathbone Street school, Mabel had an uneasy suspicion that Miss Mackie was right; some strong deterrent would be needed to stop these children from overstepping the mark.

'Shall we eat in here, or do you want to take it up to our room? The dining room's awfully big and gloomy when there are only the two of us in it.' Sandy had arranged the plates and cups on a tray and now looked enquiringly across at her friend. 'Which is it to be?'

Mabel looked out of the kitchen window. The sun was shining and the garden was a pleasant enough place, though somewhat overgrown. Their landlady had explained that the garden had always been Mr Evans's pride and joy and had been kept very neat. Since his death a couple of years previously, however, she had made no attempt to do anything out there, save to have a man in once a month to cut the grass.

'Let's take the tray outside,' Mabel suggested. 'I know it's September, but the garden is pretty well sheltered and the sunshine's beautifully warm. We shan't get many more days like this, so we might as well make the most of it.'

Sandy agreed and presently the two of them settled themselves comfortably on the grass and began to eat. It was, after all, still holiday time, Mabel told herself, munching the cheese on toast. When the schools were out, she and Sandy could be girls again; time enough to revert to being teachers when term started.

CHAPTER SEVEN

'It's the last bleedin' day of the holidays, Ginny Bennett, an' if you won't come with me, I'll bleedin' well go by myself.' Danny Levitt's face was one enormous scowl and he ran his hands, impatiently, through his curly mop of mousy brown hair, streaking his forehead with dirt. 'I'm tellin' you, there's fellers what'd give their eye teeth for a day in New Brighton an' all you've gorra do is either find the money for the ferry crossin' or sneak on board when no one's lookin'. What's it to be?'

Ginny stuck out a mutinous lip. The two of them were down by the Pier Head, watching the ships draw into the landing stage whilst streams of workers jostled their way ashore and pushed past the children, perched on the rails of the floating bridge. 'It's all very well for you, Danny,' she said crossly, 'your hair ain't bright ginger. Folks see me hair and remember it. I've gorras much chance of sneakin' on to the ferry without bein' noticed as a snowflake in hell. Oh aye, *you* could do it, 'cos you look like every other kid mooching about the waterfront, but I'm con-spicuous.' She said the last word slowly and with great emphasis. 'Conspicuous, do you understand?'

'You're just usin' long words to make yourself sound more interesting,' Danny said scornfully. 'What you mean is, you dussen't gerron the ferry wi'out a ticket, an' that stingy ole bag as you call your gran ain't likely to give you nothin', norrif she can help it. My dad said t'other day that she wouldn't give a body a cold unless they was willing to hand over cash, and it's true, ain't it?'

'She's tight wi' money all right,' Ginny admitted. 'But it ain't that, honest to God it ain't, Danny. It's—it's gettin' ready for school. I'm goin' in to a new class—I missed most o' last year—and I do truly want to look . . . oh well, like the others, I suppose. I've got me shoes, me stockings and a blouse. Nothing's new apart from the shoes, but they all look awright. Only . . . only I've gorra have a decent skirt, either grey or navy, and tomorrow's me last chance of gettin' one. If only you'd help me!'

'Tell you what, then,' Danny said, after a pause during which he stared pensively out over the dancing blue waters of the Mersey. 'If you an' me tries to earn some coppers right now, before we goes home, would you come wi' me tomorrer? I

174

know it's too late to hump heavy shoppin' home for someone, or get ourselves some old orange boxes to chop up so's we can sell 'em as bundles of kindling, but there must be something we can do of a summer evening!'

Ginny considered this. It was a generous offer because Danny had no need to scrap round for school clothes. His kecks might be worn and old, having been purchased for his brother three or four years previously, but they would be clean and patched. Mrs Levitt was always grumbling that she had more kids than was decent, but she worked hard to give them whatever she could and it sometimes seemed to Ginny that Danny's mother spent every evening darning, patching and mending for her various offspring.

'We could try, I suppose,' she said rather doubtfully. 'But a decent skirt is going to cost a bob or two. I dunno as we can make that sort of money, not this late on.'

'Tell you what,' Danny said suddenly. 'Remember them big skips at the back of the market, where the stallholders chuck out stuff they don't want at the end of the week and the dustbin men take it away to some old rubbish tip somewhere? Some of the fellers say you can pick up quite decent stuff now and then. Bobby Smith keeps rabbits and he reckons to feed 'em from old cabbage stalks an' that, which he gets from the skips.'

Ginny drew herself up to her full height, which was only a couple of inches short of Danny's, for all he was two years older. 'I don't mean to go scrabbling in the bin for filthy old fades an' then find I can't bleedin' well sell 'em, 'cos all the kids are doing it,' she said roundly. 'An' what good's cabbage leaves? D'you think I'm goin' to sew them together to make meself a skirt, eh? You're off your bleedin' rocker, Danny Levitt.' This spirited reply started Danny giggling, whereupon Ginny tried to box his ears and in two minutes the two of them were rolling on the ground, each with a handful of the other's abundant locks.

The fight ended when Danny managed to flatten Ginny, grab her by both wrists and sit on her stomach. By now they were both laughing, animosity forgotten, though Ginny said weakly: 'Let me up, do, or I might have to bite you, though I know from experience that you taste horrible.' The pair scrambled to their feet and climbed back on to the railings, dusting down their clothing as they did so. Finally satisfied that she had removed most of the dirt, Ginny took a deep breath, yawned and then said sarcastically: 'Have you any other bright ideas, cleverdick? If we gorrenough wool, I dare say you could knit me a skirt!'

This set them off giggling again but presently Danny said reprovingly, 'This won't do, we're wasting time. I know there's a deal o' fruit chucked away each night outside St John's Market—don't you hit me, Ginger, or you'll regret it—but it weren't those skips I were thinkin' of. Paddy's Market has skips too an' there's all sorts in 'em— broken china, odd shoes, clothes what are too worn to sell, bits o' rag—oh, all sorts.'

'I know, and you think that there might be a decent school skirt which would just fit me but had been chucked out by mistake,' Ginny said wearily. 'I've got rags of me own, ta very much—I'm wearin' 'em now.'

176

'Don't you jump in?' marvelled Danny. 'Ain't you never goin' to give me a chance to finish what I'm sayin'? I'm not denyin' we *might* find a skirt what'd fit you, but that ain't the point. The point is that on a Friday there'll be a full skip an' today's Friday, ain't it?'

'What's that got to do . . . ,' Ginny gave a muffled gurgle as a dirty hand was clapped across her mouth. She fought free of it, saying penitently, 'I'm sorry, I'm sorry. Go on, gerrit off your chest. I won't say another word.'

'Friday's a good market day so the bins'll be full. No one don't want those rags an' bits. The dustman takes 'em away, like I told you, but we could sell 'em to one of the raggies. There's a firm in William Moult Street—I think it's King's—what'll give us a fair price. Mind, we'll need to borrow an old pram or a handcart, or some such; what d'you say?'

Ginny looked at him, feeling her cheeks warm and her eyes glow with enthusiasm. He was brilliant, was Danny. His ideas were always good 'uns, an' this one sounded like a winner. Nicking was acceptable sometimes; she had often climbed over the wall into the station coal yard and come back with a sackful of bits when the weather was bitter and there was no money for fuel, and every kid nicked apples or a few spuds from a market stall if the opportunity arose. This was considered fair enough, though to steal from a shop was frowned upon. But Danny's idea was actually legal! No one wanted the rags in the skip; if they didn't take them they would only get thrown away— burned probably—yet she knew very well that the rag merchants would pay good money for such cast-offs. Why, there was a filthy, bearded old man, who wore a big black woman's hat and a swirling cloak, dark with grime, who came round the houses and would pay for rags by giving you either a paper windmill or a glass jar. He had a thin, white face, one solitary yellow tooth, which showed when he grinned, and a perpetual dewdrop on the end of his nose. If he knew about the skip, he would undoubtedly visit it, but it was clear he did not.

'Danny, you're the cleverest lad in the world,' Ginny breathed. 'When's the best time to go? Your mam's gorran old pram—d'you think she'd lend it us? Only if we borrow the handcart from Johnny Wickes, we'll have to pay 'im and mebbe he'll want to know why we need it.'

Danny did not reply for a moment; he was obviously considering the question seriously. Then his brow cleared. 'The best time to go to the skips is as soon as it's light in the morning,' he said constructively. 'The yard is on the corner of Maddox Street and Bevington Hill and the gates open at dawn. Because it's so early, Mam isn't goin' to need the pram and it's a good big one; I reckon it'll hold more'n Johnny's handcart. So what say you meet me under the arch as soon as it's light?'

'I'll do me best. Tell you what though, Danny, if I oversleep you could come in and give me a shake. I'll leave the door unlocked . . . we usually do.'

'Right,' Danny said cheerfully. He climbed down off the railings and Ginny followed suit. 'We'd better get back to the court an' get to bed, so's we's fresh for the mornin'.'

Ginny agreed to this and the pair of them were actually on Rathbone Street before another thought occurred to her. 'Danny, how come you know so much about Paddy's Market?' she asked

178

suspiciously. 'I'm sure I've been in there doin' messages a good deal more often than you have, but I've never wondered what happens to the unsold stuff.'

'No, you wouldn't,' Danny said. 'But remember, Ginny, I were deliverin' bread until three days ago. Bakers start work turrble early—at three or four in the mornin'—an' a couple o' times, when they were short-handed in the bakery, I were told to report there early to help unload sacks of flour and tubs of fat an' to run messages to the baker's; stuff like that. An' I see the dust cart goin' round pickin' up rotten veggies and old rags. I didn't put two an' two together until a couple o' days ago, when it just crossed me mind that there might be a few coppers in it. And then, when you went on and on about your bleedin' skirt . . .'

Ginny considered thumping him, for she had not gone on and on about her skirt, but decided against it. After all, if they fetched away a goodly supply of decent rags, then they could take them to the feller in William Moult Street and be back on the Scottie by the time Paddy's Market was opening up for business. She could buy the skirt, take it round to the Waits' and be on the ferry, legally, with the money they had earned, in time for a full and glorious day at the seaside.

'How's old Granny Bennett? Still on the booze?' Danny asked as they went into the court. 'I know she were on the wagon for weeks, then began liftin' her elbow again, but after endin' up in hospital an' all, I reckoned she might be a bit more sensible in future.'

'She's still drinkin',' Ginny admitted rather gloomily. 'But less, I think . . . or not so openly, any

179

road. I never see her tek so much as a mouthful o' the stuff, but when I get back from a trip to the shops or wharrever, she's reelin' a bit . . . and sometimes she talks squiffy, though if I say anything she gets real nasty—you know what she is.'

'Yes, nasty,' Danny said fervently. He had more than once received a clout round the ear for trying to stop the old woman hitting out at Ginny. 'Oh well, my mam says she'll drink herself into an early grave and mebbe that's what she wants.'

'It can't be a *very* early grave; she's well over seventy,' Ginny pointed out. They had reached her door now and she paused on the top step. 'See you tomorrer mornin', then.'

'And don't you be late!' Danny shouted back, as Ginny slipped inside the house.

*   *   *

Despite Ginny's fears, she woke in good time next morning, partly due to Granny Bennett. Ginny had returned to an empty house the previous evening and had made her way up to bed, guessing that her grandmother was probably at the pub, but knowing there was nothing she could do about it. If she spoke out, Granny Bennett would simply call her a nasty little liar, a right troublemaker, and with a straight face, too. Why, only the other day her Uncle George, who, to do him credit, did try to keep an eye on his mother, had congratulated the old lady, in front of Ginny, on her strength of will and abstinence.

'You'll be feelin' a lot better, our mam, wi'out a bellyful o' ale a-swishin' round inside you,' he had

180

observed. 'You're lookin' better an' all, quite bright-eyed and bushy-tailed, as they say. Oh aye, you'll be gettin' that telegram from the King one o' these days.'

Granny Bennett had laughed and said that George was right, of course he was. 'I feels much more the thing,' she had assured her son. But she had avoided Ginny's eye, and when George had said: 'Ain't your gran doin' well, our Ginny?' had given her such a threatening glance that Ginny, who had taken a deep breath to tell George that his mam still spent more money on drink than on food, wisely decided to keep her mouth shut.

So Ginny climbed the stairs and got into bed, first banging her head—gently—on the wall five times, in the hope that this would somehow manage to remind her to get up at five o'clock. Not that she had any means of knowing the time; her grandmother had pawned the big old clock which had once stood on the parlour mantel, and unless the wind was in the right direction the chimes of the nearest clock never woke Ginny, who was an excellent sleeper.

So she had settled down and slept at once, only to be woken some time in the small hours by a fearful banging and carrying-on from downstairs. Granny Bennett shouted and clattered about, the neighbours banged on the dividing wall and hollered at her to shut up and let others get some sleep, and, as the pearly light of dawn crept through her small attic window, Ginny finally decided that it must be time, and slid out of bed.

Downstairs, she found Gran sleeping at last, and snoring almost as loudly as, earlier, she had been yelling. The fire had died but since it was summer

Ginny did not attempt to light it. Tea and porridge were highly regarded by Gran first thing; she said they helped to settle her stomach and to calm her raging thirst, but, on this occasion at least, if the old girl wanted such things she could, Ginny decided, get them for herself. For Ginny's own part, she spread margarine on a cut off the loaf, poured herself a tin mug of cold water, ate and drank and then slipped out into the strengthening dawn.

Danny was there, crossing the court towards her, trundling the old pram, but when he looked up and spotted her, he gave a relieved grin. 'I were just goin' to come and wake you,' he said. 'But I weren't lookin' forward to it; Granny Bennett were on a bender last night, weren't she? We heered her comin' back, shoutin' at the top of her voice. Me dad said she knows more bad words than he does, and he worked on the docks when he were younger.'

'Yes, she were a bit wild,' Ginny admitted. 'The neighbours were hammerin' on the walls, shoutin' at her to let them get some sleep, but she don't take a bit of notice, not when she's had a bevvy or three.'

'Well, she's quiet enough now,' Danny observed as they turned into Rathbone Street. 'Why was it, do you suppose? There's gorra be a reason for her goin' on the binge like that.'

Ginny was about to reply that she could not imagine why her grandmother had leaped off the wagon so conclusively, when a mental picture came into her mind. She saw her grandmother's head laid on the table and beneath one cheek was a brown envelope. Ginny stopped dead in her tracks,

182

a hand flying to her mouth. 'Oh my Gawd! Me dad's money must have come while I were out yesterday . . . that means it came almost a week early. Ever since she were ill, I've stood there with me hand out and made her give me some of the money so's I can buy food for the pair of us. But we were out all day yesterday, weren't we, because your job were finished and I were doin' messages for folk most of the day. And then we went down to the Pier Head . . . oh, why did me dad go sendin' the money early!'

She half turned back towards Victoria Court as she spoke, with the wild idea of returning to see whether there was any money left in the envelope, but Danny, guessing her thoughts, seized her arm. 'Don't be daft, gal. It'll have taken every penny of your dad's money to get in the sort of state your gran were in last night,' he said briskly. 'What's more, you're goin' to need every bit of the rag money to keep you in food for the rest of the month. Remember, we want to be first in the yard, so let's gerra move on.'

Ginny saw the sense of this, and as they turned from Upper Duke Street into Berry Street she decided to forget her grandmother and the drink and to enjoy the day. The streets were so quiet! They were not deserted, since in front of them an elderly tom cat stalked, stiff-legged, along the pavement, and an old tramp stirred and yawned in a corner of St Luke's churchyard, where he had made a sort of bed amongst the tombstones. But it was too early for most people to be about and as they crossed St Luke's Place and entered Renshaw Street Ginny nudged her companion. 'Ain't it wonderfully quiet wi' no folks about? And look at

183

the sky!'

'Aye, them colours is grand,' Danny agreed. Above them the sky was a misty blue, but to the east the unseen sun was painting the clouds a delicate pink and gold. It was going to be a lovely day and for the first time since she had awoken, Ginny remembered that this expedition was only the start. If it was successful, the rest of the day would be spent in New Brighton, doing all the things that she liked most. Paddling came first, of course, though bathing would be even better, and then there was digging in the sand, searching for cockles, making a huge sandcastle, shell gathering; the delights of the beach were endless. They would have to have their dinner out; fish and chips would be best with an ice cream to follow, if the money would stretch to it. And then there was the funfair! They simply must save some pennies for the funfair!

They reached Lime Street, glancing at the station as they approached it, then turned into St John's Lane so that they might walk through the gardens which, at this time of year, were in full bloom, the trees heavily laden with leaves which still showed no tint of autumn. 'I reckon we've broke the back of it, 'cos it ain't more'n a couple o' miles from Victoria Court to Paddy's Market,' Danny said as they heaved the pram up the stone steps into St John's Garden and trundled it across and on to William Brown Street. Ginny looked wistfully at the free library. She longed to become a member of this institution and to borrow books which she could read at home, but Granny Bennett's habit of pawning or selling what did not belong to her whenever she was short of cash had

184

made Ginny draw back. Furthermore, on the only occasion when she had plucked up her courage and gone into the library to ask if she might join, she had been told that she must provide both a reference and the signature of a parent who would be responsible if she lost or ill-treated the books.

She told Danny about her efforts to join the library as they turned into Byrom Street but he merely stared at her, apparently unable to believe that anyone would read a book from choice. He went to school regularly though, and she supposed that this meant he could read books whenever he wished to do so.

'Did you get yourself some breakfast?' Danny asked when they reached Scotland Place. 'I only had a bit of Madeira cake and a cup o' cold water and I'm dyin' for a cuppa char. Do you suppose that little canny house on Ben Jonson Street will be open yet?'

Ginny, too, could have done with a hot cup of tea, for warm though the day might be later there was a nip in the air right now and, like Danny, she had breakfasted lightly. However, she did not imagine that the canny house would be open yet and in any event did not want to waste time since Danny had made such a point of getting to the yard early. She said as much, though glancing wistfully down Ben Jonson Street as they passed it. But they were nearing their destination and presently heard, ahead of them, the hubbub of Paddy's Market getting into its stride. By now, early trams were trundling past them as well as horses and carts in from the country, whose destination was probably the vegetable market on Cazneau Street. One or two people looked curiously at them as they slogged along with their perambulator, but though folk called a cheery 'Good morning', no one questioned them as to why they were out so early.

'Here's Maddox Street at last,' Danny said thankfully, pushing the perambulator into a far narrower street than the one they had been traversing. 'See them huge gates? They're already open, thank the Lord, so we'll go straight in and start loading up.'

As they passed between the enormous corrugated iron gates, Ginny felt the first stirrings of unease. Suppose there was someone in the yard who would query their right to be there? Suppose the bin lorry turned in through the gates just as they were loading up with rags? But Danny seemed to have no scruples whatsoever. He guided Ginny and the perambulator round to the lower side of the skip, then hauled himself up on to the rim of the thing. 'I'll pick out an armful of stuff and chuck it down to you. Then you can go through it, putting the stuff into two piles. The poor stuff we'll shove back into the skip when the perambulator's full and the rest we'll keep. Okay?'

'Okay,' Ginny echoed manfully. She had done very much worse things in her time, she reminded herself. Pinching flowers from rich folk's gardens, nicking vegetables when no one was looking, taking washing off the line when the house owners were away and flogging whatever she had prigged to the stallholders in Paddy's Market. And anyway, Danny said the stuff would be dumped and burned if they didn't take it, so they were really doing everybody a good turn.

When Danny threw down the first bundle, she examined it cautiously but very soon entered into

186

the spirit of the thing. There was good stuff here: a lovely scarlet blouse, though it lacked buttons, and floral print dresses which scarcely needed more than a few stitches to make them wearable. And just before the perambulator was completely full, a school skirt! It was extremely dirty and the buttons that fastened it on the left-hand side were missing. The hem was half down and some of the pleats were no more than lines on the material, but by now Ginny had developed a discerning eye. If she washed the garment, bought and sewed on new buttons and stitched up the hem, it would be perfectly wearable—and it was free! She hung the skirt over the handle of the perambulator just as Danny leaned over and shouted at her to chuck the unwanted stuff up quick. 'I see the bin lorry comin' down Bevington Hill,' he said hoarsely. 'We ain't stealin', nor doin' anythin' wrong, but I'd rather be out of here by the time they arrives. Gerra wiggle on, queen.'

Much struck by this advice, for she knew an angry bin man could whack just as hard as Granny Bennett, Ginny began hurling the unwanted rags back into the skip, and seconds after Danny's warning the two of them were belting out of the yard with their booty, turning into Maddox Street and then on to the Scottie. 'Left, left, not right. We ain't goin' home, we're goin' up to King's,' Danny reminded her, 'and there's no need to hurry, queen, because now we're just two kids what've been collectin' old rags round the courts, tekking 'em up to William Moult Street to get wharrever old King will give us.'

Accordingly, the two slowed from a canter to an amble and Ginny began to look around her once

187

more, no longer fearing pursuit. Who, after all, would pursue them? The stallholders had thrown the rags away and the bin men had no idea that the contents of the skip had been rifled. She looked wistfully at a large canny house—it was almost a restaurant—as they passed it, but knew better than to suggest going in for some grub. They would not be allowed to take the perambulator in, and if they left it outside she knew very well they would never see pram or contents again. Danny must have noticed her wistful glance for he said, bracingly: 'It ain't but a step to William Moult Street and as soon as we've sold this lot . . .' he tapped the perambulator handle as he spoke, 'we'll have a good blowout wi' some o' the money. It's hungry work gettin' up so early and sortin' clothes with one eye out for the bin lorry.' He suddenly seemed to notice the skirt across the handle of the perambulator. 'I say, that ain't rubbish. That's a good bit o' cloth there; shouldn't it go in the pram?'

Ginny put a protective hand on the skirt, eyeing it lovingly as she did so. That skirt represented fish and chips with ice cream to follow and maybe one of those bottles of cherryade, stoppered with a marble, which could be bought on New Brighton prom. 'No! It's mine—it'll do nicely for school. It'll save me havin' to buy one, don't you see?'

'Oh aye,' Danny said, nodding. 'D'you know, I'd clean forgot why you wanted to get a bit of gelt together, but I 'member now.' He looked at the skirt, rather critically this time. 'It is good cloth, like I said, but there ain't no buttons and the hem's down and . . . did it have pleats once? Are you sure, queen, you wouldn't rather buy one in better nick?'

188

Ginny shook her head firmly, pictures of fish and chips and ice cream still floating before her inner eye. 'No, honest to God, this one'll do. I've never sewed buttons or a hem in me life, but everyone's gorra start somewhere. In fact, I doubt there's a needle and thread in the whole of our house, but I can learn, I suppose.'

'Tell you what, I'll ask me mam if she'll give you a sewing lesson,' Danny said, inspired. 'She's a dab hand wi' a needle is me mam, and she's taught all the girls to sew and knit so I'm sure she'll do the same for you. Now, tomorrow's Sunday, so if you wash the skirt as soon as you get home and have it dry for tomorrow, you can bring it round to our place. Mam's got heaps of needles and thread, but you'd best buy your buttons in Paddy's Market as we pass.' He grinned at her. 'You'll probably buy the very buttons the old skinflint cut off of this skirt before she chucked it away. Didn't you realise why the rags in the skip didn't have buttons, and the shoes didn't have laces? The old girls on the stalls know they can always sell a pair o' strong shoelaces or a set o' six buttons.'

Ginny giggled as they turned into Bostock Street. 'No, I didn't know, but I should have guessed. Is it far now, Danny? Me legs is getting tired and it's a fair old haul back to the court and then down to the Pier Head.'

'We're almost there,' Danny said, turning the pram into an even narrower street. 'Tell you what, queen, you'd best put that skirt o' yours on and tie the waist up wi' a bit o' string, otherwise old King might chuck it on his scales and pay you for it before we knowed what had happened. See there? That's his yard.'

189

Ginny did not have a piece of string on her but managed to tuck the top of the skirt into her knicker elastic, and once this was done the two of them pushed their pram into King's yard. King himself—or the man in charge at any rate—was old and wizened with a straggly white beard and clothing quite as filthy and ragged as anything he bought. He gave the children an unfriendly stare, but when he began to rummage through the contents of the pram his expression became almost friendly. 'Good stuff, good stuff,' he kept muttering. 'Did you come by it honest? There's real good stuff here.'

He had a strange foreign accent and rather long, sinister-looking fingernails, but since he made no attempt to decry their wares, the children began to look upon him favourably.

'Yes, it's all right, it's bin collected from folk who don't want it no more,' Danny said glibly whilst Ginny was still wondering what to say. 'We can get more, too, if you pays us the right sort o' price.'

The old man gave an appreciative chuckle; it was clear that he sensed the implied suggestion that sellers of such good material could easily go elsewhere, and did not resent it. He subjected the contents of the pram to another long stare and then began to pile the rags on to the big spring-balance scale, saying as he did so: 'Grade one, grade one . . . five pounds, seven, nine . . .'

The children watched eagerly as the figures on the dial gradually rose, and when the pram was empty the old man turned to them with a benevolent smile. 'What d'you say to eight bob?' he asked, eyeing them with a mixture of cunning and hope. 'Eight bob ain't bad money for a couple o'

190

kids to earn in a day.'

Ginny would have replied that she supposed eight bob was fair, but Danny was made of sterner stuff. He gave a derisive snort. 'Eight bob? D'you know how long it takes a couple o' kids to gerra load like that together? No, shove it back into the pram, mister, and we'll see what Packy's will offer us.'

He moved towards the scale but the old man stepped forward protectively, spreading his arms wide as he did so. 'I didn't mean eight bob . . . votever vos I thinkin' of? Let's say—let's say twelve bob, eh? Ten bob would be good, but twelve bob is princely. Oh aye, you von't get more than twelve bob from anyone, apart from meself.'

Danny shot a quick look at Ginny and she thought that he was trying to say that if the old blighter offered twelve bob, then the stuff must be worth a good deal more. But suppose—suppose he called their bluff? She had no idea where Packinham's yard was but feared it might be a good deal less accessible than this one. She tried to put all these things into her answering glance and saw, by the set of Danny's mouth, that he had read her correctly but intended to take no notice whatsoever. Oh, well, she thought resignedly, he seemed to know what he was doing. When they went out together to beg orange boxes from friendly greengrocers, so that they might chop the wood into kindling and sell it around the crowded courts, he was always a far harder bargainer than she. Women who pleaded poverty, said they needed the kindling but did not have the necessary ha'penny, wrung no sympathetic tear from Danny's bright eyes. He merely offered to call again later in

191

the week and this usually resulted in some bad language, speedily followed by a ha'penny. So she would let him do the bargaining this time and see how they got on. There was always Packy's after all.

'Fifteen bob,' Danny said at last. 'I think fifteen bob's fair.'

Mr King—if it was Mr King—rolled his eyes heavenwards, shrugged his shoulder up to his ears and groaned loudly. 'Fifteen bob! You think I am made of money? If I gave every ragamuffin who came into my yard fifteen bob, soon there would be no yard, no business. What d'you say to thirteen and six?'

Danny heaved a sigh and shot out a grimy hand which Mr King immediately took, shaking it vigorously. 'Right you are, thirteen and a kick it is,' Danny said. 'And you've had a bleedin' good bargain, let me tell you, 'cos if me little partner here and meself hadn't planned to go off to New Brighton on the first ferry, we'd ha' taken our business elsewhere.'

'And you'll be back again, vith more good stuff?' the old man enquired, digging into his pockets and producing a handful of silver and a bundle of extremely dirty notes. 'You don't wanna take your stuff to Pack'nham's though; them fellers is real skinflints. They'll beat you down and beat you down, and I'll hear about it, so no use runnin' back to me expectin' me usual generous treatment, 'cos I wants first sniff at votever's goin'.' He had counted out thirteen shillings and sixpence into Danny's grimy paw and hesitated, looking at the money as though he was considering snatching it back. Ginny was quite worried and was disproportionately relieved when the old man suddenly said: 'Ve'll make it fourteen bob. Here's the extra sixpence, just so you don't go runnin' to no one else with a decent load like that.'

'It's a deal,' Danny said joyfully, cramming the money into his pocket. 'See you next week, mister.'

*   *   *

By ten o'clock, Ginny and Danny were on the ferry, heading for New Brighton. The money had been shared evenly between them, though Ginny had tried to insist that Danny should take the lion's share, since it had been his idea and his bargaining powers which had got them such a good price. Danny, however, had said magnanimously that sharing, so far as he was concerned, meant fifty-fifty. Since Ginny knew the money would probably have to buy food for herself and Granny—Granny's pension was not due again till next week—she agreed to this and tucked the cash into the pocket of her dress.

So now the children stood against the rail, watching New Brighton approach. The weather was brilliant, the sea calm, and everyone on the ferry was in a good humour. As the ferry docked, Ginny grabbed Danny's hand. 'D'you know, Danny, I've never had so much money all at one time in me whole life! Oh, I know we've made a bit from time to time, doin' messages, babysittin' and selling kindling, but I've never had seven whole shillings before. I'll put aside two bob for spuds and that, but the rest I'll bleedin' well spend.' She glanced around her, at the golden sunlight, the happy faces, the dancing water. 'Yes, this'll be the best day of me life!'

193

'Well, Ginny? It were a good day, weren't it? The sea were that warm, I could ha' stayed in it all day, and weren't the funfair grand? I reckon goin' on the big dipper dried out me kecks, though they're still a bit damp like round me waist. You were lucky, 'cos gals can swim in their knickers, but fellers can't do that. Still an' all, it were a grand day, weren't it?'

Ginny nodded blissfully and put a well-salted chip into her mouth. The day had been every bit as wonderful as she had hoped and now, in the gathering dusk, the two of them were walking up James Street and sharing a paper of chips. The two shillings which Ginny had vowed to save had gone, alas, leaving only ninepence bumping against her knee as she walked. But last night, Gran drank all the money me dad sends and most of her pension as well, she reminded herself. So it's up to her to go and see George and try to get him to part with the dibs. If she has to admit she's drunk the money, then she'll just have to face up to it.

'Ginny?' Danny's voice sounded doubtful. 'You said—you said you was goin' to save two bob o' the money towards food an' that, but we've both been spendin' like sailors. I've got ninepence left; how about you?'

'The same,' Ginny admitted. 'Somehow, it just sort of . . . went. I reckon Granny Bennett will have to tell George the dibs ain't in tune this week. She'll think up some lie—say me dad's money never arrived, or her pension rolled out of her purse and fell down the drain—but wharrever she

194

says, I reckon George will shell out, even if he don't believe a word of it. Not money, perhaps,' she added hastily. 'He doesn't give her money, in case she drinks it. But he'll come round wi' a big canvas bag of veggies, a nice meat 'n' potato pie, and an ounce or two of tea an' sugar, just enough to see us through the week. He's okay, my Uncle George, he won't let us starve.'

Danny looked considerably relieved. 'I were goin' to offer you me ninepence, but if you don't think you'll need it, I'll give it to me mam. Look, wharrabout next week? Are you on?'

'Am I on! I just wish we could go every day; we'd be rich in no time,' Ginny said enthusiastically. 'You are so clever, Danny. First of all, you found the hiding place and let me share it wi' you, so's I could save up for me shoes, an' now you've gorrus a way to make money which ain't hurtin' anyone. It's a wonder no one else has thought of it.'

'Well, they haven't, but I don't suppose it'll last for ever,' Danny said gloomily. He brightened. 'Still, we've gorra nice little earner until someone puts two an' two together an' starts to smell a rat. I don't think any of the kids is likely to twig, but the tatters, they're a different matter. But they're none of 'em too bright an' they don't get up early, what's more, so we should keep the stuff in the yard for ourselves, for a while, anyway. Old King won't tell, even if he finds out, because I'll lay he's given us less than he'd have to pay the tatters. An' don't you go sayin' nothin' to nobody, young Ginny,' he added impressively. 'We've gorra keep this to ourselves for as long as possible.'

By this time they had reached Duke Street and were hurrying along it, for the lamps were being lit

195

and casting a golden glow on the passers-by. 'I won't say a word to anyone,' Ginny said fervently. 'But won't old King smell a rat, Danny? It were real clever the way you made it seem as though we were collectin' from house to house, but *he* didn't strike me as stupid. He'll know when we're back in school we won't have the time to do that.'

Danny heaved an exaggerated sigh. 'Why should he even think about it? He's far too old to have kids in school and anyway, while the light evenings last, he'll reckon we'll collect when our lessons is finished and in a week or two, provided we keep up the supply, he won't think twice about it. I tell you we're made, if we just keep our mouths shut and carry on gerrin' up at dawn on Saturdays.'

At this point, they turned off Great George Street into Rathbone Place and Ginny beamed at her companion. 'I'll be able to save up for Christmas because now I'll have some money to put in our hiding place—real money,' she said excitedly. 'I ain't never had a Christmas present in me whole life an' I've never given one either, not having the dosh. But this year, I can do all sorts. I can buy Granny Bennett some mittens, 'cos her hands get awful cold in winter. An' I'll buy you something real good, Danny, 'cos you're me best friend and you didn't have to share your idea with me, you could ha' done it alone and had the fourteen bob all to yourself.'

'Oh sure,' Danny said derisively. 'I can be in two places at once, on the skip and loadin' the pram! And some fun it would ha' been, goin' to New Brighton on me tod. Besides, a feller what can't help a pal out ain't worth tuppence.'

By this time they were turning under the arch

into Victoria Court. Ginny squeezed Danny's hand as hard as she could, then stood on tiptoe and kissed his cheek. She turned towards her own door then looked back. 'Thanks, Danny. Will you ask your mum about teachin' me how to mend me skirt? I'll come round first thing tomorrer mornin', if that's all right.'

'That'll be grand,' Danny said bashfully. He had turned a rich shade of crimson but Ginny thought that he had not disliked the kiss. She had seen her cousin, Polly, kiss her brother Ned, and had been amused by the vigorous way Ned had scrubbed off the kiss with a grimy fist, but Danny had done no such thing. He had looked embarrassed all right, but rather pleased as well. Glad that she had not overstepped the mark by this show of affection, Ginny slipped inside her front door and made for the kitchen.

As soon as she opened the door, she knew that something was up. Her grandmother, sitting at the kitchen table and facing her, surged to her feet, her mean little eyes in their rolls of fat glittering malevolently. On one side of her sat Uncle George, looking embarrassed, and on the other side sat Uncle Lewis. They all stared at her as she entered the room, though Granny Bennett was the only one who spoke. 'So you've come back?' she said, her voice thick with spite. 'An' where have you been all day, you nasty little toe-rag? I were up betimes this morning, but there were no sign of you and you ha'n't been near nor by all day. So where have you been, eh?'

'I've been to New Brighton wi' a pal; what's the harm in that?' Ginny said. She had come right into the kitchen, but now she closed the door behind

197

her and leaned against it, her heart bumping uncomfortably. 'You—you was fast asleep when I left, Gran. I tried to rouse you to see if you wanted a cuppa but you had your head down on the table and you didn't so much as . . .'

'Don't you start on me, you lyin', sneakin' little thief,' her grandmother said fiercely. 'So it were New Brighton, were it? That were the reason you stole the remains of me pension and all the money your dad sends for your keep. Oh aye, I knew it were you the moment I found the empty envelope flung down by the fire.'

Ginny was astonished at her grandmother's accusation but realised the old woman had had to find some reason for her lack of money. Typically, she had chosen to blame someone else and, of course, the obvious person to blame had been Ginny. But that did not explain the presence of both her uncles. However, one thing must be cleared up before she could ask questions. 'I've stolen nothing, Gran,' she said, her voice steady. 'Me and my pal made a bit of money and saved up for a day out. I wouldn't take your pension nor what me dad sends.' She turned to George. 'You know I wouldn't take money, don't you, Uncle George? But what are you and Uncle Lewis doing here?'

'We went to the football, like we always do,' her Uncle George said briefly. 'Then we had a few bevvies and bought fish 'n' chips from Woudenburg's. We got enough so you and me mam could have some as well and come back here.' He glanced, half apologetically, at his mother. 'We found Mam in a rare old takin', searchin' the house for summat she'd lost . . .'

'I was searchin' for me money, o' course,' Granny Bennett said viciously. 'I were desperate for—for a nice cuppa tea . . .'

'There's tea in the cupboard, Gran,' Ginny said, as gently as she could. 'But if you thought I'd stolen the money, why did you search? It don't seem to make sense. So since I didn't take the money, it—it must have got spent.'

'Aye, our Ginny's right, Mam,' George said bluntly. 'If she didn't take it, then where's it gone?'

'I tell you she *did* take it,' Granny Bennett said obstinately. She gestured to the room around her. 'If I spent it, where's the stuff I bought, eh? I'm tellin' you, boys, the gal took it to go on the spree an' now she's tryin' to make out it were me.'

Uncle George took a deep breath, looking miserable, but before he could speak, his younger brother broke in. 'Our mam's gorra point, George; either Ginny took the money to go to New Brighton wi' her pal or else our mam spent it.' He turned to Ginny. 'You said somethin' about your gran lyin' with her head on the table when you got up early this mornin', so what did *you* think had happened? And was the money there then?'

Ginny stared from one face to the other. She had never complained about her grandmother's behaviour to either of her uncles, had never said in front of Granny Bennett that the money her father sent should go towards household expenses and not be squandered on drink. The reason she had not done so, of course, was because she had to *live* with Granny Bennett and the old woman knew all too well how to make her granddaughter's life a misery. If she incurred Granny's wrath now, her attendance at school would be patchy, to say the least. Granny would think up a dozen reasons why she should not go to classes. She would send Ginny off on messages which would take her right across the city or she would hide some article of clothing so that Ginny was ashamed to go out. On the other hand, though, Ginny did not mean to be branded as a thief, and anyway, she knew very well that Uncle George, because of his frequent visits, must have guessed at once where the money had gone. Even Uncle Lewis must have had a shrewd idea for he gave her a tight little smile.

'I—I know where it went,' Ginny said, her voice trembling a little. It seemed whatever she did or said she was going to be in trouble, so she might as well spill the beans. 'I came in quite late last night because me an' my pal had been earning a bit o' cash for today. Gran was out but she came in after I'd gone to bed. She was shoutin' an' carryin' on, crashin' around the kitchen. Mr Borrage banged on the wall and shouted to her to let folks sleep. You can ask *him* if you don't believe me; he'll tell you how it was.'

Granny Bennett got to her feet, her voice rising dangerously, and began to call Ginny a thief and a liar and to say that her boys were not to believe a word their niece said, but Lewis and George told her quite roughly to shut up and sit down. And Granny Bennett subsided, grumbling, on to her chair once more.

'Go on, Ginny,' Uncle George said quietly. 'We might as well get the truth, even if it hurts.'

Ginny cast a doubtful look at her grandmother's furious face. Oh, lor', she thought, here comes trouble, but she realised that she had to speak. 'I didn't go downstairs when I heard Gran shouting

200

because even the sight of me seems to make her worse,' she said honestly. 'But, when I came down this morning, she were asleep, with her head on the kitchen table. The envelope me dad sends the money in were under her cheek, but I could see it had been torn open an' I guessed . . .' Her grandmother gave an infuriated howl but Ginny, having burned her boats, simply raised her voice. 'I guessed that she'd been down to the Livingstone Arms and spent the money on drink.'

Granny Bennett was positively gibbering with rage; Lewis was looking shocked, but George looked devastated. 'Wharrever's the matter with you, Mam?' he said heavily. 'The drink will kill you, you know it will. Why, the doctor told you over 'n' over you were livin' on borrowed time. You've been real good, an' the money's been comin' in from Michael and bein' spent properly. Why the sudden change?'

Granny Bennett got to her feet and stumbled towards the door. Ginny, seeing retribution in her grandmother's piggy little eyes, hastily put the table between them, but it seemed Granny Bennett did not mean to attack her this time. She swung the door open and ambled, unsteadily, into the hall, and then began to ascend the stairs. Over her shoulder, she shouted that since they chose to believe their niece and to call their own mother a liar, she would thank them to get out of her house and leave her to cope as best she might, with no money and no help from anyone.

No one attempted to detain her, and when she had gone George looked rather helplessly from one to the other. 'Siddown, Ginny,' he said. 'We're goin' to have to talk this through, the three of us.

201

We can't have our mam drinkin' herself to death like this. I've offered to have her stay wi' us but she won't budge from the court; says she came here when she were wed and means to die here.'

'Which she will if she don't give the drink the goby,' Lewis said. 'I couldn't have our mam stayin' wi' us—too many kids of me own plus Amy's sister and her girls.' He chuckled. 'Ellen and Mam 'ud be chalk 'n' cheese and I reckon they'd fight like two cats if they had to share the same kitchen. It's bad enough for Amy but at least her sister don't drink.'

George turned to Ginny. 'Wharrabout you, queen? Any ideas?'

Ginny thought rapidly. She realised that she did not particularly want to live with either of her uncles, but neither did she want to find herself dumped in an orphan asylum. Granny Bennett was horrible to her but at least she gave her a good deal of freedom. And if she tries to stop me going to school, I'll get round it somehow, Ginny told herself. It would be grand if Uncle George or Uncle Lewis would take Gran and leave me here, but I can't see that happening somehow.

'Well?' George said impatiently, when she did not immediately answer him. 'Come on, Ginny, speak up.'

'It's the money that's the problem, Uncle George,' Ginny said carefully. 'I can't take me dad's money away from her—she's ever so strong, you know—and it wouldn't be right to take her pension money, even if I could. If only the money came regular . . . but it hasn't done that for ages. I think me dad's at sea again because although the envelopes are always the same—and the handwriting, of course—the stamps are mostly

202

foreign. But if you could get her to hand the envelopes over, Uncle George, then between us we could see it got spent properly.'

'It's a good idea, but it won't please Mam,' George said, after a moment's thought. 'If only we could gerrin touch with Michael, we could tell him to send the money direct to my address, but we don't know where he lives, do we? The only other solution would be to stop the money at the postman, so to speak. D'you know the name of the feller what delivers the letters round here, queen? If we knew when the money arrived . . .'

'Yes, he's Dicky Harding,' Ginny said promptly. 'It's no good me askin', Uncle George, 'cos I'm only a kid, but you could tackle him, explain the situation. And—what'll Gran and meself do for the rest of the week? Until her pension comes due again, I mean.'

'Oh, I'll see you right,' George said, getting to his feet. 'I'll bring a basket o' grub round tomorrow; I reckon you can both last till then.'

He strode down the hall towards the front door, but Lewis lingered. 'I'd still like to know where you got enough money for a day out in New Brighton,' he murmured. His bright blue eyes smiled at her and he smoothed his hair back, then glanced after his brother. 'I'm often short of a bob or two meself, what with four kids and your Aunt Amy to support, to say nothing of Ellen and her two great girls. You're a sly one, earnin' all that money an' norra word to a soul!'

Ginny knew he was only teasing but was about to reply indignantly when Uncle Lewis slipped out of the front door, closing it softly behind him, so she turned back to the kitchen. Since her grandmother

203

had stomped off upstairs, she decided it would be safer to kip down on the shabby little sofa for the night, then she could go to the Levitts' tomorrow morning without encountering her grandmother again. Fortunately, it was a warm night so Ginny turned off the lamp, lay down on the sofa and was soon sleeping soundly.

CHAPTER EIGHT

It was the first day of term and Ginny came out of the court very early that morning with a bounce in her step and a smile lighting her eyes. She and Annie meant to take great pains with their appearance because they both wanted to make a good impression on their new teacher. Ginny was on her way to Annie's home. She was wearing a decent, though faded blouse and the skirt which Mrs Levitt had helped her to make respectable. She had, rather cunningly she thought, hidden her new second-hand stockings inside an old paper bag which she had then shoved under her mattress, but now she was wearing the stockings and a pair of plimsolls so old that the soles were attached to the uppers with bits of sticky tape.

The girls had agreed that Ginny should arrive early at the Waits' flat so that she might change into her beautiful new shoes and might also have her thickly curling bush of bright hair confined in some way. She felt very envious of Annie who had recently had her thick, dark blonde hair cut in a fashionable bob, but realised that her own mop of curls was simply not suitable for such a style.

Besides, the hairdresser had impressed upon Annie that, if she was to continue fashionably neat, she must return to his premises once a month for a trim, which would cost at least a shilling. Shillings were a lot easier to come by for Annie than for herself, so bobbing was out of the question, Ginny thought ruefully. Still, long hair could be neat, if not fashionable, and she had managed to acquire a piece of navy blue ribbon with which she could tie back her locks.

She reached the Waits' side door and banged on it, and presently heard the sound of rapidly descending footsteps. There was a pause during which bolts were rattled back and a key was turned and then Nell, the sister closest to Annie in age, heaved the door open. She was panting but ushered Ginny inside and told her to run up the stairs to Annie's room whilst she relocked the door. 'We can't leave it unlocked because kids get in and misbehave on the stairs,' she informed Ginny. 'During the day, of course, folk come in and out through the shop; it's only when it's closed that we use the side door.'

Ginny was met at the top of the stairs by Annie, who dragged her into the bedroom and produced her shoes from her own wardrobe. Ginny kicked off the plimsolls and put on the shoes, then sat down on Annie's bed. 'What'll we do wi' me hair?' she asked plaintively. 'Me shoes is grand and Danny's mam made a real good job of me skirt, but me hair's a mess, as usual.'

'You're mad; I'd give me eye teeth for curls,' Annie told her. 'But if you want it to look really tidy, I'll plait it. It'll make a lovely thick plait, like a rope. I'm surprised you've not thought of it

205

yourself.'

'I have thought of it, but I can't make it stay,' Ginny explained. 'I bet you can't get it into a plait anyhow. But I suppose you could tie it back in a tail. The trouble with curls is, they've got a mind of their own.'

Annie laughed but wet a hairbrush in the water on the washstand, plied it vigorously on her friend's head and then produced a great rope of a plait, tied it off with the piece of navy ribbon and urged Ginny over to the long mirror on the wardrobe. 'Tek a look at yourself,' she advised her friend. She giggled. 'You look like one of them Angela Brazil books.'

Ginny stared into the mirror then smiled a slow, satisfied smile. The hairstyle suited her! Her face was framed with tiny, wispy curls, and somehow having her hair pulled back from her face made her greeny-hazel eyes look even larger. The freckles, which she so despised, were much in evidence but she found she rather liked them in conjunction with the thick, bright plait. She was thinner and taller than most girls of her age, but the blouse and skirt, both a little too large, made her seem more in proportion somehow, and when she looked down and saw the stockings and the wonderful new shoes, she felt a warm glow of satisfaction. She would look almost as nice as Annie, who had had new clothes for the start of the term. She turned to her friend. 'Thanks, Annie,' she said humbly. 'I never thought you could do it, but you've made a real good job of me hair. Why, I wouldn't change places with anyone; I've never looked so nice in me whole life!'

Annie looked at her critically, her eyes travelling

over Ginny from the top of her head to the tip of her toes, then she nodded. 'I never see'd you look better,' she admitted. 'But we've no time to stand chatterin' here. Let's be goin' so's we can find our new classroom and bag the best desks.'

*   *   *

'Hey! Hey, Annie, wait for me.'

Ginny came flying out of the school gates, her cheeks glowing. She and Annie always walked home together in order that she might change her shoes for her ragged plimsolls, but today Miss Derbyshire had kept her after the others had left, and Ginny was longing to tell Annie what had happened. It was October now and though Ginny had done her best to catch up with the rest of her class, she had missed so much time in previous years that she was beginning to wonder whether she would ever manage it. Joined-up writing, for instance, was still a mystery to her for it had been taught in the course of a year during which she had scarcely been in school at all. And though she could manage addition, subtraction and some multiplication, division was another closed book.

'No need to shout, I wouldn't go home wi'out you,' Annie said reproachfully. 'I've been killing time, playing hopscotch with a bit o' slate, until you come along. What did she want, then?'

'You can't play hopscotch till you've marked out the squares,' Ginny objected. 'And Miss Derbyshire wanted to ask if I'd be willing to stay late a couple of nights a week. 'Oh, Annie, ain't she the nicest teacher you ever met, though? I've haven't said much about things being difficult at home, but she's noticed. And you know the day I were late because Gran pawned me skirt so she could buy porter and hid the pawn ticket? Well, she said she guessed it was something of the sort, knew I wouldn't be late wi'out a good reason because—because you and me, we're her best pupils! She said that, honest to God she did!'

'That were nice of her,' Annie said temperately. Ginny knew that her friend did not have her own driving ambition to better herself. Annie was not even particularly interested in her schoolwork but she was quite competitive and did not mean to let her best friend soar to the top of the class whilst she herself remained at the bottom. What was more, Annie's admiration for Miss Derbyshire was very real, and after a mere six weeks of the term had passed the two girls were vying for the teacher's attention and taking it in turns to be monitors, since the other pupils in their class seemed to think it an imposition, rather than a reward for good work.

'What did you say?' Annie enquired, though Ginny thought she must have guessed. 'Your gran won't like it if you don't turn up in time to do her messages an' cook her a meal.'

Ginny slipped her arm through her friend's and gave it an admonitory shake. 'Of *course* I said I'd stay late—how could I refuse when she were being so kind? Her time is a lot more valuable than mine, you bet. As for Gran, we'll just have to come to some arrangement.'

Ginny felt a surge of despair as she said the words. Gran's behaviour made life so complicated! For instance, the pawning of the skirt, and its subsequent reclaiming by Ginny, were not events

208

which could be repeated every week, particularly now that Ginny was in school and only able to earn money at weekends. She and Danny still went to the skip whenever they could do so, and split the money evenly between the two of them, and Ginny still stored away her share behind the brick, but since Gran was drinking again—though not, so far, as heavily as she had been—Ginny often needed her rag money in order to buy food.

After the business of the skirt pawning, Ginny made up her mind that she would have to have a talk with her grandmother and, unfortunately, this had speedily degenerated into a row. The row had ended with Ginny telling Granny Bennett, bluntly, that if her gran ever laid a finger on any of Ginny's clothing again, Ginny would not only tell George why she had taken it, but would never cook another meal in Victoria Court.

Her grandmother had hissed like a snake which has been trodden on and had tried to retaliate by swearing that she would turn Ginny out on to the street, but her granddaughter had laughed at this threat. 'If you did such a thing, I'd go straight to George and he'd see to it that me dad's money went to him instead of you,' she said frankly. 'I'm warning you, Gran, I won't stand for it. I like me school and I'm doin' well, but they won't let me attend classes unless I'm decently dressed. Folk who do well in school earn more money when they leave than those who do badly and you want me to earn a decent wage, don't you? So let's have a bargain, just between us two. You'll leave me decent clothes alone and I'll go on cooking your meals and doing your messages, how's that?'

The fact that Granny had agreed was

undoubtedly due to her being sober at the time; when she was drunk, she would simply have screamed and shouted and refused to listen. And now, Ginny thought sadly, I'll have to begin all over again, because the old woman would undoubtedly notice if Ginny returned late to the court. Ginny knew that Granny Bennett could not be bothered to make herself a meal at midday but relied on Ginny's having food on the table no later than five o'clock; she would not take kindly to having to wait for her meal. And Ginny was running out of threats—and bribes, for that matter. The threat was telling George, the bribe was doing all the housework, including the cooking, and she had already used both. She could, of course, get up earlier still and prepare the evening meal—blind scouse or some other sort of stew—but that would mean leaving Granny to keep the fire going and to cook the food and Ginny knew, from past, bitter experience, that she would do no such thing. Oh, she might pull the pan over the fire, but then she would wander off and forget it, possibly setting fire to the house in the process. She seemed to have no instinct of self-preservation—Ginny thought privately that the drink was beginning to soften her grandmother's brain—so she could not be relied upon to perform even the simplest task.

'Come to some arrangement with Granny Bennett? I can't see that comin' off! I know she likes a drink, but she's rare fond of her food, ain't she, so she won't be too pleased at having to wait longer than usual. My mam was sayin', only the other day, that most fellers—and women, o'course—who drink too much stop eating after a bit and it's the drink alone what kills them. She says it's only you what keeps the old gal alive, seein' she eats at least twice a day. She should be grateful, but I know she ain't.'

'Uncle George helps as well,' Ginny pointed out. 'He comes round reg'lar as clockwork now, bringin' food, but he charges Gran for it. He makes her hand over money 'cos he says that way she can't spend it on porter. And then he gives me some o' the money for messages. Between us, we ain't managing too bad.'

'I see that,' Annie said, but she sounded doubtful. 'The thing is, queen, it's your money really. Your dad sends it so you can have decent clothes an' food, he don't send it so that your Uncle George can support his old mam, free of charge, so to speak. Why, I bet you still don't know how much money your dad sends, do you?'

'Well, no,' Ginny admitted. 'I could ask Uncle George, I suppose, but it would seem . . . oh, sort of cheeky. It's not as if the envelopes were ever addressed to me, 'cos they ain't. I'll tell you something odd though, queen. I'd made a big dinner the other day because Uncle George gave me a piece of pork to cook. I roasted it in the oven up at Sample's and boiled a lot of veggies; it were a grand meal, honest it was. Gran was stuffing the grub down her neck and chumbling away to herself—she weren't drunk—and suddenly she said to me: "I'd ha' give it to you if I hadn't been half seas over. I knowed I should ha' done but when I's gorra tankful, things look different somehow." So o' course I waited a bit, then put a few more spuds on her plate and asked her what was it she should have given me. She looked up at me, and you could see the wheels turnin', but she just said, vaguely:

211

"Given you? Oh, I dunno," and started shovelling food into her mouth again. I couldn't get any sense out of her after that, but I couldn't help wonderin'. What if me dad had put a bit extra into the envelope, tellin' her to give it to me for me birthday, or some such thing? The old girl hates me most of the time, but sometimes she seems to soften a bit. I have asked her since whether me dad had sent me something, but she just got furious and shouted, so I've not said any more.'

'Wharrabout your Uncle George?' Annie said. 'Surely he'd know if there were extra money in the envelope?'

Ginny gave a derisive snort. 'Granny may be a nasty old drunkard who don't know which way up she is half the time, but she's got quite enough sense to grab any extra money an' take it out of the envelope before Uncle George can get his hands on it,' she assured her friend. 'He don't come round till he finishes work, remember, so Gran's always opened the envelope by then. She hands it to him all right, but any extra money would have got salted away the moment the postman left.' She gave a deep sigh. 'An' now I've got to think of some way of gettin' Gran to agree to me stayin' late at school, two or three days a week, an' that ain't goin' to be easy.'

*   *   *

Mabel Derbyshire finished off the work she was preparing and opened the lid of the teacher's big desk. She slid in the books and papers which had been spread out before her, and then stood up, stretched and sighed.

212

It lacked only five days to Christmas, and she was tired, looking forward to three weeks away from Rathbone Street and her pupils, fond though she was, by now, of both. The school was a good school, the children in her class fairly good pupils, though without doubt Ginny Bennett was the brightest of them. Mabel, tidying her room, wondered what the girl would do with her three weeks of freedom; probably spend them with that horrible old grandmother of hers, trying to prevent her from getting dead drunk.

However, teachers are not supposed to have favourites, and Mabel was already doing as much for Ginny as she possibly could without her head teacher showing her disapproval. She had given the child extra tuition after school two or three days a week and, in so doing, had learned a great deal about her. She knew that Ginny lived with her grandmother; she knew the old lady drank and was both abusive and violent when in her cups. She had been told of Uncle George and his wife Mary, of the canny house and the well-loved and nicely brought up younger cousins, including poor little Polly, who would never be quite like other children, and about how Ginny and Uncle George conspired to keep Granny Bennett from drinking herself to death. She'd also heard about Uncle Lewis and his wife Amy, though Ginny had only mentioned them—and their three children—in passing, one day. All this had been passed on to Mabel in the most artless fashion; probably Ginny did not even realise how much she had told her teacher, but it had coloured Mabel's attitude to the girl.

She was desperately sorry for Ginny, who was a bright, intelligent pupil, hard working and well

213

mannered. She had speedily realised, however, that though Ginny was only ten, she had simply missed out on her childhood and was already old beyond her years. And Mabel put most of the blame for this upon Michael Gallagher, the absent father. If he had lived up to his responsibilities, come home whenever he was able to do so to see that his daughter was not being bullied and abused, then she could have forgiven him a great deal, for Michael, it seemed, was a seaman and could not be constantly in Liverpool. But though he sent money home, and though she had been reluctant, at first, to admit it, Ginny had never set eyes on her father, never received so much as a line from him. In fact she only knew he existed because of the monthly money he sent her grandmother; his share in the upkeep of his daughter.

Mabel acknowledged that, since the child had been born out of wedlock, Michael did more than a good many men, and did it willingly, it seemed. But he must have known Granny Bennett quite well, since Ginny had told her the sad yet romantic story, as it had been passed on to her by her Uncle George. How the young couple had been in love but unable to marry because they were both under the age of consent and Granny Bennett had disapproved of the match. How the only way to get married had been first to get Stella pregnant. How this had come about, how Stella had given birth to her daughter, only to die within a matter of weeks of the virulent influenza which had been sweeping the country in the wake of the terrible war. So Michael simply must have known Granny Bennett, and how on earth could a man with any sort of conscience leave a child in her filthy house, at the

214

mercy of a drunken woman's abuse and violence?

It would be easy, of course, to say that he was not a man with a conscience, had it not been for the money. He sent cash regular as clockwork—Ginny had boasted about it—which meant that he was conscious of his duty, his responsibility. That this did not extend to so much as seeing the child was terrible, unforgivable, Mabel thought. She just wished she could meet Michael Gallagher and tell him what sort of life his daughter was leading, make him do something, other than send money, for Ginny! But since the man had not visited the city once since he had left it after his young woman's dreadfully sad death, Mabel did not imagine that the pleasure would ever be hers. Sometimes she wondered if he could be traced and taken to task, but she knew so little about him! His name, the fact that he came from somewhere called Kerry and was a seaman; that was about the extent of her knowledge. Armed with that, she could probably spend years searching in Ireland without getting a whiff of her quarry.

Still. Despite the fact that she was only ten years old, and an under-nourished and ill-clad ten at that, Ginny seemed to be managing pretty well with only the minimum of assistance from anyone else. She cooked meals—though these were always stews or some other form of boiled vegetable—kept the house clean enough to satisfy her Uncle George, of whom Miss Derbyshire had heard much, bought the food, presumably bargaining with shopkeepers and stallholders, since she had made it clear that she and her grandmother never had a penny to spare, and still managed to attend school and do her homework. Probably the three-week holiday over the Christmas period would be dealt with by young Ginny as efficiently as she managed the rest of her life. And I shan't be here to interfere, or help, or anything of that nature, since Sandy and I mean to go home, at least for a week to ten days, over the holiday, Mabel reminded herself.

Having tidied away her things, she went to the staff room and took her coat and hat from their pegs, slipped them on and set off across the frosty playground. She had not been back to her village for many months, and found she was looking forward to seeing parents and brothers and sisters once more, though she knew that a week in their company would be quite long enough.

At the school gate, Sandy waited. They greeted each other and set off, walking briskly, in the direction of Canning Street and their lodgings.

*　　　*　　　*

It was Christmas which brought things to a head, Ginny reflected. She was miserably packing her meagre possessions into a couple of stout brown cardboard boxes, for she and Gran were moving out. It was Gran's drinking, of course, though Ginny could not help reflecting guiltily that, had she not bribed Gran to let her stay late at school two evenings a week, the old woman would not have had the time to herself to do what she had done.

For Gran had taken to shoplifting, and not just in the small local shops, either, where she might have been reported to the family before being handed over to the scuffers, but in bigger, more important establishments. Ginny had known nothing about it until she had returned from getting the messages two weeks after Christmas to find the kitchen crowded. Two policemen, a tall, dark-suited man with gleaming, Brylcreemed hair, a fashionably dressed woman in a tweed suit and matching cap, a police lady, looking hot and embarrassed, George and Lewis, and Gran herself, were all gathered in the room.

Even now, Ginny could not think of that day without shuddering. Gran had had a good, though probably boozy, Christmas, and when things returned to normal she had missed the drink so badly that first she had tried to steal money from other houses in the court, and when this proved too difficult she had turned her attention to the big stores.

She had been caught, naturally, but not until she had stolen a good deal of stuff. Apparently the shop people had not believed their eyes—this fat old woman, wrapped in a multitude of shawls and carrying a huge canvas bag—she had referred to it, later, with some pride as 'me burgling bag'—had been shovelling stuff inside it almost openly, and had then made her way out of the shop with surprising speed, so that the first time she had done it she had gone uncaught and unpunished.

She had taken the stuff to the nearest pawnbroker, where she was not known, and had, she told the scuffers boastfully, got a good price for it. But on the next occasion she had taken her booty to a shop nearer home, and the man had been suspicious, though he had paid up willingly enough when she said it were Christmas presents which the lady for whom she cleaned had given her to dispose of, since she herself did not want them. You had to admire Gran, when sober she was a pretty quick thinker.

Then she had been nabbed by a sharp-witted assistant—the lady in the tweed suit—who had seen her come in and had nipped out from behind her counter and established herself right by the door, grabbing Gran and her ill-gotten gains as she tried to shoot out on to the pavement once more.

George had pleaded with them, and Gran had been bound over, whatever that might mean, but it had been made clear that she must no longer live alone, or rather alone save for Ginny. And George had agreed that he and Mary would take her in.

'But we can't cope wi' the kid,' he had said gruffly. 'She's a grand girl, our Ginny, she's done her best to keep me mam off of the drink, she's fed her and seen she eats proper meals . . . she even cooks 'em . . . but there just ain't room in our place. The canny house brings in more gelt than I can earn street cleanin' for the Council, so there's no question of letting me niece sleep in what were once our front room, and I've four kids of me own . . . and my Mary's old mam lives wi' us . . .'

So it had been agreed that she—and her dad's money—would go to Uncle Lewis and Aunt Amy, though Ginny was extremely reluctant. Her aunt and uncle lived out at Seaforth, which would mean she would have a long trek in to school each day when term started, and she would be a long way from her pals, and the places and shops she knew best. But it was that or an orphan asylum, and Ginny had a dread of any such institution. It might have been all right for someone who had not had the freedom of the streets all her life, but Ginny

218

knew she could never stand it. Three meals a day, cooked for you, decent clothes, an ordered life . . . no thanks, I'd rather Aunt Amy and Uncle Lewis, Ginny had told George when he had suggested it. So here she was, packing her things and preparing to spend the coppers Uncle Lewis had handed over—with some reluctance—on a tram-ride to the other side of the city.

Presently, Ginny picked up a cardboard box and carried it downstairs. She wished that she had been able to use Gran's 'burgling bag'—at least it had handles—but Gran had been the first to leave and had taken everything that was halfway respectable. She had even taken the pots and pans—George had to hire a pony cart to get the stuff away and had grumbled mightily over it—but the only thing Ginny grudged her was the enormous canvas bag. Getting on the tram with two cardboard boxes was not going to be easy.

However, she had reckoned without her pals. As soon as she descended the steps into the court, Danny came hurrying over. He was extremely upset because she was leaving, she knew that, but he seized the larger of the two boxes and set off towards the tram stop in Great George Street. 'Your pal Annie will be along in half a mo',' he said gruffly. 'We're both a-goin' to come with you 'cos you'll hatta change trams at Lime Street an' so's we know where you are. Mam says Seaforth is a fair way off, but it won't stop us from seein' you at holidays and weekends. Why, we'll still visit the skip on Sat'days, won't we?'

'I dunno,' Ginny said gloomily. She knew how crowded Uncle Lewis's house was; she would be sharing a bedroom with three smaller girls, sharing a bed as well with her cousin, Ivy, who at eight was the eldest child in Uncle Lewis's family. Ginny just hoped that the girl was a sound sleeper and would not notice if she got up early in order to go to the skip with Danny.

They reached the tram stop just as Annie came panting up. Bless her, she was carrying her mother's marketing bag and seized Ginny's box, tipping the contents into the bag and fitting the now empty box on top. 'It'll be easier for you to carry,' she said breathlessly. 'You can give it to Danny, he'll bring it back. I'm awful sorry, queen, but I can't come to Seaforth wi' you. Mam's tekkin' us to Southport to visit Aunt Bertha. But it's only another week before school starts, so I'll see you then.'

Ginny told herself that she should be disappointed at Annie's defection, but in fact she was glad. Her friend's home was so neat and clean; her parents so sensible and friendly. She knew that Annie would not be shocked, exactly, by the sight of the house on Schubert Street, because she had been told it was a decent terraced place and Aunt Amy was a dedicated housewife. But if Annie came inside, she would see how overcrowded it was, for she knew from her grandmother's description that the house was bursting at the seams. The Bennetts were not the only occupants; Amy's sister, Ellen, and her two children, both older than Ginny, had shared it ever since Ellen's husband had run off with a barmaid, some two years previously.

'I'm awful sorry, Ginny,' Annie repeated. She looked anxious.

Ginny smiled brightly at her friend. 'It's all right, Annie. To tell you the truth, I'm not looking forward to livin' wi' me uncle and aunt so I expect I'll spend any spare time with me old pals. The thing is, you see, that they've got a nice house but—but there's too many folk livin' there. I'd—I'd rather come to you than have you come to me.'

As soon as the words were out of her mouth, she regretted them, for she saw a blush rise hotly across Annie's face, saw her eyes harden. 'Oh! Well, if you feel like that . . .' Annie turned away and set off down the street in the direction of her own home.

Ginny shouted after her, made to follow, but tripped over the box which Danny had stood down on the pavement, and as she scrambled to her feet a No. 3 tram drew up beside them. Danny began to heave himself and the box aboard, saying a trifle breathlessly as he did so: 'Don't gerrin a takin'! She'll understand what you meant and know you didn't mean what you said. Will you bleedin' well stop starin' over your shoulder and gerron the perishin' tram. I've give up a whole mornin's work to help you shift your stuff, so don't stand there moonin'.'

Rather reluctantly, Ginny obeyed. The transition from one tram to the other at Lime Street was easily accomplished since a No. 23 drew up seconds after they had been decanted on to the pavement, and soon the children found themselves wending their way from the tram stop to Ginny's new home. It was a very cold day, but walking as briskly as she could and carrying the heavy marketing bag soon warmed her up, and by the time they reached No. 14 she was warm enough and guessed, from the sweat trickling down his face, that Danny was pretty hot as well. Carrying the heavy box had plainly been extremely hard work and he dumped it down outside her uncle's door with a sigh of relief, then mopped his brow with an old khaki handkerchief. 'Phew!' he said. 'I'd rather carry that for a yard than for a mile! It ain't the weight so much as the shape o' the box which is real awkward. Still an' all, we're here now. I wouldn't mind a cup o' tea; I'm parched after luggin' that thing right across the city. D'you suppose your aunt'll give us some dinner?' He bent to pick the box up again as Ginny pushed the door open and ushered him inside.

'I expect she will, even if it's only bread 'n' marge, but she's bound to have a cup o' tea on the go,' she said hopefully. 'She said she'd be in.'

The house seemed quiet but when she opened the kitchen door and ushered Danny inside, the noise hit them like a blow in the face. The room seemed to be full of people and Ginny saw that there was a fire in the grate and a teapot steaming in the centre of the kitchen table. Danny dropped his box once more and rubbed his hands together. He looked at the oldest woman in the room, assuming it to be Aunt Amy, and remarked, cheerfully, that it were nice to get into the warm 'cos it were bitterly cold outside.

Actually, he had addressed Ellen Franklin so Ginny hastily jumped in, explaining that Mrs Franklin was her Aunt Amy's sister and her Aunt Amy was the lady sitting in front of the fire.

The uproar in the kitchen was such that her aunt had not even noticed them enter the room, but at the sound of her name she turned and subjected Danny to a long, cold stare. She was a short, wiry woman with black hair and sallow skin. She had snapping black eyes and a thin, rat trap mouth;

Ginny had often wondered why Uncle Lewis had married her for he was very good-looking, in a smarmy sort of way, and was, according to Granny Bennett, a good earner. Perhaps, Ginny thought charitably now, Aunt Amy had been ravishingly beautiful once, but if so, all traces of it had long disappeared.

'Who's this then?' Aunt Amy asked her niece, indicating Danny. Her voice was as sharp as a razor and as cold. 'Ain't there enough kids in this bloody house wi'out you bringin' in another? Tell 'im to scarper, and fast.'

'But—but Aunt Amy, he's me best pal,' Ginny objected, feeling her face flame. How could her aunt be so rude, and quite without provocation, for Danny had neither said nor done anything amiss. 'He's carried me luggage all the way from Victoria Court and it's terrible heavy. Is—is it all right if I pour him a cup o' tea before he goes home?' She was ashamed of the humble note in her voice and realised, belatedly, that she was afraid of her aunt's vicious tongue. But this was her home now and she told herself she had every right to offer her pal a drink; Uncle Lewis would be having her dad's money in future, and that would pay for a lot more than a miserable cup of tea.

Aunt Amy got to her feet and crossed over to the table. She picked up the teapot, lifted the lid and peered inside. 'There's nowt in here save dregs, but if you're set on it, I dare say there's a cup or two o' water left in the kettle,' she said grudgingly. 'But I'm warnin' you, Ginny, it'll be the first and last time I feeds one o' your mates. Me and me sister have all we can do to feed our own. D'you understand?'

223

Ginny knew that now was the moment to stand up for herself, to remind her aunt that Michael Gallagher was paying for her keep, but she hesitated, not wanting to start trouble the moment she walked into the house. In that moment, Danny, who had been transferring the contents of Mrs Wait's marketing bag back into the cardboard box, spoke. 'It's all right, missus,' he said, his voice even colder than her aunt's had been. 'If you're that hard up, I wouldn't dream o' tekkin' your tea. You'd best save it for Ginny here, 'cos I reckon she's parched an' all.' Hefting the empty bag, he turned towards the kitchen door, saying over his shoulder: 'See you around, Ginny.'

'Wait for me, Danny,' Ginny said desperately. 'I'm sure me aunt didn't mean . . . I'll make fresh tea . . .'

'That you will not, my fine lady,' her aunt said. She raised her voice so that Danny, in the act of closing the kitchen door, could not have failed to hear. 'Lerrim go; we don't want the likes of him here, the cheeky young bugger.'

Ginny would have run after her friend, apologised for her aunt's rudeness—and meanness—but when she tried to do so, Aunt Amy caught her by the shoulder and held her in a grip of steel. 'No you don't, my gal,' she said grimly. 'Just you take them boxes up to your room and stow 'em away somewhere. While you're gone, I'll make a fresh pot o' tea an' cut some bread 'n' marge for us dinners, but in future that'll be your job.' She turned to her sister's daughters. 'Norma, Belle! You'd best tek her upstairs, show her where she's to lie and then bring her down again. I won't have me word flouted and I say she's to stay in the house

224

until we've got things settled.'

The two girls advanced purposefully. Belle, who had been slouched in a chair with a newspaper spread out before her, was a plump, slow-moving girl. She and her sister both had light hair and spotty complexions, but Ginny thought Norma's expression sharp and spiteful, very like her Aunt Amy's, and resolved to steer clear of the older girl, if she could. Her Uncle Lewis had spoken, wistfully, of finding the Franklins a home of their own and she could only second this wish.

Norma gave a malicious grin as she and her sister accompanied Ginny out of the room and up the stairs. Belle had, good-naturedly, picked up the larger of the cardboard boxes, leaving Ginny to cope with the smaller one.

'It don't do to cross me Aunt Amy,' Norma said as they entered the bedroom. 'Of course, we're all right, me an' Belle, 'cos our mam won't see us pushed about, but it's different for you, Ginger. You ain't nothin' to any of us, 'cos you're Uncle Lewis's niece, no kin to us Franklins, nor to Aunt Amy.'

'My name's Ginny,' Ginny said coldly. It would have been nice to say she thought herself lucky not to be related to Aunt Amy or her sister, but she knew it would not be politic to do so. Both Norma and Belle were tall, strong-looking girls and Ginny had no wish to start off this new life of hers on the wrong footing, so she meekly dumped her belongings in the only corner of the room not occupied by beds and boxes.

The three girls went downstairs again and back into the kitchen, where Aunt Amy was handing cups of tea and rounds of bread and marge to the

225

assorted persons in the room. Ruthie, who was four, had a mug of what looked like milk and water and was having some difficulty with her bread and marge. Ginny, who liked small children, kneeled down and began to help the child with her portion, which seemed to please Aunt Amy.

'So you like kids, does you?' she said. 'Well, it's a good job you does, because you'll be givin' an eye to the kids now you're livin' wi' us. Ivy an' Millie are in school, an' Ruthie starts next term, so they won't be much bother to you. Ain't you lucky they're all girls? Boys'll sag off whenever they get the chance—you know what boys are. But the gals is all right.'

'But—but I don't see how I can, Aunt Amy— take the kids to school, I mean—'cos I've gorra get across the city to Rathbone Street each morning, once term starts,' Ginny said wildly. 'An' I goes to me friend Annie's . . .'

She stopped short. Her aunt was staring at her. 'You'll be at school in Gray Street,' she said baldly, 'wi' your cousins. We don't have no spare money for trams in this family and Gray Street's a good school. Besides, your Uncle Lewis has writ to Rathbone Street, tellin' 'em you've moved, so they won't be expectin' you.'

Ginny felt as if a great black pit had opened up in front of her. Not only was she having to live with these horrible people, she was not going to be allowed to return to her beloved school. One look at Aunt Amy's tight mouth, however, convinced her that argument would be useless, possibly even dangerous. She thought about begging Uncle George to take her in, explaining that she had had no idea of her Aunt Amy's plans when she had

226

agreed to go and live there. She could already see that none of this would be easy, but she could not simply let her aunt and uncle ruin her life without at least making a push to help herself.

'Here's your tea, chuck.' Belle pushed a mug of strong, dark tea into her hand. She had rather small, mud-coloured eyes but her smile was sympathetic. 'It's 'orrible goin' to a new school so I know how you feel. But Aunt's right, it's a decent place, the Gray Street school, an' you'll soon settle down there. Uncle Lewis told us you were bright, which is always a help, 'cos the bright ones don't get caned near as often as the dim ones. Want some bread 'n' marge? We have our hot meal at night and Aunt Amy's a prime cook.'

Ginny would have liked to refuse the bread and margarine but she did not want to hurt Belle's feelings. This was the first friendly overture that had occurred since she had entered the house. So she accepted the food and was glad she had done so as soon as she began to eat. Supper last night had been a rushed, makeshift meal and there had been nothing for breakfast since all the food and cooking utensils had been cleared away the day before.

Squatting on the hearthrug, sipping the strong tea and eating the bread and marge, she resolved to go back to Rathbone Street just as soon as she possibly could. She would tell Annie what had happened—and tell Danny as well—and then they would have to put their heads together to find a solution to the problem of her schooling. I will *not* go to another school. I'm happy in Rathbone Street and there's no other teacher who would help me like Miss Derbyshire does, she told herself fiercely.

School doesn't start for another week, so there's plenty of time. Why, I know where Miss Derbyshire lives on Canning Street so I can go there and ask her to put in a good word for me.

Ruthie had finished her bread and marge and was drinking the last of her milk. Ginny looked round the room; at the other children squabbling over a box of coloured pencils, at the Franklin sisters, eating bread and marge as though they were half starved, which they certainly were not, and at Aunt Amy and Mrs Franklin, with their heads together, hissing and whispering like two old witches over a cauldron. I'll go back to Rathbone Street tomorrow—I'll tell Aunt Amy I've left something there and need to get it back, she told herself. I won't, I *won't* just let Aunt Amy push me around!

*   *   *

A week later found Ginny miserably trailing to Gray Street School, accompanied by her three young cousins. She had done her best to get back to Rathbone Street but her aunt always found some pressing reason why she could not go.

So now, Ginny shepherded her small cousins into the playground, making sure that they lined up and actually entered the school building before making her way to her own class. Her teacher proved to be stern, elderly and unbending. He taught the children by rote, making them learn the rules of mathematics, grammar and so on by heart. He made no attempt to interest his charges and did not seem to realise that Ginny was new to the school. Furthermore, Miss Derbyshire's class of ten- and eleven-year-olds was far more advanced than Mr Reid's so that by the end of the first day Ginny realised, with dismay, that she was wasting her time. Boredom would be her lot whilst under his eagle eye.

That evening, after school, she tackled Uncle Lewis, explaining that the teacher was old and as bored by the lessons as Ginny herself had been. Uncle Lewis looked up from his paper and smiled at her. 'What makes you think you're any different from a hundred others?' he said. 'I were always bored at school, 'cept when I were bein' beaten, and so were all of us lads; ask your Uncle George if you don't believe me. It were only your mam and Lizzie who seemed to gerron well at school. The thing is, queen, that our Amy really needs you and trusts you to take care o' the kids when she ain't able to do so herself. If you went back to the Rathbone Street school, you'd be no manner o' use to us. It's the same at weekends; as you know, I work away at weekends to earn extra money so you're needed to help your aunt and give an eye to the younger ones.' He reached across the table to chuck her under the chin, smiling at her with a good deal of understanding. 'I'm sorry, queen, 'cos it's hard on you, I reckon, but everyone in Schubert Street has to put their backs to the wheel. In a couple o' years, Ivy will be ten, same as you are now, and then I dare say you'll have a bit more freedom. Until then, though, I'm afraid you'll have to stick to the Gray Street school.' And with that he dived behind his newspaper again.

Ginny sighed but realised that it was fair enough. Whatever her aunt and uncle's faults might have been, they fed her well, clothed her adequately, and saw that she had a proper share in any treats that were going. When she ran messages—and she ran a good many—she was always rewarded with a ha'penny or so and already her aunt's attitude towards her had softened a good deal. Aunt Amy still ordered her about and kept her hard at it in the house but she did so in a pleasanter way, seeming to realise that Ginny was doing her best.

'Fetch the kids in for their tea, queen,' she shouted now, bringing Ginny back to the present. 'Tell 'em it's boiled mutton an' dumplings wi' stewed apple an' conny-onny to follow; that'll fetch 'em!'

Ginny, who had been doing her homework, sighed and got up. She was already learning that instant obedience was best, otherwise it was a clack round the head and no supper, and Aunt Amy was an extremely good cook. Ginny had not realised this at first, because of the bread and marge lunch, but soon began to enjoy better food than she had ever had before, except in the homes of her friends. She no longer wondered why Uncle Lewis had married a plain woman ten years his senior, for though the house was often untidy the food was worthy of Aunt Mary, who was known as a brilliant cook by all her customers at the canny house. Anyone would have been glad to marry such a cook and besides, there was talk of the Franklins moving out. If this happened, Ginny was sure that housework would be a good deal less onerous and the place very much tidier, for very soon after arriving in Schubert Street she had realised that it was the Franklins who made most of the mess. They tramped dirt into the house but never swept a floor. They cast dirty clothing into any old corner but never thought to launder it, and though they enjoyed Aunt Amy's cooking, they would leave half-eaten bits of food where they'd put them down and then grumble that the place was full of mice, if not rats.

After a fortnight in the house, Ginny began to realise that she could have been worse off. To be sure, her aunt worked her extremely hard, but at least she was growing fond of her small cousins and always came home to a good cooked meal and a warm house. She still missed her friends and her school dreadfully, but knew there was little she could do about it. A child is always at the mercy of the adults in its life, Ginny still had a certain amount of freedom. Armed with a large marketing bag, she did the messages most days, and when her aunt wanted the children out from under her feet, Ginny took them into the jigger at the back of the house where they could play such games as hopscotch, skipping or even tag without fear of passing traffic. Life could have been worse, Ginny concluded, but she was still determined to return to her old haunts as soon as she could.

*   *   *

It was March before Ginny discovered why her Aunt Amy did not make Belle and Norma clean up after themselves, nor why Mrs Franklin never raised a finger to help. All three were working, of course, but the money they handed to Aunt Amy was surely not enough to make up for their behaviour. She might never have found out why the Franklin family seemed to contribute so little had it not been for lazy, good-natured Belle. One sunny

231

Sunday, Belle offered to take the children up to Bowerdale Park provided that Ginny accompanied her, which the younger girl was happy to do since it was such a pleasant day. If she stayed at home, she would end up doing the housework, for her aunt always cleaned the place from top to bottom on the Lord's Day, as she called it. Accordingly, she and Belle soon found themselves sitting on a bench in the park, watching the younger ones whooping and laughing on the swings and roundabouts. A man with an ice cream cart cycled slowly past and Belle hailed him.

'Go and get five ha'penny cornets, queen,' she said, handing Ginny a threepenny bit. 'I oughtn't to go splashing me money about 'cos when we move I wants me own bedroom, and Mam's so mean she won't buy me so much as a blanket. But I dunno, sometimes I wonder if we'll ever shift. We've been savin' for ages, but somehow the money gets whittled away.'

'I know what you mean,' Ginny said sympathetically. 'The house is so crowded. I used to think it were awful, living with Granny Bennett, but at least there were only the two of us. Belle, can I ask you a question?'

'Course you can, when you've fetched the cornets,' Belle said lazily. Ginny hurried off and presently they were all licking ice cream and Ginny put the question she was longing to ask. 'Belle, I know I've not been in Schubert Street all that long, but—but I can't help noticin' that it's Aunt Amy and meself what does most of the housework. Your mam . . . well, she never even dries the dishes, or carries water upstairs, or—or makes a round of toast. I don't mean to be rude, but even Gran . . .

232

well, she didn't do much, but . . .'

'Don't you know?' Belle said, her eyes rounding with surprise. 'My mam is ten years younger than Aunt Amy and after our granny died—Mam were only twelve—Aunt Amy took over the house and was like a mam to our mam. Then, later, our mam began to get thin and to cough a lot. She had just started work at the rope factory and for ages she kept on working, though she complained about feelin' ill. After a few months, she got so thin, and sort of—of listless, that Aunt Amy took fright. She took her up to the clinic on Brougham Terrace and the doctor there said our mam had TB. He were real cross with Aunt Amy, said she should have brought her there weeks ago. They whisked Mam off to a clinic in the country. She were there three years, and o' course, when she come out, me aunt were that sorry for the way she'd behaved, she waited on our mam hand and foot. Mam got married and had us two, and until our dad upped and offed she managed her own affairs. Dad left when I were twelve and Mam never even tried to cope alone. She moved in wi' her sister and I reckon things just went back to the way they had been, wi' Aunt Amy doin' all the work, even though, by then, she had a family of her own.'

'I *see*,' Ginny said. 'But wharrabout you and Norma, Belle? You—you doesn't help much either.'

Belle giggled. 'I reckon Aunt believes that Mam's chest weakness ha' been inherited by us two, an' she's scared stiff we'll go the same way as our mam,' she said. 'I reckon Mam never told her sister what the doctors told her—that it were the stuff they used to make the ropes which had brought on the illness. Aunt Amy made her stick to the job when she were desperate to quit.'

Ginny thought this over, then voiced her thoughts aloud. 'But you and Norma and your mam . . . well, you seem ever so strong and healthy,' she observed. 'Your mam must be completely cured.'

Belle giggled again. 'She never did have TB; it were just an illness caused by the rope fibres,' she said confidentially. 'But don't you go tellin' Aunt Amy or me mam will break both our bleedin' necks.' She grinned at her younger cousin. 'So now you know; if you want a life of ease, you'll have to have a horrible disease, or pretend to have one, at any rate.'

'I don't want either, thanks,' Ginny told her. 'But I could do wi' a bit more freedom, Belle. You see, I had good friends in Victoria Court an' I don't want to lose 'em. I'd love to visit me old school an' all; me teacher was prime, honest to God she was. Any ideas?'

But though Belle furrowed her brow in concentration, she could not think of a foolproof plan. 'Only the kids will play out when the weather gets warmer and that'll give you time away from the house,' she said. 'In fact now I've told you our dark secret, I don't mind takin' the kids off your hands from time to time. I like 'em, you know. Norma's awful sharp; she says hateful things—says I'm fat, an' tells tales, an' enjoys gettin' me into trouble.'

'I know,' Ginny said gloomily. 'No one at school called me Ginger until Norma went and told Ivy that it was my real name. Ivy's only a kid, she don't know any better, so now half the school calls me Ginger an' I do hate it.'

'It ain't as bad as Fatty Arbuckle,' the older girl observed, getting to her feet. 'It's not so bad now I'm at work, but at school Norma told everyone to call me Fatty Arbuckle. She told people I'd rolled on her pet cat and crushed it to death an' she's never even had a cat.' She looked shyly across at Ginny and tucked her arm into the crook of the younger girl's. 'You're a grand kid, Ginny; what say we're pals, eh? I don't have no pals at work 'cos they're mostly so much older than me. What d'you say?'

Ginny said, enthusiastically, that she could do with a pal herself and the two of them made their way home in excellent spirits, Ginny chattering away as though she and Belle had been friends for years.

CHAPTER NINE

Michael had meant to return to Liverpool as soon as the *Mary Louise* made a landfall in the British Isles but, in the event, he was unable to do so. An urgent message from his mother made him change his plans. When the ship docked in Dublin, there was a telegram awaiting him. He opened it with considerable trepidation for no one had ever sent him a telegram before and read it with a thumping heart. *Can you come Michael stop Daddy fell and broke leg stop Declan at sea stop Maeve Gallagher.*

Michael shoved the telegram into his pocket, smiling to himself at the formality of the signature. However, he could not go straight to Liverpool as he had planned. A broken leg is a serious matter

235

for a farmer; it would put all the work on his mammy and last time he had been home he had been much struck by the improvement of their holding. They now had a good flock of sheep and seven milch cows instead of the three they had owned before. His mother had always been proud of her poultry and now she was able to sell eggs at the weekly market as well as keeping the family supplied. The fields would have been ploughed and sown with crops the previous autumn, but because the weather was mild corn, potatoes and other crops would be showing above the ground and that meant that weeds would also be putting in an appearance. He might not have to stay at home long, but he could not possibly let his mother down. The fact was, he had never told his parents that Ginny existed, though he had meant to do so on his next visit home, and now, because of his father's accident, it would be a bad time to tell them he had simply got to visit Liverpool in the near future in order to see his daughter. Clearly, however, it would have to be done; he would tell them as soon as he reached home.

'Michael! I thought we were catching the ferry across to Liverpool this mornin'. Ain't you comin'? We'll lose it, else.'

Michael swung round as Nobby came clattering down the gangway and joined him on the quayside. Wordlessly, he pulled the telegram out of his pocket and handed it to his friend. Nobby read it with furrowed brow then sighed deeply and handed it back. 'Well, I'm real sorry for your old man, mate, but you were goin' to sign off for a whole voyage anyway, weren't you? A broken leg, eh? That's bad for a feller what works the land, ain't it?

236

And wharrabout your daughter? Did you write to tell her you'd be visitin' Liverpool around this time?'

'No, I never did. You see, I wrote, oh, mebbe half a dozen times last year, giving her the shipping office address so she could reply. I got a letter, just before Christmas, though it weren't from her, it were from Granny Bennett.' He pulled a face. 'I didn't even know the old devil could write, but she managed a couple of lines, though the writing were all over the place and the spelling were fearful. She said the girl was strong and healthy and doing well at school, and the money came in awful handy, though if I could spare a few bob more, they'd both be grateful. It eased me mind, so it did, but I still mean to go back to Liverpool and visit 'em, because the letters I sent were addressed to me daughter, so you'd have thought, if she were so good at schoolwork, that she would have replied herself. I know she's only a kid, an' no kid I know likes writin' letters, but she might have just penned a line.'

'She may never have got the letters,' Nobby said shrewdly. 'You said that the old grandmother hated you like poison, so mebbe she chucked the letters in the fire. After all, she's had your money all these years without doin' a thing for it, so mebbe she don't want to rock the boat. Mebbe she replied herself because she were afraid, if she didn't, you'd think they were both dead and stop sending any money at all.'

'I know. I've thought of all that, and I'm far from blamin' the kid,' Michael assured his friend. 'But I did suspicion that if I told 'em I were comin', they might hustle the kid out o' the way. Anyway, it's a

237

good thing I didn't tell 'em since now it may be a week or two before I can leave Ireland.'

The two young men set off across the quayside, making their way towards the place where the ferry from Liverpool had docked. 'Nobby . . . would it be askin' too much for you to go round to Victoria Court—it's No. 17—and check out that all's well there? I—I'll give you some money so you can telegraph me, let me know how things stand. You can tell Granny Bennett I'm comin' to Liverpool just as soon as I can get away from the farm . . . if she asks, that is.' He grinned ruefully at his friend. 'Sure and the likeliest thing is, she'll spit on your boots at the mention of me name, but I dare say you won't heed that.'

Nobby grinned too. 'Devil a bit I'll mind,' he said cheerfully. 'Any message for your sprog? I'm longin' to meet hcr, so I am!'

Michael shook his head, then changed his mind. 'You might tell her I'm goin' to get her a kitten when I come to Liverpool,' he said. 'Her mammy always did like cats.'

'I don't think I'll mention the cat, if you don't mind, old pal,' Nobby said. 'It 'ud be a turrble disappointment for the kid if you turned up wi'out it.'

It was strange how the word cat brought an immediate picture into Michael's mind, a picture he had not really thought about for ten years. Once more, he saw the darkened quayside, the shadow by the dock gates, and felt again the soft weight of the cat on his shoulder, even felt against his ear the satiny fur and the vibrating purr. And in that moment, he also saw Stella's face, only the big, dark eyes were full of tears and the mouth had a

238

reproachful droop. Michael found he was blinking back tears himself; Stella had loved him, trusted him, and he had betrayed her in the worst possible way. He had kissed her when she was expecting his child and promised that he would look after them both, and he had meant it. Then Stella had died and everything had gone wrong and now he must put everything right.

'What's gorrin to you, old feller? Cat got your tongue?'

Startled out of his reverie, Michael apologised, saying that his mind had been a thousand miles away, then bade his friend farewell and watched as he climbed aboard the ferry for England. Only when the ship was out of sight did he realise that he had completely forgotten to give Nobby his Kerry address. Sighing at his own stupidity, for he now could not possibly receive a telegram from his friend, he turned back and headed for the Kingsbridge station where he would catch the train for Limerick. From there, he would catch another train which would take him to Killorglin, and from Killorglin he would walk, knowing every step of the way, to the home which he had not seen for three years.

*   *   *

Michael's homecoming was every bit as warm and loving as he had hoped. His father was in a poor state, Michael saw; he could not use his right arm and his leg was in plaster to the thigh. His elbow had been broken in the fall that had fractured his leg, which had given him a double disability. Sean relied heavily on his favourite sheepdog, Floss, who had grown adept at keeping just ahead of her master, pushing open doors and barking to warn everyone of Sean's slow and shuffling approach. When Sean said 'stick' or 'slippers' or 'me paper', the dog would rush to bring such items to him. She seldom took her eyes from his face and Michael thought such devotion both amusing and touching.

'And when I'm on me feet again and able to work, Floss is goin' to be lost because she's treatin' me like her one an' only puppy,' Sean confided. 'Eh, old Floss is worth her weight in gold.'

Michael had been horrified at the extent of his father's injuries when he had first come home. 'I'd been fishin', climbed out o' the boat with me catch in one hand and went a purler on a slippery rock,' Sean told his son. 'It were rainin' so hard I could scarce see me hand in front of me face and, to tell the truth, I must have knocked me head an' all, 'cos I didn't come to until someone began shakin' me shoulder. It were Padraig what lives further along the coast. He and your mammy got me back to the cottage but the bone was stickin' out sort of funny, like, so Padraig brought his donkey cart up to the front door and took me into Killorglin, to the doctor's. He told me there I'd cracked me elbow an' I'm telling you, it gives me more pain than the leg.'

'Aye, he's been in a poor way, so he has,' Maeve agreed. 'I'm that sorry, son, that I had to send you a telegram, but the truth is, I were desperate. Declan was supposed to come back in April, but your dad an' me, we've got a feeling he may stay a bit longer. You see, when you wrote in August, you did say you might be comin' home for good sometime soon and I think Declan took it that he might not be needed.'

She cast a deprecating glance at her son. 'Perhaps I read too much into what you said, Michael, but it did seem as though you were missin' the farm—and us—so we thought . . .'

'Not that we dreamed of lettin' Declan go,' Sean said quickly. 'The fact is, Michael, that the farm has growed so there's work for all of us. And your mammy an' me . . . well, we're not gettin' any younger and we're findin' the work hard. Young Declan and meself ploughed and sowed last back-end, but when the warmer weather comes . . .'

The three Gallaghers were sitting around the kitchen table having just finished a large meal of boiled potatoes and fish, rounded off with marmalade pudding. Michael grinned at his father. 'You don't have to explain to me, Daddy,' he said. 'There'll be work aplenty for both Declan and meself. Mammy didn't mention the elbow when she sent the telegram but I can see it'll be a sore trial to you. How much have you been able to do since the accident? Don't say Mammy's been managin' all alone?'

Maeve snorted. 'Once I could have managed alone,' she said defensively, 'because it's a quiet time of year, so it is, and it's mainly a matter of feedin' the stock, seein' that the lambs get born wit'out trouble, and so on. But we've been payin' Padraig's son, Ryan, to give me a hand wit' the work. He's a good lad but he's only twelve.' She smiled at her son and reached over to pat his shoulder. 'Michael, even the sight of you has done us both a world o' good! When d'you have to sign on again? Only, they reckon at the hospital it'll be months, rather than weeks, before your daddy's got his full strength back.'

241

'I don't have to sign on at all, at all,' Michael said quickly. 'You were right when you thought me letter meant I wanted to come home, 'cos I do. Life aboard ship is fine; I've made good friends and had good times but now I'm thinkin' of settlin' down, comin' back to me roots.' He looked speculatively across at his mother; was this the right moment to tell her that he had a daughter who was being taken care of by her maternal grandmother across the water; a daughter he had not set eyes on since she was a few weeks old? He had been putting it off for years, knowing in his heart that his parents were bound to think badly of him. They would have loved grandchildren, and when he had been at home his mother had constantly brought girls to the house, clearly hoping that Michael might like one of them enough to begin to put Stella out of his mind.

'Well, I'd best be getting on.' His mother stood up and turned towards the back door, beginning to struggle into her heavy coat and boots. 'Going to give me a hand, Michael?'

'I will, Mammy,' Michael said. He began to put on his overcoat, relief washing over him. He would have no chance to tell his parents about Ginny now; it would have to wait until later. He opened his mouth to tell his daddy it would be like old times to milk the cows again and, to his horror, heard his voice remarking, conversationally: 'As I were sayin', I'm coming back for good this time, only I'll be wantin' two or three days off to go over to Liverpool. I've a daughter there, what I've not seen since she were a couple o' months old, an' it's time she got to know me, I'm thinkin'.'

There was a frozen silence. Sean sat in his chair,

mouth open, eyes rounding, his pipe halfway to his mouth. Maeve was half in and half out of her coat and the expression of stunned surprise on her face was so comical that Michael laughed aloud. 'I'm sorry, Mammy,' he said, his voice humble. 'I telled you about Stella an' how she died but I couldn't bring myself to admit there were a baby. She's ten years old now an' I've not seen her since I came home here, after Stella died. I send money, of course, and letters—she's a fine, strong girl an' doin' well at school, her granny tells me—but for a long time, I couldn't bring myself to go back to the city, not even to see my little girl.' He looked apologetically at his mother and was astonished to see her wearing a broad smile.

'A granddaughter!' she breathed. She turned to her husband. 'Oh, Sean, we're grandparents; did you hear what the boy said? We've got a granddaughter!' She swung round to face Michael once more. 'You say you left her with her gran, but why didn't you bring her to us, Michael dear? Farm life is a good deal healthier than city life, I'm sure o' that. And wouldn't we have give her a grand time? Why, we've missed ten years of her growin' up, but you'll bring her back now, won't you, if only for a few weeks? Her other gran won't grudge us a few weeks, surely?'

Michael gulped. He had always known that his mother loved children, that she was desperate for a grandchild, yet it had never before occurred to him how unfair he had been, both to his parents and to his daughter. The farm was a wonderful place to grow up—he should know, he had grown up here himself—and his mother a very much nicer person than Granny Bennett could ever be. But there was no point in grieving over what had happened. Now it was his duty to bring the child home.

Sean began to press the tobacco down in the bowl of his pipe. 'What's her name?' he asked. Michael could hear that he was striving to keep his voice steady. 'Your mam an' me wanted a big family, you know, but it weren't to be.'

'Stella called her Virginia but I believe she's always been known as Ginny,' Michael said, rather awkwardly. He had expected an explosion of wrath for his behaviour and realised that this would probably come later, when his parents were over the first shock. 'Look, Daddy, if I work like the devil for a week so's everything here is shipshape and Bristol fashion, can I employ young Ryan for however long is necessary, whiles I go across to Liverpool? It—it may take me a day or so to persuade Granny Bennett to let me bring Ginny back here for a while. Indeed, it might take longer than that if she's doin' so well at school, because it's term time and the kid might rather come in the school holidays.'

'Of course, of course,' Sean said immediately. 'If you can show the lad what he's to do, he'll do it. He's slow, but very willing, and if it's only for a few days . . .'

He left the sentence unfinished, and presently Michael and his mother headed across the yard to the cowshed. 'Ryan brings 'em in every afternoon and stays to help with the milking,' Maeve explained. She stopped for a moment and turned her steady, dark-eyed gaze upon her son. 'We won't say anything more just now, Michael, but I dare say you realise that you've a great deal of explaining to do.'

244

'I know, Mammy; I've behaved just about as badly as any feller could, both to you and to the kid,' Michael said humbly. 'I think I've been a bit mad, and I only came to my senses . . .' A young boy appeared in the cowshed doorway and Maeve squeezed his arm warningly. '. . . but we'll talk about it later,' he ended lamely. Raising his voice, he turned back towards the cowshed. 'Afternoon! You'll be Ryan, I dare say. I hear you've been a great help since me daddy broke his leg and I'd like to thank you.'

*   *   *

Michael stepped ashore at the Pier Head and felt an unpleasant sinking sensation in his stomach. The last time he had been in Liverpool the crushing loss of Stella had occupied all his thoughts. His one desire had been to escape, to get away from both dreadful old Granny Bennett and his strange little redheaded daughter. Time, however, had taught him the foolishness of his doubts over the child's paternity. Heredity was a strange thing and he had always known in his heart that though Stella had been innocent, she would never have played him false.

Michael had been standing on the quayside, trying not to remember how he had stood here ten years before, so full of hope, so eager to reach Victoria Court. In his wildest nightmares, he had never dreamed that Stella would not be there to meet him. He had left her with a kiss and a promise—a promise to look after her and her unborn child—and what had he done? He had abandoned her baby and escaped. All right, he had been nursing his grief, half mad with it, but there had been no justification for taking it out on an innocent babe.

However, he had returned to Liverpool to right wrongs, and he meant to do just that. He had saved up quite a nice little amount despite the monthly payments towards his daughter's keep and intended to offer Granny Bennett money so that she would not object to his taking Ginny back to Ireland with him. He remembered quite enough about the old woman to realise she would still have an eye for the main chance. If he had asked her to keep Ginny for another ten years—if she loved the child and intended to do just that—she would still have expected some sort of extra payment for the 'favour' he was requesting. Michael picked up his grip and began to walk up towards the Overhead Railway, his footsteps ringing on the frosty pavement. He grinned to himself as he did so. He remembered Stella calling it 'the dockers' umbrella', which had always made him smile. Liverpudlians, like Dubliners, had a way of nicknaming everything and everyone with their own sly humour.

He had thought about booking into the Sailors' Home as soon as he arrived but doubted whether he would be accepted since he had signed off the *Mary Louise* in Dublin. However, if Granny Bennett was not willing to let him have a bed in her house, then there were plenty of cheap lodgings to be had in the area. It was a weekday so he guessed that Ginny would be in school, but it occurred to him that if she were to walk slap bang up to him, he would not recognise her. This, for some reason, brought a sharp pang of guilt, and also a startlingly

246

clear picture of Stella. For several years now, it had not been easy to remember her.

But now in his mind, just for an instant, he saw her again; the rich fall of her night-black hair, the big, dark eyes, the way her mouth tilted when she smiled. It actually made him catch his breath, but as quickly as it had come the picture was gone, leaving behind it a warmth. It was as though she was delighted that he was back in Liverpool, as though she thoroughly approved of what he had come to do and wanted him to know it.

With a light heart, Michael began to whistle as he turned into Great George Street. Presently he swung under the arch into Victoria Court. It had not changed by so much as one iota. Young children played on the dirty paving stones and one or two older kids, who had been looking after the little ones, glanced up apprehensively as he strode towards them. They were sagging off school, he guessed, and probably thought he might be an attendance officer, for when he banged on the door of No. 17, they returned to their games, satisfied that he must be here on private business. There was a short wait during which Michael noted, with approval, that Granny Bennett had hung new, brightly patterned curtains in the parlour as well as nets of startling whiteness. The kitchen window sported red and white checks and the windows themselves were clean enough to see through. Either Ginny worked as hard in the house as he had been told she did at school, or the old woman really had changed.

Michael was still trying to peer into the kitchen to see if there were any other changes, when the front door opened. A thickset young woman with a pink and shiny face, a snub nose and pale, rather watery eyes stood in the doorway. She looked enquiringly at him, then produced a large square of cotton and blew her nose vigorously. 'Sorry, chuck, I've gorra fearful 'ead cold,' she said thickly. 'Two of me kids is off school with it, though I did send a note by one of me older boys, so I don't see why . . .' She broke off and her rather hostile expression softened. 'Oh, you ain't the 'tendance officer. I'm that sorry, mister. Now, what can I do for you? Selling insurance, are you? No, that ain't it . . . you're a sailor, ain't you? If you're lookin' for lodgings . . .'

Despite her head cold, Michael guessed that she was the sort of woman who almost never stopped talking, so he broke in as she took a deep breath to prepare for the next question. 'I'm awful sorry to disturb you, missus,' he said apologetically. 'I were lookin' for Mrs Bennett and her granddaughter, Ginny. I take it they don't live here no more?'

The woman shook her large, untidy head, then clapped her handkerchief to her nose once more as an enormous sneeze shook her frame. 'Nah, they moved out a couple o' months back,' she said. 'I dunno where they went, an' I've not been here long enough to know which neighbours were pally with 'em, like. You might try next door, though,' she added. 'Them's the Borrages; they've lived next door to old, I mean Mrs, Bennett for a couple o' years, at least. I don't say they were friends,' she added, mopping vigorously at her watering eyes this time, 'but I guess they're the likeliest to know where the old girl's gone.'

Michael was thanking her and turning away when she called him back. 'Is they in some sort o'

248

trouble?' she asked curiously. 'The old gal had a couple o' sons in the Navy, so I've heard. But if you was one of them, you'd know where she's gone, I suppose. An' if you ain't one of them, then why's you lookin' for her? I reckon it might be money . . . I know she owed money hereabouts. Yes, the Borrages might know where they've gone.'

Michael grinned at the woman. 'Curiosity killed the cat, as my mammy says,' he informed her cheerfully. 'Thanks for your help, missus. I'll try the Borrages next.'

An hour later, Michael left the courts, gnawing indecisively at his lip. The Borrages had told him a good deal, had said that the old lady had nearly driven them mad with her noisy carryings-on the previous Christmas. The kid looked after the old girl well, or as well as she could, but in the end there had been no standing it. They believed a relative from away had taken the girl; they imagined the old woman must have gone to some sort of home for alcoholics. At any rate, so far as they knew, neither Mrs Bennett nor her granddaughter had returned to the court.

'I dunno as I can tell you where they've gone,' Mrs Borrage had said doubtfully, after some thought, 'but the kid were a bright scholar, that I *do* know, and I imagine that she'll be comin' out o' school wi' all the others in an hour or so. Why not try and catch her there?'

Michael had only the vaguest idea where the school was but he went into the corner shop to buy some Woodbines and the woman behind the counter gave him directions. Then, seeing that it was an hour before school came out, Michael booked himself into a room in a small guest house, just for the one night, and went and had a meal at the nearest dining rooms. All the time he was eating, he was conscious of a glow within him which he knew was because, at long last, he was keeping his promise to Stella. He would find Ginny and arrange to take her home to Ireland. If she did not want to go, then he was not sure what he would do, but he could not imagine any child not being attracted by the thought of living on a farm.

The children came out of Rathbone Street School in a rush, as children do the world over, and Michael scanned the faces anxiously as they streamed past him. He stepped forward at one point, meaning to stop a girl with bright red hair tied into a knot on top of her head, then stepped back, realising she was far too young. And anyway, he was going the wrong way about it; he should have gone into school and asked to be conducted to her classroom. He could have explained who he was to the teacher in charge so that the introduction could be made properly.

Nevertheless, he remained by the gate until the last child had passed him. Then he straightened his shoulders and crossed the schoolyard, entering the building through the doorway the children had used. Inside, the familiar smell of chalk and rubber plimsolls greeted him, reminding him, nostalgically, of his own school days. He glanced about him, uncertain what his next step should be, and was still standing near the entrance when two young women approached him, chattering animatedly as they came. One was short and square with dark hair pinned into a tight little bun on the nape of her neck. The other was taller and slim, with a thin pale face, large tortoiseshell-rimmed spectacles and hair so fair that at first he had thought it white. The pale hair was shoulder length and Michael noticed, detachedly, that the young woman's eyebrows and lashes were also white.

As the two approached him, he stepped forward. He had already removed his cap upon entering the building and now he turned it in his hands, suddenly feeling like a trespasser. 'Excuse me, ladies, I wonder if you could help me?'

Both young women smiled at him but it was the taller of the two who spoke. 'Certainly we'll help you if we can. Are you searching for the head teacher's office? I know the skylight over the infants' cloakroom had been leaking again . . .'

Michael smiled deprecatingly. 'No, no, it's nothing like that, miss. I'm a seaman, just come ashore and wantin' to see me daughter. I watched the kids comin' out of school but I'm pretty sure she weren't among them. Me daughter's name's Virginia Bennett and I've visited the house, only it seems they moved out a couple of months ago . . .'

The fair-haired woman interrupted him. 'I knew Virginia Bennett well. She was in my class,' she said, and Michael could not help noticing how icily cold her voice had become. 'You'll be Michael Gallagher, I take it?' She turned to the smaller woman beside her. 'You go off home, Sandy, and get the tea started; Mr Gallagher—I take it you are Mr Gallagher?—and I have some—some business to sort out.'

The dark-haired one left them, though she shot her friend an apprehensive glance as she did so. Michael said haltingly: 'Yes—yes, I'm—I'm Michael Gallagher, so I am. Does me daughter talk of me, then? The truth is, miss, that I've not seen

251

her for a long while, and—and . . .'

The fair young woman gave him a contemptuous glance, then turned away and retraced her steps along the corridor, moving so fast that Michael had to lengthen his own stride or be left behind. She flung open the door of a classroom and jerked her head at him, indicating that he should pass inside, ahead of her. Michael obeyed, feeling confused. He had done nothing wrong, had not been rude or impatient, had done his best to explain his errand to this snooty bitch, and she was treating him like— like a leper. She's only a bleedin' schoolmistress, he told himself savagely, staring across at her as she seated herself behind the teacher's big desk. She's treatin' me like one of her perishin' pupils—the bad one, the one in the corner wearing the dunce's cap—an' I won't stand for it.

However, he realised that it would not do to comment; instead he began to explain again that he had searched for Ginny and her grandmother in Victoria Court without success. 'No one was able to help; no one seemed to know where they'd gone,' he said, speaking slowly and trying to eradicate as much of his brogue as he could. 'Then I thought of the school and I thought she was such a good scholar that she'd come here every day, no matter what. Only—only when the kids came tumblin' out I couldn't see her, so I thought mebbe—mebbe her teacher might know her address.'

She had been looking down as he spoke, but now she lifted her eyes from their contemplation of her desktop and looked challengingly at him. 'But how would you have recognised her, Mr Gallagher? After all, you've not set eyes on her since her mother died, so why this sudden desire to get in

252

touch? You've been happy enough to ignore her for ten years.'

Michael felt a rich tide of heat sweep over his face, no doubt dyeing it crimson, he thought savagely. So this snooty English schoolma'am knew about his behaviour—perhaps it was the talk of the neighbourhood! But he did his best to answer calmly, with as much politeness as he could. After all, she must have the information he needed; he could not afford to antagonise her further.

'I t'ought I'd know her by the colour of her hair; it was bright ginger when I last saw her and I didn't think it would change that much,' he said slowly. 'You're right, of course; I've not seen her for a—a longish while, but—but I've sent money regular, sometimes more 'n' I could rightly afford, and I've written, oh, a heap of letters and only ever had one reply. But now I'm leavin' the Merchant Navy and moving back to my daddy's farm, and I t'ought . . .'

The young woman seated at the desk gave a little crow of triumph. 'So *that's* why you've come back!' she said. 'Of course, I should have guessed! Ginny's ten years old now, old enough to be useful. You're going back to your farm, so you need an extra pair of hands, and a child of ten who's been brought up as she has is a capable, useful creature. I understand now why you are so anxious to find her.'

Michael's fury was so great that he had to stop himself from simply turning round and marching out of the classroom. Instead, he adjured himself sternly to count to ten, a maxim which his mother was always preaching. Anyway, it was no use flying off the handle and leaving the place without the information he so badly wanted. The wretched

253

woman had totally misjudged him, was happy to believe the worst of him, but explanations could come later. Right now, the important thing was to find out where his Ginny had gone. So he made no attempt at self-justification. Instead, he spoke with a calmness he was far from feeling. 'I'm afraid I don't know your name, miss, but I've told you mine. If you're goin' to abuse me, which I admit you've every right to do, I'd like to know your name, at least.'

For the first time there was some softening of her expression and he realised, with considerable surprise, that some men might even think her not bad-looking, though he was not one of them. He liked dark girls, gentle girls with sweet expressions, not sharp-tongued termagants who never let a feller get a word in edgeways, not even in their own defence. But she was speaking, answering; he had best be as nice as pie, else she would deliberately keep from him the information he needed.

'Well, Mr Gallagher, I'm surprised you don't know my name, since your daughter was my star pupil and, I like to think, very fond of me, as I was of her. You did say you'd received a number of letters? I got the impression that she did not know your address. Oh, and my name is Miss Derbyshire. Does that ring a bell?'

On firmer ground now, Michael shook his head. 'No, but it wouldn't. You misunderstood me, Miss Derbyshire. I told you I've writ a grosh o' letters, but I've only ever had one reply, and that was from the old . . . from Mrs Bennett. Ever since it arrived I've wondered whether her grandmother ever passed on any of me letters to Ginny. To own the truth, the old lady never did like me, didn't think me good enough for her daughter, so it were always

254

on the cards that she'd just chuck the letters in the fire, never hand 'em on to Ginny. That's one o' the reasons I've come searchin' for me daughter now,' he concluded, gazing earnestly at the pale, disapproving face before him. 'So if you could tell me where they're livin' I'll be on me way.'

'I can tell you nothing, Mr Gallagher,' Miss Derbyshire said crisply. 'For I don't have the foggiest notion. Virginia simply did not come back at the beginning of the winter term, but her grandmother—or likelier, I think, one of her uncles—had written to Miss Mackie, our headmistress, telling her that they were moving away, staying with a relative of some description, I believe she said.'

'O-oh,' Michael said. He told himself that she must know, she simply must, yet he did not think the teacher would stoop to telling lies, not deliberate lies, when it might be very much to Ginny's advantage to see her father. 'But—but she must be at school somewhere . . . couldn't you find out, Miss Derbyshire?'

The young woman looked pensively at him. 'I doubt that I could do so,' she said, after thinking it through for a long moment. 'But—forgive me—you must have known Virginia's relatives fairly well. Wouldn't it be quicker to find them? I know Virginia had at least one uncle in the neighbourhood, though I've a feeling he didn't live round here. She mentioned an Uncle George . . . or was it Joseph? Did you never meet him?'

'It was George, so it was,' Michael said, his brow lightening. 'D'you know where he lives?'

'I've no idea,' the teacher said briskly.

Michael gave her a cold look and turned towards the door. There was no longer any need to be

255

polite to the woman; she knew as little as he. 'Good afternoon, Miss Derbyshire.'

'Wait a moment!' Her voice, firm and commanding, brought his head round sharply. Had she thought of some clue, remembered a chance remark, perhaps?

'Yes? Was there some pal who might know where they've gone?'

'It isn't that. You still haven't told me, Mr Gallagher, just why you have decided to try to find Virginia after all these years. I think you owe me that much, at least.'

Michael was a patient man, and a fair one, but he simply did not see why he should tell this Miss Derbyshire anything at all. How had she helped him, for a start? She had said she didn't know where Ginny was and couldn't—or wouldn't—help him to find out. She had accused him of wanting the child only now she was old enough to be useful, and had not said a word about his generosity in sending money for his daughter's upkeep. It was high time, he felt, that he told high and mighty Miss Derbyshire a thing or two—and that would not include the strange events which had led him to think, for the first time in ten years, of his small daughter.

'Well, Mr Gallagher? I'm waiting.'

Michael turned back towards her. He was not a man much given to cutting speeches, but right now he felt entitled at least to defend himself. 'Then I'm afraid you will have to continue to wait,' he said, his tone reasonable. 'Because I've nothing more to say to you; I'm not one of your pupils, thank God.' He turned to the door once more.

Behind him, he heard the crash as she jumped to

256

her feet, knocking her chair over backwards. 'How dare you!' she gasped. 'Why, if I were a man ...'

Michael turned in the doorway. 'If you were a man you'd be nursin' a bloody nose be now,' he said grimly. 'Darin' to suggest that I'd use me own daughter like a little slave. If all I've done is speak frankly to you, then you've got off light, I'm tellin' you.' And before she could say a word, he was out of the door and slamming it behind him with a bang that echoed through the empty building like a thunderclap.

*   *   *

Mabel stood behind her desk, her fists clenched, literally trembling with rage. So that was Ginny's beloved father, who sent her money and had ignored her existence for ten long years! She had been all the more shocked to find the young man was Michael Gallagher because her first impression of him had been so favourable. He was tall and sturdily built, with a mop of thickly curling black hair and dark eyes which had seemed to look at her with gentleness and interest. He had a straight nose, very white teeth and a strongly cleft chin; in short, he was most girls' idea of an extremely handsome man.

She had thought so herself, had been admiring him as he walked towards them and had been pleasantly surprised by his deep voice and soft Irish brogue. Then, of course, he had told her his name and her admiration had fled. She had sent Sandy off home and had accompanied him to her empty classroom, honestly meaning to tell him how his child was being neglected. She had not meant to

257

flare up at him the way she had—not at first, anyway. But her temper had got the better of her, perhaps because he had shown interest neither in herself nor in Ginny. In fact, he had only wanted to know where he could find the child.

Sighing at her own hot temper, Mabel righted her chair and glanced around her classroom, finding her hands still unsteady. Quickly, she left the room and hurried along the corridor, half hoping, half fearing that she would catch him up. If she did so, she knew she should apologise for treating him like a recalcitrant pupil, for that was what she had done. Her indignation over his neglect of her favourite pupil had swamped common courtesy and she felt ashamed of the way she had behaved. But he had been rude, really rude, and she dreaded having to face him again, so was relieved when she crossed the playground and turned towards her lodgings and saw no tall figure ahead of her, no one waiting.

As she put her key into the lock, she told herself that she had behaved badly and decided, in fairness to Ginny, to do a little searching on her own account. If she could find Ginny, she would contact Michael Gallagher and . . .

With her foot already on the stairs, she stopped short, dismayed. She had been so eager to embarrass him, cut him down to size, that she had completely forgotten to ask for his address.

* * *

Michael set off for his lodgings, still fuming over the sheer impudence of the woman. She had attacked him without reason, apparently taking a

258

dislike to him on sight, and she had been completely useless to him. He hoped he would never set eyes on her again and, indeed, probably would not do so, since he could not simply abandon the farm where his parents needed his help so badly. Today was Tuesday; he would remain in the city and continue his search all day tomorrow but would quit it on the first ferry to leave on Thursday.

Reaching his lodgings, Michael went straight to the landlady to inform her that he would stay for one more night.

The following day was spent in a completely fruitless search. That night, when he got back to his lodgings and went to his own room, he slumped on to his bed, feeling despair creep over him. No one at any of the schools he had visited that day had heard of Virginia Bennett; she seemed to have disappeared. He was bone weary, hating the city he had once loved so well and eager to return to Kerry. Yet despite his fatigue, he kept re-enacting in his own mind the scene between himself and Miss Derbyshire. Had he been less than fair to the woman? When he thought about it, she had heard only of his negligence, his apparent indifference to Ginny's welfare, so, in a way, she had a right to her indignation. Shamingly, because she had seemed so antagonistic, he had deliberately tried to paint a brighter picture of himself and his actions by letting her assume that he had written regularly for many years, whereas, in fact, he had never written until the previous summer. And he supposed, grudgingly, that it was not so odd for Miss Derbyshire to leap to the conclusion that he had waited to contact Ginny until she reached an age when she could be useful.

Sighing, he lay down on his bed, linked his hands behind his head and gazed broodingly up at the stained ceiling. Perhaps he should have gone back to the school and apologised, explained how his eyes had been opened to the possibility that Ginny might not be a happy, well-loved child. But he found that the idea stuck in his craw. He still felt, hotly, that Miss Derbyshire had prejudged him and had been extremely unfair. Why, she had not listened when he had tried to explain . . .

But you didn't try to explain, a tiny voice said inside his head. *Oh, I know she talked like a schoolteacher, but that's because she is one. You should have told her what happened in the African market . . . you should have remembered the promises you made.*

Michael felt the hair prickle erect on the nape of his neck. He had thought it was his conscience speaking but now he was beginning to think differently. From the start of his search, he had believed in his heart that Stella was with him, encouraging him to greater efforts, expecting him to find their daughter. Michael closed his eyes and immediately a picture of Stella as he had never seen her, smiling down at the babe in her arms, came into his head. He gasped, opening his eyes, and the picture of Stella fled. The little voice was still. But it had done its work.

Michael knew he must go back to the farm next day, but he would return to the city and if it meant bearding Miss Derbyshire in her den again, then he would do it. What was more, he would not hold back this time, but would prove to her that he wanted Ginny for her sake and not for his own.

And next time, he would spend longer here, search harder. He closed his eyes once more and though the picture did not reform and the small voice stayed silent, he spoke to Stella as though he knew she were in the room, attending to every word he said. 'Don't worry, acushla, me darlin' girl,' he said softly. 'I won't give up and I won't be beat. I've failed you all these years but now I'm keepin' me promise, so I am. I'll find our little girl and see her right if it's the last thing I do on this mortal earth.'

*   *   *

When Michael arrived home to announce to his parents that he had not found Ginny, Maeve immediately began to plan a campaign whose goal was to discover her granddaughter and bring her back to Headland Farm.

'It's no use you sayin' that the child probably never received your letters,' she said crossly. 'They've been getting the money all right or I'm pretty sure there would have been more than one letter once Granny Bennett knew she could write to the shipping office. She's obviously made some arrangement to have her post delivered to wherever she's living now. You give up too easily, son. You must write to the old lady and say you have to have Ginny's new address, or you'll stop sending her allowance. She'll let you have it all right, and then you can write to the child direct an' I'll be bound you'll get an answer just as soon as she can put pen to paper. Once you do, you can tell her all about the farm and suggest she comes to us for some of her summer holidays. No kid could resist an adventure like that. So just you sit down

261

right now, young Michael, and write to your little girl.'

Michael agreed that this was a good idea and sat down to start the letter immediately, feeling a surge of hope and anticipation. His mam's ideas always worked, and to his way of thinking this was her best yet.

His tongue protruding with effort, Michael began to write.

CHAPTER TEN

It was a mild, windy day in April, and the strong salt smell of the sea made Ginny feel lively and full of hope. As she came out of school, where she had spent another boring and useless day, she saw her cousins clustered around the school gates and remembered why she felt so cheerful; she was going to visit Aunt Mary in her canny house on the Scotland Road, taking the kids with her. Aunt Amy would be cleaning at the big insurance offices until eight or nine that evening. The Franklins might have wondered where she had gone, but she knew they were going to visit an aunt, straight after work, so she was safe enough from them.

She did not often visit Aunt Mary and Uncle George, for it was a long walk from Seaforth to the Scotland Road. But she had decided she really ought to try to have a word, on the quiet like, with her aunt.

Ginny knew that Aunt Mary would be delighted to see her nieces and would immediately produce her stock of shortbread biscuits and lemonade. She would sit the kids in her nice big kitchen, give them jigsaws and puzzles to play with and the biscuits and lemonade to eat and drink, and then she would turn her attention to Ginny and ask how the family in Schubert Street were getting along.

And what exactly should I say, Ginny thought, as she began to round up her small charges and head towards Crosby Road South. For recently, to her great dismay, she had discovered something which she was not supposed to know.

As they made their way towards the Scotland Road, she pondered on what had happened when Mrs Franklin had sent her on an errand on the previous Friday evening. Mrs Franklin was clever with her needle and did embroidery for a certain dressmaker in Crosby. She rather enjoyed the work since she was given all the materials necessary, and all the silks and cottons too. The dressmaker would send her a large parcel of collars and cuffs with a letter telling Mrs Franklin which designs and colours to use. Mrs Franklin would do the work and despatch the finished products back to Crosby, usually using Norma to fetch and carry. But on this occasion, Norma had had a nasty cold and refused point blank to go. 'It ain't fair to ask when I'm poorly,' she whined. 'Make Belle do it, or send Ginger—yes, why not? She never gets sent further than the end o' the road . . . make her go, Mam.'

It had been a chilly evening, with a gale blowing off the sea, which made it impossible for Ginny to suggest that one of the younger children might run the message. Instead, she had looked hopefully at Mrs Franklin, whereupon that lady blew her nose vigorously, remarking thickly that she had caught Norma's cold and didn't mean to get pneumonia by

263

going out after dark.

Aunt Amy, rolling out pastry for one of her famous meat and potato pies, had looked up. 'You've gorra choice, chuck,' she had said breezily. 'You can tek me sister's 'broidery to Crosby—I'll give you a penny for the bus 'cos you can't skip a lecky when you've a parcel of delicate stuff in your arms—or you can get me big marketing basket and take these pies up to Sample's for bakin'. You'll have to go back again an' fetch 'em when they're cooked, o' course, so tek your choice.'

Listening to the howl of the gale outside, Ginny had decided to take the embroidery. It was not terribly heavy and it would mean a bus ride, which was infinitely preferable to slogging all the way to Sample's and having to hang about in the windy street until her aunt's pies were cooked. Of course she could return to Schubert Street and then go back to Sample's, but that would double the journey.

'I'll tek the embroidery,' she had said. 'But who's goin' to tek the pies?'

'I'll give Totty Barnes, what lives down the road, a big piece o' one of the pies when they's baked an' she'll go like a shot,' Aunt Amy had said. Ginny knew Totty, knew she would be glad of a piece of pie since her father was out of work and food was hard to come by. She reflected, rather smugly, that she, Ginny, would have a share of the pie wherever she went, but still looked hopefully at Mrs Franklin. Surely, if her aunt was prepared to pay Totty to take the pies to the baker, then Mrs Franklin should be prepared to shell out for her own errand?

Mrs Franklin had caught her eye and grinned

suddenly. 'You can have a penny for chips,' she said gruffly. 'Only you'll have to go out again to get 'em 'cos I don't want greasy fingers on me embroidery —understand?'

Ginny had understood. Mrs Franklin was well paid for her embroidery but the work—and the condition of the collars and cuffs—had to be immaculate or she would lose the dressmaker's patronage. So she had taken the proffered penny and battled her way to the bus stop in the teeth of the gale, glad to board the first vehicle, Crosby bound. The bus had drawn to a halt in what she took to be Crosby town centre, where all the shops were firmly shut. She had asked directions from a friendly woman who told her that she was not far from her destination, and presently she saw a public house from whose doors light streamed. As she reached it, the doors opened and a man and woman came out. Ginny glanced at them casually, then turned hastily away. It was her Uncle Lewis and he had an arm round a plump, jolly-looking blonde, whose bright green dress showed in the opening of her dark coat.

Ginny had scarcely believed her eyes; it was Friday evening so Uncle Lewis ought to be miles away, possibly even in Ireland, doing his weekend job. She knew he had to stay away over the weekends because his work took him a great way from Seaforth . . . but Crosby wasn't a great way from anywhere, so what on earth was he doing here, when he could have been cosily at home?

The couple had passed Ginny without seeing her, the woman remarking contentedly: 'It's been a grand evening, Lewis. I misremember when I've enjoyed meself more. Fridays is the high spot of me

265

week—I just wish your work didn't take you abroad once the weekend's over.'

Uncle Lewis had chuckled. 'Aye, you can't have enough of a good thing, Dolly,' he had said. 'But we don't have the sort of money to go out drinkin' all weekend . . .'

His voice had been lost in the howl of the gale and Ginny realised they were heading in the direction which she herself would be taking, so she had followed them. The streets were not well lit and she found herself flitting from shadow to shadow listening to their upraised voices as they fought to be heard above the wind. They were passing down a street of small terraced houses and Ginny was just beginning to think the whole thing unimportant—she knew married men occasionally did have friends of the opposite sex, and Uncle Lewis was very attractive—when the couple climbed the steps of one particular house and Uncle Lewis produced a key with which he opened the front door. As he did so, a fair haired child had come running up the hallway and cast itself, ecstatically, at her uncle's legs. 'Daddy, Daddy, tell Stevie I'm allowed to play with the cat,' the child had shouted. 'He's always bossin' me about when you ain't home. I loves the cat, I does.'

Ginny had felt stunned. Was it possible that Uncle Lewis was leading a double life, that he had a young, yellow-headed wife in Crosby and an older, dark-haired one—her Aunt Amy—in Seaforth? Clearly, Uncle Lewis had accepted the child's greeting and he had gone into the house and shut the door behind him as though it was his own home. For a moment, Ginny had simply stood in the shadows, staring across at the house. Then she had

266

given herself a shake and remembered her errand. She had made her way to the dressmaker's establishment, handed over the parcel of completed embroidery at the door and had taken the bundle of work still to be done. 'Got the money for your bus fare home?' the dressmaker had asked. 'But you ain't one of Mrs Franklin's girls so I s'pose you've been well paid for this evening's work already?'

'She give me a penny for chips and me aunt give me me bus fare,' Ginny had said, raising her voice to combat the howl of the wind. 'But I ain't to buy the chips till I've been home again so's not to put greasy fingerprints on the stuff.'

The woman had tutted, and given Ginny a silver threepenny piece. 'You can spend that tiddler on sweets, but not tonight, tomorrer,' she had said kindly. She had looked curiously at her young visitor. 'You reminds me of someone . . . it's that hair. I knew a gal once . . .' But the gale had whipped the words out of her mouth and she had stepped back into the shelter of the hallway.

Ginny had thanked her profusely for the money and told her that though she was not one of Mrs Franklin's girls, her Aunt Amy and Mrs Franklin were sisters. She thought such magnificent generosity deserved an explanation for it was not often that so much money was paid for running a message. With Mrs Franklin's penny, she now had fourpence, and could have splashed out on a great many sweets, had she desired to do so. Aunt Amy's cooking, however, and the generous helpings she dished out, meant that Ginny was rarely hungry now so that sweets, though still a treat, could be bought a few at a time whenever the fancy took her.

For some time now, Ginny had begun to realise that despite the crowded house and her dislike of her new school, she was both better off and happier than she had been in Victoria Court. Because she was expected to look after the younger children, she was able to indulge in many of the games she had previously only been able to watch others playing, since in Victoria Court all the messages and household chores had fallen on her shoulders. Now, provided she kept an eye on the young ones, she was able to take a turn at skipping, hopscotch, cherry-wobs or cat's cradle. This meant that she did not wish to upset the apple cart in any way, and if she began tale-clatting about Uncle Lew it would undoubtedly change the even tempo of life in Schubert Street. Yet to hold her tongue, when Aunt Amy worked so hard—apparently in order to support another woman and her children—seemed wrong too.

Presently, she had climbed aboard a bus and, no longer battling with the gale, had time in which to think about what she had seen and decide what best to do about it. All the way back to Seaforth, she had mulled over Uncle Lewis's strange behaviour. She could not possibly say anything to Aunt Amy or Mrs Franklin, but she honestly felt it was her duty to tell someone. If her uncle was keeping two families, then of course it was important for Aunt Amy to have the money which Mrs Franklin and her daughters paid to her at the end of each week, and this answered a question which had been niggling at Ginny's mind for some time: why Mrs Franklin and the girls stayed in Aunt Amy's house when surely, by now, they could have rented a place of their own. But if Aunt Amy needed the money, Ginny guessed that family feeling would keep the Franklins in Schubert Street until times were easier.

By the end of the journey, Ginny had made up her mind that she would swear Aunt Mary to secrecy and then describe to her what she had seen. Her aunt was a sensible and kind-hearted woman; she would advise Ginny what she should do.

Having made her decision, it had occurred to Ginny to wonder how much of her uncle's doings was known to Aunt Amy, for the older woman was not slow-witted, far from it. She must have a fair idea of what her husband earned, which meant she must realise that he brought home only a percentage of his wages. Would that fact alone not make her suspicious? Aunt Amy had said her husband had a really good job and, if she thought he earned at weekends, surely she must wonder where the rest of the money went.

By the time she had reached Schubert Street, however, Ginny had remembered how some of the wives in Victoria Court had grumbled that 'The old feller drinks half his money and gambles the rest, which is why I has to work, no matter that I've got half a dozen kids to look out for.' Aunt Amy probably took it for granted that Uncle Lewis spent the money on himself. She knew he liked good clothes and always dressed impeccably, went to a good barber to be shaved each day and generally took care of himself.

As she had entered the house on Friday evening, thankful to be out of the biting wind, and smelled the rich aroma of the meat and potato pie, Ginny had decided that at least Uncle Lewis was not wasting his money. It had seemed, to her, very

269

much better that a feller should feed two families rather than pour bevvies down his own throat or gamble his cash away on the horses or in a Pitch and Toss school. As she had settled down at the kitchen table to eat the meal that Aunt Amy had kept hot for her, she had decided that she would definitely visit Aunt Mary as soon as it could be arranged.

Having made up her mind on this point, she had finished her meal and gone to bed without having said a word on the subject to anyone.

'Ginny! Ginny, I thought you said we was goin' to see Aunt Mary, but you've just walked straight past her canny house, an' oh, I do love seein' Aunt Mary, 'cos she gives us nice things an' lets us play games wi' her kids. You promised, you did, you know you did!' It was Ivy, tugging resentfully at her cousin's arm, and Ginny realised, with some surprise, that the younger girl was right. She had indeed marched straight past the canny house whilst her mind was still occupied with what had happened in Crosby the previous week.

'Oh, queen, I'm so sorry,' she said repentantly, clapping a hand to her forehead. 'I were that engrossed in me own thoughts, I clean forgot where I were goin'.' She had turned on her heel and retraced her steps. Ruthie's legs were getting tired and she was dragging on Ginny's arm and Ginny guessed the child would be glad enough to sit down in Aunt Mary's kitchen after her long walk; all the children must be quite hungry for they usually went straight home after school and had bread and jam, or a piece of plain cake if their mother had baked one.

Ginny shepherded the children through the

270

canny house, ducking under the long counter where the food was served. Aunt Mary greeted them kindly, for it was a quiet time of day, and accompanied them into the kitchen.

'Where's Gran?' Ginny asked curiously, glancing around her. The kitchen was empty, save for Polly, who sat meekly in a corner, doing a jigsaw on a wooden tray balanced across her small knees. Despite her disabilities, the child was fitting in the pieces both quickly and accurately and looked up and smiled vaguely in the direction of her cousins as they came tumbling into the room. Polly wore thick pebble glasses which made her eyes look enormous, but even so her sight was so poor that Ginny guessed she was putting in the pieces of the jigsaw more by touch than by what she could see of them.

'Didn't you see your gran as you came through?' Aunt Mary said. 'She's sittin' at a table in the corner, gossipin' with a couple o' pals. And she's peelin' a big barrel o' spuds at the same time.'

Ginny went back and peered into the canny house. Sure enough, there was Gran, actually doing something for a change. She had not noticed Ginny but continued to work and to talk to the two old shawlies at her table, but it occurred to Ginny at once that Granny Bennett looked healthier and happier than she had ever seen her.

Ginny turned back to the kitchen and beamed at Aunt Mary. 'She looks grand, an' real happy, so I won't disturb her,' she said. 'Where's the twins, Aunt Mary?'

'They're playin' out,' Aunt Mary replied. She turned to Ginny's charges. 'Come up to the table, kids, and I'll get you your teas.' She began swiftly

271

placing various ingredients on the sideboard. 'Well, this *is* a nice surprise! It isn't often we see you down this way, but your mam's workin' late tonight, I dare say.' She turned to Ginny. 'Or are you doin' messages down the Scottie for your Aunt Amy? Ivy, run an' fetch your cousins, there's a good gal, then you can all have your teas together.'

Ivy, who had been standing by Polly, stroking the younger girl's hair and chattering away to her, promptly rushed out of the kitchen, and Aunt Mary took the tray from Polly's knees, picked the child up and sat her in a chair by the table. Ginny noticed that the chair was the only one with arms and that the arms kept Polly securely in position, for she knew that as a result of a serious illness at birth, Polly could not walk unaided and was usually taken around in a converted pushchair. She also knew that Polly was bright as a button, knowing a great many books by heart when Aunt Mary had only read them to her a couple of times. Because of her disabilities, she did not attend school, but despite the canny house and all her other responsibilities Aunt Mary put aside a period each day during which she was teaching Polly all sorts of things, so that the child was always happily occupied and had little time to brood on her situation.

With tea on the table and the younger children eating and chattering, Aunt Mary gestured to Ginny, drawing her to one end of the kitchen where it was quieter. 'Everything all right at home, queen? Only, as I said earlier, it ain't often that you bring the whole fambly down this way and it were clear from the start you'd not come to see your gran! Amy's a good woman, hard-workin' an' that,

272

but no one could call her easy and that sister o' hers . . .' She shook her head and clicked her tongue disapprovingly. 'Well, least said, soonest mended, I always say. But if there's anything I can do . . .'

'I—I rather wanted a word wi' you,' Ginny said hesitantly. 'There's something I think you mebbe oughta know, something I found out by accident . . .'

Aunt Mary looked shrewdly at Ginny's flushed face. 'Sometimes, something you find out by accident is best kept to yourself, best forgotten in fact,' she remarked. 'Just think on, queen. If you saw someone cheatin' in a school examination, would you feel it your duty to tell the teacher?'

Ginny shook her head; she had no need to even consider, she knew very well what her reaction would be. She might disapprove strongly, she might say something to the child in question, but she would never, never tell a teacher. Clearly, Aunt Mary could read her reaction in her face for she smiled and patted Ginny's shoulder.

'There you are, then. You'd not tell on a pal, you wouldn't even tell on someone you dislike, if you're honest. You're fond of your Uncle Lew and Aunt Amy, aren't you? Well, you're right to be fond of them, and if you can't confide in them, it's gorra be somethin' connected wi' one of them, I suppose.' She sighed gustily. 'It'll be Lew, I reckon, still up to his old tricks.' Ginny began to speak but her aunt shook her head. 'No, no, you don't have to tell me, because if it were something you aren't meant to know, then I guess it applies to me and George as well. I dare say, though, queen, that every married couple have their disagreements from time to time and mebbe someone marches out an' goes to the

273

pub, and does somethin' daft. That's married life, gal, and married life is something you've had no experience of, right? So just you put whatever you saw, or heard, right out of your head an' gerron with your own life. That's my advice, chuck. All men are weak, an' if a woman makes up to 'em when they's had a bit of a barney at home . . . well, it don't mean a thing, it'll be forgot by next day— unless someone tale-clats an' makes trouble. See what I mean?'

Ginny nodded slowly, relief washing over her. So Aunt Mary knew what Uncle Lew was up to and was advising Ginny to do just what she realised she most wanted to do; mind her own business and keep quiet. 'All right then, I'll keep me gob shut.'

Aunt Mary nodded, satisfied, then turned anxiously back to her niece. 'I think I'm readin' you right, chuck, but mebbe I'm not, mebbe it's somethin' different. It—it ain't nothin' *illegal*, is it?' she hissed beneath her breath. 'I mean nothin' that would get the scuffers a-knockin' on the door?'

Once more, Ginny did not even need to think about it. 'No, it's nothing illegal, just—just a bit unusual and like what you said,' she assured her aunt, choosing her words with care. 'Something Uncle George would never do,' she added.

A look of complete comprehension passed over her aunt's face. 'Oh, I *see*,' she breathed. 'I've always known Lew was a great one for the judies when he were in the Navy . . . oh, don't you worry your head over that, queen; it don't mean a bleedin' thing.'

*　　　*　　　*

274

At home once more in Schubert Street, tucked up in bed with her cousin Ivy's back snug against her own, Ginny decided that she was glad she had not told on Uncle Lewis. After all, what harm was he doing? And though Aunt Amy seemed to be neither warm nor loving, she was a good deal better than Gran had been. She expected a great deal of her niece, taking it for granted that she would be at her beck and call twenty-four hours a day, but she fed all her family, including Ginny, extremely well, and saw that she was respectably dressed and shod. Ginny often thought, wistfully, of the beautiful shoes which were still, presumably, in the wardrobe at the Waits' flat in Washington Street. Sometimes she worried that she might outgrow them before she was able to wear them again, but she did not intend to bring them back to Seaforth. Her aunt would think them far too fine for her niece and would probably put them away for Ivy to wear when she was old enough. Aunt Amy provided all the children with plimsolls for school and ugly old boots for winter wear, and now that she came to think of it, Ginny realised that no one in her present school wore shoes as good as those she had left behind. But one day she meant to get back to the Rathbone Street school and her dear Miss Derbyshire, and when she did she would need the shoes again. She had no idea how she was to perform this miracle but remembered how impossible she had once thought it that she should be able to go to school in respectable shoes. Surely, if she was prepared to walk all the way from Seaforth to Rathbone Street, she could find someone willing to take charge of her young cousins to and from school. There were girls in her

275

own class, friendly, pleasant girls, who looked after their younger brothers and sisters. If she managed to earn some money and could offer to pay them, surely one of those girls would be willing to give an eye to the young Bennetts.

Despite her hopes, she had never been able to get back to Rathbone Street on a Saturday, so that she might join Danny at the rag skips, and so had not been able to earn any real money. She had thought that if she woke at the crack of dawn and sneaked down the stairs, she might elude both her cousins and her aunt, but this had not proved to be the case. She had tried it twice; the first time, the Bennetts' dog, Rufus, a skinny mongrel with so much hair that he looked like an animated hearthrug, had bounded to his feet, yelping with delight. The row had brought Uncle Lewis down, hair on end, a poker in his hand, convinced that they had burglars. She explained, rather lamely, that she needed to go to the lavvy, but Uncle Lewis had reminded her that there were chamber pots under each bed and advised her, curtly, to make use of them rather than disturb the whole house.

That had been appallingly bad luck since Uncle Lewis was almost never at home at weekends; she now knew the reason for his absence and where he went, though she had not done so at the time. He seldom came in for a meal on Friday evening and did not return until late on Sunday. Ginny had known that he had a really lucrative job—he was chief buyer for a firm which manufactured yachts, cruisers and the like, for the holiday market—and thought it just her luck that he should have been at home on that particular Saturday.

She had returned to her bed, red-faced, and next

time she tried it, had thought to bribe Rufus with a bone. However, Rufus's delight over the bone had been almost as noisy as his reaction to her sudden appearance crossing the kitchen, and this time it had been her aunt who had descended the stairs, which meant that Ginny had received a clack round the ear which made her head spin. Clearly, escape in the early hours was out of the question, and the worst of it was, she had had no opportunity to tell her pal that she would not be joining him.

Ivy turned over in bed, pushing the covers impatiently down to waist level, for the night was warm. Ginny sighed to herself and burrowed her face into her thin flock pillow. Now that the evenings were growing lighter, she thought it might soon be possible to visit her old haunts and explain the circumstances of her new life to the Waits and to Danny. Her aunt had many tasks for her but she was not ungenerous; when Ginny came in, staggering beneath the weight of a large canvas marketing bag, they would check the contents together on the kitchen table and Ginny would hand over whatever change she still had. Invariably, Aunt Amy would push a copper or two back across the table, saying: 'Buy yourself some toffee or a bag o' sherbet. You done awright, queen.'

Such praise was delightful to Ginny, quite as welcome as the pennies, and these were not spent on sweets but carefully saved up. When she first came to Schubert Street, she had hidden the money in a hole in the mattress on her side of the bed, but soon realised that this was not necessary. On one occasion, when she and Ivy were turning the mattress, a penny fell out and rolled across the floor and Ivy, pursuing it, gave her big cousin a reproachful look. 'Why d'you put money in our mattress, Ginny?' she asked plaintively. 'Mam will give you a tin if you ask—haven't you seen our tins on the window sill? Us puts our money away so as we can go to the seaside, and the penny rush on Sat'days, and have some money to buy presents with, birthdays and Christmas. And sweeties, of course,' she had finished.

Ginny had noticed the tins on the window sill. One had originally contained baked beans, another sardines, and a third, cough drops. Ivy had pointed proudly at the baked bean tin. 'Mine's the beans,' she had announced. 'Ruthie's is sardines, 'cos you don't get much money when you're only four, and Millie's is the cough drops. We gerra Sat'day penny, o' course, but me and Millie has ha'pennies and farthings sometimes when we get messages or when we're 'specially good.' She had turned large blue eyes up to her cousin's face. 'Ask Mam to give you a tin.'

Ginny had accordingly asked and been given an old tobacco tin and a quizzical glance from Aunt Amy's small, bright eyes. 'You're learnin', queen,' she had said, quite gently for her. 'There's no thievery in this house; your money's as safe in that tin as if it were the Bank of England.'

Ginny had felt her cheeks burn. 'I know, Ivy told me,' she had muttered. 'But wi' Granny Bennett . . . well, it were different. There weren't nowhere in the house that she'd not search.'

Aunt Amy had nodded grimly. 'Aye, an' well I know it. I feel downright sorry for poor Mary. There's the money she takes in the canny house as well as your Uncle George's wages which have to be—to be kept safe. Still, the old gal's got her

278

pension, and knowin' George, he won't interfere wi' how she spends it.'

Ivy turned over restlessly once more, bringing Ginny's mind abruptly back to the present. It still puzzled her how Uncle Lewis explained away the fact that despite having a well-paid job, his wife only received a modicum of his wages, or so Ginny imagined. She decided that at the very next opportunity she would try to find out a bit more about the household finances. It might actually be possible to ask Aunt Amy outright about her own father's contribution. She had noticed that Aunt Amy was almost easy-going when she was doing some simple domestic task, such as preparing cake mix to carry up to the baker or making drop scones on the hot griddle. Yes, next time her aunt was in a really good mood, she would see what she could find out.

Satisfied, Ginny relaxed once more and was soon asleep.

*   *   *

'Here you are, Aunt Amy . . . by golly, but this bag's heavy.' Ginny heaved the big marketing bag on to the kitchen table and then took the packages from Ivy's arms and set them down beside the bag. 'I wish we had a pram; although Ruthie walks as far as she can, she's only got little legs and I do have to carry her from time to time. Haven't you ever thought of getting one? My pal, Danny, back in Victoria Court, shoves the younger ones into this big old pram and then piles the messages round 'em.'

It was a warm day and Ginny mopped at her

279

brow with the back of her hand, then began to empty the marketing bag, chanting out the list of contents as she did so. 'Ten pounds of flour, two pounds o' raisins, two pounds o' currants and a five pound slab of margarine.'

Her aunt, checking the shopping and the prices with her, said musingly: 'Aye, a lorra folk I know use a pram and I must say when the messages is heavy, like today, you could do wi' some help. You didn't think to ask Norma to go along, or Belle?'

'They're in bed still,' Ginny said briefly. She did not add that the last thing she wanted was Norma's spiteful and grudging company. 'You might think about a pram, Aunt Amy; you can pick one up cheap at Paddy's Market, any day o' the week.' She looked curiously at her aunt, then decided that the moment was ripe. 'You could use some o' me dad's money; I'm sure he wouldn't mind. Now that I know his address I could write and ask him, if you wanted.'

Aunt Amy laughed, sounding genuinely amused. She must have realised, Ginny thought, that her niece still did not know exactly what her father's contribution was, and was curious. She must also have realised that Ginny could not possibly ask such a question herself, though she knew that father and daughter now corresponded quite regularly.

'Well, I'll think about it, have a word wi' your Uncle Lewis,' Aunt Amy said.

'Thanks, Aunt,' Ginny said demurely. 'Uncle Lewis has got a real good job, hasn't he? I've heard you say so, many a time. I expect he gets good wages as well, doesn't he?'

Her aunt glanced round the kitchen but the

room was empty save for Ginny and herself. 'You're sharp as a monkey, Ginny Bennett,' she said, almost approvingly. 'You've lived wi' us a fair while now, more 'n four months, and you're beginnin' to wonder why we lives squashed into this house, considerin' the money we've got comin' in.' She had been rolling out pastry but now she stopped work and looked Ginny straight in the eye. 'Can you keep a secret, queen?'

'Yes, I'm sure I can,' Ginny said readily. She had kept Uncle Lew's secret, hadn't she? 'Wharris it, Aunt Amy?'

'The fact is, chuck, I were a country girl before I married your uncle and I've always hankered after livin' in the country again, so we're savin' up, your uncle and me. That's why he works away, weekends. I miss him, o' course I does, but it's in a good cause.'

'Gosh,' Ginny breathed. 'I'd like to live in the country an' all, Aunt Amy. As you know, my daddy's got a farm in Ireland so I've read up on it quite a lot. But would the rent be so much more than this house costs? And how would me uncle get to his work? And there's your work too; how would you manage, eh?'

Her aunt smiled a trifle grimly and began to line a tin with pastry and to pour golden syrup and breadcrumbs into it. 'That's the whole point, chuck,' she said. 'What we're after ain't just a house in the country, it's a farm . . . well, I suppose it's more like a smallholding . . . which your uncle's had his eye on for many a long day. We wouldn't need to work outside o' the place because farmin' is a full time job. I'd have charge o' the fowls, we'd keep pigs, goats, cows . . . and there'd be plantin'

281

out crops such as corn an' barley. It 'ud be hard work, I don't deny that, but we'd be workin' for ourselves, d'you see? We wouldn't need to leave the place, though at first Lew might have to keep on his weekend job, just until we've got the farm sorted out.'

'It sounds wonderful,' Ginny breathed. 'Would you rent it, Aunt Amy?'

'Normally we'd rent, that stands to reason, but this place has been abandoned—the old couple what owned it died eighteen months back—so it's on the market. It ain't a big enough acreage for most folk but it 'ud suit me and your uncle down to the ground.'

'I say! But how long will it take you to save up enough money?' Ginny asked breathlessly. Her aunt's exciting news had put all other worries out of her head. 'I'd dearly love to live on a farm, wi' pigs and cows and that. So is that why Belle and Norma and their mam live wi' you, Aunt? And when you and me uncle get the farm, will the Franklins come too?'

'No, they'll be stayin' here. Ellen will take over the rent of the place and she means to let rooms, 'cos the three of 'em, all bein' female, can share the room Uncle Lew an' meself has now an' let out the others for a decent rent.' Aunt Amy had recently bought a contraption called a camp oven which could be suspended over the fire and in which one could bake cakes, pies and so on, provided one kept a careful eye on them, turning them if a side browned too quickly. Now, she took her treacle tarts, placed them in this contraption, and turned back to her niece. 'So you see, there's a reason behind everything we're doin',' she said with a

282

touch of complacence. 'Ellen's stayin' in this house because she don't want to see the landlord rentin' it to someone else an' I purrup wi' your uncle bein' away weekends 'cos the money's goin' towards our new life. Gerrit?'

'Yes, I understand a lot more now, Aunt,' Ginny said. 'Will—will it be long before you can afford to buy the place you've got your eye on, d'you think?'

Her aunt shrugged. 'That's your Uncle Lew's business, queen. He's waitin' till the price is right. The farm's a long way from here—it's over the border, into Wales—which means it's cheaper, so you never know. Every time he comes home, I look at him and he gives a little shake o' the head so I know it ain't yet awhile. But I'm content to wait 'cos I know we're headin' in the right direction. An' now let's gerron with gettin' dinner ready or the kids will be comin' in an' not so much as a spud cooked.'

It was not until she was in bed that night that Ginny had the leisure to think over what her aunt had told her. She had been carried away by the thought of living on a farm in Wales because she felt that it would be a much pleasanter life than the one she now lived. She thought a small village school would suit her a good deal better than the one she now attended, and, as she had told her aunt, she had now started reading books about farming from the Seaforth library in Crescent Road, so that if her father ever came for her, she might be useful.

But of course, if Uncle Lewis was using his spare money to keep his Crosby family, then the farm was no more than a cheap way of keeping Aunt Amy quiet and this was wickedly unfair. She knew her aunt frequently handed at least a portion of her own wages to Uncle Lewis to put in the Post Office, and she felt furious at the thought that this money, too, could be being misappropriated.

At first, she had not liked her aunt at all, much preferring friendly, easy-going Uncle Lewis, but as time went on she had begun to appreciate her aunt's many good qualities. She did not see why Uncle Lewis should get away with his deception and wondered, again, why Aunt Mary, who had appeared to know all about it, had seemed to consider it of no importance.

She was still undecided whether it was any of her business when she saw the boy getting off the bus. She had been going, attended by the two older Bennett children, to the Broadway Cinema on the Stanley Road. The Saturday rush usually included a comic film and quite often a western, but on this occasion it was to be the adventures of 'Rin Tin Tin'. She and Ivy were discussing the marvels the dog could perform when a bus pulled up beside them and a number of people got off. One of these was a boy of twelve or so, holding a child of four or five by the hand, and one look at the older boy's face made Ginny stop in her tracks. He had blond wavy hair, very blue eyes and a cleft chin. For a moment, she thought she knew him, then realised he was a stranger but must bear a strong resemblance to someone she knew, or had known once. She was still staring at him when the younger boy spoke. 'If we's goin' to see the fillum, where's the sweeties Mammy said I could have?' he asked aggrievedly. 'Don't you be mean to me, Stevie Bennett, or I'll tell Mammy when we get home and she'll gi' you a good clack.'

284

Ginny gasped; she could not help it. All of a sudden, a number of things clicked into place. The boy's resemblance was to Uncle Lew and since his surname was Bennett it seemed likely, too, that he and the small boy were the people Uncle Lew had been visiting when she had seen him in Crosby a few weeks earlier. Ginny fell into step behind them, listening intently. Was it possible that these boys were actually some sort of cousin, that Uncle Lew had just been visiting them as an uncle might? But she remembered the little lad calling him 'Daddy', and also the affectionate way in which he had hugged the plump blonde woman. What was more, she had never heard of any Bennett relations living in Crosby. But the younger boy was speaking again, and this time Ginny realised that she recognised the petulant whine of his voice.

'Where's the sweeties, I say?' he said querulously. 'Daddy give us money for sweeties, you know he did.'

'I'm goin' to buy you some sweeties when we reach the shop near the Broadway,' the older boy said patiently. 'You're a spoiled brat, Roly, but I'll buy you some anyway. And when we get in the picture house, you're not to start whining that you're bored or that you want the lavvy, understand?'

Ginny now turned her attention to Roly. He was not particularly like his brother, save that both were fair and blue-eyed, but he was, she realised, very like Ruthie. The likeness, Ginny concluded, was in their features.

Ginny and her small cousins were now on a level with the two boys, as if about to pass them, and Ginny was just wondering whether she could start a

285

conversation when Ivy piped up, reaching out to tug at the bigger boy's sleeve as she did so. 'Hoy, mister, if you're going to buy the kid sweets, why don't you come wi' us? Mrs Butler across the road on the corner of Malvern Road sells the best taffy in Liverpool and you gets a great big slab, enough to last right through the Sat'day rush, for a ha'penny. We'll show you where she is, won't we, Ginny?'

After that it was easy. The five of them strolled along the pavement together and bought slabs of toffee at Mrs Butler's. Without having to ask too many questions, Ginny learned that Stevie and Roly did indeed live in Crosby, in the very street where Ginny had seen Uncle Lewis. Stevie—who preferred to be called Steve—explained that his mother worked in a factory during the week so he had to keep an eye out for Roly and that his father was a travelling salesman, who was only ever home weekends. 'Me dad's savin' up so's we can buy a little farm in the country,' he said confidingly. 'Me mam were a country girl afore the war but then she wanted to do her bit so she took a job in a munitions factory in Liverpool and that's where she met our dad. He were in the Navy. Because he ain't home much, he an' Mam usually have a day out on a Sat'day, so I get to take care of Roly all day long,' he explained rather gloomily. 'Roly's awful spoiled. He'll have a trantrum if his will is crossed, I can tell you, so me pals don't want him taggin' along with them, which is why I'm bringin' him wi' me to the Sat'day rush, even though he'll be a blamin' nuisance once the fillum starts.'

'But there's a picture house in Crosby, isn't there?' Ginny said. Steve's mention of the farm had

286

brought cold certainty into her mind. Uncle Lewis was playing a deep game which she did not understand, but it worried her. 'Why don't you go there? It's a long way for you to come just to see a film, isn't it?'

'Yes, it's a fair way, but the picture house in Crosby is showing *Nanook of the North* and one of me pals told me that the Broadway is showing a Rin Tin Tin film this week and I think that dog's grand. If I ever had a dog, it 'ud be an Alsatian an' I'd train it to obey only me. Not that there's much chance of me having a dog until we get the farm,' he added sadly.

'Did—did you tell your dad you were comin' into Liverpool?' Ginny asked curiously. Her uncle must be well aware of the extraordinary likeness between this boy and himself, so surely would not encourage Steve to go to the very cinema his other family frequented. She gazed enquiringly up at Steve and was not at all surprised when he shook his head.

'No, I didn't tell him we were comin' into the city because he always says it's a dangerous place, full of lads what'll start a fight wi' a stranger at the drop of a hat. He and Mam think we've gone up to Southport . . . not that I told any lies,' he added virtuously. 'Because when I asked for money for a bus fare, they sort of took it for granted that we were goin' up to Southport for the day and Dad gave me a bob so's I can buy us dinners, an' off we came.'

Ivy glanced curiously up at Steve. Ginny's stomach tightened with apprehension—was Ivy about to remark that Steve reminded her of someone?—but Ivy only said in an awe-struck tone: 'A bob? Just for your dinners? Why, you could have

287

a penn'orth of chips each, and ice creams an' sweeties an' all sorts. Is you rich, Steve?'

Steve laughed and rumpled Ivy's smooth brown hair. 'No, we ain't, you little goose. When we're out for the whole day, we has our tea out an' all. Wharrabout you three, then? You've not said much about yourselves. Where do you live? Near here, I suppose.'

'No, we're from Seaforth,' Ivy told him. 'We likes Rin Tin Tin best, just like you do, but we walked, 'cos our mam can't go handin' out dosh for tram rides as well as toffee money. What'll you do when the fillum is over, Steve? There's a good chippie on the Stanley, or you could come back to Seaforth wi' us. We could play on the beach later, or go to Bowerdale Park.'

Ginny felt the hair on the back of her neck bristle with horror at this suggestion and was very relieved when Steve shook his head. 'Thanks, chuck, but I reckon Roly an' me will stroll on an' tek a look round the area; we doesn't often get the chance, you see.'

Soon after this, they reached the Broadway Cinema and went in together, but in the press of children surging down the cinema aisles they got separated. Ivy, who had taken a great liking to Steve, loudly bewailed the fact but Ginny, watching Steve's blond head bobbing down towards the front seats, could only feel glad. She had wanted to know about her uncle's other family but now she realised, with a sickening jolt, that she had learned a good deal more than she had bargained for. She had always thought that Uncle Lew's second family lived in Crosby but now she knew that this was not so; his second family lived in Seaforth, for how could it be otherwise? Steve was about twelve and Ivy, the eldest of Uncle Lew's Seaforth family, only eight.

*   *   *

Two days before the end of term, Ginny decided that she would simply have to skip classes and go back to the Rathbone Street school, otherwise she might not see Miss Derbyshire, since once the holidays started she supposed that the teacher would return to her own home, wherever that might be. Even at her present school, things usually became more relaxed as the summer holidays approached. They had Sports Day and various classes gave concerts, or performed small plays, and since the weather was fine Ginny found it easy to slip away directly after the register had been called. She had confided in Ivy, promising to return before school ended, and knew the younger girl would keep her secret. Indeed, Ivy had said immediately that there was no need for Ginny to hurry back since she was quite capable of getting her sisters home herself and making their tea.

Ivy was a good kid, Ginny reflected, hopping aboard the tram which would take her to Great George Street. She always did her share of the housework and was quite happy to accompany her cousin when doing the messages; very different from the Franklin girls, who spent most of their time plotting to get out of every possible task.

The tram drew up with a screech at Ginny's stop and she hopped down and set off towards the school, feeling warmth and excitement growing within her. Soon, now, she would be seeing her beloved Miss Derbyshire and explaining all the changes which had taken place in her life. She realised it would not be fair to mention her big problem to the teacher—that of her Uncle Lew's two families—but fully intended to tell her that she was now in touch with her father and actually meant to stay with him in Ireland during the summer holidays.

Immensely excited, she trotted across the playground and headed for Miss Derbyshire's classroom.

*   *   *

At the end of the school day, Miss Derbyshire took Ginny back to her own lodgings where she made them a cup of tea and a plate of sandwiches. She had very much enjoyed seeing her old pupil again after so long, and was much struck by the improvement in Ginny's appearance. The child looked neat, clean and well cared for, and though she was obviously very disappointed with the standard of education at her new school, she had become a member of the local free library and would, Miss Derbyshire thought, educate herself so far as she was able.

The news that she was now writing to her father was excellent and Miss Derbyshire was glad to be able to tell her former pupil that she herself had met Michael Gallagher.

'He's a very handsome man,' she told Ginny. 'He's got curly dark hair, very dark blue eyes and nice, even teeth. I was rather angry with him, at the time, for not getting in touch with you sooner, but looking back on it I realise I had no right to criticise him. I promised him that I'd try to find you and let him have your new address but I'm afraid though I did try asking round some of the local schools, I had no luck. I meant to start searching and asking questions in the holidays but since you are already in touch with him, that obviously won't be necessary.'

'It was awful kind of you to think of it,' Ginny said rather thickly, through a mouthful of sandwich. 'Oh, I can't wait to see me dad, Miss Derbyshire, though as I telled you, I'm ever so happy wi' me Aunt Amy an' Uncle Lew, an' me little cousins is grand kids. I miss Rathbone Street School and me pals in Victoria Court, but I'm beginnin' to see why me aunt and uncle didn't want me coming back here whenever I got the chance. I'm makin' pals where I am, you see, and I reckon that's better'n tryin' to get back here all the time. But fancy him bein' dark; I thought he'd be ginger, like me. Though now I come to think of it, me mam and Uncle George and the others have all got black hair, but me Uncle Lewis is yellow as a corn cob, so I s'pose you don't have to have the same colour hair as one of your parents.' She looked ruefully across at Miss Derbyshire. 'It were a bit of a shock to find that Danny and me old pal Annie had got together. They spend most of their time in and out of each other's houses, Annie was telling me when I spoke to her earlier, and they've all sorts of schemes goin'. They told me it were all right for me to join 'em during the holidays, but I reckon they were just being polite. And anyway, we—we may not be in Seaforth all that long. You see . . .'

Mabel watched her visitor's small, animated face, as she told her, in strict confidence, of Lew

Bennett's plans to buy a farm on the Welsh hillside and to move his family there just as soon as they were able to stock it. 'So you see, if I go back to Ireland wi' me dad and have to come back to England when the holidays is over, I'll bring a whole lot o' farming experience wi' me.' She looked shyly across at her companion. 'Only . . . only there's something I know, something I found out, which could mean Uncle Lew won't never get that farm. I've not said a word to Aunt Amy, nor to anyone else o' course, but—but I think mebbe I'll tell me dad when he comes for me in August.'

Mabel was only human and longed to ask the child just what she had discovered, but realised that it would be unfair to do so. Probably, Ginny had seen her uncle spending money on drink when he should have been saving up, or something similar. So instead of asking the question which hovered on the tip of her tongue, she said reassuringly: 'That's right, Ginny love, you tell your daddy about it. He's a sensible man and will advise you what's best to be done.'

Ginny gave her the sweet, three-cornered smile which lit up her small face and made her look almost pretty. 'I'll do that, Miss Derbyshire,' she said joyfully. 'It's grand to see you again, miss; if I can get away, I'll come again and let you know when my daddy's picking me up.' She looked a trifle anxious. 'You *did* like him, didn't you? You weren't just sayin' it to ease me mind?'

'I'm sure he's an excellent sort of man,' Mabel Derbyshire said, rather stiffly. It most certainly would not do to let Ginny see that she had thought Michael Gallagher selfish and overbearing. 'Now you'd best run along, love, or you won't be home in time to get a meal ready. And just you come back whenever you are able, because it's a great pleasure to see my favourite pupil, even though you aren't, strictly speaking, my pupil any more.'

CHAPTER ELEVEN

AUGUST 1929

Michael stood on the headland above the small bay, chewing a piece of grass and watching, with some dismay, as a veil of soft summer rain swept in from the sea. So far, it had been a wet summer and though this was by no means unusual in Kerry, Michael was extremely keen to introduce his daughter to the farm in sunny weather. She was a city child and he imagined would be dismayed to find lanes, meadows and copses ankle-deep in mud.

His father only grew sufficient corn to feed his stock and, though the weather had been wet, the rain had been gentle so the crop was not laid flat. If we get some sun in a week or so, we'll maybe harvest it towards the end of August or the beginning of September and all the kids love a corn harvest, Michael told himself, turning away from the headland just as the rain began to blow gently into his face.

Declan was a grand lad and was doing Sean's share of the work, never grumbling at the long hours which every farm worker has to put in when days are long and nights short. Sean was doing his best to give what help he could but his leg needed a good deal of rest and though he would have

293

pushed himself mercilessly had his son not been present, Maeve had told her husband, severely, that this was foolishness: a short-term view which would end up with the leg permanently weakened. Sean saw the point of his wife's remarks and reluctantly agreed not to try to do too much. 'For wit' Michael and Declan keepin' up wit' the work so grand, and wit' you managin' the stock almost as well as I could meself, I might as well be sensible,' he had told his wife. 'I t'ought we'd miss young Ryan turrble bad when Padraig had to have him back—young Ryan had a way wit' sheep, so he did—but I don't t'ink we've lost a lamb, thanks to you and Floss, and only two o' the ewes were barren, so we're building up the flock better than I dared hope.'

His wife had laughed, raising her eyebrows comically as she replied. 'So I'm bracketed wit' a sheepdog, am I? Still an' all, things seem to be goin' all right for us Gallaghers, one way and another. And as soon as he's able, our boy will fetch Ginny home and we'll be a proper family.'

Michael skirted the cottage, smiling to himself. He had gone up to the headland to see whether his father had taken the *Orla* out, and sure enough, the boat was not at her moorings in the tiny harbour. Sean was probably checking his lobster and crab pots and Michael's mouth watered, hopefully, at the thought of a crab or a lobster for his tea. But there was no point in standing here dreaming. He and Declan meant to dip the sheep some time this week and since the other task which awaited them was that of digging peat, and everyone knew that peat could only be dug when the moor had dried out, they had best get on with the sheep dip today.

The rain continued to fall, softly but steadily, for a further three days and then, to Michael's joy, it ceased; the skies cleared and a brisk wind began to blow. After a couple of days, Michael announced that the peat would be cutting just fine, and he and Declan took the donkey and cart and their slanes and spent the day, in company with many other villagers, cutting the big squares of turf and piling them into the donkey cart.

It was at the end of the second day, with the weather still fine, that Michael decided to write to Ginny, telling her that he would not be able to come and fetch her much before the second or third week in August because they would be frantically busy on the farm lifting the main potato crop, although they would not be cutting the corn until early September since the summer had been so wet. In actual fact, he thought that if the weather continued good, he would get away much earlier than that, but he reasoned that it was better to surprise her by an early arrival than to have the kid being disappointed over his failure to turn up.

Michael finished his letter, sealed it and fished a stamp out of his wallet. He would take the letter into Killorglin in the morning and put it into the post office. He tried to imagine its journey. It would travel by train across Ireland and then it would be carried on the ferry over the Irish Sea. From there it would, he supposed, go into a sorting office and thence would be carried, by the postman, to the town of Seaforth, wherever that might be.

As he made ready for bed that night, he wondered about Seaforth, wondered what sort of place it was. Town? Village? But really, its only interest for him was that his daughter was there. He remembered his last visit to Liverpool and the dragging weariness of his unsuccessful search. He also remembered, with some annoyance, that stuck-up, bossy schoolteacher, who had been so unpleasant to him. Well, at least there would be no occasion for him to visit her this time round. This time, he would go to the very house just as soon as he came ashore, and meet his daughter at long last.

Satisfied, he climbed into bed and was soon asleep.

*   *   *

Ginny managed to visit Miss Derbyshire a couple more times at the end of July and on Thursday, 1 August, they actually had a day out together. Miss Derbyshire had been much shocked to discover that Ginny, despite living within a stone's throw of Liverpool Cathedral, had never so much as glanced at it and was surprised to learn that although work had started on it in 1904, it was still not finished. She was also amazed that Ginny had never visited the Walker Art Gallery or the Liverpool museum, and said they would have an enjoyable day seeing the sights and educating themselves. Since she also planned that they would have lunch at a Lyon's Corner House, Ginny was naturally delighted by the scheme but rather to her surprise, as the day approached she began to be nervous about leaving Schubert Street for any length of time. The thought that her father might come and find her not at home was a horrid one, but she realised that Miss Derbyshire was looking forward to the outing and so merely left Ivy on watch, with a promise of tuppence if she detained Michael Gallagher, should he happen to arrive in his daughter's absence.

'I don't suppose he'll be staying in the Sailor's Home this time, like he did when he were courting my mam,' she told Ivy. 'But he's bound to be staying in a lodging house somewhere because I telled him when I wrote that your mam's house was packed just as full as it can hold.'

Ivy agreed enthusiastically to watch for her cousin's dad and Aunt Amy, who was working mornings in a large greengrocery shop on the Scotland Road, promised to do her own messages so that her niece could enjoy her rare outing.

The day dawned brilliant with sunshine and a clear blue sky, which was a bonus, since Ginny had been telling herself all week that even bad weather would not spoil her enjoyment of the treat ahead. As it happened, Miss Derbyshire whisked her round the art gallery and museum and then announced that they would go for a boat trip on the Mersey since the weather was so fine.

Trailing home that evening, Ginny thought she had never been happier. They had had a wonderful day and now could she could settle down to wait for her father with what patience she could muster.

As she turned into the jigger which led from Caradoc Road to the backs of the houses in Schubert Street, Ivy came flying to meet her. She cast herself into Ginny's arms, saying breathlessly: 'Did you 'ave a luverly time, queen? Ooh, we did miss you, 'specially me, 'cos I forgot to buy a pot o' jam yesterday, so it were just bread 'n' marge for us an' Ruthie howled louder'n Rufus did when I shut his tail in the door.'

'I had a grand time, thanks, me luv,' Ginny said contentedly, giving her little cousin a hug. 'We had our dinners out, like Miss Derbyshire said we would, but that were ages ago and now I could eat a perishin' horse. Has me aunt gone out yet? What's for tea, eh?' She did not bother to ask whether there had been any visitors; she knew very well that had her father arrived from Ireland Ivy would have blurted out the news the moment she had set eyes on Ginny—and would have held out her hand for the tuppence, no doubt.

'It's boiled beef an' carrots, wi' a big pan of spuds and a great old cabbage what Mr O'Keefe gave me mam this morning,' Ivy disclosed. 'Mam's working at the Caradoc this evening so we'll have our food as soon as me dad gets home. Oh, I forgot.' She plunged a small and grimy hand into the pocket of her pinafore. 'There's a letter from your da'; d'you think it'll say when he's comin' over, Ginny?'

Ginny took the crumpled letter and ripped the envelope open. She leaned against the wall which bounded their courtyard and read it eagerly, then turned to Ivy, trying not to sound as disappointed as she felt. 'He isn't comin' for two or three weeks, so Aunt Amy won't have to start makin' arrangements to see someone's at home of an evening for a while yet,' she said cheerfully. She so longed to see her father and her grandparents, longed to see the farm, for that matter, and now she would not be present at what her father thought was one of the busiest times of the farming year. Still, he had said he would fetch her before the corn harvest and she knew from her book reading that harvesting was one of the nicest

298

farming events. All the farms in the district banded together so that everyone's harvest could be gathered in whilst the weather was clement, and this meant that she would meet everyone in the area, for even the children followed the reaper and binder from field to field.

'Oh, poor Ginny . . . but it's awful nice for us,' Ivy said, as the pair of them went through the back gate and began to cross the yard. 'I does love the summer holidays, though, and we'll have a good time, won't we, Ginny? I loves to play on the beach, paddle in the sea and dig castles, and then there's the park. Tell you what, our Ginny, Crosby's seaside, ain't it? I 'member that boy, Steve, sayin' their beach were cleaner than ours, wi' not so many people on it. We could catch the train or a bus to Crosby, couldn't we? I did like that Steve and it 'ud be fun to have a day out and mebbe meet up wi' Steve an' Roly.'

Ginny grinned to herself and rumpled Ivy's hair. 'I dare say we might have a day out somewhere,' she said, a trifle guardedly. She had realised that Ivy had taken a great liking to Steve but had hoped that the child would forget him if they did not meet up again. Clearly, Ivy's liking had gone rather deeper than Ginny had thought, for it was some weeks since the two families had met up.

The two of them went into the kitchen. Uncle Lew was hanging up his cap and jacket and rolling up his shirt sleeves, remarking jovially that since his wife had cooked his favourite tea, he did not intend to lose a moment, and the kids must all get round the table so he could start carving the silverside. He grinned across at Ginny, removing her own jacket and hanging it on the hook behind the kitchen

299

door, and told her to give her Aunt Franklin a shout. 'No need to shout the girls,' he added, 'since they're never backward in coming forward when there's food on the table. Oh, that reminds me; I picked up some o' them sherbet dabs you kids are so fond of. I'll hand them round after the meal.'

Ruthie squealed with pleasure but Aunt Amy frowned at her husband, lifting the small child on to a chair with two cushions on the seat. 'Now why ever did you tell 'em you'd bought sherbet before they'd ate their teas?' she said peevishly. 'I want to see every plate clean as a whistle or no matter what your dad says, there'll be no sherbet dabs for anyone tonight.'

Ruthie began to whine that it was too hot and that salt beef always made her thirsty, but before Aunt Amy could do more than frown at her the Franklins erupted into the kitchen and very soon the meal was under way. Despite the warmth of the day, everyone made short work of their food, though when Aunt Amy put a boiled pudding on the table and began to cut sticky wedges for each person, there was more than one doubtful glance cast at their helping.

'Get outside of that lot and don't let me hear no grumbling,' Aunt Amy said, sitting down and beginning on her own portion. 'I'm workin' tonight so you'll have to get the meal washed up and cleared away wi'out me.' She turned to her sister. 'Don't let the kids buzz off until you've made sure all the work's done,' she instructed.

Mrs Franklin nodded, though her daughters both said at once that they would be unable to help since they were off to the cinema as soon as the meal was finished. Aunt Amy shot a quick glance at

300

her husband, but said nothing, and very soon Uncle Lewis got to his feet and produced a brown paper carrier bag. He began handing round the small packets of sherbet, each with a liquorice stick protruding from the top. The Franklin girls had already made themselves scarce and Aunt Amy was preparing for her evening's work at the Caradoc, taking off her big white apron, loosening her hair and brushing it fiercely before pinning it back into its usual bun. Mrs Franklin was at the sink, piling up the dishes, when Ivy, peering into the carrier bag, announced gleefully: 'There's two more in there, Dad. Don't you know you've only got three girls an' our Ginny?'

Ginny, stacking plates, spoke before she thought. 'Oh, the extra two will be for Steve and Roly, of course,' she said blithely. 'I expect Uncle Lew will take them at the weekend.'

There was a moment of frozen silence; Mrs Franklin swung round from the sink and stared, then shrugged and turned back again. Ivy began to say that the sherbets couldn't possibly be for Steve and Roly because our dad didn't know them and Ginny, desperate to cover up her awful mistake, said hastily that she must be going mad; she had meant Belle and Norma, of course.

It was unfortunate that Aunt Amy had been looking straight at Uncle Lew when Ginny had dropped her bombshell. Ginny thought that if ever a man had looked guilty, it was her uncle. He reddened to the roots of his hair but said, feebly: 'Yes, of course, they were meant for Belle and Norma . . . I—I knew they was off to the flickers so I—I thought I'd buy them a little treat, like.'

Aunt Amy had been staring at Uncle Lew but

301

now she swung round and her scorching gaze transferred itself to Ginny. 'I think you'd best explain just what you meant, young woman,' she said furiously. 'I were goin' happily off to me work wi'out a care in the world, but now I want an explanation.'

Ginny's mind darted wildly about, seeking for a good reason for what she had said. She began to mumble that the boys were a couple of pals she and Ivy met sometimes in Bowerdale Park but Ivy, all unknowing, was having none of it.

'They ain't, Ginny,' she said reproachfully. 'They comes from Crosby, you know they does. Why, weren't we plannin' to meet up wi' them one day during the holidays?'

Uncle Lew turned on his daughter. 'Shut your mouth,' he said roughly. 'Your mam asked Ginny what she meant, not you.' He turned back to Ginny. 'And if you go tellin' lies or makin' trouble, I'll beat you within an inch o' your life. You ain't like me own kids, what ha' been taught never to lie or steal; you've had a bad upbringing and your mam were a spoiled little piece what thought the world revolved round her. Now! Let's be having the truth.'

There was a look in his eyes which terrified Ginny. But though she was frightened she was beginning to be angry, too. What right had Uncle Lew to threaten her, call her mother names and insinuate that she was not to be trusted? After all, it was the truth he feared, and with so many eyes upon her Ginny knew she would not be able to lie convincingly. She took a deep breath. 'Ivy's right; them boys do live in Crosby an' Uncle Lew . . . well, they're his boys.'

302

She waited for an explosion of wrath from her uncle, but instead it came from Aunt Amy. Her aunt shot across the room and slapped Ginny's face so resoundingly that she cannoned into the table, giving a cry of pain as she did so. 'You wicked, brazen little hussy!' Aunt Amy hissed. 'And after we've been so good to you, too. Your uncle took you in and we've treated you like one of our own an' now this is the way you reward us! Well, my lady, you've spent your last night under this roof and so I'm telling you. You can go back to your grandma, and when your Uncle George hears what you've been saying he'll likely break your neck, for he's rare fond of Lew and won't have you spreading your lies when he's by to prevent it.'

Ivy burst into tears and clutched at her mother's skirt. 'What's the matter, our mam?' she hiccuped between sobs. 'Why are you so cross wi' our Ginny? She don't tell lies, you know she don't. I've heered you tellin' people wharra good girl she is an' how 'liable. An'—an' them boys does come from Crosby, they told us so.'

'It don't matter where they come from,' Aunt Amy said tightly. 'It's—it's what your cousin's sayin' about them being your dad's boys.' She glared at her niece but Ginny could see there was a flicker of doubt in her eyes. 'I ain't goin' to pretend your uncle's a saint but there's no way . . .'

'Ask him where he goes weekends,' Ginny said. Her voice was shaky but determined. 'Ask him to show you the savings book with the money you've saved towards—towards . . .' She remembered, belatedly, that she had promised her aunt not to reveal the secret about the Welsh farm and ended, rather disjointedly: 'Towards what the pair o' you have been saving up for. Please, Aunt Amy, I'm norra liar an' I never meant to say a word . . .'

Aunt Amy was staring at her, not moving, but Uncle Lew came across the kitchen like a tiger. He grabbed Ginny by her shoulders and lifted her off the floor then ran across to the back door and flung her into the yard. 'You heard what your aunt said; gerrout an' stay out!' he bawled. 'Why, you trouble-making little bitch. If I'd knowed what you were plannin' to do, I'd ha' given you a dose o' somethin' a deal deadlier than sherbet.' With that, he retreated into the kitchen, slamming the door behind him.

For a moment, Ginny lay where she had fallen. She had cracked her head against the water butt, but then she scrambled to her feet. She turned towards the back door and actually had her hand on the latch when she heard her aunt's voice. 'P'raps I'd best take a glance at your savings book, Lew,' Aunt Amy said. 'I'm off to me work now but I'll tek a look at it when I get home. Just to satisfy myself, like, that there's no jiggery-pokery goin' on; awright?'

'Awright, queen,' her uncle said in a subdued voice. 'You'll gerra pleasant surprise when you see how well we're doing . . . but you'd best get off now or you'll be late. I'll walk down to the pub at closing time so's we can have a talk on the way home.'

Ginny was still hovering by the door when she heard the sharp tap of her aunt's shoes on the kitchen bricks and hastily beat a retreat. She scooted into the jigger and ran for all she was worth towards Henley Street, knowing that her aunt would head in the opposite direction. For the moment, Ginny's main thought was to get away

304

from Schubert Street, to lick her wounds and decide what she should do next. Her head was still singing from Aunt Amy's slap and her ribs ached where she had cannoned into the table. She had bumped her head against the water butt and cracked her knee, which was bleeding copiously. Still sobbing beneath her breath, she headed for the grounds of Seaforth Convent, knowing that no one would think of looking for her there, not even Ivy, for she had never taken her young cousins when she climbed the high wall and trespassed into the enormous neglected grounds, for the convent had been deserted now for nearly two decades. She seldom ventured near the house itself, which she thought spooky and was probably dangerous, but she knew the outbuildings and grounds like the back of her hand and often came here, armed with a book, when she needed peace and quiet. The light was fading by the time she sought refuge in a grove of birches. Ginny sat herself down, leaned against the trunk of one of the trees, and examined her wounds. What a sight I must look, she thought, spitting on the hem of her faded blue cotton dress and trying to rub off the blood from around the wound on her knee. She put a hand up to her head to trace the outline of an enormous bump just above her eyebrow. Yes, she must indeed look absolutely dreadful, and with the thought came the realisation that she did not want *anyone*—anyone at all—to see the state she was in.

When Uncle Lew had said she must go, she had thought at once of her old home in Victoria Court and of her friends there. But now she realised that not even Danny or Annie could be expected to understand unless she told them the whole story,

305

and to do this would be letting her aunt down and blackening her cousins too, for if she was right, and Uncle Lew was really married to Steve's mother, then Ivy, Millie and Ruthie were love children, as she herself was. She remembered nasty remarks she had overheard about her begetting. Some children at school had called names and some parents had muttered behind their hands. She had asked Aunt Mary, when she was quite small, why a fat and blowzy neighbour with seven kids of her own and a drunken husband frequently told her children off for playing with 'that kid what's mam was just a cheap little tart, for all her pretty looks'. Aunt Mary had snorted disdainfully and replied that it was a case of a pot calling the kettle black, since Mrs Snelling's eldest child had also been born out of wedlock. At the time, this had not meant much to Ginny, but now she understood and was determined that her little cousins should not be tarred with the same brush, if she could possibly help it.

Having decided that she could not return to Victoria Court, she also realised that it would not do to go round to Canning Street and beg Miss Derbyshire to help her. Nor could she go to Aunt Mary and Uncle George because, if she did so, no doubt Uncle Lew would get to hear of it and would come down on her like a ton of bricks.

Thinking it over, she had decided that Uncle Lew would simply falsify his Post Office savings book, putting off the evil hour when he would have to admit to his wife that he had very few savings. So it was no use relying on the Post Office book to prove that it was Uncle Lew who was a liar and not she.

306

Presently, since it was now pretty well dark, Ginny got to her feet and made her way to where a large pool, surrounded by trees, had once been a focal point for the garden, but was now overgrown with rushes and flag irises. The moon was out and she kneeled by the water and had as good a wash as was possible, flattened her untidy hair with her wet hands, and then sat down on the low wall which flanked the pool and considered what she should do next. Going back to Schubert Street was out of the question, and unless she was prepared to tell her friends what had happened, she could not expect any help from them. But when her father came, she would be safe. She could go back to Ireland with him and tell him and her Irish grandparents why Uncle Lew had thrown her out and they would understand and sympathise with her, but would be in no position to pass on the awful news to anyone in Liverpool. Ginny's hand dug into her pocket and felt for the letter. It was all very well to think about awaiting her father's arrival, but unless she returned to Schubert Street she was unlikely to discover that he had arrived. And then there were the two to three weeks before he came. She could not live on air and dreaded to think of the terrible fuss and the gossip which would result if she were picked up by the police and either put into an orphan asylum or handed back to the Bennetts to face her aunt and uncle's fury.

There was a small summer house overlooking the pool, and Ginny made her way towards it. She sometimes came here to read her book, because at some stage the summer house had become a repository for the dried grass and bracken which, at first, the gardeners had cut down. The foliage was old, dry and crackly but Ginny knew, from experience, that it would make an excellent couch. She lay down on it and made herself comfortable, wondering for the first time whether her aunt and uncle had reported her as a missing person, or were scouring the streets for her. But she no longer cared, for weariness assailed her. She would let tomorrow take care of itself, but right now she simply had to sleep.

She was on the very edge of dreaming when a thought occurred to her which had her snapping upright, eyes wide open. Of course! If her father was not coming to England for two to three weeks, then she had best go to him. She had his address and imagined, since he lived by the sea and had often written of it, that all she would have to do to find him would be to catch the Irish ferry and travel a few miles to Headland Farm. Once there, she could explain everything and she was sure that her father would sort things out.

Satisfied, she lay down again and was soon asleep.

*   *   *

They searched for her, of course they did. Uncle Lew swore he hadn't expected her to take him seriously, but Amy thought he had known very well what he was doing. He had wanted the kid so cowed that she would take back the words she had uttered and leave the whole matter alone, but Amy considered that he had gone too far.

She had gone off to work, too upset by what had happened to worry much about her niece. She had told herself that Ginny would return by bedtime, that she had nowhere to go except, possibly, to Mary and George. But that would mean sharing a house with Gran, and explanations . . . Amy's blood ran cold at the thought.

When the pub closed and Lew stepped out of the shadows and tucked her hand into his arm, she asked him at once whether Ginny was home yet, never even thinking about the Post Office book which had seemed so important earlier on.

'No, she ain't come back yet, but don't worry, queen, she'll turn up in time for breakfast,' he said. 'I walked along to the canny house and had a word with Mary, but they'd seen neither hide nor hair of the kid.'

'Well, thank God for that,' Amy said fervently. Almost without realising it, she had begun to believe that there was some truth, at least, in Ginny's accusation. 'I wouldn't want no gossip— norrif we can avoid it, that is. Now where's this Post Office book, eh?'

Lew muttered something beneath his breath. She heard the words 'always been considered trustable' and 'a man of me word, don't see why you have to doubt me', but he did not sound as if he believed what he was saying and, after a perceptible pause, dug into his jacket pocket and produced a small and shabby Post Office savings book.

Amy took it and stopped under a street lamp, examining the pages. It seemed as though, in the early days, money had certainly gone in each week, but since most of it was drawn out the following week the actual sum still in the savings account was likely to be small. And so it proved; when she reached the last page, the balance showing was £8

7s 9d, not exactly the sort of money one could use to purchase a farm.

Amy sighed deeply and handed him back the book. He took it without a word and rammed it back into his jacket pocket. Then she said gently: 'Ginny weren't lying, wcrc she, Lew? You're havin' a bit o' fun on the side, ain't you, an' me an' my kids have been payin' for it. I've done me best to be a good wife to you, I've worked me fingers to the bone to keep a decent table and to bring up your kids right and this is the thanks I get for it. The—the boys Ginny mentioned ain't your get though, are they? They'll be the woman's kids; the woman Ginny must have seen you with?'

Lew began to agree, to say that he had quite enough children already, and then he seemed to crumple. By now, they were crossing the yard and heading for the back door, and as they entered the kitchen he said miserably: 'It's no use, Amy love, I'd ha' done anything to keep it from you, but the truth is I—I gorra girl into trouble years back, before ever I met you. She had a boy—he's the Steve Ginny and Ivy talked about—and—and we—we rented a little house in Crosby, so's she could be comfortable like. Then—then I met you and—and I knew you were the gal for me. Y'see, Dolly's a sweet woman, in her way, but—but I were only a lad so I kept on supporting her, but I married you and . . . well, we've been happy, haven't we? I've done me best as well, you know, because I couldn't just abandon Dolly to starve. She works, o' course, but Steve's a big feller now—eats her out of house and home—and the rent's not cheap, and . . .'

Amy slumped into a chair. She realised that if she did not press the point now, she would never

310

learn the truth. But she was so tired! She was also, if she was honest, not at all eager to learn the truth, but it was no good burying one's head in the sand. She would have to face up to whatever Lew had done right away, before he could start inventing half-truths which might be difficult to disprove.

'Sit down, Lew,' she said, trying to keep her tone calm, though her heart was racing in her breast. 'Now that we know where we stand, I want the whole story. Ginny or Ivy, I can't remember which, said there were two boys. Are—are they both yours? And how old are they?' Lew leaned forward and tried to take her hand but Amy shook her head at him and clasped her hands in her lap. 'Come along, Lew; at least you know I'm not going to turn *you* out of the house, even if you have deserved it.'

Lew gulped and Amy saw that there were tears in his bright blue eyes. 'Steve's twelve and Roly's five,' he said humbly. 'And—and Roly *is* my son—I didn't mean—it were only the once—oh, Amy, I'm that sorry.'

'So am I,' Amy said numbly, with her world collapsing around her ears. I'll never be able to trust him again, she told herself, but I can't imagine life without Lew, so I suppose I'll have to forgive him. Only—only he'll have to promise to give her up, never to go near Crosby again. And how can I possibly make sure he sticks to it? I can't spend the rest of me life spyin' on him.

Lew had been gazing at her appealingly, but now he said uneasily: 'If I promise to stay away from Dolly and the boys, d'you think it would be possible for us to go on as before? I mean, it would break me mam's heart if she knew I'd got—I'd got two families, like, an' there's George an' Mary; they're

311

real strait-laced and wouldn't approve at all. When we were both in the Navy, I—I had a girl or two in different ports—you know how it is—but George just weren't like that. From the moment he first set eyes on Mary it were her or no one . . . and I were the same wi' you,' he added hastily. 'Only—well, I met Dolly first, that were the trouble.'

'The trouble were, you wanted to have your cake and eat it, Lew Bennett,' Amy said severely. 'And it's got to stop. D'you understand? You'll have to tell this Dolly you're a respectable married man and can't carry on the way you've been doing. I agree you can't let your boys go hungry, but in another couple o' years the elder one will be workin' an' if you ask me she'll just have to learn to manage; you can send her money by post, like Ginny's dad does. Now I'll just pop upstairs and make sure she's come home.'

Amy hurried up the stairs, truly expecting to find Ginny in her bed, and was honestly dismayed to find she was not. Making her way slowly downstairs once more, she recollected that it had been she, in the first flush of incredulous rage, who had told Ginny to get out. However, she knew how eagerly Ginny was awaiting her father's visit and was certain that, even if the child had sought the hospitality of a friend for this one night, she would return in the morning.

Now that things were becoming clearer to her, all the affection that she had felt for her niece reasserted itself. She felt ashamed for the way she had spoken to Ginny and meant to apologise handsomely next morning, for on thinking it over she was pretty sure that the child would not have told anyone else what she had discovered. After all,

312

she had hugged the secret to her own breast for many weeks, judging by what she and Ivy had said.

Returning to the kitchen, she sat down at the big, scrubbed wooden table and eyed Lew steadily across it. 'She ain't in bed, so she's not come home,' she said abruptly. 'She'll mebbe have gone to that schoolteacher pal of hers, or one of her friends in Victoria Court. But I tell you what, Lew, she *is* a good kid, you know. I'm pretty sure she won't split on you, for all you behaved like a brute and a bully to her.'

Lew hung his head. 'I'll tell her I'm real sorry when she comes back, Amy,' he said humbly. 'And I'll keep me promises, I'll swear it on the Bible if you like, not to go near nor by Dolly and the kids.'

Amy nodded grimly, then gave vent to a little human curiosity. 'Does—does this Dolly woman know about me?' she enquired. 'Is she—what does she look like?'

'No, of course she don't know about you,' Lew said, sounding shocked. 'She's blonde, plump, easy-going, norra bit like me lively, lovely wife!'

Amy gave a disbelieving snort at this but she was secretly rather pleased. After all, he had married her and merely had a child—two children—by the other woman. So presently, when the two of them headed for the stairs, she told herself that they did have a future together, might even own that farm one of these days. But when Lew tried to follow her up the stairs, she shook her head reprovingly. 'You're sleepin' on the sofa tonight,' she told him. 'I'll need a lot more than empty promises before I take you back into my bed.'

*　　　*　　　*

313

Ginny woke when a ray of early sunshine crept through the window of the little summer house and fell across her face. For a moment, she could not think where she was or what had happened, but then she remembered. Leisurely, she got up and made for the high wall; no point in getting into more trouble by being seen and recognised as a trespasser as she dropped on to the paving stones. If she was to abide by the decision she had made last night, however, and make her way to Ireland, then she could no longer try to hide away from everyone she knew. She was aware that, in books, children stowed away on ships, but she was perfectly certain that if she tried it, she would be discovered and would get into all sorts of trouble. Therefore, it behoved her to decide which of her friends was the most trustworthy and appeal to them for help.

Making her way along Crosby Road South, she thought wistfully of the house in Schubert Street. She could tell by the position of the sun that it was still very early, guessed that no one would be about yet, particularly after the sort of night they had probably had, but she knew that if she tried the back door, Rufus would immediately start to bark. Besides, though the money in the tobacco tin was her own, she would still feel like a thief if she took it from her aunt and uncle's house. Instead, she decided she would make her way back to Victoria Court and consult Danny. He had always been generous and she thought he would quite probably lend her his savings, secure in the knowledge that she would certainly pay him back.

And so it proved. It took Ginny a fair while to

314

walk to Victoria Court whilst around her the city woke up. She found Danny kicking a ball about with one of his younger brothers, but as soon as she had explained her predicament he went indoors and produced a quantity of money. 'Is it just money for the ferry you're wantin'?' he asked, counting a princely sum into a scrap of faded linen and handing it to her. 'You'll have to eat, queen, and it may take you a day or two to reach that farm you've talked about. What'll I say if your aunt and uncle come round enquirin' about you? Before all this blew up, you were real happy in Seaforth; Annie an' me both thought so. Why, when your aunt and uncle gerrover bein' furious with you, they'll likely start to worry. They'll have the police out, an' if you ask me they'll go first to your Aunt Mary and Uncle George and then they'll come here. I won't let you down, queen, but I doesn't fancy pretendin' I know nothing if they're real concerned you've drownded yourself in the Mersey or got yourself took off to South America to be a white slave.'

Ginny laughed. She had not told Danny the whole story, still thinking this would be very unfair, but had merely said she had seen her Uncle Lew with a young woman and had mentioned it without thinking, in Aunt Amy's presence. It seemed that this explanation was quite sufficient for Danny, who had whistled, told her she'd not got a ha'p'orth of sense and applauded her decision to go to her father in Ireland until things blew over.

'They will, o'course,' he had said confidently. 'Your Uncle Lew were always a one for the gals; me mam used to say he'd got a girl in every port durin' the war, though Dad couldn't see what the

315

gals saw in him.'

'Ye-es, Aunt Mary said something of the sort, too,' Ginny admitted. 'But I'm better off out of it, Danny. As for what you should say, you tell 'em I've gone to me dad. Don't say you lended me the money, say I've got savin's from when I lived in Victoria Court and came back to fetch 'em out.'

'Yes, I'll do that,' Danny said contentedly, pushing the rest of the money back into the pockets of his ragged kecks. 'Now are you sure that money'll see you through, chuck? Only Annie don't fancy gettin' up before dawn to raid the skip on Maddox Street, so I've had no one to share the money with, which means I've got a fair amount stowed away. I'm willin' to lend you another quid if you like.'

Ginny, however, already weighed down by the responsibility of what she felt to be a very large sum, shook her head. 'No thanks, Danny, this'll be fine,' she said firmly. 'Mind you, if they come questioning you in the next couple o' days, I'd rather you didn't tell them too soon. I don't want to be caught this side of the water and hauled off to an orphanage or back to Schubert Street to be beaten up by Uncle Lew.'

Danny looked a little self-conscious. 'Actually, I'm off on a campin' trip wi' my scout troop, later on in the morning,' he admitted. 'They're takin' us by coach into the countryside and we'll put up our tents on a farm. It's grand fun, we make all our own meals, light fires, fetch water from the stream . . . oh, it's great, I'm tellin' you. There's sing-songs round the camp fire of an evening, and of course we work for our badges. But the thing is, queen, we'll be gone three days, so no one won't be able to

316

ask me wharr I know for a while.'

'That's a bit of luck,' Ginny observed. 'You're a real pal, Danny; I won't ever forget what you've done for me and you shall have your savings back as soon as I reach Headland Farm.'

*   *   *

Despite Ginny's fears, she managed the business of buying a ticket on the Irish ferry quite well. She knew she would be half price but rather doubted whether she would be able to purchase a ticket without facing a barrage of questions as to why she was not accompanied by an adult. Therefore, she waited until she saw a motherly-looking woman join the queue and then ran up to her, saying breathlessly: 'Oh, missus, would you mind buyin' me a half fare to Dublin, please? Me aunt has gone ahead of me—she sent me back to the chemist to get her some pills, 'cos she's always sick on the sea—an' I can see her up there on the boat deck, waving to me to gerra move on.'

The woman turned and looked at the long queue behind her, then tutted indulgently and took the money Ginny was holding out. 'Awright, you young devil,' she said cheerfully. 'At least this way your aunt won't be worryin' in case you miss the boat altogether.'

Twenty minutes later Ginny, and everyone else, was aboard the huge ferry. Ginny settled herself comfortably at the prow of the ship, and hung over the rail, at first peering eagerly into the water as it creamed against the bows and then staring ahead for the magical first glimpse of that even more magical island which lay ahead.

317

CHAPTER TWELVE

It was the beginning of August and the weather continued bright and sunny. Michael and Declan simply threw themselves into the task of getting as much routine work as possible done on the farm, so that Michael could set out for England earlier than he had promised. His mother and father had both tackled the work with equal enthusiasm, for they could not wait to see their granddaughter and were planning all sorts of treats for her arrival.

Michael set off on the cross-country journey bearing presents—a box of new-laid eggs, a couple of chickens plucked and trussed ready for the oven, and a large bag full of ripe Victoria plums. In addition, his mother, who was an expert needlewoman, had made a couple of dainty lawn aprons for Aunt Amy, and after a great deal of thought he had purchased a tobacco pouch filled with his father's favourite shag for Lew. Michael had never met the older man, but remembered that George had once made a mocking remark about Lew's addiction to pipe smoking, so hoped this might be a suitable gift. Judging from Ginny's letters, both Amy and Lew had been good to her, and though he had paid them so that the cost of her upkeep had not fallen upon them, he was still extremely grateful. Granny Bennett had been paid, too, but she had given Ginny neither love nor care so Michael felt no impulse to buy a present for her. He was rather proud that he had managed to get aboard the ferry without breaking so much as one egg and when he eventually arrived at the

Liverpool quay he felt even luckier, for the first tram which met his eyes had 'Seaforth' on its destination board.

It was mid-afternoon, and Michael settled himself and his parcels on one of the slatted wooden seats near the entrance, deciding that he would ask the conductor to warn him when Seaforth was approaching, so that he might gather up his bundles and packages in good time.

The conductor looked a little dubious at this request, beginning to ask Michael which stop he wanted, then changing his mind. 'I'll put you off at the Rimrose Bridge. Anyone will give you directions from there,' he said cordially. 'Reckon I ought to charge you a double fare since your parcels is takin' up a whole seat, but seeing as the bleedin' lecky is half empty, I'll let you off this time.'

He grinned and Michael grinned back and thanked him, and presently he announced that the Rimrose Bridge were comin' up and Michael found himself on a busy stretch of road, with a number of people hurrying in various directions. He stopped an elderly man with a cigarette apparently glued to his lower lip, and a filthy cap pulled so low over his eyes that he had to tilt his chin to see who was addressing him; but he gave Michael concise directions and very soon the young man found himself turning into Schubert Street. As he approached the Bennetts' house, he suddenly realised that he was nervous. Suppose the child didn't like him? Suppose she had grown used to living in comparative luxury with her aunt and uncle and did not much want to leave the comforts of city life for the hardships of the country? Worse,

319

suppose he did not like her? On the whole, he thought he rather liked children, but he could not bear whining kids or the loud-mouthed, spoiled sort, who were never happy unless they were causing their parents grief.

Without realising it, his footsteps had slowed. Suppose she was a pink-eyed, pink-nosed, snivelling kid who complained about everything and was never really happy? Suppose she thought him a country bumpkin, and showed contempt? Suppose her letters had been dictated by a wish to keep the money coming in rather than a desire to meet him?

But by now he was standing directly in front of the door, and he raised his hand to rap sharply on the faded wooden panel; how ridiculous he was being! It was pointless to conjecture when, within minutes, he would be meeting his daughter for the first time. And she isn't just my daughter, he reminded himself as the echoes of his knock faded away, she's Stella's daughter as well and I simply don't believe that a child of Stella's could be anything but perfect.

Heartened by this thought, he knocked again and then stood back as footsteps came rapidly along what sounded like a linoleum-covered passage towards the front door.

The door shot open and a woman appeared. She was small, skinny and dark but even when she only said, sharply, 'Yes?' Michael could feel her concentrated energy and guessed at once that this must be Aunt Amy. Ginny had not described her but had said she never stopped working and never seemed to get tired. Michael looked down into the narrow, intelligent face and thought she was very different from Granny Bennett, whom he

320

remembered as being both lazy and malicious. But even as he opened his mouth to speak, the woman forestalled him.

'Oh my Gawd!' she said and a thin, work-worn hand flew to her throat. 'Oh dear God, you don't have to tell me . . . you're our Ginny's dad, Michael Gallagher, and you've arrived early.'

'Aye, that's me, so it is,' Michael said, 'and you'll be Mrs Amy Bennett. I know I've come before me time but I were able to get away early because o' the fine weather, you know.' He heard a commotion in the passageway behind her and saw a child's shape as a door within the house was opened. 'Is that me daughter? Eh, I'm longin' to see her, so I am.'

He expected that this remark would bring forth some similar reply to the effect that Ginny, too, was longing to see her daddy, but instead Amy Bennett's eyes darted past him and for a moment she stood irresolute, still blocking the doorway. Then, almost grudgingly it seemed, she stood aside and beckoned him to enter the house. 'You'd best come along in,' she said gruffly. 'It's—it's a long story and you ain't going to be pleased but, honest to God, we've done everythin' we could. In fact, only this mornin' . . .' She was ahead of him now and entered the room with the open door, saying over her shoulder as she did so: 'I'll send the kids outside and we'll talk in the kitchen. Oh, I wish Lew were here!'

*   *   *

It was a long story but Amy told it concisely, making it clear that she no longer blamed Ginny

321

for any of it. 'For once I got down to doin' a bit of investigatin' meself,' she explained, 'it were clear that Ginny had discovered the whole story, an' a pretty nasty one it was so far as I were concerned. Ginny had said the boys were Lew's sons and she were right. Not only that, but he had married Dolly as soon as they found she were in the family way, which means, o' course, that when he married me it were—it were bigamy, an' that means I ain't married at all.'

'I see,' Michael said slowly. 'So you say Lew threw Ginny out? I'm sorry, Mrs Bennett, but I don't quite see . . . surely me daughter came back? Or did she go to George and Mary? I quite believe she wouldn't want to live with old Mrs Bennett, but she were always fond of her Uncle George and Aunt Mary, or so she said in her letters.'

'Aye, that were what we thought,' Amy agreed. She had round, brown eyes as bright as a robin's and now they met Michael's own, squarely. 'The fact is, Mr Gallagher, that she must have believed Lew would really do her harm, and since the old woman is living with George and Mary, I reckon she was scared to go there an' all. We told the scuffers and all the neighbours and so on, that there'd bin a family row and she took herself off, but . . . well, you know what kids are like; in a great big city like Liverpool, one little girl can just disappear. I hope to God no harm's come to her but Ivy, she's me eldest, don't seem to think so. Ginny's gorra lot of pals, an' I reckon one of 'em's got her hid away somewhere. She's only been gone three days . . . today's the fourth day, so I'm expectin' news of her any time now.'

Michael sat for a moment in deep thought, then

322

scraped his chair back and stood up. He had listened to Amy, but at first had been unable to take in what had happened. At first, too, slow anger had burned within him, making it difficult to think clearly. But now he had thought and had decided what he should do next. 'Has anyone been round to her old schoolteacher, that Miss Derbyshire?' he asked huskily. 'I didn't take to her meself—well, she didn't approve of me and said so —but Ginny were rare fond of the woman. And there were kids in Victoria Court that she mentioned once or twice; has someone tried them?'

'I reckon the scuffers have been round,' Amy said after a moment's thought. 'But no, I don't reckon the family have tried her old schoolteacher, nor yet her pals from the court. Ivy said our Ginny had gone back to meet up wi' some girl called Annie, or Nellie, a couple of times, or some such, but the gal had made new friends and Ginny felt kind o' out of it.' She brightened. Not only did she have a robin's round eyes, but she had a sharp little beak of a nose as well, Michael thought, and decided that he liked her and felt very sorry for the way Lew had treated her. 'If you want, I could send our Ivy round to ask the kids; I reckon they'd tell her a good deal more'n they'd tell you or me.'

'Aye, you're right there. Kids will talk to one another quick enough,' Michael agreed. 'But I'll go meself to have a word wi' Miss Derbyshire, so if Ivy cares to come along o' me . . . oh, by the way, I brought some eggs an' a couple of fowls and that, from the farm.' He indicated the brown paper bags which he had set down on the table. 'I hope they'll be of some use to you.'

Amy smiled gratefully. 'Thanks very much,' she said. 'And Ivy would be glad to help. She's rare fond of her cousin, is Ivy. Why, after the row, she cried herself to sleep, an' now she won't talk to her dad, just turns her head away when he speaks to her.' She grinned suddenly at Michael and her narrow face looked almost pretty for a moment. Michael had found himself wondering what Lew had seen in her, for he remembered Stella telling him that her brother liked easy, flamboyant women, but now he understood. Amy might not be the type Lew usually went for but she had her own subtle charm and, anyway, he guessed it had been she who had made most of the running during their courtship.

'I'll fetch her,' Amy said. She bustled over to the back door and flung it open, screeching her daughter's name so loudly that Michael thought the kid would have heard it even if she had been down at the Pier Head. But as it happened, the child must have been hovering just outside the back door, for she came into the kitchen at once, saying eagerly as she did so: 'Was that Ginny's da' at the door, Mam? Wharrever did he say when you . . . ?' Oh . . .' She saw Michael, clapped a hand over her mouth, then grinned apologetically up at him. 'Sorry, mister, I thought you'd gone.'

'Well he hasn't,' her mother said briefly, and outlined the proposed expedition to Victoria Court. 'And then he'll want to see that there teacher—I can't remember the woman's name— what your cousin were so fond of,' she added. 'I dunno where she lives but I reckon it won't be far from the Rathbone Street school. Here, I'll give you tuppence for the tram.'

'I'll pay her tram fare willingly,' Michael said gruffly. 'By the way, did Ginny have any money on her? I know she was saving up because she told me when she wrote.'

Aunt Amy shook her head sadly. 'She didn't have a penny; nor a jacket nor nothin'. She were wearin' an old blue cotton dress and plimsolls, and though we checked, she hadn't come back for her savings nor for a warm coat. Oh, Mr Gallagher, we've been that worried!'

'I can imagine,' Michael said, a trifle grimly. 'But at least if she had no money she can't have gone far. Well, if it's all right by you, Mrs Bennett, an' if your daughter don't object, I think we'd best be going. The trail's cold as it is; I don't want it to get no colder.'

So, presently, the two of them set off and arrived at Victoria Court half an hour later. Michael began to make enquiries of the neighbours and was told that Ginny's closest friend had been a lad called Danny, in the house opposite.

'But he ain't here at the moment,' Danny's mother told Michael. 'He's gone to scout camp but he'll be back later in the day. An' I can tell you where Miss Derbyshire lodges 'cos Danny's mentioned it once or twice. It's in Canning Street.'

Ivy was all for finding Annie Wait, saying she had been great friends with Ginny, but Michael thought that a child in trouble was not likely to run any risk of parental interference and since the only way to reach the Waits' flat was through their grocery shop, he thought it unlikely that Ginny would have visited them. Besides, had she done so, Annie's parents would have undoubtedly have told the scuffers when they were asking questions.

However, he left Ivy playing hopscotch with a number of other children in the court, asking her to come and fetch him at Miss Derbyshire's lodgings as soon as Danny arrived home, and then set off for Canning Street and rang the bell on the front door of the large, dilapidated-looking house in which he had been told Miss Derbyshire lodged. He was in luck, in one sense at least. Miss Derbyshire answered the door herself. For a moment he did not recognise her, was about to ask her if the teacher was in, then he realised that she had bobbed her thick, ash blonde hair and darkened her brows and lashes. But he was too anxious to give much thought to her appearance, and immediately told her that he would like to have a word about his daughter. Miss Derbyshire gave him a long, penetrating look, and then said briskly: 'You'd best come in. The last time I saw Ginny, she was full of how you and she were exchanging corre- spondence, so you clearly know her address. But a policeman called a couple of days ago, said she'd run away from home and asked if she'd visited me.'

She was preceding him up the rather steep stairs as she spoke and Michael followed hard on her heels. 'They were after havin' a terrible row in the Bennett household and Ginny got mixed up in it and lit out,' he explained briefly. He did not think that the true reason for Ginny's flight was any of Miss Derbyshire's business. 'Ginny were rare fond of you, Miss Derbyshire, so I thought she might've telled you where she were going.'

By now, they had reached a small, square landing and Miss Derbyshire ushered Michael into a neat bed-sitting room, with a vase of flowers on the window sill and a kettle steaming on a small gas ring. Once inside, she gestured him to a chair and then began to spoon tea from a japanned caddy into a brown teapot. 'I was just about to have a cup of tea when I heard the bell ring. The house is almost empty at the moment since the other lodgers are teachers, too, and have either gone home or are on holiday, so I knew if I didn't answer it, no one would. Sugar, Mr Gallagher?'

Michael accepted a cup with one spoonful of sugar, though he did so rather resentfully. She was the bossiest woman he'd ever met, so she was! He hadn't wanted tea, had wanted simply to ask his question, but the unexpected offer of hospitality had made this impossible, and like most of the Irish, Michael seldom refused a cup of tea. Now, sipping it, he said bluntly: 'Just where do you think young Ginny would have hidden herself, Miss Derbyshire? She knew I were comin' to fetch her towards the middle of August and she were lookin' forward to seeing Headland Farm an' meetin' her grandparents for the first time. I can't think she'd go far from Schubert Street when she knew I'd arrive there in a couple o' weeks.'

Miss Derbyshire stared at him and he thought he read derision in her glance. 'And you, no doubt, think yourself an intelligent man, Mr Gallagher,' she said softly. 'If you meant to arrive in a couple of weeks, then Ginny would have no idea that your plans might change, because I take it you've given her no hint?'

'No, I said nothing for fear of disappointing her,' Michael said, defensively, after a moment's thought. 'Why should I?'

'Well, I suppose you couldn't guess that Ginny would run away,' Miss Derbyshire admitted, somewhat grudgingly. 'But don't you *see*, man? She will imagine she has two whole weeks in which to cross Ireland and find your farm in Kerry. She's run away to find *you*, of course! Isn't that what any bright, brave child would do?'

'I'm afraid you're out there, Miss Derbyshire,' Michael said triumphantly. 'Didn't her aunt tell me that Ginny went wit'out so much as a coat to her back or a penny in her pocket? Why, wit' no money, she'd never get aboard the Irish ferry, let alone off t'other end. No, no, you're out there.' He would like to have added, 'Miss Know-it-all', but knew it would be impolite to do so whilst he was drinking her tea.

And as it turned out, it was fortunate that he held his tongue for before Miss Derbyshire could answer him the doorbell pealed again and she jumped to her feet. 'Blow!' she said crossly. 'Yesterday, I was indoors all day, marking end of term examinations, and would have welcomed a visitor. Today, if the bell has rung once, it's rung six times and my legs fairly ache with hurrying up and down those wretched stairs.'

Michael had half risen to his feet, meaning to answer the door for her, but she was out of the room and clattering down the stairs before he could do so and, it seemed to him, was back in the room in no time at all, pushing Ivy Bennett before her. Miss Derbyshire was smiling so broadly that it could have been called a grin and before the child could so much as open her mouth, the woman spoke. 'I told you so, Mr Gallagher! Ivy says young Danny arrived home ten minutes ago and explained where Ginny had gone. It's to Ireland, of course.'

328

Michael stared at her for an unbelieving moment, then transferred his gaze to Ivy. 'Tell me what Danny said, me darlin',' he said gently. 'Can you remember his exact words?'

'Yes, easily,' Ivy said. 'He told me Ginny had gone to Ireland to find her daddy because my mam and dad were cross with her. Danny said she had some savings which she kept in a secret place in Victoria Court and she took 'em and went off to catch the ferry. He axed her if she knew the way to the farm and she said it were by the seaside, so it couldn't be far from Dublin. That's all.'

'Well I'll be damned,' Michael said slowly. 'If I'd known about the money, o' course, I might ha' guessed. Well, at least I'll know where to search, only—only Ireland's a mortal big country when you're searchin' for a needle in a haystack, and if Ginny thinks Kerry is near Dublin . . . why, it's the opposite side of the country, so it is! Oh, Lord, she's only a kid, when all's said and done. Her money will run out . . . she'll get into bad company . . . I must go at once.' He slammed down his mug of tea and headed for the stairs, propelling Ivy in front of him. 'If I give you tram money, alanna, can you get yourself home?' he asked his small companion. 'I hadn't even booked into a lodging house, and I've still got my grip with me, so I don't need to go back to Seaforth. I can catch the next ferry right away.'

Ivy raised no demur at this but as Miss Derbyshire stood in the doorway, seeing them off, she said mockingly: 'Don't be in *too* much of a rush, Mr Gallagher. There's something I'll be bound you've not thought of, which might give you pause when you do think of it.'

329

Ivy was already heading for the nearest tram stop, plainly longing to be able to tell her family where Ginny had gone, but Michael turned reluctantly back towards the teacher. He did not like her but admitted, to himself, that she was a clever woman and might well have spotted a flaw in his plan. 'Well?' he asked, trying not to sound belligerent, but failing, 'What is it this time?'

'How are you going to recognise Ginny, if you do catch up with her before she reaches the farm?' Miss Derbyshire asked sweetly. 'Come to that, how do you expect her to recognise *you*? Just think, Mr Gallagher, a strange man walks up to a child of ten, in the streets of Dublin, and tries to tell her he's her father. You wouldn't do it, it would be far too liable to misinterpretation!'

She was laughing at him again and Michael longed to be able to tell her she was wrong, talking through her hat, hadn't thought the problem through. But it was useless and he knew it. She was absolutely right; without some help, he was never going to find Ginny.

*   *   *

They left on the first ferry the following morning, Miss Derbyshire carrying a neat little suitcase and Michael with his grip. Looking across at his companion as they stood on the deck he was still amazed that things had come to this. Of course, her remark about his not recognising Ginny had completely floored him, but he had not admitted as much to her. He had muttered something about 'making arrangements', and had still been wondering how on earth to solve the problem when

Miss Derbyshire had said: 'Surely some member of the Bennett family will go with you? Perhaps young Ivy?'

He had swung round on her, irritation making him speak before he had really thought of the wisdom—or otherwise—of what he was about to say. 'I can't burden meself wit' a child even younger than Ginny,' he had said roughly, his brogue much in evidence. 'Why don't *you* come with me?' 'Tis the start of the summer holidays so you'll not be teachin' classes for a while yet. You know Ginny better'n most and you say you want her found, so why don't *you* come along?' He had not been serious, of course he hadn't. The last thing he wanted was the company of someone who had criticised his every action and might turn Ginny against him when they did catch up with her, so he was struck almost dumb by her quick response.

'Why not, indeed?' she had said coolly. 'At least I can stop you making a real fool of yourself, and if we find her quickly, then it needn't take more than a day or two. As it happens, I've nothing planned, though I always spend a couple of weeks during the summer holidays with my parents, but that's a movable feast; in other words they expect me when they see me.' She had given a small, tight smile which seemed to him to hold very little humour. 'Thank you for your kind invitation, Mr Gallagher, which I accept. I've never been to Ireland let alone Dublin, so it will be a pleasant change.'

Michael had goggled at her for a moment, then said uncertainly: 'Are you sure, Miss Derbyshire? 'Tis a great sacrifice I'm askin' of you, to give up your free time to go chasin' round after me daughter. If—if you'd like to change your mind . . .'

Miss Derbyshire had laughed, but this time far more pleasantly, and then she had leaned over and patted his arm in an almost friendly fashion. 'I'm sorry, Mr Gallagher, I wasn't being very kind,' she had said, her eyes sparkling. Again it had struck Michael that she might, by some, be considered a very pretty girl, though for his part he liked a woman to be dark, dramatic, and thought the pallor of Miss Derbyshire's hair and skin insipid. 'I dare say you don't realise it, but I'm just as worried about Ginny as you are and I've been fretting for two days, wondering what I should do and to whom I should confide my fears. Now you've offered me a role to play and I promise you I shall play it with all my heart. For a start, I'd better call you Michael, and you can call me Mabel. And I'm sure that, working together, we'll find Ginny before she gets into any sort of trouble.'

So here they were, setting out for Ireland like two friends, whereas in fact they scarcely knew one another and would, Michael felt sure, find even a few hours in one another's company a considerable strain. However, there was no doubt about Miss Derbyshire's—Mabel's—ability both to recognise Ginny and to talk sense into her, if such was necessary. And so far they had rubbed along quite well. Michael had insisted that he would pay all the expenses of the trip and Miss Derbyshire, after an initial hesitation, had agreed that this seemed fair. After all, he had asked for her help, even if he had not expected to get it, so the least he could do was to see that she was not out of pocket as a result of her kindness—if kindness it could be called.

'Michael? I know it's August, but I've begun to feel a trifle chilly. Would you . . . could we go

332

below? I believe they are serving hot drinks in the saloon, and I think I should feel better with a warm drink inside me.'

Miss Derb— Mabel, he corrected himself hastily, had spoken quite pleasantly and so he accompanied her below and bought them each a cup of hot coffee and a large iced bun. His companion ate her bun rather quickly, drank her coffee and then remarked uneasily that she did not much care for the way the floor kept surging up and down and suggested that they should return to the deck. Michael, who had never felt ill aboard a ship in his life, was blind to these signs, but accompanied her back on to the deck and was unflatteringly astonished when she suddenly returned both coffee and bun, not even making the rail but throwing up within a couple of inches of his boots.

'Hey!' he said involuntarily. 'Mind me boots, they're the only ones I've brought.'

He had meant it as a joke but Mabel did not seem amused and cast him a malevolent glance before tottering over to the rail where she proceeded to lose her breakfast to the surging waves of the Irish Sea.

Michael was a kind young man and had heard about the agonies of seasickness from friends who did not have his strong stomach and presently, when Mabel's agonies seemed to be abating, he put a strong arm round her waist and half led, half carried her to the nearest deck chair. He settled her into it, telling her comfortingly that now she was empty she would be all right, but his words proved unduly optimistic. For three hours, his companion retched and retched, refusing all offers of food and drink with a visible shudder, though Michael assured her that she would be a deal more comfortable if she had something inside her.

The weather continued fine, though windy, and presently, to Michael's relief, the teacher fell into an uneasy doze and he was able to leave her in order to go below to buy himself a large cheese and pickle sandwich and a pint of Guinness. He carried his meal back on deck and was tucking in when Mabel awoke. She glanced at him, saw the food and once more tottered to the rail, where the most dreadful sounds almost put Michael off his dinner. Almost, but not quite. He was extremely hungry and realised, for the first time in their acquaintance, he was actually the stronger of the two. It was a good feeling and it made him more sympathetic towards the young woman. In fact he took himself and his food out of sight, behind the funnel, in order not to upset her further, and when he returned, she actually gave him a pallid smile before sinking into sleep once more.

Michael stood at the rail and looked forward; he could see on the far horizon the bank of frail cloud which meant that land lay below; in an hour they would be in Dublin Bay, where the surge would be very much less. He returned to Mabel's side and told her that her troubles would soon be over, but she made no reply and he concluded that she really was asleep at last. Satisfied on this score, he settled down on the deck beside her and was very soon asleep himself.

*   *   *

Ginny's adventure had started aboard the ferry

heading for her father's country. No one had queried her right to be aboard for, because it was the summer holidays, a great many families, accompanied by their children, were returning to Ireland on this ship and Ginny guessed that each group assumed she was with another such party.

Like most children, she welcomed new experiences and forgot her own troubles in the pleasure of exploring, examining the lifeboats, the great funnels and the large saloons below deck. The sea surge worried her not at all and presently she fell into a game of hide and seek with a rowdy group of children of her own age. Soon she was able to ask them where they lived in Ireland and how long it would take them to reach their homes.

After four or five hours, it occurred to Ginny that one of the boys in the group was looking at her with rather more interest than seemed necessary. A little nettled, she stared back at him curiously, thinking that if he was going to say anything rude about her mass of bright red hair, she could easily reply in kind, for he was a strange-looking lad. He was very brown and his hair was brown too, though there was a sheen of gold over it caused, she imagined, by the strength of the summer sun. He was a thin boy, dressed in ragged kecks, ancient plimsolls and a threadbare grey shirt, which he wore unbuttoned to the waist and tied in a knot. But the really odd thing about him was his eyes, which were large, of so light a brown that they were almost gold, and slanted sharply upwards at the outer corners, giving him a sly look. Ginny noticed that his eyebrows, too, slanted upwards and decided to ask him why he was staring. She would have done so, too, except that he spoke first.

'Well? Know me again, Ginger?'

The remark was made in a Liverpool accent, yet Ginny was pretty sure the boy was Irish, though she could not have said why. There was just something in his face which reminded her of various Irish people she knew. 'I don't want to know you again,' she said coldly. 'An' if you call me Ginger once more, you nasty, slant-eyed tinker's get, I'll darken your daylights for you.'

Rather to her surprise, the boy looked at her approvingly; clearly he had not expected a girl to attack so briskly. 'I say, you're a fierce 'un,' he said admiringly. 'What's your name, then, if I ain't to call you Ginger, that is?' He grinned at her. 'Wharrabout Carrots? I've heered fellers in school callin' redheads Carrots; would you darken me bleedin' daylights for that?'

Ginny giggled; she could not help herself. He had spoken in such a droll way that despite her resolve to stand no nonsense, she had had to laugh. But she said as gravely as she could: 'Me name's Ginny and before you says another word, it ain't short for Ginger. Me real name's Virginia but all me pals call me Ginny, 'cos the other's so long. What's your name, then?'

'Conan O'Dowd, and in case you're wonderin', I'm off to seek me fortune in the land of me forefathers.' He cocked an intelligent eyebrow at her. 'Is that what you're doin'? Only I couldn't help noticin' that you're by yourself, same as me.'

'How d'you know I'm by meself?' Ginny said at once, the fear of being handed over to authority rising up in her again. 'I'm—I'm wi' me dad, only he's downstairs in the bar an' don't want me hangin' around.'

336

The boy grinned. 'You ain't with your dad at all,' he announced baldly. 'I see you come aboard wi' a fat old woman, but you left her as soon as your feet touched the deck and haven't been near nor by her since. Don't worry, there's nothin' wrong with being alone—I am meself.'

There was a moment's pause whilst Ginny considered what to say and decided the truth was probably best. 'All right, I *am* on me own,' she admitted. 'But I'm crossing to Ireland to find me daddy; his name's Michael Gallagher and he's gorra farm down by the sea. He were comin' over to Liverpool to fetch me back, only—only there were reasons why I couldn't wait, so I come by meself. Wharrabout you, then? Or are you really seeking your fortune?'

'It's a long story,' Conan admitted, 'same as I 'spect yours is. It's odd though: we're both searchin' for our fathers. Mine's called Eamonn O'Dowd. He came over to Liverpool to do navvying work, met me mam—she were a Liverpool girl—an' they had me. Only when I were five, me mam died an' me dad left me with me Aunt Deb, and went back to Ireland. I were happy enough, even after Aunt Deb married Uncle Tom and they had half a dozen kids of their own. But last year, Aunt Deb died an' Uncle Tom married the woman next door. She don't like me an' I don't like her, so I stole the housekeeping money, bought me a ticket on the ferry, an' when I gets to Ireland, I'm goin' to start looking for me dad.'

'Cor,' Ginny said reverently. 'That's a story and a half, ain't it? I wonder if it's true?'

Conan grinned. 'Well, I mebbe prettied it up a little,' he admitted. 'But I am searchin' for me dad,

337

honest to God I am, only he could be anywhere because Aunt Deb always said he were an Irish tinker an' they travel all over the country. They work on the little farms, steal a few peats and the odd hen, whittle clothes pegs an' linen props to sell, picks bunches o' white heather—that's for good luck, you know—an' turn their hand to anything what'll make 'em a few bob.' He looked speculatively at Ginny. 'What say we team up, the two of us? We can search for our dads an' keep one another company. It's summer so I reckon we won't starve, not with the orchards full of apples an' the rivers full of fish. What d'you say?'

Ginny looked at her companion doubtfully, realising as she did so that she did not trust him an inch. But what was the harm, after all? Poor Conan had no idea where his father might be found but she had a name and address. If he liked to accompany her to her father's farm outside Dublin, she was sure there could be no harm in it and the Gallaghers might have heard of a band of wandering tinkers. She said as much to Conan who nodded enthusiastically, eyes brightening. 'You're right there, Ginny,' he said. 'From what me Aunt Deb's told me, all the tinkers know one another. Once it gets about that young Conan O'Dowd is searching for his dad there'll be a dozen folk what'll tell me where he's to be found. Now, where does your dad live?'

For answer, Ginny pulled the much-crumpled letter out of her pocket and held it out. Her companion took it, looked at it for a moment or two, and then nodded sagely, handing it back to her. 'Aye, well, that's clear enough,' he said, rather gruffly. 'How long d'you reckon it'll take us to reach the farm?'

Ginny stared at him thoughtfully. 'An awful long time if it's left to you, since you were holdin' the letter upside down,' she said accusingly. 'You can't read, can you? Why didn't you say?'

Conan grinned again, looking not in the least discomposed. ' 'Cos I sagged off school whenever I could to help me Aunt Deb,' he said cheerfully. 'Readin's no good to a tinker, anyhow. Tinkers read in different ways. They look at the sky an' tell you if it's goin' to rain or if there's a storm blowin' up. They look at the hedgerows an' can tell whether the farmer's a sharp one who'll notice if a few turnips go missin'. An' they look into people's faces an' read their minds, and that's a lot more useful than book learning.'

Ginny was about to demand that, if he was so clever, he should tell her what she was thinking right now, but fortunately for their future friendship the ship's bucking movement suddenly ceased and they found themselves gliding into the mouth of the River Liffey.

'C'mon, we're goin' to dock,' Conan shouted excitedly. 'Let's see if we can be first ashore.'

*   *   *

Dublin was a surprise to both children. They had been brought up in a city whose waterfront towered high into the sky, with resplendent buildings seeming almost to touch the clouds, but Dublin was very different. It was smaller, lower, and a good deal more compact so that the children felt none of the awe which they experienced when passing the Liver buildings, the Custom House, the great town hall and, of course, St George's, up on its plateau. As soon as they were ashore, Ginny bought a large loaf of brown, rustic-looking bread and a chunk of creamy local cheese from a small shop. Then she and Conan squatted on a low stone wall and began to plan their next move. Ginny read her father's address to Conan and was relieved when he nodded wisely. 'Aye, I've heard me Auntie Deb speak of it often and often,' he assured her. 'I dunno, offhand, exactly where it is, but I do know it's no more'n a couple of miles from the city itself. D'you want to go there at once, queen, or can we take a look round this place first? Only, we're none too flush for cash, either of us. An' I reckon we might make ourselves a few bob here, because when we're in the country it'll be all turnips and fields of corn and we shan't get much of a price for *them*.'

Ginny agreed to this, though rather doubtfully. For her own part, she was pretty sure she had sufficient money to last her until she reached Headland Farm, but fair was fair; Conan might have to search for many weeks before running his father to earth and he only had 1/6d left out of the housekeeping money he had stolen. Ginny did not approve of his action in taking the money, but guessed that circumstances had forced him to behave the way he had. So she agreed that they should search the city for some means of making a bit of money before abandoning the place and making for her father's farm.

That first day, they explored their surroundings, trying to find somewhere to spend the night, and came upon a large park with benches set amidst trees and shrubs, and a big pond full of gold, white and red fishes, which Conan told her were carp. 'They make good eating,' he said wistfully, gazing at the sinuous shapes in the watery depths. 'But I dare say folk 'ud notice if we started haulin' 'em out, so we'll make do with bread an' cheese an' a few apples tonight, I reckon.'

Ginny insisted upon paying for the food, secure in the knowledge that she would soon be with her father, particularly when they found a market in a place called Capel Street. 'The only snag we're goin' to come across is the language,' Conan remarked after they had purchased more bread and cheese, a bottle of ginger beer and two large oranges. 'The old shawlies is bad enough, but I scarce understood a word them kids were sayin'. I know there is a language called Irish, but they weren't speakin' that, were they? It's goin' to make it mortal difficult to find our way to your dad's place.'

Ginny, rather chastened, admitted that this was so. Coming from Liverpool, the children were both used to a certain amount of Irish brogue, but she supposed that Dubliners spoke slowly and with more care, when in England, than they did on their native soil. 'It's all right when you're buyin' somethin', 'cos you can guess, more or less, what they're sayin',' she admitted. 'But askin' the way . . . well, that's goin' to be a lot more difficult.'

'Aye; an' from what Aunt Deb told me, the tinkers have a language all their own,' Conan said. 'Still, I dare say we'll get by. Shall us eat our supper sittin' by the fish pond or shall us take it to a nice, cosy bench under the trees, where we won't be spotted if a scuffer comes by?'

It was growing dusk and Ginny decided it would

be more sensible to find shelter for the night. Presently, the pair of them discovered not a bench, but a thicket whose branches were so cunningly entwined overhead that, even if it rained, she doubted that they would get wet. The thicket was floored with dried leaves and the children sat under its canopy, ate their food and drank their ginger beer and then snuggled down for the night, curling up back to back to share their warmth, like a couple of puppies.

'No one's goin' to spot us here,' Conan mumbled, just before sleep claimed them. 'Tell you what, queen, I'm rare glad we found each other, ain't you? Sleepin' rough's all very well in the countryside, but if it weren't for the fact that we're together, I don't think I'd care to kip down in a public park, not wi' scuffers an' park keepers an' such on the prowl.'

Ginny was much struck by this piece of good sense and agreed that meeting had been a bit of luck for them both. She had meant to keep a weather eye open for any figures of authority passing their nest, but sleep overtook her within five minutes of settling down and both children slumbered soundly till morning.

*   *   *

When Conan had first suggested making some money before beginning their search, Ginny had felt some reservations. She was not at all sure how they could possibly make money because all the methods by which children at home earned a penny or two would be barred to them. They could not run messages, beg wooden boxes off greengrocers and chop them into kindling, carry heavy baskets for neighbours, or even offer to help swill down the fishmongers' stalls when trade was finished for the day. Well, perhaps they could do one or two of these things, if they could make it plain to the locals that they wanted some sort of paid work.

However, she accompanied Conan back to the big indoor market they had found the previous day and soon realised that, so far as her companion was concerned, the language spoken and the understanding of adults was immaterial. Conan meant to steal and was so good at it that, at first, Ginny did not realise where he had obtained the large canvas bag, or its contents. When she asked him, Conan was frank enough. 'I robbed 'em,' he said cheerfully. 'No use looking so po-faced about it, queen, 'cos there ain't no other way, not for us there ain't. But if you don't like it, just steer clear o' me in the next shop. You can watch though,' he added, with a gleam in his eye which told Ginny that he was not the least ashamed of his actions, was, in fact, quite proud of them. 'If you do, you'll learn a thing or two, I'm tellin' you.'

Ginny said, loftily, that she did not wish to learn a thing or two, not if it concerned stealing from shops, but she was curious and hovered in the doorway of the next grocery store Conan entered. Having seen him at work, she had to admit— though only to herself—that he was a very skilful operator. He stood the large canvas bag down at his feet, gaping open, then purchased a screw of tea, taking his time over the transaction. Had she not been watching closely, she would never have spotted the quick dart of his hand towards the pile of goods being purchased by a woman standing

343

beside him, nor have seen how neatly it fell into his shopping bag. He did this two or three times, netting a bag of dried fruit, some extra strong mints and some broken biscuits. Watching him, Ginny doubted whether he actually knew what he had stolen, for he never seemed to take either his eyes or his attention away from the various teas which the shop assistant was showing him, though when the pair of them were outside on the street once more and Ginny pointed out that he might have stolen half a dozen candles and a tin of boot polish, he shook his head chidingly at her.

'You don't have no faith, you don't,' he said accusingly. 'I've been robbin' shops since I were knee high to a grasshopper an' I took a good long look at the sort o' stuff the old gal were buyin' afore I touched any of it. Have a biscuit; there's some of them ones wi' icing on the top, or you might find a chocolate one if you delve about a bit.'

It would have been nice to refuse, to tell Conan that she would not accept stolen food, but she realised that she was in no position to criticise. As Conan said, the shop was a large and successful one and the woman he had robbed was smartly dressed and buying a great quantity of things. 'I wouldn't rob folks as poor as us,' he said righteously. 'Tinkers don't do things like that an' besides, me Aunt Deb wouldn't've liked it.' He helped himself to another biscuit and rattled the bag under Ginny's nose. 'Go on, have another,' he urged. 'And then we'll start lookin' for your dad's farm.'

* * *

344

Two days later, they had thoroughly searched the immediate area of Dublin without any success. They had asked a number of people, mostly kids like themselves, whether they knew of a place called Headland Farm, somewhere in the vicinity of Killorglin, but the most they got were blank looks and a suggestion that they should try somewhere else. Though they raided orchards and stole root crops from the fields, their food was running out and Ginny was becoming more and more convinced that they were searching the wrong area altogether. Conan suggested that they should offer to work on one of the farms for a bit, so that they could earn enough money to catch a bus or train, which would enable them to search further afield, but Ginny's faith in her new-found friend was fast running out. She knew, now, that he would always be reluctant to admit to ignorance, that when she had asked him if Headland Farm and Killorglin were near Dublin he had not had the foggiest notion, but had simply replied in the affirmative, determined not to admit that he had no more idea than she.

And by the same token, it occurred to her that asking kids was unlikely to get them far. She was a kid herself, and though she knew the area around Victoria Court intimately, and was beginning to know Seaforth too, she would have been hard pressed to say where Wavertree was, or Aigburth or Allerton, though she knew they were all to be found somewhere in the vicinity of the city. But if a questioner had asked the way to St Helens or Manchester, she would not have had the vaguest idea in which direction such places lay.

So when they had managed to get enough money

together to take a bus ride, Ginny told Conan, with unusual crispness, that she meant to ask a grown-up in one of the shops to put them on the right road . . . mebbe even a post office, if there was one, and to take a bus as far as they could on their way. 'I know you don't want us to make enquiries in Dublin, partly because of the thievin' and partly because you're afraid the scuffers might hand us over to an orphanage or something,' she told him defiantly, 'but a village or town will be different.'

Conan demurred, but only half-heartedly. He clearly realised he had been rumbled and did not want to lose Ginny's friendship, for the fact that there were two of them was becoming increasingly important as the days passed. Fortunately, the weather had remained mild and sunny but Ginny thought, shrewdly, that a couple of rainy, chilly days would make them both begin to think wistfully of the charms of a roof over one's head, three meals a day and a soft bed at night.

So early on the morning of their third day in Ireland, they climbed aboard a country bus heading for Portlaoise and descended from the vehicle when it reached the town. There was a main street lined with respectable-looking houses and a scattering of small shops, including a linen draper's, a post office and a general store. There was a pleasant green with two slatted wooden seats upon which sat half a dozen elderly men, smoking their pipes and enjoying the early sunshine, and the usual group of children crouching on the pavement and playing some complicated-looking game which involved sticks, string and a pile of small, shiny pebbles.

'We'll ask them kids . . .' Conan was beginning,

moving towards them, when Ginny seized his arm.

'No!' she said vehemently. 'You stay and watch the kids if you like, but I'm going to try the post office.' The post office was on the further side of the green, and she was only halfway across when there was a triumphant shout behind her.

'Hang on a minute, chuck,' Conan panted, arriving breathlessly at her side. 'No need to go to the post office; them kids told me there's a group o' tinkers camped out on a bit o' wasteland not all that far away. They've been helpin' wi' lifting the potato crop and it ain't finished yet—the work, I mean—so they'll be here for a day or two. And tinkers travel the whole country, so if anyone knows where this here Kill place is, it'll be them.'

'It's Killorglin,' Ginny said. 'Well, what are we waitin' for? Oh, Conan, with a bit of luck, I could be wi' me daddy by nightfall.'

CHAPTER THIRTEEN

By the time the ferry arrived at the quays, Mabel was so worn out and empty that the only thing she could think of was how soon she would be able to lie down. Michael helped her ashore and then led her, tottering, to the nearest bench, where she collapsed, clutching her hollow stomach and not even thinking to thank her escort for carrying her little suitcase as well as his own grip.

After a moment, Michael sat down beside her. 'Are you feeling more the thing?' he asked. 'Because if so, we'd best be makin' tracks. The kid ain't likely to be hangin' round the quays. Are we goin' to ask folk in Dublin if they've seen her or are we goin' to make for the nearest railway station and ask there? The trouble is, I can't read Ginny's mind and I reckon you can't either. So what's best to be done, eh?'

Mabel leaned back against the sun-warmed wooded seat and closed her eyes, but as soon as she did so the ground seemed to surge beneath her feet and her head swam. Hastily, she opened her eyes once more, narrowing them against the sunlight, and regarded her companion with hostility. Had he no sensitivity, the great Irish lump? Here was she, sick unto death, simply longing to lie down in a darkened room and all he could do was ply her with unanswerable questions and suggest courses of action which she was simply not capable of carrying out.

She opened her mouth to say all these things but, rather to her surprise, all that came out was a sound very like a miaow, followed by a small but definite groan. Michael patted her shoulder but she could see he was stifling a smile and, had she been capable, she would have said something cutting, something to wipe the amusement from his face. However, she was clearly not capable so had to content herself with saying, in a husky whisper: 'I— I don't think I can help much right now. I feel terribly ill. I've got awful pains inside, my throat feels as if someone's cut it and there's no strength in my legs. I thought I was dying aboard the ferry and I still think I am.'

Michael laughed. 'Well, of course you've got pains in your inside because you chucked up everything, bar your liver and lights,' he said, with hateful cheerfulness. 'You'll feel better when

348

you've some grub inside you though, I can promise you that.' He put a strong arm round her and heaved her to her feet, ignoring her squawk of protest. 'Come along now, I'm tellin' you, no one ever died of seasickness yet, especially on dry land. Tell you what, we'll book into a lodging house, get ourselves a bit o' dinner and then begin to ask questions. What d'you think of that?'

'It's a bloody awful idea,' Mabel said resentfully. She had been brought up never to swear but felt that only strong language could convey her feelings to this great dolt. 'I can't even face a cup of tea, let alone anything more solid. Oh, dear God, and I can't even turn round and go home because it would mean getting back on that bloody ship and crossin' that terrible bloody ocean again.'

Michael was still holding her upright, pressed against his side, and though he did not actually laugh again she felt his amusement and would have liked to push him away, though she dared not do so for fear she would simply collapse on the cobbles at his feet. However, he said, encouragingly: 'Don't worry, I know what I'm talkin' about. There's a little café not fifty yards away—we'll go there first, if you like. Then, when you've got some of your strength back, we'll carry out the rest of me programme, awright?'

'I shan't eat anything, nor shall I drink so much as a cup of tea,' Mabel muttered, but she took care to keep her voice below the range of his hearing. She did make an abortive effort to take her case from him, but he shook his head, chidingly, assuring her that it was 'light as a feather, so it is', and continued to almost carry her across the cobbled quays and into what she took to be a workmen's small dining room, since it was crowded with men whom she imagined to be dock workers, whilst the only woman in sight wore a cheerful checked apron and was serving the food across a wide—and very dirty—wooden counter.

'Can someone find this lady a chair?' Michael bawled. 'She's not feeling too good but I told her a plateful of Ma Mulligan's stew and a nice hot cup o' tay would soon put her right.'

Mabel, gazing with lacklustre eyes at the dockers and other working men, was pleasantly surprised when a table was hastily cleared and she was pushed into a wooden kitchen chair whilst the aproned woman came clucking from behind the counter with a cup in her hand, remarking that the poor young critter looked green as a cabbage, so she did, and would benefit from strong, sweet tea which she must drink up immediately, whilst it was hot.

The kindness and hospitality behind the words was so plain that Mabel actually found herself taking the cup and sipping at the burning liquid. She did not normally take sugar in her tea and thought it had a very strange taste, but it was wonderfully warming and presently she looked across at Michael, sitting opposite her at the small table, and managed a watery smile. He smiled back and lifted his own mug to her as if in salute. 'Feelin' better?' he enquired. 'Ma Mulligan's tay is famous, for she always puts a drop of something in it and it settles your stomach like nothin' else can.'

Mabel put her cup down hastily. What could the woman have put in the tea? Ever since moving to Liverpool, she had heard stories of innocent girls doped by seemingly friendly strangers who had

350

then shipped them off to South America. But surely this would not apply in Ireland? And Ma Mulligan had a round, rosy-red face, devoid of guile. Lowering her voice to a whisper, Mabel asked Michael what had been put into her cup and was only partly reassured when her companion told her that it was nothing more dangerous than a tot of rum. At any other time, Mabel, who had never touched alcohol in her life, would have been appalled by this information, but now she simply concluded that the spirit must be medicinal and continued to sip at her drink.

By the time a large plateful of stew and dumplings had been put before her, she realised that she really was hungry, and, though it went against the grain to admit Michael was right, she soon began to feel a good deal better, though her longing to lie down quietly for an hour or so had not left her. Still, she reminded herself as Michael paid the bill and the two of them left the stuffy little room, she could scarcely expect her companion not to worry over his small daughter, alone in this strange city.

'I know a neat little lodging house where they'll give us a clean bed and only charge a couple of bob,' Michael said presently, as they made their way through the crowds thronging the quays. 'The place is owned by a Mrs Connell an' she's a grand cook, so she is. I dare say we shan't be in Dublin long, for it's not a big place and a wee girl, on her own, is bound to be noticed, but while we are here, Mrs Connell will feed us right well.'

'I hope you're right,' Mabel murmured. 'But there do seem to be an awful lot of children about, Mr Ga . . . I mean, Michael. And I don't know if you've noticed, but more than half of them seem to be redheaded girls. I thought Ginny would stand out, with that long, thick plait of red hair, but now I'm not so sure.'

Michael laughed. 'Aye, they say that red hair is typical of the Irish,' he admitted. 'But I've not seen many plaits, have you? Lots of girls, though, and a grosh o' freckles.'

'Ginny isn't freckled . . .' Mabel was beginning when Michael steered her gently into a side street and presently she found herself entering a small, clean house, where she was greeted by a grey-haired woman in a blue wrap-around overall, who led her guest to a tiny bedroom, sparsely furnished, with a small truckle bed, sprig muslin curtains at the window and a wash stand.

'You'll be on the next floor up, Mr Gallagher, dear,' Mrs Connell said, preceding them down the stairs. 'No need to show you your room; you've stayed in it often enough. Now what was the problem you mentioned when I was showing this young lady the kitchen where me guests have their dinners?'

Rather to Mabel's surprise, Michael told their landlady the story of Ginny's flight from Liverpool and the puzzle of her whereabouts, whilst Mrs Connell listened with bright, intelligent eyes fixed on his face. 'It's a frightenin' thought, so it is, to have a wee lass on the loose in Ireland, not knowin' a soul an' innocent as a new-born lamb of the wicked ways of men,' she said solemnly when Michael had finished his tale. 'But I'll put the word around, m'dear, and get the priest to do the same, and afore you know it we'll have run the child to earth an' no harm done. You did say she were

352

alone?'

'She was definitely alone when she left Liverpool,' Mabel said, putting her oar in for the first time, 'but we asked at the ferry terminal and they couldn't remember a child by herself. Apparently there were a great number of family parties crossing the Irish Sea that day, so I suppose she might have palled up with someone.'

Michael, however, said that he was doubtful of this. 'I don't believe she'd confide in a grown-up because if she'd felt inclined to do so she could have gone to you, Mabel,' he pointed out. 'I think she'll make her own way to Kerry, but what really worries me is how she'll live on the journey. Oh, I know country kids can live off the land for weeks at this time of year, but my Ginny isn't a country kid an' she may see nickin' a few apples or munchin' on raw potatoes as thievery and prefer to go hungry.'

Mrs Connell laughed at this and shook her head. 'Kids is kids. I've no doubt even English kids box the cox from time to time,' she assured her guests. 'Besides, kids see growin' things as everyone's right, so I don't think she'll starve. But as I said, I'll put the word around an' if she's lyin' up anywhere in Dublin, don't you worry yourselves, it'll come to my ears soon enough.'

With this Michael and Mabel had to be content, but as soon as Mabel felt sufficiently rested, the pair of them set off. At every street stall and corner where a news vendor or a lad offering to polish one's shoes stood, Michael stopped and gestured to his companion, who promptly went into her soon familiar spiel. 'Have you by any chance seen a thin little girl of about ten years old, wearing a faded blue cotton dress, with a long braid of red hair? Or

353

her hair might be loose, because it is very curly and difficult to restrain. She has blue eyes and a Liverpool accent. She's not in any sort of trouble except that she missed her father and went aboard the ferry by herself, and now we're anxious to find her again.'

One or two people thought they might have seen such a child, but since no one had watched which way she went, this was of very little help. In fact, Mabel was doubtful whether the child they thought they had seen was, in fact, Ginny. As she had already remarked, there seemed to be even more kids on the streets of Dublin than there were in Liverpool and at least half of them had curly red hair. As evening approached, she and Michael returned to their lodgings, very much discouraged. 'I don't reckon she's spent long in the city,' Michael told his companion. 'Oh, I'm not sayin' she would have set off for Killorglin immediately—and anyway, the farm's a fair way from Killorglin—but I am saying I reckon she'd have more sense than to hang around here. I told her in all me letters about the fishin' and the mussel beds. She'll know she won't find such things in Dublin.'

'Well, she'll know once she's had a good look round,' Mabel said. 'But there's a lot of—of seaside around here, wouldn't you say? If she's searched all of that she might still be in the neighbourhood.'

'Aye, there's Booterstown . . . but every kid in Dublin knows Booterstown, and they'd tell her soon enough that it's not Killorglin . . . and then there's Bray, only that's a bit further off . . . Oh, I dunno! I reckon we ought to spend one more day here, and then set off for Kerry.'

Mabel and Michael got their first real lead early on the following day. They had tried a great many different places without any success at all, so when they approached the bus stands on Aston Quay Mabel very nearly told Michael that this would be yet another useless enquiry. However, they approached a young news vendor, squatting cross-legged by the bus stand, and Michael launched into the now familiar questioning. Had the lad noticed a young, red-haired girl, probably in shabby and faded clothing, with a long mass of ginger curls and a Liverpool accent.

The boy looked up at them, then scrambled to his feet, holding out a newspaper. 'Would you be wantin' a copy of the *Irish Independent*?' he asked hopefully. ' 'Tis only a penny to you, sir.'

'No, I'm not after wantin' a paper, only some information, but I'll pay you a silver sixpenny piece if you can help me,' Michael said. 'I'm lookin' for a girl of ten or eleven wit' long . . .'

'I know, I heered you,' the boy said. He grinned up at Michael. 'A sixpence, eh? Well now, would she be a girl wit' a long, red plait, wearin' a blue cotton dress an' plimsolls wit' her toes poking out? And would she have a rare funny sort o' voice . . . I heered her say *Gerralook at the timetable, Conan* to the young feller she were with.'

'That sounds like my Ginny,' Michael said, after a quick confirming nod from Mabel. But—but we t'ought she was on her own, so we did. Who was this she were with? Was he young? Old?'

The boy considered. 'He weren't a lot older than her, I shouldn't think,' he said, after a moment. 'He was wearing plimsolls—better ones'n hers—blue shirt and raggedy trousers. I noticed him 'cos he had an Irish name but he talked just like she did.' He gave a derisive crow of amusement. 'No, he weren't Irish; he were as English as she were.'

'You're a noticin' sort of young chiseller,' Michael said, producing a silver sixpence from his pocket and handing it to the boy. 'You didn't happen to notice where they went next, I suppose, 'cos if you did, I've got another sixpence in me pocket which is almost burnin' a hole, it's that eager to jump into your palm.'

This time the boy did not even have to consider. 'I know 'xactly where they went, 'cos they stood close by me, countin' their money,' he said. 'They wanted to go to Glyn-something-or-other but they couldn't afford the fare, not to go all the way. So they boarded a bus for Portlaoise—leastways the bus were bound for Limerick but they only had enough money to get to Portlaoise.'

Michael gave a deep, contented sigh, rooted around in his pocket and produced a shilling. He handed it to the boy, thanked him very much for the information and took Mabel's arm. He led her away from the bus stands and down towards the Liffey, but then it seemed he could contain his exuberance no longer. He flung both arms round her, lifted her off her feet and whirled her round, then set her gently down. 'I'm sorry for takin' such a liberty, Mabel,' he said, but the humble words did not match the excitement in his tone or his broad and triumphant grin. 'So we're on the trail at last! We must go straight back to our lodgings, pay what we owe and catch the next bus to Portlaoise.'

Ginny and Conan reached the tinkers' camp as the sun was setting. It had proved to be a good deal further from the town than their informants had supposed, or perhaps the tinkers had moved on, for naturally they would set up camp close to where the work was. As they neared the spot, Ginny began to feel distinctly apprehensive. The tinkers had a couple of ancient caravans but it seemed that they mostly lived in stained and ragged tents. Ginny had been impressed by the beauty of the countryside and, though she did not say so, thought the tinkers' camp a blot on the landscape. They had erected their tents in a small valley beneath a stand of pines and a river wound its leisurely way not twenty feet from the encampment. A number of livestock, mostly ponies and donkeys, grazed desultorily nearby, and as the children approached the camp half a dozen skinny, vicious-looking dogs hurtled towards them. None of the animals made a sound, which struck Ginny as very queer, but they surrounded the two children and Ginny could hear muttered growls whenever she or Conan moved.

'Here boy,' Conan said uncertainly to the nearest dog. It was a mean-eyed lurcher, grey and gaunt. Ginny thought it had a good deal of wolf in its make-up and was careful not to move, but as though Conan's words had been some sort of introduction the dogs suddenly ceased to bristle and growl and the largest of them—the lurcher-cross wolf—turned to look back at the encampment, almost as if it were waiting for instructions, and Ginny saw, with some relief, a tall, thin man holding a hefty stick, coming towards them. She thought he looked menacing, but when he reached them his tanned face broke into a broad grin and she realised he was probably no more than twenty or twenty-two and seemed well disposed towards them.

'Evenin', kids,' he said. 'Is your da' lookin' for someone to give a hand wit' his spuds? Or mebbe he's wantin' to buy a nice little mule? We only moved here today, so we ain't fixed up for work yet.' He held out a grimy hand. 'I'm Flann Kavanagh; who's you?'

'I'm Conan and this is Ginny,' the boy said, taking the proffered hand before Ginny had done more than open her mouth to reply. 'We've come to Ireland to find our famblies. My dad's a tinker so I thought mebbe you'd know where I can find him. His name is Eamonn O'Dowd.'

Flann, who had been staring, curiously, from one to the other, suddenly seemed to remember himself and took Ginny's small paw in his. 'You'll be brother and sister; you've both got a look of the O'Dowd family,' he said genially. 'An' aren't you the lucky ones? For Flann Kavanagh knows your daddy right well, though where he is now, I'm not so sure.' He grinned widely at them, revealing amazingly white teeth. 'Mebbe in gaol,' he ended, giving them a glance so sly that Ginny flinched. He saw the movement and grinned again. 'Only coddin' you,' he added hastily.

'So you know him? But you can't tell us where he's likely to be?' Conan said uneasily. 'Won't he be workin' the farms, same as you?'

Flann shrugged. 'Mebbe, mebbe not,' he said guardedly. 'But as we're movin' across the country, we'll meet other tribes and one of 'em's bound to know where your daddy's liable to be found.' He glanced curiously at them, his light eyes flickering over them both from head to toe. Ginny felt that every article of clothing she wore had been assessed and probably found wanting. 'Got any money, have you? You can stay wit' us but we don't carry passengers. You'll have to pay, or work.'

He was looking at Conan as he spoke, but this time it was Ginny who answered. She did not see the point of letting this man believe she was Conan's sister, since it could scarcely help in her search for her own father. Besides, if these people were moving across the country in the wrong direction, she might find herself worse off than before. 'I'm not his sister. Me name's Ginny— Ginny Gallagher, and me daddy's Michael,' she said bluntly. 'He's gorra farm near somewhere called Killorglin. Is that near here?'

Flann had taken very little notice of Ginny but now he stared at her as though seeing her for the first time. Staring back, Ginny saw that he had a broad forehead and high cheekbones tapering to a jutting and determined chin. His eyes were a very light brown and they had the same tilt to them that Conan's had. Ginny had never seen a fox but suddenly she thought that there was something foxy about this young man and realised that she neither liked nor trusted him. His smile was friendly but it never reached his eyes. But now he was speaking, and to her for a change. 'Michael Gallagher. Michael Gallagher,' he said slowly. 'You're not after tryin' to cod me that he's a tinker, like meself? 'Cos Gallagher ain't a tinker's name.'

Does this man think I'm a fool? Ginny asked herself inside her head. Doesn't he listen when

359

someone speaks to him? But she did not mean to let her annoyance show; if this man could tell her in which direction Killorglin lay—if it was not far— she would be off at once and have no more need of him. 'How could me dad be a tinker when I just told you he has a farm?' she asked reasonably. 'Don't you listen when a girl talks to you, mister? All I'm really askin' you is if you know Killorglin? It's in Kerry,' she added belatedly.

Flann grinned ingratiatingly at her but Ginny continued to stare at him and did not return the smile. She was disliking him more with every moment that passed and was already determined to get away from here just as soon as she was able. But the man was speaking, his tone no longer mocking. 'Killorglin? I know it well; a grand town, so it is. And the countryside around it, grand country. But it's a fair way off—several days' journey, in fact. Us tinkers travel great distances, so we do, and we're headin' for Kerry, but we shan't get there tomorrow, nor yet the next day. Still, if you come wit' us, you'll get there in the end. And now, come over to the fire and you shall have a hunk o' bread and a plate o' stew and a warm place in a tent. Then tomorrer, we'll talk about how you're goin' to work your way wit' us.'

For the first time, Ginny looked past Flann and realised that whilst he had been talking to them, most of the other members of the tinker tribe had come forward and were listening curiously to the conversation. They were a wild enough looking band with flashing eyes, gleaming teeth and ragged clothing. Most of the men carried cudgels and the women, though not as shabby as the men, still seemed dirty and unkempt beside the townspeople that the children had met earlier in the day. Ginny clutched Conan's arm and glanced uneasily behind her, only to realise that they were completely surrounded. All in a moment, she knew that they had got themselves into real trouble. If they ran, the dogs would undoubtedly pull them down before they could get more than a few yards, but if they stayed, they would be completely in the power of the tinkers. The only good thing is that no one's goin' to believe I'm a tinker's brat when they see me red hair an' white skin, Ginny found herself thinking. But this is mad, what can they want with us, after all? We're only a couple of kids and even if we work for them, we'll eat our share. I remember Aunt Mary saying gypsies stole children but I didn't believe it then and I don't believe it now. So I reckon it's best just to pretend to go along with them and get away later when they think we're staying with them of our own accord.

She had clutched Conan's arm, and now she felt his hand take hers and give it a reassuring squeeze. The whole group was moving back towards the fire now, taking the children with it, and Conan muttered into her ear: 'It's awright, chuck, don't you fret yourself. They look pretty rough but they won't harm us 'cos I'm one of 'em, don't forget!'

'No, I won't forget,' Ginny said rather grimly. She decided that she would not tell Conan she meant to escape. As he had said, he was at least partly a tinker and was probably as sly and untrustworthy as these men and women appeared to be.

And presently, Ginny realised that she was actually enjoying herself. Sitting cross-legged in the firelight, amongst a group of children of similar age to herself, with a tin plate full of the most delicious stew in front of her and a hunk of coarse brown bread in one hand, the romance of it all brought a flush to her cheeks. It was a mild night and the stars twinkled in the dark sky and a large, orange moon shone through the branches of the pine trees. The tinker children smelled a bit high but the perfume of grasses, water and the pine needles upon which they sat masked the unwashed odour of the tribe.

The stew was excellent and Ginny asked her neighbour what was in it. She was a plump, golden-skinned girl wearing a ragged red dress, her long black hair reaching almost to her waist, and she smiled at Ginny's question. 'Everything,' she announced after a moment's thought. 'Rabbit, pigeon, squirrel, hedgepig . . . and there's carrots, onions, taties, turnip . . . everythin' we can get hold of. Good, ain't it?'

'It's grand,' Ginny said fervently. 'I never tasted anythin' so good in me whole life an' me Auntie Amy's a first-rate cook. Who made the bread?'

'It's sody bread; I prigged it meself off the baker in the village while me mam were buyin' flour,' the girl said offhandedly. 'There'll be tea in a moment when the kettle boils.'

It occurred to Ginny at this moment that she was fortunate indeed to have sat down by this particular girl since she had understood every word her companion had uttered, whereas most of the children might have been speaking Chinese for all the sense she could make of it. But this girl was different.

Presently, when she had finished her stew and was drinking strong, sweet tea out of a mug, Ginny

362

said as much. The girl grinned. 'That's why I sat by you,' she said. 'Mammy and I lived in Liverpool for several years 'cos me dad were a Chinese seaman and Mammy were that fond of him, she'd have followed him anywhere, but then he jumped ship— or mebbe he were killed in a brawl, we never really knew—so a year gone, Mammy came home to her tribe and brought me with her,' she finished.

'What's your name, kid?' Conan interrupted. He was sitting by Ginny and leaned forward to speak across her. He indicated Ginny with a jerk of his thumb. 'She's Ginny an' I'm Conan. What's your moniker?'

'I'm Nan,' the girl said briefly. She drained the last of her tea, set her mug down and stood up. 'C'mon, Ginny, we'll get to us tent afore everyone else piles in.' She turned to Conan. 'The boys' tent's next to our'n,' she told him. 'G'night; see you in the mornin'.'

It was stuffy and not very pleasant in the tent though the smell of trodden grass was sweet. 'I'd rather sleep near the entrance,' Ginny told her new friend, as other females, both young and old, began to enter.

Nan said something to one of the older women, not one word of which Ginny could understand, and the woman replied at some length. Whereupon, Nan turned to Ginny, shaking her head. 'No, we're to sleep right at the back, agin the canvas,' she said. 'The older women has to be up first to make the fire and start the breakfast. Kids allus sleep at the back.'

Ginny shrugged and took the ragged piece of blanket which Nan was offering her. 'Okay,' she said resignedly. 'G'night, Nan.'

363

Ginny awoke next morning and could not, for a moment, think where she was. Just above her was a piece of very dirty brown canvas. She had an ache in her back from lying on the hard ground, and judging from the noises she was sharing her abode—whatever it was—with a family of pigs, for there were snorts, grunts and squeals coming from somewhere. Groggily, she sat up and looked about her and memory came rushing back. She was in a small tent, sharing it with . . . she counted . . . half a dozen girls ranging in age from four or five to fifteen, and three elderly women. Even as she watched, however, one of the old women yawned, stretched and stumbled out into the morning, then another followed. Neither of them had glanced in her direction, and Ginny lay quietly down again. She needed time to think, to consider what she should do, and if there was an opportunity to escape, she must take it, so it would be best to pretend to be asleep whilst she worked out a plan.

When the third woman left the tent, Ginny shed her blanket and crawled over to the entrance. Outside, the camp was already astir and the sounds, which she had thought had come from her fellow sleepers, were explained. A tinker who looked about twelve or thirteen was driving a lean sow with half a dozen scrawny piglets at heel into the encampment, and it was from these animals that the various squeals and grunts had come. In fact, her first guess had been correct for the sow and her brood must have been passing the back of the tent as Ginny had woken. The boy turned and grinned at her as she stood up and looked slowly about her. The huge stew pot of the night before had been taken off the fire and a smaller vessel was in its place. The elderly women were fussing round the fire and a younger woman, wrapped in a scarlet shawl, came towards them with her arms full of sticks and began to poke them into the flames beneath the blackened pot. Breakfast, judging by the smell which came from that direction, was to be oatmeal and Ginny realised that despite the good supper she had eaten the night before she was hungry once more. When someone jerked her elbow, she turned quite crossly, for the scene before her was fascinating. She had thought that tinkers were a pretty feckless lot, but they were moving quickly and neatly now. Men were hustling the sow and her brood into the shelter of the pine wood where, Ginny now saw, they had already made a rough enclosure which they were disguising, in what she considered to be a masterly fashion, with branches of pine and bundles of sticks, until it resembled nothing so much as a fuel store. The children were beginning to emerge from their sleeping quarters and they, too, were going about their business speedily and efficiently. Two of the bigger boys seized buckets and carried them off in the direction of the river whilst younger boys disappeared into the woods and the girls began to spread out, a couple making off, armed with buckets, towards the meadows which lay above the little valley and others moving the livestock's tethers so that they might have fresh grazing.

'Hey, queen, wharra you starin' at?' It was Conan, rubbing sleep out of his eyes and looking around him at the bustle with a good deal of

365

interest. 'Them pigs woke me up, a-snufflin' and a-snortin' as they was druv into the camp.' He grinned wickedly. 'Some farmer, somewhere, won't believe his eyes when he finds he's a sow short—a sow and her piglets.'

'You mean they're stolen?' Ginny said. She sounded shocked, which was exactly how she felt, for though they had passed a good few farms before they reached the tinker camp, they had all been small, poor affairs. She could not imagine a farmer failing to realise he had lost a pig, and as soon as he did so, surely he would make straight for the nearest tinker camp? She said as much to Conan, remarking indignantly that it was a mean thing to do, stealing from folk poorer than themselves. She added that she had no doubt the tinkers would speedily find themselves in prison if they continued to thieve from local farmers.

Conan, however, gave a derisive snort. 'It ain't like farmin' in England, what they do round here,' he explained. 'In summer, the farmers drive their pigs into the forest and on to common ground to fend for themselves. And besides, they're afraid of tinkers. They know tinkers thieve but they know, too, that unless they want to find their haystacks on fire or their calves and lambs carried off, they're best to keep quiet about the odd critter goin' missin'.'

'How do you know?' Ginny asked aggressively. 'An' don't go tellin' me your daddy told your mam and your mam told you, 'cos I shan't believe it. I already know you're a liar, Conan, so don't go makin' it worse.'

Conan grinned again. I believe he thinks it's a compliment to be called a liar, Ginny thought. One

366

thing is for sure, the sooner I can get away from the tinkers and Conan, the better I'll be pleased.

'No, queen, but I don't waste me time sleepin' when I need information,' Conan said boastfully. 'You know the feller who prigged the pigs? I talked to him last night, askin' 'im about the tribe and how they go on. He told me no end; he told me they're mainly horse dealers and go to all the horse fairs, buyin' an' sellin' what they can. That's why they're on their way to Kerry, 'cos there's a grand horse fair there. He told me they don't have no permanent place of their own so they reckon that gives them a right to take what they can between fairs. How else can they live, eh? They'll take eggs from beneath the sitting hen, but they'll always leave her one or two; clothing off the line, if the wife is mad enough to leave it unattended, and peats off the pile. Unless they've gorra grudge against a farmer, they won't take his lambs or calves, but pigs wanderin' in a wood, well, they could belong to anyone.'

'Oh,' Ginny said, rather doubtfully. 'Well, it ain't what I'm used to and I don't like it. Shall we—shall we go our own way, Conan? I can't see it's goin' to help us—well, not me, at any rate—travellin' with this little lot. An' they can't want us; they've gorra dozen kids of their own, if not more. We're just two extra mouths to feed.'

'I think we're a good deal safer in a group, like,' Conan said. 'After all, they know this country like the back of their hands so we'll end up at your dad's farm, no problem. As for meself, I'm happy to stay with 'em until we come across me daddy.'

'Ye-es, but it could take weeks and weeks if they keep wanderin' around to different horse fairs,'

367

Ginny pointed out. 'And my daddy will be leavin' to go to Liverpool quite soon I should think, though me grandparents will still be there. Honest to God, I dunno what to do for the best.'

'I'll have a word wi' one or two of the fellers,' Conan said eventually. 'Flann said your dad's farm were some way off, didn't he? I reckon if I has a word wi' one of the chief ones and explain the situation, they'll mebbe go straight to this Killorglin place. Especially if I tells 'em your daddy will be so pleased to lay hands on you that he'll be likely to give 'em a bob or two for their trouble.'

This sounded pretty sensible to Ginny and since one of the elderly women began beating on her tin plate at this point, indicating that the food was ready, she neither argued nor questioned further, but took her place in the line-up and was soon sitting on a fallen tree trunk with Nan on one side of her and Conan on the other, gobbling oatmeal and drinking the strong tea which seemed to be a staple of the tinker diet.

When the meal was over, a group of men set off to do fieldwork for which, Nan explained, they would be paid in potatoes, eggs and similar commodities. The women finished such tasks as they considered necessary and then seemed to melt away, leaving two old women to keep an eye on the encampment, and the children to look after the livestock and move the tethers as the animals cropped the grass in large circles.

The day wore on. Mostly, it was an enjoyable time, though Ginny still found it difficult to understand the tinkers, for their brogue was the broadest she had heard yet. But Conan told her that he would be unable to speak to the chiefs until evening, when they returned from their fieldwork, and since Ginny had no idea in which direction Kerry lay, she did not attempt to strike out for herself.

Besides, it would be difficult. Conan and Nan never left her side for one moment and though she realised that this was just friendship, it still made it impossible for her to simply walk away and return to the nearest village. When evening came and the fieldworkers returned, Conan went off to talk to the men he referred to as 'chiefs'. Ginny had noticed a grizzled man with a blue spotted handkerchief round his neck and another, younger one, who reminded her of pictures she had seen in her school book of a Red Indian chief, so dark his skin and flashing eyes, so long, straight and black his hair. She guessed that they were discussing her, saw them glance constantly in her direction, and was immensely reassured when Conan came over to her presently and assured her that the men had agreed the tinker band would make its way straight to Killorglin.

Satisfied on this score, Ginny began to play a hilarious game of cat's cradle with Nan, which several of the other girls joined in, and presently made her way to the tent, wrapped herself in her ragged blanket and settled down. Nan had told her that the tribe would be moving on next day and she felt pretty sure that this move was on her account, since there had been no indication that they meant to up sticks until Conan had spoken to the chief. But already, the men had begun to pull rough wooden carts from their hiding places in the pine wood and to load them up. Sure now that the tinkers meant her nothing but good, Ginny fell

369

asleep as soon as she lay down.

*   *   *

She was woken, what felt like hours later, by a voice. It was a familiar voice, speaking in a husky, chuckling whisper, and it must have been the mention of her own name which had woken her. She sat up on one elbow, suddenly alert and listening with all her might. It was Conan's voice and she was pretty sure he was talking to one of the boys in the other tent, completely unaware that voices carry through canvas as though through thin air, for as he continued to talk his voice grew louder and more boastful, despite his companion's telling him every few moments that 'there be no need to shout' and wondering why he couldn't tell a plain tale, ' 'stead of 'broidcrin' it up all the while'.

As she listened, Ginny felt her entire body grow cold. Conan was telling his pal just what he and the chief had been discussing and what they intended to do.

'I brung that there gal—that Ginny—to the tribe acos I knew her da' were in a big way o' farmin'. He's a warm man, I'm tellin' you, an' mortal fond of 'is only child. He'll pay up handsome to get her back unharmed. The chief says he'll get Nan's mammy to write him a letter, sayin' he's got the kid an' tellin' her da' what he'll do to her if a good bit o' money ain't forthcomin'. We can send the letter right away, 'cos the chief says the longer this Gallagher feller has to sweat it out afore we gets within easy reach, the more willin' he'll be to pay to get her back unharmed.'

Conan's companion grunted. 'Is that why young

370

Nan's stickin' closer to her'n porridge to the pan?' he enquired. He gave a hoarse chuckle. 'Well, if it works, we'll be in the money, but if it don't, I reckon we'll all be behind bars. Has the chief thought o' that?'

Conan gave a derisive snort. 'Course he has,' he said scornfully. 'How many bands o' tinkers are there roamin' the countryside in summer? An' Killorglin's a long way from anywheres, the chief says. Likely they'll have one fat old scuffer—that's a Garda to you, Liam—who'll be as scared of the tinkers as everyone else is. He's a wise feller, the chief, he's not takin' chances, he knows what he's about.'

For a moment, Ginny stayed exactly as she was, feelings of fury fighting with fear within her. She should never have trusted Conan but had not believed even he capable of such wickedness and deceit, but at least she knew now why the tinkers were willing to take on board a couple of kids, and that meant that she could, to some extent at least, protect herself. She looked round at the sleeping children and at the three large women, one of whom was lying across the entrance to the tent. The flap had been left open, because it was another mild night, but it would be extremely difficult to get out through the narrow opening without awaking at least one of the sleepers.

Very, very slowly and cautiously, Ginny sat up. She thought she had made no noise at all but Nan, beside her, stirred and sat up too. 'You awright, Ginny?' she said. 'It's a warm night, I don't need my blanket.'

'Nor me,' Ginny mumbled. So unexpected had Nan's awakening been, that Ginny's heart seemed to have doubled its pace so that when she spoke her voice was a little breathless. 'You didn't half give me a fright when you sat up like a bleedin' jack-in-the-box, Nan,' she exclaimed. 'I want to go out for a pee but I dunno as I can get past that old woman wi'out wakin' her.'

'Then wake her; why not?' Nan said equably. 'It's all that tea you drunk, gal. But ne'er mind, I'll give Granny a nudge wi' me knee an' we'll both slip past. 'Twon't take a moment; we'll be back agin afore Granny's had a chance to get back to sleep.'

'Awright,' Ginny muttered and followed the other girl across the tent. Nan gave Granny a poke and the older woman seemed to wake immediately, to be instantly alert. 'Whass goin' on?' she said thickly. 'Oh, it's you, Nan . . . and the young 'un from Liverpool. Want to have a piddle? Well don't you be long, spoilin' me beauty sleep.'

The two girls sidled past her and made their way to the edge of the pine wood. Ginny wondered whether she might simply slip away deeper into the wood as soon as Nan took her eyes off her, but Nan did no such thing. 'We'll go here,' she said, indicating a clearing. 'Then we'd best get straight back or Granny'll be rousin' the camp an' sendin' out search parties.'

'Why should they do that?' Ginny asked, though she thought she knew the reason. 'It ain't as though the woods is full of bears an' tigers. We can't come to much harm, can we?'

'No harm at all, so long as we stick together,' Nan said cheerfully. 'Finished? C'mon then, let's be gettin' back.'

Ginny began to follow her, keeping a little to the rear, but Nan reached back a friendly hand and

372

tucked it into Ginny's arm. 'Best stick together unless you've got eyes like a cat an' can see in the dark,' she said breathily. 'The dogs know me, y'see, but to them you're just an intruder an' might easily be attacked. That's why I come out with you, 'stead of leavin' you to piddle alone.' She gave Ginny's arm a squeeze. 'Another time, if you feel the urge, just you give me a shake. It were lucky I woke this time—I don't suppose I'd gone properly to sleep— or you might ha' ended up wi' a nasty bite.'

By now they had regained the tent, squiggled past Granny's bulk and settled themselves into their corner. 'The dogs must be gettin' to know me as well as you, though,' Ginny pointed out, as they settled down. 'I dare say I'd ha' been safe enough.'

Nan giggled. 'I wouldn't risk it if I were you,' she said. 'An' you don't want a broken leg, either. Haven't you noticed that there's little pits an' mounds all round the camp? The fellers dig 'em every time we put up our tents. We don't want no intruders comin' round after dark, to try and get their pigs back . . . or to steal our ponies,' she added hastily. 'But you can break a leg just as easily sneakin' out as you can sneakin' in.'

'I wasn't sneakin' anywhere,' Ginny said immediately. 'Why should I?'

Through the darkness, she saw Nan's shoulders lift in a shrug. 'I dunno, but I thought I ought to warn you,' she said, her tone still friendly. 'Now for Gawd's sake, stop chatterin'; tomorrer's movin' on day, so we should get some sleep while we can.'

CHAPTER FOURTEEN

Mabel and Michael began to ask questions as soon as they reached Portlaoise. They had decided that they would stay there for the night and meant to get lodgings at one of the neat houses which lined the main street, but before doing so they went round the shops asking the usual questions . . . had anyone seen a redheaded ten-year-old in a faded blue dress. Several people remembered seeing Ginny but it was in a baker's that a small boy buying a bag of buns followed them out and jerked at Michael's sleeve. 'Please, sir, I seen 'em,' he said huskily. 'There was two of 'em: a boy who talked strange and a gal wit' long, curly ginger hair. The gal were goin' to go into the post office but the boy stopped by me an' me pals and axed if we knew of any tinkers hereabouts. We telled 'im yes, so we did, and sent 'im off in the right direction.'

'Which direction?' Michael said excitedly. 'Did they ask for Killorglin or Kerry? Was it the girl who asked or the lad?'

'No one said anything about Kerry or Killerwotzit,' the boy said, after a moment's thought. 'One o' the fellers took 'em out o' the town and set 'em on the right road. It were Mick O'Casey; d'you want me to fetch 'im so's you can ask if either of 'em mentioned that there place?'

Michael and Mabel looked at one another, then Mabel nodded. Her heart began to beat faster; it had to be a sign that they were on the right track.

'That's a grand idea, so it is,' Michael said. 'You go an' fetch your pal, an' I'll search through me pockets to see if I can find a nice, bright shillin' to thank you for your help.'

The boy trotted off and presently returned with an older lad who eyed the shilling his companion was given greedily, and immediately began to tell the adults everything he could remember about his meeting with the two children.

'Dey axed me if I could take 'em to where de tinkers was camped,' he said, his brogue so thick that Mabel had to use all her powers of concentration to understand a word. 'It were de young feller what talked most so it were; the gorl said scarce a word. But she come along wi' us, an' when we got to de top of de rise, by ole Hilton's medder, I pointed out de path dey should take, an' left 'em to foller it.'

'And what sort of tinkers were they?' Michael asked, his tone telling Mabel that it was not just an idle question but might be terribly important. 'Were they a small band, mending pots an' pans, selling bunches of lucky heather, mebbe stealing an egg or two when a hen laid astray? Or—or a bigger group? Did they have much livestock . . . ponies, mules, and so on? Because I don't suppose they'll still be where you saw them, no matter what tribe they belong to. They're wanderers, all tinkers.'

The boy shrugged. 'I'm after tellin' you I never went wit' 'em into the valley, so I didn't see de tinks, not proper I didn't. Dey come to help wit' de harvest an' got paid same's always, wit' taties o' course, an' eggs, an' mebbe a sack or two of turnips. But me daddy said we was to keep away from 'em—he didn't care for 'em at all at all—so we did as we was bid, for once. Tinkers can be powerful mean an' spiteful, if dey takes agin you.'

'I know it,' Michael said fervently. 'When was this, exactly?' He began to delve in his pocket again and this time produced two sixpenny bits. 'How many days ago, I mean?'

The older boy glanced at the younger, then they both said together: 'T'ree days ago,' whilst the smaller one added: 'An' the tinks were in the fields next day but on the followin' one they was gone. Ain't that right, Mick?'

After some thought Mick said that it was and got his sixpenny bits, and then he agreed to go with Michael to show him where the camp had been. 'Though I dunno whether you'll be able to foller dem,' he said rather doubtfully. 'Except there were a lot of dem, and dey'll mebbe leave a trail. And o' course I dunno that the kids—de ginger girl an' de boy—went wit' de tinks. Not if dey had sense dey didn't.'

Michael said that they would have to take a chance on it.

'Den I'll take youse as far as I can . . . youse an' your good lady,' Mick said, glancing curiously from one to the other, and Mabel realised, with a shock of surprise, that Mick thought she and Michael were married to one another. Well, he's out there! I wouldn't marry Michael Gallagher if he were the last man on earth, she told herself.

Even as the thought crossed her mind, she realised that she was simply paying lip service to a feeling she no longer harboured. She had disliked Michael—and distrusted him, too—when they had first met, but she acknowledged that that had been blind prejudice, mostly caused by his treatment of Ginny. Knowing him better, she had begun to like him better, too. He had many virtues, and the sensitive way he had behaved towards her during their journey had influenced the way she felt about him.

'One t'ing, if dey're wit' de tinks no one else will interfere wit' dem,' the boy said, bringing Mabel's thoughts back to the present. They were hurrying along a dusty lane and striking off it on to a narrow track which led into wild, unfenced country. When the track came out on to moorland, Mick stopped and gestured ahead. 'Dis is as far as I went wit' dem kids,' he announced. 'See dat hill, slopin' down to a pine wood? De tinks was campin' in de valley, close agin' the stream.'

Michael squinted into the middle distance, then gave the lad another sixpence and thanked him for his services. Then he and Mabel set off in the direction the lad had indicated. It was a warm day and Mabel, wiping perspiration from her eyes, remarked that when they reached the stream she was jolly well going to take off her shoes and stockings and have a cooling paddle, and Michael grinned at her, agreeing that a paddle would be pleasant. 'These perishin' boots are a lot hotter than your shoes,' he observed. 'I could do with a paddle meself.'

They reached the valley and saw that the boy had been right. There were obvious signs of tinker occupation, for the tribe had not bothered to clear up after themselves but had simply abandoned their mess.

'And it's clear enough which way they went,' Michael said exultantly, as the two of them quartered the camping ground. 'They may have been careful, though I doubt it when you look at the mess, but their animals have left a pretty clear

377

trail. They skirted the pine wood and then followed that track, the one that climbs right up and over the shoulder of the mountain.'

'Oh, Michael, it looks as though we're on the right trail at last!' Mabel exclaimed. She could feel a broad smile spreading across her face.

'Ye-es, but the trail, as you call it, is two days old,' Michael pointed out soberly. 'And we can't follow 'em on foot because we'd not catch them up. Still, we're better off than we were . . . and now, Miss D., let's be havin' that paddle you talked about, because me feet are on fire, so they are, and I could do wit' a drink of that water as well.'

Mabel took off her shoes and her stockings and ran down to the stream. Even in the valley, it was a mountainy stream, she thought, the water dashing over smooth, rounded pebbles and around the mossy rocks. She splashed in, revelling in the icy chill on her hot feet, went to sit on a boulder, slipped, and fell into a deepish pool. She gave a squawk of alarm and floundered helplessly for a moment, then felt herself seized and pulled upright. Her rescuer was laughing; she could feel the reverberations of it through the hands which held her so firmly.

'Oh, Mary, Mother of Jesus, I'm after thinkin' you and water just don't get along,' Michael said, lifting her up and carrying her across to the bank. 'First, you're on the sea and sick as a dog, and now you find the only deep pool in a mountain stream and go head first into it! Janey, and now you're soaked to the skin.' He sat her down on the grassy bank and stood back, smiling ruefully down at her. 'What a good t'ing it's a warm day so you won't catch your death, but we can scarcely follow the tinks wit' you half drownded.'

Mabel began to wring out her heavy cotton skirt, looking up at him as she did so. He would have every right, she thought, to be annoyed, but he did not look cross, only amused, with sympathy lurking. 'I slipped,' she said apologetically. 'But it was bad luck, wasn't it? As you say, I did seem to find the only really deep pool to fall into. But don't worry about me; I'll soon dry off and it's such a lovely hot day that I'm not likely to catch a chill. How far is it along that track before we reach another village, though?'

'A goodish way, I shouldn't wonder,' Michael said. 'If only I'd thought, we could have bought some food and had a picnic.'

Mabel suddenly remembered that they had not found themselves lodgings before setting out with the boys, so she still had her suitcase and Michael his grip. 'If you'll turn your back, like the gentleman I know you are, I can change into dry things and spread the wet ones out on a handy gorse bush,' she said. 'That way, they'll dry a good deal quicker than if I kept them on. And then we can follow the track until we reach the next village and ask there for Ginny and the tinkers.'

Michael nodded slowly, though he still looked a little uncertain. 'Ye-es, but we may be mortal hungry before we reach civilisation again,' he pointed out. 'You don't find many villages on mountains.'

But Mabel treated this remark as unimportant. 'We'll walk all the better if we're hungry and needing our dinner,' she said briskly. 'Now turn your back, Mr Gallagher, and let's hope there's no wandering farmhand peering at me from behind a

379

bush!'

It was not easy, struggling out of her wet clothing, but Mabel managed it somehow. She put on a blue cotton dress but decided against such items as stockings, let alone the fawn cardigan which she had been wearing over her white blouse. Realising that her shoes would be uncomfortable to her bare skin, she decided to go barefoot, for a while at any rate, and presently told Michael that he might turn round, since she was respectable once more.

Michael turned and his eyes travelled slowly over her, from her cropped golden head to her bare pink toes. Then he came towards her with a glow in his eyes that Mabel had never seen there before. She waited, conscious of a small frisson of excitement as he held out a hand, but he merely picked up the bundle of wet clothing, saying prosaically as he did so: 'Good girl, you'll be a great deal more comfortable in that loose dress. Now I'll spread your wet stuff out on the bushes and we'll sit in the sun until it's dry.' He cocked a quizzical eyebrow. 'Unless there's something you'd rather do?'

Mabel felt the heat rush to her cheeks but shook her head. 'No, there's nothing I'd rather do because I don't mean to paddle and get another soaking,' she said firmly. 'Thank goodness it's such a heavenly day. Even the breeze is warm.'

Michael agreed that this was so and presently the two of them sat down, leaning against a rock. Mabel immediately fell asleep, only waking when her companion gently shook her shoulder. 'Your things are dry,' Michael said softly, as she yawned and sat up. 'I didn't want to wake you, you looked so peaceful lyin' there, but I think we had best go back to Portlaoise and then set off again first thing. I don't fancy trekking along narrow pathways by moonlight!'

Mabel got to her feet and began stuffing her now dry clothing into her suitcase. 'Yes, I think you're right,' she said reluctantly. 'I don't much fancy a walk by moonlight myself. Especially with my sort of luck; I'd probably go head first into a ravine, which wouldn't help us to catch up with Ginny and we've lost too much time as it is.'

Michael chuckled. 'I'm goin' to keep me eye on you from now on, so there'll be no more accidents,' he said firmly. 'I know I've not said it before, but I'm that grateful for your help and companionship that if you did fall into a ravine, I'd carry you the rest of the way on me back sooner than abandon you to your fate.' He glanced shyly at her, his dark eyes questioning. 'Mabel . . . I don't know how to say this . . .'

'Then don't say anything,' Mabel said, with a crispness she was far from feeling. The look in his eyes had made her feel soft and vulnerable; two sensations which had previously been completely alien to her. 'We really must get on, Michael, if we're to overtake the tinker band before . . . before . . .'

'Sorry; for a moment I was forgettin' that Ginny's our first priority,' Michael said with a humility which tore at Mabel's heartstrings. She saw him pick up his grip and her suitcase as though it weighed no more than a feather, and felt a sharp pang of regret that she had not let him continue with whatever it was he had been going to say. But she knew he was right; Ginny was their first priority. Their own situation—and feelings—could be dealt with later, when they had Ginny safe.

She stretched out a hand and caught Michael's. 'Give me that suitcase,' she said in a scolding voice. 'You can't carry everything, it's not fair.'

Michael grinned down at her and squeezed her hand and she realised, with a mingled sense of relief and disappointment, that they were now back on a normal, friendly footing.

'I can carry a good deal more than this wit'out strainin' meself unduly,' he assured her. 'Best foot foremost, Mabel!'

*   *   *

During the days that followed her arrival at the tinker camp, it became more and more clear to Ginny that, no matter how friendly and casual everyone seemed, she was, in fact, a prisoner. She was still furious with the two-faced Conan, who had pretended to be her friend but had plotted with the tinkers against her, but she did realise that it would not be sensible to show her animosity openly. Conan did not know she had overheard his conversation with the older boy and she felt, obscurely, that it would probably be easier to get away from Conan than it would from Nan. Nan went with her everywhere as a rule, but there were occasions when her mother gave her a task which meant she could not keep her eye on Ginny all the time and it was then that Conan took over. He was growing useful, she supposed, since he was frequently sent to take a group of ponies, mules or donkeys off into the nearby countryside and release them in a farmer's meadow, distant from the farmhouse, where he would remain with them as they grazed their full on stolen grass. If she had been taking the ponies to graze in a farmer's meadow without his permission, Ginny would have been terrified that the farmer would appear and give her a good beating or even hail her off to the nearest police station, but Conan told her that he positively enjoyed such encounters. He carried a cudgel with which he threatened anyone who approached too close and whistled up reinforcements from the tinkers' camp if such threats failed. If he saw that none of this deterred the angry landowner, however, he would mount the leading pony, crouching low over its neck and whipping the rest of his small herd into frantic flight. He often boasted of his exploits as the tribe sat around the camp fire eating the delicious stew, and though this sometimes earned him contemptuous glances from lads of his own age, the older men seemed more tolerant. Ginny heard two of them discussing Conan one evening and it appeared that they thought him much like his father and were prepared to put up with his boastful talk because they hoped he would one day be truly useful to them.

'Eamonn O'Dowd is just the same, so he is; but he's a rare 'un, a horse caller,' the older man told the younger one. 'When I goes after a horse, I has to get right up to him and even then he'll sometimes take fright and bolt. But Eamonn just stands by the gate and calls and the horses come over to him, all of 'em. He'll reach out a hand wit' the rope halter in it, and the horse he's chosen will drop its head into the loop and trot off at his heels, as though they'd knowed one another all their lives.

I think young Conan may be just such another, and if he is, he'll be worth his weight in gold to the tribe, no question.'

It all sounded very strange to Ginny but it was clear that, should Conan decide to stay with the tinkers, he would soon become valuable to them whereas she, so far as she could tell, was to be sold to her own father when the tribe got near enough to Headland Farm.

She wondered whether to tell Conan that his usefulness to the tinkers was not dependent upon the ransom they might get from her father, but decided that this was a card she would hold in reserve.

And then, when she had been with the band several days without once having an opportunity to escape, the chief called her to his tent. He and his brother, Abe, were sitting cross-legged on the ground. Both men had greasy black hair, sharp black eyes and swarthy skin, but Abe's hair hung to his shoulders and his face was thin and crafty as a fox. Ginny disliked him intensely and knew him for the cheat he was, for though he frequently came into the camp bringing in horses which he claimed to have bought, she had seen him using dye on their coats to change their appearance. The dye was made by the women of the tribe and was much prized since it did not wash out in the rain and so transformed a stolen horse for many months. Indeed, Nan told her that the secret of its manufacture was much envied by other tribes.

Ginny had hung around the fire one day when a brew of dye was boiling up. Her antagonism towards the band was such that she had stolen one of the tiny bottles full of dye and slipped it into the

384

deep pocket of her skirt. It was evidence, she told herself grimly, that all the tinkers were thieves, and if she ever managed to escape from them she meant to take the dye to the scuffers as proof of the Kavanagh tribe's perfidy. However, escaping did not seem likely as yet.

But right now, she looked enquiringly across at the chief, avoiding even a glance at his brother. The chief told her that he had written to her father—or rather that he had caused Nan's mother to write—saying that Ginny was safe with the tinkers and would be returned to him as soon as possible. 'So there's no need for you to t'ink of leavin' us,' he said, giving her an oily smile. 'Because you'll get home a deal slower if you're by yourself, and Conan's happy wit' us and don't mean to leave.'

'I see,' Ginny said, rather inadequately. 'I'd like to write to my father meself, but I don't have no paper, nor no pencil.'

The man laughed. 'Nor no stamp, nor no ennylope,' he said mockingly. 'But I told you, a letter's gone to your pa' so you'll be safe home awright and tight, if you sticks with us, that is.'

After that, Ginny realised that keeping a constant eye on her was growing as irksome to the tinkers as it was to herself. She decided to do her best to calm their fears and besides, unless she could get to talk to someone who could tell her in which direction Kerry lay, there was little point in trying to escape. She determined that the next time the women went into the nearest village for supplies, she would offer to accompany them, suggesting that she should help to carry back the provisions they bought. But mature reflection that

385

night, as she lay in her blanket, told her that any such suggestion would be greeted by either doubling up the guard on her or simply refusing her offer of help. No, the best to thing to do was to allay their suspicions totally by voluntarily remaining in the camp. She would go with the girls on wood-gathering expeditions and accompany either Conan or Nan when they went stealing vegetables, but she would not wander off—not until she was ready to make her bid for escape that was—for she realised that if she tried to escape, and failed, she would be very unlikely to be given a second chance.

The next morning Ginny woke to hear a strange sound, a sort of gentle pattering upon the roof over her head. She was staring at the canvas when a large drop hit her smack in the middle of her forehead and she realised, with a small pang of dismay, that it was raining.

It was the first rain she had seen since arriving in Ireland, and presently, when she got up and made her way to the tent entrance, she saw that it must have been raining for some time, for the camp fire was out and large puddles had formed in every little hollow. Ginny shivered, wrapping her arms round herself. Shortly, she would have to go out into the rain and fetch dry wood to get the fire started, she supposed dismally, and it wasn't like rain in the city, where one could dodge from doorway to doorway, or catch a tram to one's destination. Here, it would be impossible to escape the rain, and since they would be packing up the tents and moving on, even that temporary shelter would soon be denied them.

'Wharrever are you doin', Dreamy? Oh, how I

386

hate rain, but we'd best get a couple of armfuls of dry wood, or there won't be no breakfast for anyone. Everyone hates strikin' camp in the rain, but Abe brought back a chestnut mare—she's in foal, too—so the chief won't let us linger, although Abe has dyed her mane an' tail black, so she does look a bit different.'

Ginny turned and grinned at Nan. 'Awright, awright,' she said placatingly. 'But by the look o' the puddles, there won't be much dry wood about, norreven deep in the perishin' forest. Still, we can try, I suppose.'

Nan giggled and squeezed past her, then gestured towards the nearest trees. 'Don't you notice nothin', girl?' she asked derisively. 'The men allus pulls one of the carts into wharrever shelter there is and slings a canvas over it. They puts all the dry wood in the cart first, o' course, so we can allus have a fire. Tinkers ain't fools, you know; we live outdoors the whole year, not just in the summer.'

As she spoke, she had been leading Ginny towards a red and green painted cart, and presently the two girls, laden with dry wood, came hurrying back into the centre of the clearing. Nan got one of the thickest branches and began to sweep the ash to one side. It was still warm, and working quickly, she showed Ginny how to build a pyramid of the pieces of wood. Then she shouted and one of the old women came hurrying through the rain, carrying what proved to be a box containing dry leaves, hay and even some bits of old newspaper. She pushed these in at the bottom of the pyramid, lit a match, and very soon the fire was roaring and the contents of the porridge pot beginning to simmer.

No doubt to everyone's annoyance, the rain continued unabated all morning, though the tinkers seemed to take the weather very much in their stride and continued to strike the tents and bundle them into the carts, along with all their other possessions. Since these included pigs, poultry and the younger children, it was quite a lively and even a noisy proceeding, though the children never murmured, leaving the livestock to voice their grievances.

Determined to keep up her efforts to make a good impression, Ginny worked with a will. And though, at first, she hated the rain, she soon grew accustomed to it. Besides, in its way it was beautiful, she decided, watching as a great curtain of it swept across the hills and valleys, bringing the scent of wet growing things to her nostrils. Because of the long period of dry weather, she thought she could almost see the weary trees lifting up their branches to drink in the rain, and already the grass, which had begun to flag and grow pale, was greening up once more. The river at the foot of the hills, which had seemed no more than a stream yesterday, was beginning to fill its bed, and by the time they were ready to leave, the noise of its onward rush was loud enough to intrude upon conversation and made it necessary for everyone to shout.

Usually, when the tribe were on the move, Nan and Conan were extra specially careful to stay close to Ginny, for though their path took them along unfrequented ways and quiet country lanes, they seemed to realise that in the hustle and bustle of a move Ginny could easily slip away unnoticed.

Because of the rain, however, they were late setting off and very soon tempers grew frayed. The heavy clouds were actually resting on mountain and hilltops, so that as the path climbed the tribe—mules, donkeys and all—disappeared into a thick white mist and it became increasingly important for the children to check on the animals constantly. Every now and then a shrill, piping voice would announce: 'The strawberry roan's gorn off. I casn't see her nowhere, I casn't.'

Tinker children never made a noise or fuss, presumably having had it knocked out of them at an early age. Ginny had noticed that a boy would receive a clack across the head violent enough to send him crashing to the ground, but though he might scowl and mutter, he would never wail or complain vociferously. It was odd, because the adults, particularly the women, could be both noisy and aggressive. They sometimes fought amongst themselves, or a man would give his wife a clout, and then the women shrieked like wildcats whilst the men shouted and blustered; but children, it seemed, did everything quietly—except when searching for animals in a dense, white cloud. Then they whistled and hallooed to each other and very soon returned to the line of carts, the straying animals driven before them.

The tinkers never stopped for a meal when they were moving from one camp to the next, but one of the women would come round with a big jug of cold tea and a number of tin mugs, whilst another handed out great slabs of soda bread, smeared with margarine, which was enough to keep everyone satisfied until they reached their new camping ground. Ginny had no idea how such places were chosen but imagined that the tinkers tended to stop at the same spots, time after time. They must know the countryside like the backs of their hands for they always camped near a river or a stream, with a good thick stand of trees at their backs and plenty of grazing near at hand. At one point, she and Nan met, both of them trying to persuade a couple of mules that it would be more sensible to rejoin the train, and she asked Nan how long it would be before they were able to snug down somewhere for the night.

'Dunno; mebbe an hour, mebbe two,' Nan said vaguely. Rain was running down her face and beading her long, dark lashes and she had one arm around the neck of a recalcitrant mule, but Ginny reflected that she did not look unhappy with her lot, as a city child would have done. Nan accepted the rain, the dense fog of the clouds, the awkwardness of the animals and the steepness of the stony track up which they scrambled as no more than slight—and temporary—annoyances. Ginny guessed that the other girl would uncomplainingly help to erect the tents, make the fire and cook the food, stake out the horses, donkeys and mules, and finally crawl into bed in the wet and chilly tent, waking to more rain next morning and simply accepting it as a part of a tinker's life.

But I shan't, Ginny found herself thinking. If I can't get away in all this confusion and with the cloud so thick, then I don't deserve to escape at all. And a grand thing it would be for me daddy to have to pay a ransom to get his own girl back just because I hadn't the wit or the courage to run away from a band of tinkers.

Presently, the track, which had been winding upwards, began to descend. They were in wild country now and even when they emerged from the cloud, there was not a farm or a cottage in sight. But I'm sure there's nowhere in Ireland where you can walk for miles and see no sign of habitation, Ginny told herself. And there's certainly nowhere suitable here to put up tents, and no wood for a fire either, because the only trees I've seen this high in the mountains are puny things which wouldn't shelter a cat, let alone a crowd of tinkers.

It was at this point that the old women began to slosh cold tea into mugs and hand round the bread and marge. No one even thought of stopping whilst they ate, but continued to trudge. Ginny thought that this was fair enough, since she could imagine, with horror, the difficulties of erecting tents and staking out the livestock with darkness as well as rain to combat.

'The tea's got milk in it,' Nan's voice said in Ginny's ear. She giggled, giving Ginny's shoulder a friendly shove. 'I wonder who gorrit?' She giggled again. 'Someone's going to think their cow's gone dry when they milk it tonight.'

Ginny giggled too. She knew that tinkers would frequently nip over a hedge and milk any unattended cows into a bucket before moving on, and though she might disapprove of the habit, on occasion she was extremely glad of it. Tinkers made strong tea and sugared it lavishly but to Ginny's city-bred taste the addition of milk was welcome. So now she sank her nose enthusiastically into her mug, drained it and handed it back to the old woman in exchange for her share of soda bread. 'It were cow's milk, too,' she said, speaking rather

391

thickly. 'Goat's milk is okay, but it's kind o' strong, wouldn't you say?'

'Aye, that it is,' Nan agreed. 'But you can't see a fat old milch cow keeping up with a tribe, can you? The goats is allus ahead of the rest and young Snicky—he's our goat herder—stays well up the front with his goats, no matter how bad the path. So that means when we do reach our camping ground, there's always fresh milk to hand.'

But soon the track began to climb once more and Nan fell back a little. Her plumpness meant that she was slower on an upward slope than Ginny and, though both girls were assisted in the climb by hanging on to the manes of the mules they were leading, she still could not quite keep up. Ginny, realising this, began to move a good deal faster. She heard Nan's plaintive cry and called reassuringly over her shoulder that she could see Conan ahead and meant to get him to lead her mule so that she and Nan might walk together. In actual fact, she could see nothing ahead, save for a dim shape through the muffling whiteness, and she began to look about her, realising that because of the cloud, the rain and the narrowness of the track, here was an opportunity to get away which might not come again. She told herself that she was bound to find a cottage or a farmhouse if she descended into the valley, and glanced cautiously about her. There was no one really near, for Nan had fallen a good way behind. Ginny felt the heat rush to her cheeks as she contemplated what she should do for the best. Mules are tricky beasts; if she let go of her companion and began to descend into the milky whiteness of the cloud, someone—Nan or Conan—might remark on an unaccompanied mule and set everyone searching for her; but if she took the mule with her, the sound of its unshod hooves on the mountainside might give her away. If she had been able to ride, the mule could have been a real advantage, but Ginny had tried on a couple of occasions to ride one of the ponies and had been unable to stay aboard for more than a few minutes. This particular mule was a large animal and capable, as she well knew, of putting on quite a spurt. No, riding the beast was out of the question. She decided to simply release it and begin to scramble as quietly as possible down the mountainside, trusting that no one would see her go and that the mule would continue doggedly climbing upward. If, on the other hand, the mule followed her and she was spotted, she would say she was trying to recapture the animal and would almost certainly be believed. Heaven knew, she had chased enough mules today to make it the sort of story even the suspicious chief would be unable to fault. Ginny peered down over the side of the path and saw, with some relief, that a grassy bank stretched below her as far as her eyes could see, which was not particularly far. She let go of the mule's mane and gave it an encouraging pat on its rump, then sat down on the edge of the path, meaning to begin a gentle descent, if necessary on all fours.

She had reckoned without the wetness of the grass and the steepness of the slope. The moment she sat down, she began to slide, with increasing rapidity, into the unseen valley below.

Five breathless—and quite painful—minutes later, Ginny's hurtling speed began to slow and she came to a halt amongst tufts of heather and gorse.

Fortunately, it was the heather which had stopped her rather than the gorse and, glancing about her, she realised how extremely lucky she had been. Not only were there a great many gorse bushes, but there was a multitude of rocks, their grey noses protruding up above the heather. Had she struck one of them, Ginny reflected, she could not have escaped quite serious injuries. She glanced up towards where she guessed the track must be but could see nothing save the swirling white cloud, reminding herself that since she could not see the tinkers, then it was clearly impossible that they should be able to see her. For a few moments longer, however, she sat just where she was, listening intently for a shout which would indicate that she had been missed, but she heard nothing. Oh, she could make out the tribe's almost silent progress, the occasional clatter of hooves, the creak of the wagons, a quiet murmur of speech, but other than that, nothing. No shouts of alarm, no shrill ejaculations—in fact, no sounds of pursuit.

The desire to get up and run for it, to get as far away from the track as possible, was almost irresistible, but Ginny was firm. If they suspect, that's just what they'll be listening for, she reminded herself. And it doesn't sound to me as though they do suspect, so sit tight, shut up and let them get well away before you move a muscle.

Another reason for not moving, if she was honest, was that she had done herself quite a lot of damage as she slithered at speed down the mountainside. She was pretty sure nothing was broken, but equally sure that she was bruised all over, and she feared that when she eventually did stand up she would find walking both painful and difficult. Accordingly, she lay cautiously down in the heather, actually wriggling deeper into it so that most of her body was hidden, and simply waited. Soon enough, the slight sounds of the tinkers' progress faded into the distance and at long last Ginny hauled herself, carefully, to her feet. To her relief, she had been right and she was not badly injured; indeed, after she had walked twenty or thirty yards, the slight stiffness caused by remaining still for so long disappeared and she felt sure that the grazes and bruises she had suffered would soon cease to trouble her.

Looking around, she realised she was alone in wild and mountainous country; she was without food or warm clothing and she had no idea in which direction she should go, yet despite all this she felt triumphant. She had escaped from the tribe, which was something to be proud of, and she was certain she would find both shelter and help very soon. It was unfortunate that she would have to turn back rather than go on, but if she continued in the same direction that the tinkers were taking it would only be a matter of time before she was recaptured. She had gone a couple of hundred yards when something else occurred to her. The river lay now to her left and she thought that the tinkers were probably following its course since they always liked to camp by water. She had seen the tribe in the heat of summer, fetching water from the river, occasionally paddling in it, but she had never seen any of them bathing, no matter how hot the day. I don't believe tinkers are very keen on water, she told herself, changing direction so that she presently stood on the river bank. The water was brown now, with tiny, creamy-topped wavelets, and probably, in the centre, it was quite deep. But there were still plenty of rocks jutting above the water and Ginny decided that no one would ever dream that a girl of her age would cross a river in flood.

For a moment she hesitated on the bank, but the thought of the dogs decided her. She knew them fairly well by now but she had heard stories of fugitives being hunted by dogs and had no desire to feel the mangy tinker pack snapping at her heels. She remembered stories in which the hero had escaped detection by dogs by crossing water and was more determined than ever to do just that. Resolutely, she stepped down into the swirling river.

Ginny had never learned to swim so she clung to the rocks, thinking that, if the worst came to the worst, she could probably scramble aboard one. They were not close enough for her to leap from one to another, but she thought that she could manage to launch herself across the short distance between them without coming to harm. However, the river was a good deal more powerful than she had supposed. The rushing water tore her legs from under her and she realised that it was considerably deeper in the narrow channels between the large rocks.

Clinging to the first rock, soaked to the shoulders and doing her best to resist the water's desire to prise her fingers from their limpet-like grip, Ginny began to realise that she had done a very foolish thing. Even had she been able to swim, she could not possibly have done so against the force of the current. I'd best go back, she thought, and immediately realised that the moment she released her hold on the rock she would be swept downstream, regardless of which bank she was trying to reach.

Ginny had greeted every obstacle she had met on her journey with courage and determination. When Aunt Amy and Uncle Lew had accused her of telling lies and kicked her out of the house, she had gritted her teeth and decided that somehow she would find her father and explain to him what had happened. She had got aboard the ferry—and off the other side—without being detected as a runaway and had survived in the city of Dublin by accepting the help Conan offered and doing her share of the work, and pilfering, which had been necessary. Her biggest challenge had come in the tinkers' camp when she had realised that they meant to demand money from her father for her safe return. She had known then that she must escape and had planned and plotted how she would do so with grim determination. She had never allowed herself to despair or to think that she was the unluckiest girl in the world; she had certainly never wept one tear for herself.

But now, with her hands slowly but steadily slipping down the rock and her feet totally unable to find bottom, she acknowledged that she had met her match. She could go neither forward nor back and she could feel her strength ebbing. Desperately, she tried to get a knee-hold somewhere below water so that she might pull herself further up the rock, but her knee found a spur so sharp that she cried out as it gouged into her flesh and she lost her grip. Triumphantly, the river seized her, whirled her round, dragged her along and sent her spinning, helpless as a rag doll, off on its course towards the sea.

Conan discovered Ginny was missing when he turned back to take a look at a loose mule, tapping gently along the path behind him. Although he had only been with the tinkers a short while, his affinity with horses, mules and donkeys was such that he knew each one and was fond of them all. This particular beast, known to Conan as Velvet, because of its soft and velvety muzzle, was definitely the one he had seen Ginny leading an hour or so before. The track was winding downhill now which meant that the cloud cover was lessening. Frowning a little, Conan reached out a hand and patted the mule's neck, letting it pass him. He slowed his pace, telling himself that the girls had probably dropped back a good way, but as the tail of the procession reached him he saw that Nan was alone. Immediately, warning bells rang in his head. He knew very well that Ginny had been behind him when they started to climb the mountain path, yet she was nowhere in sight, and he knew, too, that Nan would have stuck to her, stuck closer than glue, because, like himself, she was still trying to prove that she was every bit as much a tinker as those kids who had been born in a tent and reared to the wandering life.

Nan reached him and he saw at once that she looked anxious. 'Where's Ginny?' he said, without preamble.

'She went ahead, said she were goin' to catch up wi' you and then wait for me. Only . . . only I'm slow, walking uphill. Haven't you seen her, Conan?'

398

Conan shook his head and for a moment the two stared at one another, wide-eyed, and when Nan spoke it was in a husky whisper, with tears coming into her eyes. 'Oh my Gawd,' she breathed. 'Oh, me mam will half kill me if we've lost her. I dunno if you know it, Conan, but they's goin' to get a load of money off o' her daddy. A hunderd pounds, beside a horse and cart packed wi' farm produce an' good, dry peats. That's what one-eyed Ben telled me mammy, anyhow, and she telled me that if it come off and I'd made sure Ginny didn't gerraway, I should have a pair of golden-hoop earrings for me very own and a red shawl just like Minnie's.'

Conan stared at her, almost unable to believe his ears. 'A hundred pounds?' he breathed. 'An'—an' a horse an' cart . . . farm produce . . . peats? Oh, Nan, wharrever made 'em think Ginny's da' were that rich?'

'You did,' Nan said, not mincing matters. 'You telled 'em he had a great big farm in Kerry and were a rich man. You said he had beautiful horses, a big flock of sheep and a grand house and a big fishing boat . . . you said . . .'

Conan put his head in his hands and groaned. It would have been wonderful to be able to deny that he had said any such thing, but he knew very well he had said as much and probably more. He remembered his Auntie Deb warning him that one day his lies and boasting would turn back and bite him, but as time had passed he had become more and more convinced that she was wrong. But now . . . Conan groaned again. The tinkers had believed every word he had said—the more fools they—but now he realised that if he couldn't find Ginny, his chances of becoming a trusted member of the tinker tribe would be utterly lost. He said as much to Nan, who looked at him for a long, hard moment and then slowly shook her head. 'Losing Ginny means they won't find out about your lies,' she said positively. 'If you ask me, it's a bleedin' good thing she has got away—for you, I mean. For me, it couldn't be worse. I shan't get the pretty things my mam promised me and everyone will have a swipe at me and one-eyed Benny will use his leather belt. And they'll never accept me. I'll never be one of 'em.'

They had been continuing to walk down the track as they talked but now Conan stopped. 'When, exactly, did she get ahead of you . . . how long ago, I mean?' he asked. 'An hour? Two?'

Nan shrugged helplessly. 'I dunno,' she said. 'It were after the old 'uns had come round wi' the grub. And we was goin' uphill . . . an hour or two, I guess.'

Conan nodded briskly. 'Right; I'm goin' back,' he said briefly. 'I'll find her, see if I don't, an' bring her back, too.'

'Shall I come with you?' Nan asked hopefully, but Conan shook his head.

'No fear, you're too slow, you'd only hold me back,' he said cruelly. 'If anyone asks where I've gone, say I'm after a likely-lookin' pony what I saw grazin' in the valley.' He turned away, raising a hand in farewell. 'See you later, Nan.'

'Will I say you took Ginny wi' you, to help catch the pony?' Nan said, her voice echoing off the rocks around her. 'How long will you be, Conan? Oh dear, I hopes you catches her.'

Conan did not answer; there was no point, but

he had already decided that no matter how long it took, he would fetch Ginny back to the tinkers. He was happier with the tribe than he had ever been and thoroughly enjoyed the wandering life and the closeness with the animals which such an existence brought. I won't be slung out because a bleedin' girl decides she'd be better on her own, he told himself savagely as he hurried up the path. She shan't ruin me life, norrif I can help it.

CHAPTER FIFTEEN

Conan slogged on up the mountain path and down the other side, and as he descended the cloud thinned and cleared and he was able to scan the countryside for his quarry. There was no sign of her but if Nan were to be believed she had at least an hour's start on him, so he did not despair. He did wish he had thought to bring one of the lurchers; dogs, he knew, could pick up a scent trail and follow it when people were unable to do so. However, it had not occurred to him, so now he must manage alone. For a moment he stood still, staring about him. Ginny was escaping from the tinkers. She did not wish to be caught yet he was pretty sure she still wanted to get to Kerry. If he had been in her position, what would he have done? I'd cross the river, he thought triumphantly. Tinkers always seem to stick to the same side of the river. They use the water all right but you never see them swimming in it and they seldom cross, so far as I can see. So if it were me getting away from the tribe, I'd cross the river just as soon as I came to a ford or a shallow place. Therefore my best plan would be to go down to the river and follow it. She won't think of being pursued so soon, so she isn't going to hurry. If I jog-trot I'll maybe catch her up in thirty or forty minutes and if I keep my eyes open I may see her on the opposite bank, though if it were me I'd move inland. Tinkers follow the tracks over the mountain because they're usually quicker than the windings of the river—at least, I suppose that's why they do it.

Hurrying along in what he devoutly hoped was Ginny's wake, he presently came to a patch of marshy ground and here, to his immense relief, he began to think that he really was on the right track. Someone small and light had been this way before him. He could see her footprints dancing along, jumping from one firm patch of ground to another. He remembered Ginny had worn plimsolls with her toes protruding through the ends and was pretty sure that these were her footprints. Unfortunately, however, the weather was worsening. The cloud was pressing lower so that he could barely see the far side of the river and it had begun to rain; a gentle misty rain which nevertheless soaked everything as effectively as a stronger downpour would have done. Conan rubbed it out of his eyes and cursed all women. He was just rehearsing in his mind what he would say to Ginny when he caught her up, when he rounded a bend and realised, for the first time, how swollen the river had become and how dangerous. Up here, he entered a rocky defile in which the river was probably at its narrowest, but as a result it was both deeper and faster than it had been for many miles. The water was brown with churned up silt and streaked with creamy foam where it dashed against the rocks. It no longer looked the sort of river that a grown man could cross, let alone a skinny bit of a kid, and Conan was about to turn away and go back to the track when something ahead caught his eye. At this particular point the river was strewn with large boulders and one of the boulders seemed to have what looked like a round dark object balanced on top of it. Below the round dark object was something which, at first, he took to be some sort of plant clinging to the rock, yet even as he thought this he realised he was wrong. The round dark object was a head and the two plant-like projections below it were the desperate fingers belonging to the owner of the head.

Even as he realised, terror shot through Conan like the blade of an icy knife, almost stopping his heart. The little idiot! She could not have chosen a worse place to try to cross the river, yet even as he broke into a run he guessed why she had done it. Here, there were boulders actually above the water and the river was at its narrowest. Knowing nothing of what happens to rivers when they narrow, she had thought this a good place to cross and now was well and truly stuck.

Even as he ran, Conan was beginning to blame himself. He remembered how sweet and trusting Ginny had been when they had first set out on their adventures. She had bought them both food and had shared everything with him, uncomplainingly. She had helped him to steal though she had strongly disapproved of such actions, and even in the tinkers' camp she had never let him down, never told the tinkers that he was a liar and a boaster. And what had he done in return? He had used her—and her farming father—as a means to make himself popular with the band. He had known that the chief meant to sell her to her own father and had not even had the decency to warn her. He had kept her a prisoner and had dogged her footsteps, determined not to let her get away, whereas had he been a real friend he would have done everything in his power to help her.

Never before in his whole life had Conan actually looked at himself and realised that he was not a nice person. Many and many a time his Aunt Deb had said that his lies and his boasting would come home to roost, but in his wildest nightmares he had never thought that someone else would suffer as a result of his behaviour. Now it seemed that Ginny had been forced to run away from the tinkers and might easily lose her life as a consequence.

Sick with guilt and fear, Conan reached the spot at which Ginny had entered the water. Not even thinking of his own personal safety, he splashed down the bank and just as he was whirled off his feet by the current he saw Ginny's hands slip from their precarious hold, saw her swirl downstream and found himself following her, keeping afloat with the greatest difficulty, and realising, as the current channelled between the rocks, that Ginny could not swim. He glanced round desperately, praying for help, and heard what sounded like a faint mew, perhaps a gull or a distant creature, for there was no one within sight. Then the water dragged him down and the last thing he saw was Ginny's out-flung arm before the water closed over his head.

*   *   *

Nan watched Conan disappearing up the track and felt despair. It was her fault that Ginny had escaped, or at least one-eyed Ben and all the others would say it was. Her own mother might not; at first in agreement, she had changed her mind and had not approved of the chief's desire to ransom Ginny to her own father, and told Nan that she should refuse to guard the girl. But Nan was trying to make a place for herself; all she would make by losing Ginny was enemies. And she had enough of them, simply by not being a true member of the tribe. Sticking closer to Ginny than glue had brought approval from the older tinkers and such approval was sweet. So even as she watched Conan disappear into the mist, Nan decided to follow him. She might not be able to help Conan to recapture Ginny, but with two to one it would be a good deal easier to get her back to the tribe. And anyway, if the three of them returned together, everyone would know she had at least been willing to do what she could.

It was tough going though. For the first ten or fifteen minutes, Nan managed to keep the mule by her side, but the animal was plainly uneasy at being separated from its fellows and by the time Nan reached level ground it had clearly worked out its own next move. It whipped round so quickly that Nan lost her balance and landed with a painful thump on the track. By the time she had scrambled to her feet, it had disappeared into the mist once more, braying defiance as it did so.

Nan cursed softly and glanced ahead of her up

405

the track; it looked uncommonly steep and she guessed it would take her a good deal longer without the mule's help. However, she could just make out Conan's small figure ahead of her. Grimly, Nan set off in pursuit.

She could not have said how long it was before Conan turned towards the river, but his action put Nan in a quandary. The land at this point was flat and marshy and if she followed him, one glance back would be sufficient for him to spot her. I'll stick to higher ground, Nan decided. After all, it isn't as if he's likely to try to cross the river. Nan had all the tinkers' aversion to water and seldom paddled, even on the hottest day. Gaining higher ground was not difficult but with the soft, fine rain blowing into her face, it was hard to make out what was actually happening. She saw Conan suddenly break into a run, however, and guessed that he must have seen Ginny. She was still wondering whether this was the moment that she herself should make for the river when she realised that Conan had disappeared. She stopped short, a hand flying to her throat; her first thought was that if she lost him, she would also lose her chance of a triumphant return to the tribe. But then she thought she heard a shout and, peering through the rain, saw that Conan was up to his knees in water and actually going in deeper yet.

To do Nan justice, she immediately set off as fast as she could towards the water. It was hard going through the marshy ground but she gained the bank just in time to see what looked like two bundles of rags fairly hurtling along downstream. Desperately, miserably aware that she was no runner, Nan began to hurry along the bank. She saw an out-flung arm—she could not tell whether it belonged to Conan or Ginny—and then she reached a bend in the river and lost sight of them. By the time she had negotiated it, the rain was so heavy that she could only see a few yards ahead, and though she trudged along the bank for another half hour, there was no sign of anyone, either in the water or out of it.

With a heavy heart and tears mingling with the rain on her face, Nan turned her weary footsteps back to where she imagined the tribe would now be making camp for the night. It was several hours before, footsore and exhausted, she managed to join them again and then she found the place in a real uproar, for they had realised that the three children were missing and though Ginny only meant money to the elders of the tribe, they had no wish to see her making trouble for them by telling the authorities they had kept her with them against her will. What was more, they valued Conan for his abilities as a horse caller, and Nan herself because she was an obedient child who did her best to help. Indeed, her mother pounced on her and gave her a tight hug before beginning to rail at her for her absence. Nan, exhausted and in a state of considerable nervous excitement, promptly burst into tears. 'C-C-Conan an'-an' Ginny an' me went down to the river after one o' the mules,' she said, hiccuping and stammering but keeping in mind the story she had carefully rehearsed. 'C-C-Conan saw a grand, black horse wi' a white star on its forehead on t'other side o' the river. I c-c-can't swim so they told me to stay on this bank while they crossed to fetch the pony. I did what they said but when they was halfway across the water took Ginny and whirled her away and Conan went in after her. Th-the bleedin' mule gorraway from me but I follered Ginny and Conan from along the bank un-until the water dragged 'em under. Even then I follered, hopin' they'd be swept ashore, bu-but the river got deeper an' faster . . . Oh, Mam, they was both drownded dead before me eyes and there weren't nothin' I could do, nothin'!'

Nan had to repeat her story many times before nightfall but since most of it was true, she did not mind too much. Of course, she had had to make up a lie about the reason they had all taken off in the first place and she supposed that some people probably realised that it was a lie; guessed that Ginny had been fleeing from the tinkers and that Conan and Nan herself had been trying to recapture her. But none of that was important; what mattered was that the two children had been drowned and there was no point in searching for them further.

To be sure, as soon as Nan's mother had heard her story, she had insisted that a group of tinkers be sent to the river and this had been done, mainly, Nan thought, to keep her mother quiet. There had been little hope by then, of course, since darkness was falling and rain still drummed steadily on the hard earth. When the men returned to say that the river had now overflowed its banks in several places and was thundering towards the sea in a torrent of dirty foam and debris—broken branches, great chunks of bank and even some dead animals—Nan and her mother had to agree that there was no point in searching further. Indeed, Nan, who had seen the pair being carried along at a terrifying rate, had never doubted for one moment that they were dead. When she crawled into her tent that night, having refused to eat any supper, she was aware of an enormous weight of loneliness. Ginny might have resented Nan's guardianship, but Nan had been truly fond of the other girl and had wished her nothing but good. She did not see why Ginny should have tried to escape, for since the chief had said he would take her all the way to her father's farm, what did it matter if he then asked her father for money and stock to make up for his having taken good care of her? If only Ginny had said she meant to run away, I'm sure I could have talked her round, told her it were a daft thing to do, Nan told herself wretchedly. Oh, Ginny, Ginny, you were me best friend and now you're drownded and I'm so lonely!

Just before she fell asleep, Nan thought about Conan, another friend. She had not been as close to him as she had to Ginny, but they had had a good deal in common. They had both been outsiders, trying to get in, and Conan had been happy to chat to Nan sometimes, of an evening. And Nan had been happy, in her turn, to begin to teach him the language that the tinkers spoke. She had picked it up piecemeal herself, but she had begun to teach Conan properly and had been pleased when he had proved to be an adept pupil.

Beside her, the tinker girl known as Missie called out in her sleep, something about water in her mouth, and then began to mumble, and Nan guessed she was having a nightmare and realised that she, Nan, was not the only person to mourn the passing of Ginny and Conan. Missie's mammy had a tongue like a whiplash and was quick with a cuff or a blow, and the younger girl had sometimes hung around with Ginny and had seemed to want to be friends. In the dim light, Nan could see Missie's tear-wet cheeks and was a little comforted. She put her arm around Missie's shoulders and gave her a gentle shake. 'It's awright, Missie, Nan's here,' she whispered. 'You go off to sleep like a good gal, an' Nan'll take care of you.'

The younger girl muttered something to the effect that she had been dreaming she was drowning in the river, then curled up within the circle of Nan's arm. Very soon, both children slept.

*   *   *

When Conan had seen the water close over his head for a second time, a sort of fury possessed him. Whilst he had lived with Auntie Deb, he had been the best swimmer amongst all the neighbourhood boys. From the time he was three or four, he had been swimming in the canal whenever he got the opportunity. He had never feared water, had considered it his friend, and now it had turned on him and was showing him how strong it was and how puny and ineffectual was Conan O'Dowd. And what was more, if he didn't do something fast his friend Ginny would be nothing but a dead body in a tumble of soaked clothing, for he knew that very few girls ever learned to swim. Above him, he could see the silver gleam of the surface and fought his way up to it, realising as his head emerged that he was in what appeared to be a deepish pool under some overhanging trees. The river here was calmer, for it was out of the main stream, though he could hear the furious roar as the water surged past this quieter spot.

He could not see Ginny and was about to set out again when he happened to glance towards the bank and there she was, on a little bit of sandy shore. She was lying on her back, her head turned to one side, and he reached her in two strokes and hauled himself out beside her. He realised at once that she was not breathing and turned her on to her face, beginning to squeeze the water out of her as he had been taught, whilst muttering over and over: 'She mustn't die, don't let her die! It weren't her fault . . . it were all *my* fault. Oh please, whoever you are, don't let her die!'

He was not praying, or not in any accepted sense of the word, but he was definitely pleading and the pleading paid off. Ginny made a terrible, hoarse, crowing sound, spewed a great quantity of water on to the little beach, jerked as convulsively as a landed fish and began to breathe.

Conan sat back on his heels and felt a wide and ridiculous grin spread across his face. A surge of hot and dizzy exultation filled him. She was alive! It had all been his fault, he had acknowledged to himself, but now he had made up for it. If it had not been for him, she would have croaked; even if she did not know it, he did. And suddenly, he wanted to tell Ginny that he was sorry, had never meant her harm, and was just about as glad as a feller could be that she was alive and kicking.

Though Ginny was now breathing, however, she still had not opened her eyes, so Conan bent over her and pulled her into a sitting position, with the vague idea that she would breathe more easily upright. She had clearly not recovered consciousness completely, for she leaned against him, a dead

411

weight in his arm, and he was just beginning to worry, and to wonder what his next move should be, when her eyelids fluttered apart and she began to look round her, and to speak.

'Where . . . ? What . . . ?' Before he could answer, her gaze fell on the river and she gave an enormous, convulsive shudder. Plainly, she had remembered her ordeal. Conan moved round so that he could look into her face, saying gently as he did so: 'It's awright, queen, you're safe wi' me. Wharrever was you doin', tryin' to cross the river where it ran fastest and deepest? I thought you were a goner, so I did, but we was dead lucky if you ask me. The current swirled the pair of us into this here pool . . .' He pointed. 'And when we was both ashore, I remembered me old life-saving class at the Burlington Street Baths and squeezed the water out o' you, like what I were taught.' With the arm which still encircled her shoulders, he gave her a bit of a squeeze. 'Feelin' better? If so, I think we oughter to move, 'cos we're both soakin' wet an' I don't want to save you from drownin' just to have you die of exposure.'

It was then that he noticed the look in Ginny's eyes and realised, uncomfortably, that it was neither a nice nor a friendly look. In fact, she was glaring at him as though he was her worst enemy, and at the same moment she shrugged off his encircling arm. 'Leave me alone, Conan O'Dowd,' she said fiercely, though her voice was thin and weak. 'Saved me from drownin' indeed! Why, if it hadn't been for you, I wouldn't have had to try to cross the river. Oh, you think you're so great, makin' up to your friends the tinkers, plannin' to sell me back to me own daddy, but I've got your measure, boy! An' now

412

you think you're goin' to take me back to the band, but you're wrong, you ain't goin' to do no such thing! So you can leave off lyin' an' pretendin' to be me friend, 'cos all you are is a cheat and I won't go one inch towards the tribe, not even if I have to throw meself back in the river.'

Conan was dumbfounded. He had known Ginny to be a girl of spirit but had thought her both gentle and easily led. And the ingratitude of it really hurt him because, though he had meant to recapture her when he had first realised she was missing, in fact he had changed his mind as soon as he saw her trying to cross the river. And he bleedin' well *had* saved her from drowning, and though he didn't expect to get a medal he had thought she might at least thank him. However, since this was not to be, he had best explain that he had no intention of dragging her back to the tribe.

He began to speak but stopped short before he had said more than a few words. If she was listening, which he doubted, he realised that it would take more than words to convince her of his change of heart. There was a mulish set to her mouth, and though she was shivering with cold and reaction he could read contempt in her eyes. Sighing, Conan got to his feet and held out his hands to her. 'C'mon, we'll find ourselves a nice dry barn full of hay and snug down for the night. There's cows in the fields but my cup has gone; I suppose the river tore it off of me belt, which means I've nothin' to milk a cow into. But I reckon anyone settin' eyes on us would let us have a sup o' milk and a bite o' bread because when we tell 'em we nigh on got carried away by the flood they'll feel sorry for us.'

413

Tinkers usually carried a cup on a leather thong. Ginny, not being a tinker, and being totally unable to milk a cow in any case, had never possessed one, but she did nod briefly at Conan's words before struggling to her feet. Conan admired the way she forced herself to take a few wavering steps but he could see she was very unlikely to get far from the river without help. He put an arm about her waist and when she tried to pull away, told her roughly that she'd best behave herself. 'I seen a barn not more'n fifty yards away,' he told her. 'If you let me help you we can both reach it, but if you're goin' to pretend you can make it alone, we'll neither of us see tomorrer mornin'. Good God, girl, you're shakin' like a bleedin' leaf an' cold as ice. I know you don't trust me, you won't listen to what I were tryin' to tell you, but you've gorra let me get you to shelter.'

For a moment, Ginny compressed her lips and continued to try to drag herself up the slight slope, but then she sagged against Conan, clearly recognising the truth of his words. With his help, she managed to reach the barn and Conan, with an enormous sense of relief, pushed her into an untidy mound of hay, covering her well over with it and then draping a couple of old sacks on top. 'I'm goin' to find the farmer what owns this barn,' he said briefly. 'I'll get some grub o' some sort . . . no, hang on a minute!'

Even as he spoke, Conan pounced on an object half hidden in the hay. It was an old meal scoop, dinted and rusty, but Conan knew at once that he could milk a cow into it and get the milk back to Ginny a good deal faster than if he had to find a farm, explain his needs to the farmer, and then carry a cup of milk some considerable distance without spilling it. For though Conan regarded himself as tough, he was beginning to feel extremely cold and was fighting a lethargy which was tempting him to curl up in the hay and simply sleep and sleep.

'Shan't be long,' he said cheerfully to his companion, hefting the meal scoop. 'You stay there and give your arms an' legs a rub, try to get yourself warm. I'll be back in two ticks.'

It was horrible leaving the shelter of the barn for the windy darkness, since night had now fallen and, though the rain had ceased, the wind had a sharp nip to it. But Conan knew that they needed to eat or drink before they slept, so he plodded determinedly on, and presently was able to return to the barn with the scoop more than half full of rich, warm milk. It had not been easy, getting that milk from a cow whose mind was set on moving slowly across the meadow, cropping the sweet grass, and it was not easy getting back into the barn, for the door had managed to slam shut and Conan was afraid to stand the meal scoop down in case it tipped and he lost his booty. But he managed it in the end and was chagrined to discover, when he lifted the sacks off her, that Ginny was fast asleep. She was curled up in a tight little ball, shivering as she slept, and Conan stood for a moment, wondering whether he should wake her. The shivers decided him. He leaned over her, calling her name, and shook her briskly, though he could only do so with one hand since the other was fully occupied with the scoop of milk.

* * *

415

Ginny awoke from a frightening dream in which she was being chased by a herd of maddened, red-eyed bulls, to find Conan bending over her and holding what, to her frightened eyes, looked like a huge axe above her head. She had honestly intended to run away from the barn and hide herself somewhere else as soon as Conan had left, but this had proved quite impossible. She could not move a limb without pain and realised that she would have to stay with Conan until at least a measure of her strength returned. She had cuddled down in the hay again, therefore, and had fallen into an uneasy sleep from which she was glad to be awoken, especially when she realised that Conan was offering her a drink of warm milk and not threatening to cut her head off, as she had at first feared.

Sitting up in the hay, with her teeth chattering so loudly that they sounded like castanets, she managed to drink her share of the milk and watched as Conan downed his own portion. She had been telling herself that he was wicked, would hand her over to the tinkers just as soon as he was able, but somehow, when she looked into his white and weary face, she began to believe that he could not possibly be all bad. As he settled down in the hay beside her, she asked him, in a small voice, whether he had really saved her from drowning and found herself believing him when he said 'Yes' without his usual elaboration.

'Then thanks very much,' she said, after thinking the matter over. 'How far away is the camp, Conan? Because there's no need for you to stay here, you know. You're stronger'n me an' you could get back to the camp tonight, I dare say.'

'I'm goin' to see you safe on the road to your da's farm afore I does anythin' else,' Conan said firmly. 'If you remember, queen, I came to Ireland to search for me own daddy. Oh, I've liked bein' wi' the tinkers all right but I'd just as soon see you settled and then find another band, mebbe a tribe who can tell me where Eamonn O'Dowd is, an' don't keep sayin' that he might be in prison an' such, the way the Kavanaghs have done.'

Ginny heard the bitter note in his voice and smiled to herself. She had thought Conan had taken that remark as a joke but it had plainly rankled. Once, she would not have believed that he meant to leave the tribe and help her on her way to Kerry, but suddenly she found that she did believe him, after all. She might be wrong, he might be planning to trick her into returning to the tinkers' encampment, but she did not think so and presently, curled up together like two puppies in a box, the pair slept.

*   *   *

Ginny awoke at dawn the next morning, feeling very much better. Her clothes had dried on her and the bruises, sustained as she hurtled downriver, had begun to show. Indeed, she was one enormous bruise from her neck to her ankles. Yet she managed to crawl to the barn door and peer through it, eager to see just where they were and whether there was human habitation at hand.

It was a beautiful morning. The rain had cleared, leaving the countryside sparkling. A hawthorn tree, leaning out of the hedge, was diamonded with a

417

million drops, and every time the little breeze stirred its branches the drops fell, pattering, into the ditch at its foot. The sky arched overhead, a gentle misty blue, and the golden rays of the sun shone not only on the fields and distant hills, but on a nearby farmhouse, its cob walls whitewashed and its golden thatch steaming gently in the sun's rays.

Ginny gasped. Whilst with the tinkers, she had often marvelled at the beauty of the Irish countryside but, perhaps because she was free from their unwelcome presence, the landscape before her looked lovelier than anything she had ever seen. She eased herself out of the barn door and padded, with some care, round to the back, so that she could take a look at the river. To her satisfaction, it was, if anything, wilder and more turbulent than it had been the day before, and she remembered hearing Granny Dido, the oldest of the tinkers, telling the children that they should beware of the river three days after the rain. 'For it takes three days for heavy rain in the mountains to work its way down to the plain and then the water comes in a great, wicked wave which uproots trees, tosses boulders as though they weighed no more than apples, and can drown a young tinker whilst he or she is fillin' a bucket for to make a cup o' tay,' she had told them. 'Oh aye, the river in flood ain't no friend to tinkers, so when you go down to fetch water on a mild an' sunny day, just you remember that the mountains can unleash a great wave on you when you least expects it.'

Ginny had left Conan sleeping, but even as she stared down at the turbulent river she heard his voice at her elbow. 'Mornin', Ginny! Everything's too wet to light a fire—and that includes me little box o' matches—so I reckon we'll ha' to go down to the farm, see if they'll feed us. I wish we had shoes, because if they guess we're tinkers, they'll mebbe keep themselves to themselves and set the dogs on us.'

Ginny had felt quite well disposed towards Conan, but at these words she stiffened angrily. 'I am *not* a tinker, Conan O'Dowd,' she said coldly. 'An' neither are you, not a proper one. If we tell the folk in that farm that the tinkers caught us and meant to ransom us to our daddies, then I reckon they'll take us at our word. After all, I don't believe we look much like tinkers, an' we certainly don't sound it.'

She turned back towards the barn but Conan caught hold of her arm. 'Meant to ransom us to our daddies?' he said. 'Wharrever makes you say that?'

Ginny sighed. 'I heard you tellin' one o' the other kids that that was what the chief meant to do—to sell me to me daddy,' she said patiently. 'And I reckon, if it were worth doin' to me, then it might be worth doin' to you, an' all. Oh, I know they said you were a horse caller, wharrever that may be, an' that makes you valuable, but that's an even better reason to demand money from your daddy, don't you *see*?'

There was a long moment of silence whilst Conan thought it over, frowning down at her as though he could not believe his ears. Then his brow cleared and he smiled. 'D'you know, I believe you're right,' he said. 'Oh, ain't I glad I decided to leave the Kavanaghs an' stick wi' you. Ain't I glad we met up on that ferry, an' all? Oh, Ginny, it's goin' to be awright, I know it in me bones!'

Later that morning, they set off, keeping well clear of the river. Conan took the meal scoop so that he might milk cows as they went, and they managed to find enough vegetables in the fields to sustain them, for a while at least. But one thing was worrying Conan and at last Ginny noticed his frown and asked him what was the matter.

'I'm worried about the tribe,' he said at last. 'We're valuable to 'em, as valuable as though we were made of gold, pretty near, so it stands to reason they'll search for us. I know we've crossed the river, but the truth is, we're all headin' in the same direction. When we come to a village, we'll have to go into it, see if we can nick some clothes off of a line so we won't be so easy to spot. But goin' into a village is dangerous, see? Because the tinkers go into villages to buy grub an' to sell bits an' pieces an' if they see us . . . well, the game 'ud be up, wouldn't it?'

Ginny agreed, rather mournfully, and suggested that they should make straight for the nearest village, reconnoitre it carefully, and then go in and see whether they might beg, borrow or steal some sort of disguise. 'I could get a dark headscarf, or something, mebbe,' she said vaguely, then her face brightened. 'Oh Conan, I've had a grand idea, so I have! We'll take a leaf out o' the Kavanaghs' book, do what they'd do. That way, I'm sure we'll be safe as houses!'

CHAPTER SIXTEEN

It was the terrible wind and rain, Mabel thought, which had actually brought herself and Michael closer together, for there had seemed little point in tramping in the tinkers' wake when they could scarcely see more than ten feet before them.

'I reckon the tinkers will lie up under the cover of a wood whilst the weather stays so bad, because they can't expect to be given fieldwork in conditions like these,' said Michael. The two of them were in a pleasant lodging house in a small village, enjoying an excellent breakfast of boiled brown eggs, bread and butter and strong tea. 'We have to work on the assumption that Ginny is still with the tinkers because now we know they're headin' for Kerry, Ginny might as well be with them as not.'

Mabel, with her mouth full of crusty bread, nodded. They had been told, at the last village, that the tinkers would be making their way to Killorglin, in Kerry, for the August Puck Fair, since this particular tribe were horse dealers. The Puck Fair, Michael had explained, was the most important event of the year, not only for local people, but for the tinkers, horse dealers, stall holders and side-show entertainers who flocked to it.

'Everyone wit' livestock to buy or sell goes to the Puck Fair,' the farmer they had questioned assured them. 'The Kavanaghs are bad lot, though, stop at nothing. Most tinkers is all right, but if you sup wit' the Kavanaghs, you need a long spoon, so you do. There are so many of 'em that it's nigh on impossible for any poor farmer to guard his stock. We're used to tinkers takin' the odd hen that lays astray, as well as her clutch of eggs, diggin' a sack o' spuds out o' a field durin' the night, milkin' the cows an hour or so afore we brings 'em in, but this lot ain't content wit' such trifles. They'll steal your best bay mare an' by mornin' she'll be skewbald, 'cos they'll bleach white patches here an' there. Even donkeys an' mules disappear from their pastures when the Kavanaghs are in the neighbourhood.' He had grinned suddenly, his mouth twisting with wry amusement as though, in a way, he admired the cunning of the Kavanaghs. 'But they're well thought of at the horse fairs, 'cos they only steal the best . . . well, it don't do to ask too many questions or to wonder aloud why the black gelding's coat feels harsh to the touch.'

'Why harsh to the touch?' Mabel had asked, curiously, as they had left their informant behind and set out to get themselves lodgings. 'Does that mean the horse isn't well?'

Michael had laughed. 'You're an innocent, so you are,' he had said teasingly. 'A harsh coat is usually a sign that dye has been used, perhaps to turn a nice little snow-white horse into one black as pitch, whose own master wouldn't recognise him. Oh aye, there's no doubt these Kavanaghs are up to all the tricks. We'd best get our Ginny out of their clutches before they think of a way of turning her to good account.'

Mabel had agreed and they had continued their pursuit though now, as Mabel said, Ginny's presence with the tinkers made a good deal more sense. Since the tinkers were heading for Kerry, the child's best possible move would be to stay with them until they were within shouting distance of Michael's home. Then she could make her own way to the farm, sure of her welcome and with no further need of the tinkers' company.

Over breakfast, Michael put forward the suggestion that they should actually take advantage of the terrible weather and the fact that the tinkers would probably be lying up in some sheltered spot. 'If we catch a long-distance bus, it'll get us well ahead of the tribe. What's more, it might take us to a decent-sized town where we can buy ourselves wet weather gear, and then we can discover from the locals where the Kavanaghs usually camp when they're in that area. We can hide ourselves somewhere handy and, in all the bustle of setting up camp, I reckon we could get in and get Ginny away without any bother. I keep tellin' meself that no harm can come to a child whilst she's with a large group of adults, but from what folks have said, these Kavanaghs aren't the sort o' people anyone would willingly associate with. If we're honest, they're more like thieves an' robbers than ordinary tinkers, so the sooner we find 'em an' take Ginny away from 'em, the better.' He looked enquiringly at his companion across the table. 'What d'you think?'

'I think it's an awfully good idea,' Mabel said. The thought of visiting a town, of seeing shops and people instead of rain-drenched meadows, cows and sheep, was an attractive one. It had been her own fault she had not thought to bring a waterproof, but the thought of some protection against the rain was exceedingly welcome. And a really long bus journey, when they could settle into a warm, dry seat and watch the rain through the bus windows, was pleasant, too. Irish rain, Mabel had heard, was the most penetrating in the world; it would be good not to be out in it, and still feel they were getting closer to Ginny.

So later that day they boarded a bus and set off on their journey the easy way. The bus was old and rickety and filled not only with humanity, but also with livestock. The rain beat against the windows but by late afternoon the weather had changed to a nippy sunshine full of gusty breezes. Mabel was so happy not to be on foot that she scarcely noticed. They had intended to go to Nenagh but since the rain had stopped they got off the bus at the village of Toomyvara. They climbed down, got themselves rooms in a local bar and then started asking whether tinkers ever camped nearby on their way to the Puck Fair. 'We'll ask about the Kavanaghs,' Michael remarked, 'where they stay, an' so on, when they're in the neighbourhood. That way, we won't have to waste time tomorrow.'

They asked the locals for information about the tinkers and, as usual, were rewarded with pungent opinions of the Kavanaghs and their like. Fortunately, the villagers were also able to direct Michael and Mabel to the very spot where the Kavanaghs had set up their camp in past years. The two of them slogged out and examined the site; Michael even going so far as to choose a vantage point from which they could watch the camp whilst remaining unseen themselves.

'I bet they'll arrive tomorrow,' he told Mabel, 'now the weather has improved.' He grinned down at her and Mabel was struck by how much his attitude towards her had changed. At first, he had been prickly, difficult, quick to take offence and slow to respond to any friendly overture. Now, they were like two old pals, thinking along similar lines, sometimes even anticipating what the other was about to say so that they spoke in chorus, breaking off and laughing together. She realised that, much though she wanted to find Ginny, she was beginning to dread parting from Michael. She told herself that it was simply that she'd grown used to him, but she was beginning to suspect that it was more than that. She had not meant to like him, far less love him, but she was very much afraid that she was in danger of being far fonder of him than was wise. After all, when they found Ginny, he would return to his Kerry farm and she to her classroom. There was little chance that they would ever meet again, for Michael had made it plain that, if Ginny were willing, he meant to keep her in Ireland. So the sensible thing was to treat him with friendliness whilst never forgetting that they were soon to part.

'Mabs? Will you stop dreamin', girl! Do you or do you not think that the weather's going to be fine tomorrow?'

Mabel, rudely jerked back to the present, said that she certainly hoped he was right. Then the two of them returned to the village, arriving at their lodgings in time for an evening meal.

*   *   *

They ate their breakfast with sunshine pouring in through the window and Michael felt, optimistically, that today might see the end of their search. He beamed at Mabel as he told her that he thought they ought to go straight to the camping ground as soon as breakfast was over and Mabel smiled back, though not, he thought, quite as

425

enthusiastically as he. But of course Ginny was only her pupil, not her little lost daughter, so he could scarcely expect an equal show of excitement from her. He thought she looked extra specially pretty today, with the sunshine glinting on her golden head and a flush on her cheeks. For the first time, he realised how the good weather had improved her. In Liverpool, she had been pale with the pallor of a plant kept too long in the shade, but now she was gloriously sun-kissed, her skin golden-brown, even her hair seeming to have an added lustre. But it would not do to sit mooning here; they had work to do. He glanced interrogatively at his companion. 'Finished your breakfast? If so, we'd better be after makin' tracks for the camping ground. Tinkers get on the move before the sun's up so we'd best get into our hidin' place in good time.'

Mabel stood up. 'Right. I'd better get a jacket,' she said briskly. 'And if you're right, Michael, and we do find her today, I suppose I ought to start looking up the times of buses back to Dublin.'

Michael had been about to turn away to go up to his room, but at these words he stopped short and turned to stare at her. 'Back to Dublin?' he asked in an incredulous tone. 'Whatever would you be wantin' wit' a bus to Dublin?'

Even as he said the words, he remembered that of course, for Mabel, there had been one reason and one reason only for accompanying him on his search. She knew Ginny and he did not. With a heart plummeting into his boots, he realised that her presence had made the search into a happy, shared adventure and that he had not once thought that it must end when they found Ginny. But—but why should it end? Surely she would agree to come home with them, to meet his parents, see the farm, settle Ginny in? Surely she did not mean to simply point Ginny out and then desert him? But of course, right at the start of their trip, she had told him her parents expected her to go home to Suffolk for some part, at least, of the summer holidays. He supposed that he should have realised she would do what she had come to do and then return to England to take up the threads of her normal life. She was a bright, intelligent woman with a good job and excellent prospects and he was just what Granny Bennett had called him—an ignorant, Irish bog-trotter with straws in his hair. He could offer her nothing, save the hard life lived on the land, but even so . . .

'You know very well why I'll want a bus to Dublin, Michael,' Mabel said. Her voice sounded impatient, but there was a little break in it too. 'Once Ginny's found, my job's over. I came to introduce the pair of you, if you remember, and . . . and . . .'

'Oh, but you can't just turn round and leave me wit' a daughter I've never set eyes on before,' Michael said eagerly. 'Ginny an' meself is strangers, so we are—she may even be afraid of me! You'll come wit' us to Headland Farm, surely? Me parents would never forgive me if I didn't introduce the young lady who helped me in me search . . . we'll catch a train or a bus, you won't have to walk . . . an' you've never seen Kerry—'tis the most beautiful place in Ireland, so it is. You can't come all this way and . . .'

Mabel smiled at him. 'We're jumping the gun a bit, aren't we?' she said gently. 'We haven't even found Ginny yet. Don't—don't let's argue, Michael,

427

because we've been good friends, haven't we? But—but you knew I'd have to go home once Ginny was found, didn't you?'

She was looking up at him and it was on the tip of Michael's tongue to say that there was no need for her to go home, that she could make her home in Ireland with him, that he loved her, had loved her pretty well from the moment they'd first met although he hadn't recognised the feeling for what it was. But then he remembered the calm, authoritative schoolteacher who had shown, all too clearly, what she thought of Michael Gallagher, and his courage failed him. He mumbled that he supposed she was right but that there was no point in discussing it now, and made for the stairs and his room.

*   *   *

Their landlady made them sandwiches and a bottle of cold tea so that they should not starve during their vigil, and the two of them made their way to the ground where they had been told the tinkers would camp. It was an ideal spot, but though they waited until dusk began to fall, no one came into the clearing below them. They saw squirrels, a good few rabbits, and a wary dog fox who came down to the river to drink, but no tinkers. Because their hiding place was halfway up a hill, they had a good view of the track along which the Kavanaghs would come, so they were able to relax, to chat and to discuss how they would extract Ginny from amongst her companions just as soon as they were able.

At first, the atmosphere between the two of

428

them had been a little tense because of their breakfast time conversation, but it soon eased once more into normal warmth and friendship, and by the time they were descending into the village again all their differences had been forgotten.

'We'll get up early tomorrow and return to our hiding place as soon as we've ate our breakfast,' Michael said, as they made their way to the boarding house. 'Mrs O'Mara is a good sort, she'll do us a packed lunch again, so we can stay there all day. But I feel in me bones that tomorrow we're going to be lucky.'

'Lucky in one way, unlucky in another,' Mabel said.

Michael looked at her curiously. 'What does that mean?' he asked bluntly. He watched with interest as the rose deepened in her cheeks. Could it be that she was enjoying their adventure as much as he was? Was it possible that, much though she wanted to find Ginny, she would regret that their journey through this now sunny land would be coming to an end? But it seemed that Mabel had been thinking along more practical lines.

'We-ell, judging from what folk have said about the Kavanaghs, we may not find it too easy to get her out of their clutches,' she explained. 'Everyone has said there are good tinkers and bad and the Kavanaghs are obviously very bad indeed. I know we haven't discussed it, but it's been in my mind for a while that they might be holding Ginny against her will. They might even demand money from you for her safe return. I know it happens a lot in books, but it happens in real life, too,' she ended, giving Michael a look which was half frightened, half apologetic.

Michael stared at her. The same thought had constantly occurred to him but he had not said anything to her because somehow it seemed so far-fetched. The Gallagher farm supported the family and allowed them to save a little but they were always dependent on a good harvest, on the ewes lambing well, on the weather being kind. A bad season could nigh on ruin them, and there had been years when only the fishing had enabled them to carry on. True, they were more established now but even so, he could not imagine that any ransom worth having could be paid to the tinkers from their few precious acres.

He said as much to Mabel, who shook her head sadly at his innocence. 'Remember, Michael, these people have never lived in one place for longer than a few days. To them, anyone with a roof over their heads must seem rich beyond compare. They steal a couple of hens for the pot and a clutch of eggs from the nest, but they see the farmer with twenty or thirty hens, with a couple of pigs in the sty . . . apples on the tree . . . meadows with stock grazing upon it. To them, a tiny holding of an acre or so must seem to represent unheard of wealth.'

Michael snorted. 'Then it's sorely disappointed they're goin' to be,' he said roundly. They had reached their lodgings and he ushered Mabel in ahead of him. 'But I understand what you mean, because of course it's occurred to me too—that they might be holdin' her against her will, I mean. Still, we'll find a way round it, you see if we don't. And now let's be havin' a good tea to build up our strength for tomorrow.'

*   *   *

They were there by the time the sun had climbed above the hills, and saw the first signs of an approach within half an hour of their arrival. There were a couple of caravans, eight or ten horse-drawn wagons, a good few horses, mules and donkeys and, of course, a great many tinkers. So far as Michael could see, no one was riding in the caravans although a man sat up in front of each, idly slapping the reins on the horse's neck, whilst the women and children walked alongside, the women carrying heavy burdens, the children minding the livestock with the aid of half a dozen skinny, savage-looking dogs.

Mabel and Michael scanned the arrivals eagerly but, as Mabel said, Ginny's fiery head would have stood out a mile and there was no sign of her. 'But of course, if they are keeping her captive, they aren't likely to let her wander around the encampment,' Mabel pointed out. 'I'd not thought of caravans . . . oh!'

For even as she spoke, the caravan doors were pulled open by a couple of women climbing ponderously aboard. They then began to bring out such a quantity of goods that Michael doubted whether even a mouse could have found space to remain within. The tinkers began to erect tents and to build a fire in the middle of the clearing; plainly, they were settling down here for a while, at least. Michael guessed that it was conveniently near the village of Toomyvara, where they would sell bunches of lucky heather to the superstitious, hand-whittled clothes pegs to the housewives and bass brooms, clothes props and other such items to anyone willing to part with a few coppers. He knew

431

they would steal what they could, but there were some things which must be bought and these things could be obtained in a village. Yes, he thought the tinkers would be here for a day, possibly more.

When the sun was at its height, he and Mabel agreed that even if Ginny had once been with the Kavanaghs, she was with them no longer. Michael was tempted to go down into the encampment and ask questions, but Mabel was against it. 'I can't explain why I think it's a bad idea, but I'd much rather you didn't,' she said urgently. 'They look such a dirty, disreputable lot. I'm sure if they knew you were searchin' for Ginny, they would search for her, too, and that might lead to all sorts of trouble. I mean, there are dozens of them, and if they found her first . . .'

'Awright, but if they come into the village—and I'm sure they will—mebbe I could stop one o' the kids and ask 'em if they'd seen a red-haired girl in a blue dress,' Michael said rather diffidently. He saw Mabel's point about not alerting the tinkers to the fact that his daughter was lost, but he had been deeply disappointed to find that she was not with the band and was rather at a loss what to do next.

Mabel made up his mind for him. 'If we want to have a word with one of the kids then I think we ought to make our way back to the village as quickly as we can,' she said. 'The chances are they'll send someone out to the shops as soon as they've made camp, and you know what kids are— one or two of them are bound to tag along out of curiosity, if nothing else. The only thing is, we don't want the tinkers to know they're being spied on, do we? So can we get away without alerting them, do you think?'

432

Michael looked at the surrounding terrain. Their little copse was just below the top of a small hillock. 'We'll be fine, so we shall,' he said bracingly, standing up and beginning to gather their belongings together. 'After all, it's no sin to walk through the Irish countryside. For all they know, we could be trekking from town to town, doing fieldwork whenever it was offered—just like themselves, in fact. Tell you what, you take hold of me arm an' we'll look like a couple out for a stroll on a sunny day.'

Mabel caught hold of his arm and smiled up at him. 'There's trees and bushes between us and them, once we're over the hillock,' she observed. 'I doubt if they'll catch more than a glimpse, if that. They're still awfully busy, Michael. Making camp takes a while and now they're fetching water and beginning to prepare a meal, I imagine—see the woman in the purple skirt? She's skinned and jointed a couple of rabbits and she's putting the pieces into the pot and her friend, in the grey shawl, is plucking pigeons and a hen, and the kids are gathering up the feathers ever so carefully—I wonder what they use them for?'

'I know they're busy; it's fascinating watching them because you wouldn't expect tinks to be so organised,' Michael said as they stole quietly away. 'One of the girls—the plump one, with long, brown hair—washed a huge bunch of carrots in the river and then fished a knife out of her pocket and chopped 'em straight into the pot, as quick an' neat as any butcher.'

'I wonder whether Ginny was ever with them?' Mabel asked idly, once they had regained the narrow country lane which wound down towards

Toomyvara.

Michael shrugged. 'I was certain, but now I'm not so sure, but I would like to find out for definite, so we'll try to have a chat with one of the kids if they do come into the town.'

Despite the fact that their search for Ginny at the tinkers' camp had been fruitless, Michael found himself whistling a tune beneath his breath as they walked down the lane and was delighted when Mabel, recognising the melody, began to sing the words. They were thus engaged, still sauntering along, when something made Michael glance behind him and he saw the young girl from the tinkers' camp, who had been washing carrots, following them. She was carrying a string bag full of pegs and smiled as she saw him watching her. She looked a good deal cleaner and more neatly dressed than the other children in the camp and Michael smiled back, deciding that she was probably the result of a mixed marriage. As she drew level with them, he put a detaining hand on her arm. 'Hang on a moment, alanna! Are you after sellin' them pegs, because if so, I'll relieve you of, say, three dozen.'

The child's smile had been a little guarded but now it widened joyfully and she said, her voice holding no trace of an Irish accent, 'Thank you kindly, mister. That'll be a shillin' to you.'

Michael guessed that she expected him to bargain but he did not intend to do any such thing. Instead, he nodded agreeably and watched as the girl set down her bag on the grassy verge and began, painstakingly, to count out thirty-six pegs.

'Dicky Diddlum whittled these pegs,' the child said conversationally, as she counted out the first dozen and began on the second. 'He makes the best pegs out o' the whole tribe. When he's done 'em, he rubs 'em wi' sandpaper so you'll get no snags on your washing from *these* pegs. And that's why they're a bit pricier than most,' she finished triumphantly, setting out the second row of a dozen. She looked curiously up at Mabel, who had sat down on a mossy log beside her. 'Has your feller bought all these pegs for you?' she enquired. 'D'you have a heap o' kids so you need a heap o' pegs? Us Kavanaghs don't use washin' lines; we spreads our clothes over the bushes and the big boulders down by the river.'

Mabel fingered one of the pegs admiringly. 'They are really fine,' she said. 'The pegs are for me, of course, but we don't have a heap of children. In fact, we've only got one and—and we've lost her. We wondered, my fellow and me, if you might have come across her? Her name's Ginny and she's got long, curly red hair and . . . why, whatever is the matter, my dear?' For with Mabel's words, Michael saw that the child's round and rosy face had drained of colour and the capable, though dirty little hands doling out the pegs had grown still as stone.

Even as he watched, he saw large tears appear in the child's eyes and roll down her cheeks, and at the same moment she threw down an extra handful of pegs and scrambled to her feet.

'I—I dunno nothing,' she muttered, staring fixedly down at the ground. 'There's—there's no kid called Ginny in our—in our fambly and we's all Kavanaghs, you know. You—you can have the pegs for nothin', mister . . . oh!'

For Michael, realising that she was about to depart, and at speed, had grabbed her arm and was

435

hanging on to it firmly. 'No you don't, my girl,' he said. 'It's clear as daylight you know a deal more about my Ginny than you mean to tell me, but it ain't on. We *know* she were with the Kavanaghs because she were spotted in Portlaoise—she were with a young chiseller—so there's no use lyin' to us.' He took hold of her other arm, turning her so that she was forced to face him. 'What happened, eh? And let's have the truth this time, or I'll take you straight into the village and hand you over to the nearest Gardai as a liar and a kidnapper. Unless you tell us the truth, that is, and quickly.'

The girl looked wildly from one to another, but she must have read the resolution in both faces for she bent her head once more, then jerked up her chin and looked Michael straight in the eye. 'She were nice, were Ginny,' she muttered. 'I did me best to make her happy so's she'd stay wi' us and so did Conan—he were the young feller what brung her in. But she didn't want to stay wi' us—I dunno why—and the other day it rained and blew a gale, and the tribe was on the move, an'—an' she ran away. Conan went after her, meanin' to bring her back, 'cos we woz goin' to take her to her daddy, honest to God we woz. Only, the river were in flood an' she an' Conan—they—they tried to cross. Ginny slipped, Conan tried to grab her . . . and they—and they . . . were carried away.'

Michael was so appalled that he released the child's arms and, quick as a flash, she snatched up her bag of pegs and began to pelt down the lane. He ran after her and would have caught her up had he not heard a sound from behind him and, turning his head, seen Mabel, running in his wake, go flying over a loose stone. He turned back at once, though

436

Mabel shouted to him not to do so. She began to scramble to her feet, assuring him that she would be fine, that he must leave her and catch up with the child, but Michael put his arm round her and supported her for she was much shaken by the violence of her fall. Blood was pouring from the palms of both hands; she had grazed her chin and her knees looked to be in a shocking state. 'The tinker brat doesn't matter; she's told us all she knows,' he said brusquely, 'and besides, you know what tinkers are. She might have been lying just to put us off the scent. But right now it's you that matters.' Michael swallowed the lump in his throat and tried to concentrate on Mabel's various hurts. 'Me poor darlin', what a horrible thing to happen. I hope to God you've not broken anything.'

First he must make sure that Mabel had, indeed, not broken any bones, and do his best to patch her up so that they might return to the village where, if necessary, he could take her to see a doctor before continuing their search. After all, if Ginny had indeed fallen into the flooded river, she might well have been carried a considerable way before managing to scramble out. That she might have been drowned was something he refused to consider. Besides, she had had a companion: the boy, Conan, who would have managed to get them both ashore somehow, he told himself firmly. He could not bear to think that his little girl had set out to cross Ireland and find her daddy, and had found only her death. No, no, she would be alive and keeping well away from the tinkers, he was sure of it.

Tenderly, Michael picked Mabel up, despite her protests, and carried her to the nearest bank where he set her down and carefully folded back her dark blue cotton skirt. He got out his handkerchief—it was clean, fortunately—and began to mop at her knees. He was remarking, as cheerfully as he could, that though she had taken a nasty tumble he did not think that her hurts would need more than cleaning up, when he glanced up at her face and saw that she was crying. Immediately, he jumped to his feet and sat down beside her, putting an arm about her shoulders and giving her a comforting squeeze. 'Don't cry, alanna, don't cry,' he crooned. 'Sure an' 'tis a terrible t'ing when a child falls into the river but I'm sure she was out again in no time and hiding somewhere from the tinkers. The boy, too, probably. Tinkers are afeared of water, they say, so I doubt they'd waste time combing the river bank for a child that was not their own.'

Mabel rubbed her eyes and said, shakily: 'I'm sure you're right and we mustn't give up hope. If only we knew where she'd fallen in, we could follow the river ourselves.'

'We'll make our way back into the village and mebbe find the tinker girl,' Michael said determinedly. 'And this time she won't get away until she's told us all we want to know. Can you walk, alanna?'

Mabel sniffed, then fished a handkerchief out of her sleeve and blew her nose resoundingly. 'I can walk all right,' she said stoutly. 'Oh, Michael, we ought to kneel down right now and say a prayer and ask God to look after her, wherever she is.'

This, however, seemed pretty impractical to Michael. 'We'll pray as we go along,' he said briskly, helping her to her feet, though keeping a supporting arm about her. 'I want to get into the village as soon as possible and find that kid. I want to ask her . . . well, about what we've just been discussing. Are you sure you're fit to walk all the way, though?' His arm tightened about her for a moment and he touched her cheek gently with his free hand. 'Poor little Mabs. Shall I carry you?'

'No indeed,' Mabel said. 'My knees are a bit stiff and my hands sting like billyo, but I'll be right as rain by the time we've gone a few yards. Oh, Michael, I do so hope you're right and Ginny was just carried along with the river and managed to scramble out somewhere. After all, the last thing she would do would be to return to the Kavanaghs to tell them she was still alive. I'm sure you're right and she'd be more inclined to hide from them.'

Michael agreed, and presently they entered Toomyvara and headed towards a general shop. Michael was just saying that it seemed likely to him that the tinker child would have made first for the houses, hoping to sell her pegs and thus have money for shopping, when Mabel clutched his arm. 'Look! Isn't that her, coming out of the shop with something in her arms?' They both started forward, but within a few yards of the girl Mabel pulled him back. 'Oh, no. I'm so sorry, Michael, that's quite a different girl. I don't think she comes from the Kavanagh camp, either; I've never seen her before, I'm sure.' She began to say something else, then realised that Michael was staring at the young girl as though he could not believe his eyes. Mabel stared in her turn. She was a pretty little thing, of probably ten or eleven, with a pointed, elfin face, large blue eyes, and a tumble of rich, coal-black hair, curling down almost to her waist. Mabel smiled tentatively at her, but Michael still stood

439

where he was, as though turned to stone.

*   *   *

As Michael's eyes rested on the child's face he felt the years roll back and he was standing once more on the quayside in Liverpool, facing a beautiful girl who held a white kitten between her hands.

'If it isn't me darlin' Stella,' he breathed. 'Oh, Stella, Stella!' And then he covered the space between them in a couple of strides, and took the child's hands in both of his, for all in a moment he knew her for who she really was—the little daughter he had last seen when she was only a few weeks old. 'Ginny?' he said wonderingly. 'It *is* Ginny, isn't it? I don't know what's happened to your lovely red hair, but, oh, Ginny, you're so like your mammy! I couldn't be mistaken, I'd know you anywhere!'

*   *   *

Ginny gave a strangled yelp and flung her arms round her father, hugging him with all her strength and half sobbing as she did so. Michael had thought she might be shy with him, might need, so to speak, an introduction, but she seemed to accept him immediately, looking up at him with frank and loving eyes.

'Oh, Daddy, Daddy! You're just like I thought you'd be . . . and we was headin' for Kerry and your farm just as fast as we could, only so many things have happened . . . were you huntin' for me? Oh, I can't believe it's you at last—I'm so happy!'

'Me little girl, me little Ginny . . . and ain't you

440

the image of your mammy?' Michael crooned, returning her hug and feeling the tears standing in his own eyes, beginning to trickle down his cheeks. 'Oh, we've found you at last and you're safe and sound, t'anks be to God.'

Ginny sniffed and wiped away her own tears, then turned astonished eyes on his companion. 'Miss Derbyshire!' she said. 'It's grand to see you so it is, but what the devil are you doin' here?'

Mabel smiled lovingly down at her erstwhile pupil. 'Your daddy thought he might not recognise you so I came along just in case, but it was me who didn't know you,' she said. 'It's the hair—you look so different, I'd have walked straight past you if Michael here hadn't spotted you. And you've a friend with you as well . . . are you going to introduce us?'

She indicated the small boy standing awkwardly nearby and Ginny clapped a hand to her mouth. 'Oh, Conan, I am sorry! This is Miss Derbyshire, who used to be me teacher back in Liverpool, and—and this is me daddy! Conan is Conan O'Dowd, and he's been a real good pal to me. He—he was bringin' me to Kerry . . . the tinkers were after us, though . . . oh, can we go somewhere quiet? We know the Kavanaghs are somewhere near because we walked slap-bang into Nan earlier, only she didn't recognise us, thanks be to the Holy Mother.'

'We'll go to our lodgings,' Michael said, taking his daughter's hand and indicating to Conan that he should follow them. 'And then you can tell us everything, because we heard a story just now . . . but all's well that ends well, you're alive, and very soon we'll be on our way!'

CHAPTER SEVENTEEN

'It's an awful long story though, Daddy, an' I'm not quite sure where to begin.'

Ginny and Conan sat side by side on Michael's bed and the two adults sat opposite them, on the small upholstered chairs provided by the landlady. Now Michael smiled encouragingly at his daughter, then reached out and took Mabel's hand. 'Perhaps it would be best if Miss Derbyshire and meself told you what we've learned,' he said. 'Then you can correct us if we go wrong and explain what really happened. Does that sound all right, alanna?'

'It sounds grand,' Ginny said contentedly. Miss Derbyshire and her daddy were both beaming at her as though she were the crock of gold at the end of the rainbow. 'Go on, then. Start at the very beginning, when you got to Seaforth and found I weren't there. I'm dyin' to know what they telled you, because they were pretty mad wi' me when I lit out.'

Michael grinned. 'Oh, all that was behind them by the time I arrived an' they were mortal worried about you,' he said. 'But they thought you might have gone back to Victoria Court and be hidin' wi' one of your old pals, so . . .'

He outlined the story of his own search, his finding of Mabel, and her decision to accompany him to Ireland.

'Because you see, dear, your daddy hadn't set eyes on you since you were a tiny baby and it would have been difficult, finding you by himself,' Mabel explained, looking rather self-conscious, Ginny

442

thought. 'I knew I'd know you amongst a hundred others . . . or thought I would! But the hair colour foxed me completely. And it was your likeness to your mother which gave you away, in the end.'

'I didn't know I *was* like me mammy,' Ginny said, knowing she must look as amazed as she felt. 'Granny Bennett was always on about how beautiful Stella was, and how I weren't in the least like her, and no one else ever said anything different, so I thought . . . besides, I *know* I'm not beautiful!'

'Well, you are then,' Michael said firmly. 'Anyway, to cut a long story short . . .'

He told the tale of their search well and quickly, but when he got to Nan's part in it his voice trembled and he made a mute sign to Mabel, who took over. 'Nan said she'd followed the pair of you to the river and seen you swept away,' Mabel said. 'We—we were horrified, but even then your daddy didn't believe you were dead. We were coming into the town to find Nan . . . is she the plump little girl with long, light brown hair? . . . yes, we thought that was who you meant. Well, we were going to ask her where you'd fallen in the river when we walked into you coming out of that shop, cuddling that loaf as though it were a baby,' she ended, with a laugh.

'Cripes!' Ginny said inelegantly. 'Well, now for our story! We joined the tinkers 'cos Conan's daddy is a tinker and 'cos they were headin' for Kerry and said it would be awright for us to go along with 'em. We didn't have money for buses or trains, but the tinkers work on the land as they go and we thought we could do the same. Only it didn't work out, and when we realised the Kavanaghs were liars and

443

cheats we decided to escape if we could. We got away from 'em on the journey over the mountains, because the cloud came down and the rain pelted and they couldn't see us when we nipped off. Then we tried to cross the river and I slipped and Conan came after me and managed to pull me out, somehow or other. He squeezed the water out of me and we found a barn and hid in the hay until morning. Then we realised that the tinkers and ourselves would all be heading for Kerry and Conan said we'd best be disguised. I—I'm afraid we nicked a dark skirt and blouse for me, off a washing line, and some navy kecks and a tattered blue shirt for Conan, only—only me ginger hair's a dead giveaway, wouldn't you say? I mean, Conan said I'd stand out like a lump of coal in a snowfield, and that gave me an idea. Whilst I were with the tinkers, I saw them usin' the dye often and often, on the ponies they stole, so I nicked some of it 'cos it were evidence that they were a real bad lot and not honest horse dealers, like they kept sayin'. I meant to show it to the scuffers if the Kavanaghs tried to say I were with 'em of me own accord, but it never come to that, 'cos Conan an' me got away. Only when Conan said that about me hair, I thought o' the dye, an'—well, we used it. See?'

'I wonder why the tinkers were so keen to hold on to you?' Michael said slowly. 'I mean, you're only a couple o' kids and they've got kids of their own in plenty. It doesn't seem to make sense.'

'It does when you know what we know,' Conan said gruffly, speaking for the first time. 'The Kavanaghs got the idea that the Gallaghers farmed in a big way and were rich. They meant to ask a hundred pounds and a good deal of stock for the

444

return of your daughter. So you see, Ginny were valuable to them. I expect they're mad as fire that we've got away,' he added, with satisfaction.

'Right, I've got the picture now,' Michael said. 'You're safe enough now though, because Nan said they believe you were drownded, and anyway you've found us. So now the four of us will get ourselves to Headland Farm just as soon as we can.'

'The three of you,' amended Conan. He was very flushed but spoke up nevertheless. 'I'm still searchin' for me own daddy, remember.'

'The two of you,' Mabel said quietly. 'I really do have to get back to England, Michael. My parents will be expecting me any day now, and—and . . .'

'Ah, but surely the pair of you can spare us a few days?' Michael said coaxingly. 'After all our wanderings, you'll be wantin' to see the home where Ginny will be stayin' for a good part of her life—if she wants to, that is. You can't let me down now, Mabel! Say you'll come back wit' us, if only for a few days, and then I promise you I'll take you back to Dublin and put you on the ferry meself, if that's what you want.'

* * *

Despite their protestations, Mabel and Conan accompanied Michael and Ginny when they walked up the path to Headland Farm next day. Mabel had agreed that it would be a sad shame to miss meeting Mr and Mrs Gallagher and admitted, with a faint flush, to curiosity over the Gallagher farmhouse. What was more, journeying back alone across Ireland did not appeal to her at all; it would

445

be far better to have Michael's company as far as the ferry, she told him.

Conan did not take much persuading either. Having admitted that he had no money and no idea of his father's whereabouts, it seemed only sensible to go to the Gallagher farm and make what enquiries he could from there. So it was four people who ascended the sloping lane which led up to Headland Farm, and were presently ushered into the large and homely kitchen. Here, Michael introduced Mabel, Conan and Ginny to his beaming parents. He had telegraphed them twice since returning to Ireland; once to let them know he was in Dublin and searching for his daughter, who might well arrive at the farm before him, and the second time to say he had found Ginny and would be returning with her quite soon. He meant to explain Ginny's falling in with the tinkers, but as soon as she had got them all down to the table, with a hot meal in front of them, Maeve Gallagher forestalled him. She produced a very dirty sheet of yellow notepaper and read it aloud. It said, quite simply, that Ginny had been found by a good-hearted family of travelling folk who meant to deliver her safe and sound to her father's farm.

She is costin us considrable in time and money and going out of our way to fetch her to you, the letter went on. *So we'll be asken that you pay us bak some o the money we laid out. Us reckons she worth a 100 pounds to you and mebbe a coupel o thay fancy horses what your gal have talked about. It'll be mebbe a month afore we reaches you so you've time aplenty to get the money together and oblige a good friend.*

The letter, if you could call it that, was signed with a straggly cross. Michael read it aloud, then

446

gave a contemptuous snort and tossed it into the fire. 'Well, Ginny, my girl, you've saved us a deal o' trouble,' he said gruffly. 'So now we all know for certain just what their little plan was, but you and Conan, between you, have foiled them very neatly.' He turned to his mother. 'Mammy, I just want you to know what a good friend Mabel has been, both to me and to Ginny. If it hadn't been for her, I don't believe I'd ever have found my girl. And Conan saved her life . . . but we'll make a real tale of it as soon as we've ate our supper and are sittin' round the fire, relaxed.'

*   *   *

Later that evening, the whole story was told, yet again, to an admiring audience, though Maeve Gallagher confided to her husband, when they were alone in their goose-feather bed, that she could not imagine why Michael was taking Mabel Derbyshire back home to Liverpool in a few days. 'For it's plain as the nose on me face that our lad's in love wit' the girl an' she wit' him,' she announced. 'Neither of 'em has ever been married, though I know Michael was in love wit' Ginny's mammy, but she's been dead these ten years. Surely he isn't holdin' back because of Stella?'

'I dunno,' Sean Gallagher mumbled. 'I know you say he's fond o' the colleen, but he's so dazzled over Ginny—ain't she the prettiest thing, Maeve?—that I don't reckon he's thinkin' straight. I reckon she's all he wants right now. And you, Maeve—how are you after feelin' towards your only granddaughter?'

'She's the best thing that's happened to me since

our Michael were born,' Maeve said contentedly. 'Did you see her give me a great big hug and a kiss when I showed her the little room we'd made ready for her? There's nothin' sweeter than a lovin' child.'

'And did you see her give *me* a great big hug and a kiss,' Sean said, 'when I said she could have Floss in her room, just for one night? And tomorrow she swears she'll get up early so you an' she can collect the hens' eggs from the nests, and then she wants me to teach her to milk the cows.'

Maeve chuckled. 'I wondered if she'd want to go wit' Michael when he takes Mabel to catch the ferry, but I don't think she even considered it and I'm sure they won't really want her company,' she admitted. 'It's grand to know she'd rather be wit' us though, Sean. She says she won't call me Granny, because of Granny Bennett back in Liverpool; she's goin' to call me Mammy Maeve, which is just fine by me.'

'She'll mebbe call me Granddad, since she's got her own daddy wit' her at last,' Sean said sleepily. 'The little lad ain't bad, either. But he won't be wit' us long. He really means to find that no-good tinker father of his and though I told him he were welcome to stay, I think mebbe leavin' is the right thing for him. He's a born wanderer, you know, and Michael said, after the kids had gone to bed, that the boy's a horse caller. If he is, he'll never lack for work in Ireland.'

*   *   *

Michael got into bed that night feeling completely happy. His mother had made him a shakedown on

448

the couch in the kitchen so that Mabel could use his room, and young Conan, at his own request, had been given a blanket and had been allowed to doss down in the hay store where, no doubt, he was snug as a bug in a rug.

Despite the exciting day he had had, or perhaps because of it, Michael lay awake for a long time. There was so much to think about and consider! He had been so lucky to find his little daughter, and to persuade Mabel to accompany them to the farm. Yet he had still not managed to tell Mabel how he felt about her. She had said she would stay for a few days and Michael knew that he must pluck up his courage. Naturally, he feared a rebuff, but he knew that if he let the opportunity pass, let Mabel return to Liverpool without knowing he loved her, he would never forgive himself.

He had loved Stella deeply and truly, had thought he could never love another, yet during their journey across Ireland he had begun to realise, more and more, that though his love for Stella could never die, it had begun to take its proper place as a part of his past. Life is for living, he told himself now, watching thin threads of smoke wandering lazily upward from the banked down fire. I've got Ginny and the farm and me good parents, but a man needs something more. I must tell Mabel how I feel or I will lose her, and she's become important to me—in a way, more important than Stella ever was. My love for Stella was first love, fragile and beautiful. But my love for Mabel was forged in a hotter fire. I didn't even like her at first; I thought she was bossy and a know-all. Even her looks didn't attract me; I told myself she weren't my type. Yet now . . . oh, she's me golden girl and I love her from the top of her head to the tip of her toes. Why, when I think about the two of them, Stella is moonlight—hair midnight black, skin silvery white—whereas Mabel is sunshine. Oh, I must, I must pluck up me courage and ask her to be me wife.

Having made up his mind to act the very next day, he began to doze at last and presently slept, to dream of a life with Mabel always at his side and the sun always showing.

*   *   *

Mabel, lying in Michael's bed, watched the moon rise, huge and yellow, in the dark sky outside the window and thought she had never been so miserable. I'm the only truly unhappy person in this whole house, she told herself, because the others have all got just what they wanted. Mr and Mrs Gallagher have got the granddaughter they've longed for, and Michael's got his little girl back again. Ginny's so like her mother that she will be a constant reminder of how much he loved Stella, and how much he misses her. For my part, I've made a complete fool of myself. I've gone and fallen in love with a man who isn't free to love me back because he's still in the thrall of the woman he loved ten long years ago. Several times I thought he was beginning to like me, thought I had a chance with him, but that was before Ginny turned up. I realised then that Stella must have been incredibly beautiful, the sort of woman a man can never forget. I'm just ordinary, I'm not even pretty, so the best thing I can do is get myself back to Liverpool and try to forget the whole Gallagher family. No matter what the Bennetts may think, I don't believe Ginny will ever return to live with them; she's got too much sense. No one in their right mind would move away from this beautiful spot if they could possibly help it and Ginny's a sensible child. Oh, how I wish . . . but it's no use wishing, and the longer I stay here, the harder leaving will be. So I'll go first thing in the morning, before anyone's up, and make my way back to the ferry alone. If I linger, Ginny will try to persuade me to stay on for a few more days and I just don't think I could bear it. Life here could have been wonderful, but I can't, and won't, play second fiddle to a woman who's been dead ten years. And anyway, Michael isn't going to ask me to stay. Why should he?

The hours slipped by but still Mabel could not sleep. At one point, she even considered that Michael might ask her to marry him simply to provide Ginny with a mother figure. Even if he doesn't love me, I could be useful, she told herself, and perhaps, in time, he might begin to feel as I do . . . wouldn't that be worth staying for?

But she knew, in her heart, that she could not take such a risk; she loved Michael far too well. No, her best course would be to go away, to leave right now, so that the pain of goodbyes would be spared her.

Quiet as a mouse, she slipped out of bed, dressed, packed her small case. Then she took pen and paper and wrote a note, thanking the Gallaghers for their hospitality, saying that she would no doubt meet Ginny and Michael again when they returned to Liverpool to see Ginny's relatives, and that she had decided to leave at once in order to save Michael the trouble of accompanying her back to the ferry when she knew he was so busy. She signed it, *Your friend, Mabel Derbyshire*, stuck it in a prominent position on the pillow, and then turned to the small window which she opened to its widest extent. She had not taken a great deal of notice the previous evening as to the layout of the farmhouse, but was pretty sure she would have to cross the kitchen in order to get out through the door. And that would mean passing the slumbering Michael. If he woke . . .

There was a chair in her room. She climbed on to the seat and eased herself out through the window, dropping lightly on to the hard packed earth beneath. A dog trotted over to her, sniffed curiously at her legs, and then returned to the shed whence it had come. Even the dog isn't really interested in me, doesn't care whether I come or go, Mabel told herself bitterly, heading for the lane which led to the nearest village. I'm best out of here; perhaps everyone should stick to their own place. After all, it wasn't Michael's idea that I should accompany him on his search—oh, he was the first to suggest it, but I'd put the notion in his head—so if I've got hurt, it's entirely my own fault.

Glancing round, she saw that the gentle hills ahead of her were already standing out boldly against the lightening sky; dawn could not be far distant for already the stars were paling and a little wind had got up. The verges were thick with wild flowers and as she walked the tall creamy spires of meadowsweet brushed her skirt, sending its heady fragrance billowing around her. Unaccountably, tears came to her eyes; she had always loved the country and the thought of living, once more, in a

452

great city dismayed her. But there are other country lanes, other beautiful spots with the sea close at hand, she told herself, beginning to walk more quickly. I'm doing the right thing, I know I am!

*   *   *

Michael did not know what had awoken him; he just found himself wide awake. He knew it was not time to get up though he could see through the kitchen window that a new day was dawning. He sat up, stretched and yawned, and in mid-yawn stopped short, listening. He had heard a very slight creaking sound and then, he could have sworn, a very soft footfall. He stared intently at the lighter square of the window, but heard nothing more. The farm was so remote that fears of an intruder seemed ridiculous, but he remembered that the tinkers had been heading for Kerry, and knew the address of this farm. He did not think the Kavanaghs could possibly have reached them already, but he knew there were other tinkers and that often such people, though they would not break into the house, had no such compunction regarding hay stores, shippens and hen houses. If he was right and there was an intruder, then it behoved him to get up and tackle them before the Gallaghers found themselves a couple of pigs short. He got out of bed, remembering that his mother had told him the previous evening that Jet, the black mare, had recently dropped a fine foal. If tinkers were sneaking around by the stable . . .

It was the work of a moment to pull on a thick jersey and his old flannel trousers, to shove his feet

453

into boots and to pick up the heavy shillelagh which his father always left by the back door. As soon as he was outside, he realised that it was no longer truly night. The stars were paling and the sky in the east showed a pink flush. He noticed the little dawn wind which was already stirring the summer foliage on the gnarled trees which surrounded the farm garden, then he crossed to the hay store remembering, belatedly, that Conan was sleeping outside. It's stupid I am, thick as a short plank, he told himself. If Conan got caught short in the night, he will have come out of the hay store and gone to the midden. It'll be him I heard, and besides, there are clearly no intruders around or the dogs would have been going mad. He turned back towards the house and immediately noticed the open window. Ah, so it was that he had heard. Mabel had undoubtedly flung it open because she was feeling the heat, so that was one mystery solved.

He was actually crossing the yard when it occurred to him that the window was too wide open. He stood for a moment, wondering what to do, then he thought that the girl might be feeling unwell. He knew no intruder could have got in without rousing the dogs, so had no fear on that score, but if Mabel had felt ill . . .

He was across to the window in three or four strides, too worried to wonder about the propriety of peering into a young lady's bedroom, and saw at once that the room was empty. He also saw the note on the pillow and all his forebodings came rushing back. Whatever had happened? Something must have upset her . . . but what could it be? Whatever could cause her to climb out of a window, in the middle of the night, and leave his home? His parents had made it plain that they wanted her to stay for as long as she could be spared—he had made it plain too, surely. But there was no point in dithering here; he must read the note and find out if she had left because of something someone had said or done.

Seconds later, he stood in the small bedroom, reading the note whilst his heart sank into his boots. Why, oh why, had he not told her how he felt before they even reached the farmhouse? He had known in his own heart that she was the only girl for him, yet he had not had the courage to tell her so. Well, he would be served out if she had made up her mind to have nothing more to do with him, though he still could not understand why she had left so abruptly.

He was still standing in the middle of the bedroom, wondering what he should do next, when someone behind him coughed. Michael swung round, heart hammering, half expecting to see Mabel standing there, but it was Sean. His father cleared his throat and said apologetically: 'I heard you come in through the back door like a whirlwind and I thought there must be something the matter, because you're a thoughtful lad, Michael, always have been, and wouldn't want to wake the family.' He looked at the empty bed, the note in his son's hand, and finally at Michael's face. 'So she's gone, has she? Well, what did you expect, lad? Three times durin' supper last night, you called Ginny "Stella" and three times young Mabel looked as if you'd hit her. Women need a feller to put into words what's in his heart an' I don't believe you've said anything about how you feel to that poor young thing. But you told Ginny, over and over,

455

how like her mammy she was. Was that sensible, Michael? Was it kind?'

Michael felt his face grow hot. 'But—but Stella's been dead ten years,' he muttered. 'Oh, Daddy, she were a beautiful creature, and I loved her truly, but—but time has moved on, and so have I. Mabel's intelligent, she knows her own mind and isn't afraid to act on it, and she's beautiful. I were thinkin' last night that Stella was moonlight an' Mabel sunshine, an' that's how I think of her: a warm, glowing, golden girl, the one person I want to spend the rest of my life with.'

'Then tell her,' Sean urged his son. 'Tell her *now*, don't let wrong feelings grow up between you, else you'll lose her.'

'But—but she's gone,' Michael mumbled. 'She—she could be anywhere. And if it's what she wants . . .'

Sean caught hold of his son by both shoulders and stared into his face. 'If she means a t'ing to you, you'll go after her this minute and tell her what you've just told me. You've been afeared to say a word in case she rejected you, but now it's sink or swim, and you're no son of mine if you don't make a push to put things right.'

Michael grinned shamefacedly down at the older man. 'I'll go at once; she can't have got far,' he said, striding towards the door. 'Wish me luck, Daddy!'

* * *

He caught her up by the little stone bridge across the tumbling stream. As he hurried along, he had been rehearsing what he meant to say, but, in the event, he said almost nothing. She was walking

456

head bent, shoulders drooping, but she must have heard his boots on the stony track and turned towards him. In the grey of the dawn light, her face was a pale blur, but when he reached her he could see the tears on her cheeks and somehow he knew there was little need of words. He gathered her into his arms and kissed her and kissed her, muttering disjointedly between kisses, until his mouth finally homed on to hers and they clung together, no longer needing any words at all. Explanations could come later, but for now the love between them simply blossomed as their mouths clung and their bodies seemed to fuse into one.

Presently, Michael sat down on the stone parapet of the bridge and pulled Mabel on to his lap. 'Will you marry me, Mabs?' he asked humbly. 'I've loved you ever since I first set eyes on you, despite knowing that you thought me a pretty poor sort of fellow. I've been afraid to ask you in case you said no, and broke me heart into a million pieces, but when I found you gone I saw what a fool I'd been. Mabel? I swear I'll be the best husband in the whole world, so I will.'

Mabel snuggled against him, tucking her head under his chin so that she could hide the tears of joy which had formed in her eyes. 'Of course I'll marry you, you great eejit,' she said in a scolding voice. 'Haven't I been in love with you ever since we first met? That was why I was so cross with you, because I didn't understand why even the sight of you made my tummy turn over. Oh, Michael, I'm so happy!'

Michael began to kiss her again and for some moments there was silence, save for their quickened breathing. Then Michael raised his head. 'You can't be any happier than me,' he said contentedly, lifting her off his knee and standing up. He glanced around him, realising that the sun had risen whilst they kissed, bathing the countryside with gold. He took her hand in a firm clasp. 'We'd best be gettin' back, me little darlin', before the family wakes up, and we'll tell them the news at breakfast time.'

The two of them began to retrace their steps, whilst around them the birds shouted their greeting to the new day.

PART III

CHAPTER EIGHTEEN

The week which followed their arrival at Headland Farm was a busy one—so busy, in fact, that no one had a chance to go down to the Puck Fair, though Michael admitted he was very interested to see the Kavanaghs for himself. But in his absence his parents and Declan had not quite managed to keep up with the work, so as soon as he returned he, Ginny and Mabel had thrown themselves into the tasks which awaited them. Because the weather had remained brilliant, they began to harvest their corn and everyone was busily occupied. And then, of course, there were wedding arrangements, for Mabel and Michael had decided to get married towards the end of September, when the harvest would be over and done and work would be less pressing.

Conan had not stayed for more than a couple of days, though the Gallaghers had pressed him to do so. He had no intention of visiting the Puck Fair since he had no desire to be questioned by the Kavanaghs as to Ginny's whereabouts, but meant to attach himself to another tribe heading away from Killorglin. He intended to ask for his father but had taken the precaution of smearing his own light brown hair with Ginny's black dye and planned to tell the new tinker tribe that his name was Declan Delaney and Eamonn O'Dowd was his uncle, and by this means to find his father without any risk of the Kavanaghs' beginning to suspect that he was not dead after all.

Before a wedding there is always a great deal of

work to do and in this case, since Mabel and Michael were to marry in Ireland, Mr and Mrs Derbyshire were going to come and stay at Headland Farm, arriving two days before the ceremony and leaving two days after. Ginny and Mabel were already sharing a bedroom but they intended to vacate it for the Derbyshires and to move into Michael's room whilst he had a shakedown on the sofa in the kitchen once more. The wedding breakfast would be provided by Maeve, though the Derbyshires insisted that they should pay for all the ingredients and Mrs Derbyshire had promised to do a great deal of the baking herself, once they arrived at Headland Farm.

'I wish we had been able to go to the Puck Fair,' Mabel said dreamily, a couple of evenings after the fair had closed. The whole family were sitting in the kitchen; Michael reading a newspaper, Sean smoking his pipe and fondling Floss's ears, whilst Maeve and Mabel knitted socks for their menfolk, and Ginny sat cross-legged on the floor, industriously stitching away at a tray cloth which she meant to give Mabel as a wedding present.

At Mabel's words, Michael lowered his newspaper and smiled across at her. 'Don't fret, alanna, you'll probably attend every Puck Fair for the next twenty years,' he reminded her gently. 'Why, with the way the farm's expanding you might even sell honey from your own bees and fresh vegetables from your own garden, to say nothing of bunches of herbs and cheeses from your dairy.'

'What about my career?' Mabel said, trying to sound indignant. 'I thought we'd agreed that when a job came vacant in Killorglin School I was to ask for an interview. Don't you go forgetting I'm a professional teacher, Michael Gallagher!'

Michael, who was bare-headed, pretended to doff an imaginary cap, saying in a squeaky voice as he did so: 'Sorry, miss, sorry, miss, I didn't mean to offend your teachership.' He dropped his voice to his normal level. 'But what's to stop you doin' both, Miss High and Mighty? I'm sure a girl as clever— and beautiful—as you could do both jobs wit'out blinkin' an eyelid. Why, only the other day . . .'

Outside, Skipper began to bark, and Floss raised her head and growled just as someone knocked at the back door. 'I wonder who's that,' Maeve said, laying her knitting in her lap. 'Shall I go, Sean?'

Sean began to reply but Michael shook his head and got up. 'No need, Mammy. I asked Mr Farrell to come round this evenin' 'cos he's t'inkin' of sellin' his bay pony. I expect this'll be him.'

He went to the door, then slipped out into the yard, closing the door behind him. Mabel heard the low murmur of voices and glanced across at Ginny, her eyebrows rising. Who on earth could it be? If it had been Mr Farrell, or any other neighbour, he would have been asked in at once, so it had to be a stranger, and not a particularly welcome one at that, for Mabel already knew that Irish hospitality would not let even a stranger remain outside the house for long.

She turned an enquiring face to Maeve, who could only shake her head, clearly as perplexed as she, but just when Mabel was about to take a peep through the window the back door opened again and Michael came into the room. He was ushering before him a very dark-haired man of medium height, with overlong greasy hair hanging down to his shoulders.

Mabel stared at him for a long moment, thinking there was something familiar about him, but before she could say a word, Michael spoke. His voice was silky sweet but Mabel could hear amusement behind the gravity of his tone. 'This here is a friend of our'n what wrote us a letter some while back,' he said gravely. 'I don't know his name, because he signed his letter with an X, but I believe it's probably Kavanagh.' He turned to the stranger, beginning to grin. 'That's right, isn't it, Mr Kavanagh?' The stranger nodded and Michael continued. 'Mr Kavanagh has come all the way to Kerry to bring my daughter, Ginny, home,' he said impressively. 'As he said in his letter, he's asking a hundred pounds for her safe return as well as a couple of our best horses.' He turned once more to the stranger. 'Would you prefer a mare with a foal at heel or a mare and a stallion?' he asked the uninvited guest. 'I want to be quite sure just what you think me daughter's worth.'

The man's crafty little eyes swivelled anxiously around the room and flickered over Ginny without a sign of recognition. It was plain, Mabel thought, that the child's midnight black locks had completely fooled the tinker and she could see that he was puzzled by the fact that every face now wore a smile.

'Well?' Michael said the word gently, caressingly almost, but the tinker was too wily a bird not to recognise danger when he heard it.

'Oh sure and the girl's a wonderful wee worker, so she is; we'll not want to part wit' her but we know what's right and she *is* your daughter,' he said, in a whining, sing-song voice. 'To show good faith, we'll say not'in' about the horses, but if you'll give me the hundred pounds, I'll go back to me people an' she'll be knockin' on your door within the hour.'

Mabel could see Ginny was giggling now, a hand clasped over her mouth to stop her laughter escaping. The child jumped to her feet and ran over to the back door, gave the panel a couple of sharp raps and then turned, grinning, to the astonished tinker.

'Why, if she isn't here already!' she exclaimed. 'It's clear enough you didn't recognise *me*, Abe Kavanagh, but I'd know you anywhere. So clear off afore we call the scuffers . . . Gardai, I mean!'

The man gasped as comprehension dawned, and turned to flee. Michael reached for him and actually grabbed his shoulder, but the tinker was quick as an eel and as slippery. He twisted out of Michael's grasp, dodged round Ginny and was out of the door and pounding down the path in a moment, whilst the family roared with laughter and Michael shouted after him that if he ever came near Headland Farm again, he'd find himself chucked into prison and left there for a hundred years.

'Ain't he the foxiest thing, though?' Ginny said; Mabel thought she sounded half-admiring, half-shocked. 'He thought I'd been drownded, but he still tried to gerra ransom out of me daddy! If that ain't tinkers all over.'

Michael put an arm round her shoulders and the other round Mabel's waist. The three of them stood, crammed in the doorway, watching the tinker's figure grow gradually smaller as he sped away down the lane, over the small stone bridge

465

and out of sight.

'Well, there's one good t'ing. The word will get around that we found the Kavanaghs out in a cheat and likely we won't see them in these parts for the next twenty years,' Michael said philosophically. 'If there's one t'ing all tinkers hate, it's bein' laughed at, and when this story gets around there'll be plenty who'll mock at the Kavanaghs.'

He turned back indoors, taking his womenfolk with him, and Mabel took her seat again with a sigh of contentment. 'It's all over at last, and we're all safe,' she remarked, picking up her knitting once more. 'But the cheek of the fellow. I wonder whether he would have tried to palm off one of their own kids as the missing Ginny . . . I dare say he knew you'd not know her?'

Michael began to reply but Maeve, getting up to pull the kettle over the fire, interrupted him. 'Blood's thicker'n water, alanna,' she said. 'Me son would ha' known. Let's just be thankful we've seen the last o' the tinkers! And now who's for a nice cup o' tea?'

466